Hades & Seph

EILEEN GLASS

All rights reserved. No part of this publication may be reproduced in any form or by any means without the prior permission of the author.

© Eileen Glass

www.eileenglass.com

Edited by Jennifer Smith.

One

Seph huddles in his bedroom closet, listening to his mother's voice crash against the floorboards, booming underneath him, brimming with the strength of an angry goddess who must be obeyed.

"What do the perversions of two incestuous cousins have to do with the virginity of my son?!"

The man's answering voice, while calmer and almost soothing, holds as much power as hers. It is a harmless, even jovial voice that promises a formidable will if you wrong the man who speaks.

"*Four* cousins. Apollo and Eros are also asking for him now. I must set up the games for a proper courtship. He's too beautiful, so they say, and his cousins are starting to spar amongst themselves."

"My son will not choose one of those lice-infested barn animals!"

"Demeter. Discontent from the gods causes chaos in the lives of mortals. And you are the caretaker of many such lives. This disturbance is aimed directly at you *and my son*. That is why I'm so concerned. It is best—"

"You do not get to play the role of father now!"

Something crashes. Seph imagines it's one of the large vases sitting on the floor in the entryway. Not a suitable thing to heft and throw, but an eight-foot goddess requires a sizable object to hurl at her ex-lover.

Demeter grows bigger as she gets angrier.

Zeus replies with a hint of sighing impatience. "You have not let me get to know the boy. That was not my choice—"

His mother's roar, so loud the house supports must rattle, startles Hibus, the white rabbit in Seph's arms.

"You are not his! And you are not *mine*! And you have nothing to do with this family! I have made this clear."

"Shhh, Hibus," Seph whispers, stroking over the bunny's head

1

and down his long ears, across his back. The rabbit squirms once, afraid, but then trustingly stills. His little heart hammers against Seph's arm, which cradles him under his body, against Seph's chest.

And his father responds with that same calm tone, the slightest perceptible frustration giving it that deep mysterious power.

"I am the boy's father, Demeter. No matter the distance of where I've been, or the fact that you've shut me out, I am his *father*, and I care for you both—"

"You are a scoundrel! A liar! A play actor and a dirty dog! You couldn't be the father of anything, even if your seed is fertile! You don't have the heart. You don't even know what it is!"

Seph holds his breath, fearful for his mother.

She has had this rant many times. All it takes is a curious question or two from him, spoken when he was very young, for Seph learned long ago that he doesn't have a father. And he never will. It is an undeniable, absolutely irrefutable fact.

That is, according to the goddess who just called Zeus a dog.

"He is mine, Demeter!" At last, that anger shows. But even in this, it is quiet. When the God of Storms truly rages, you will know. This is only a darkened sky on what should be a clear day. The sign of a warning. "And I am the King of Gods, or have you forgotten?"

"You are the King of Mount Olympus," his mother corrects. "And that is where you belong, beside your jealous wife, Hera. Or did you forget?"

"I am the one who looks after all of you—" he starts to reply. But his mother isn't done.

"And you are some special kind of ass to be down here talking to my face about chaos amongst mortals, you dingy old street mutt. How much time do you spend on Mount Olympus, Zeus, hm? How much time a year do you spend overseeing that kingdom you claim to run?"

The powerful voice gives in to petty squabbling. But it is different than his mother's fury. More like the great God of Gods is enjoying strong wine and suffering the ribbing of good friends.

"What am I, Demeter? An ass or a dog? That is two animals in one sentence, unless you mean I am the ass of a dog, which would have been far more creative. You may use it if you like."

"You are all of that!"

Something wooden creaks. Either his mother's great weight is breaking the floor, or her head has finally bent against the high ceiling and she is growing into the shape of the room. She must be huge now.

"All the things that are slimy and wicked and devoid of any kindness or positive, real emotion! You are a creature of lust, Zeus. It is the only thing you've felt since you killed our father."

"Oh my gods, here we go again..."

"Hah! You use the mortals' swears. That is how long you're gone, Zeus. Every year. Creating chaos for mortals. So don't come at me thinking you have some kind of authority to marry off my son!"

"Our son."

"Get out! Get out, get out, get out—!"

A number of things break. A housemaid downstairs shrieks. She will not be underfoot amongst the quarreling immortals, so it must be the sight of precious pottery pummeled against the walls that frightens her.

The door opens, heavy footsteps descend the steps outside, and Seph looks up from sweet Hibus, who must trust him very much not to run off in all this clashing and yelling. He only sees the back of his dark closet door, but he imagines the balcony overlooking the front steps. It is not so far.

He has never seen his father before.

"Will you tear up the pillars and hurl them too?" The strong voice is getting angry, but that doesn't change Seph's mind. Surely he should see his father one time? The father he doesn't have, according to the furious Demeter.

He doesn't know *anything* about Zeus except that he's a *dirty dog who humps anything in heat. And he's not your father. And he doesn't feel anything, Seph. He's hollow inside. He looks beautiful, and happy, and if you met him, you'd love him. But he's like... the shadow of a man. Or a creature pretending to be a man. He doesn't love. Not like you or I. He doesn't care for the girls he loves, or how he twists them up inside. He's perpetually bored. And he's extremely dangerous.*

Seph sets Hibus aside. "Shh," he tells him, as though the rabbit is upset. And then he crawls, quickly, for standing up would let the god Zeus see him from a window. *Stay down. Stay out of sight.* Those are the rules for those few times when Zeus comes to visit. And *that monster is not your father.*

He knows it's the truth. He's not expecting his father to be any better than the monster she described. But he has heard other things from the townspeople and the servants and slaves and all the mortals who help them here on their land.

Zeus is beautiful. Like an enormous statue, an artist's perfect vision of a man, but better. Uncapturable. Seph has seen the statue of Zeus in the center of town. His mother idly told him that even the best mortal hands cannot sculpt his features.

No matter how evil she tells him he is, his mother has never argued against his form.

And Seph would like to see it. Just once. Just quickly.

Like a thief, he sneaks through his own house, bent over, his bare feet moving fast. He goes into the upstairs hall and looks over the railing at the pottery scattered below, pretty flowers strewn about like ruined maidens in a pillaging. His house looks ransacked. And if the goddess had stayed here, she would have grown up to the ceiling and eventually exploded out of the roof.

If Zeus still remained, she would have to shake the house off her foot like a dirty sandal.

But the god is smartly leaving before a small war is waged.

A small war for them. A catastrophe for mortals. The entire countryside and the large town nearby would be obliterated.

Seph sneaks to the lightly billowing curtains on the front balcony and huddles inside them. He creeps ever so close, ever so carefully, to the balcony's edge. The figure through the gauzy haze is just as Seph heard from the villagers. Bronze. Tall. Muscular. Thick, curly hair. Gorgeous locks. People go on for a while about his hair and the matching beautiful beard on a young but manly, broad-boned face.

The back of his head does not disappoint. His hair is indeed curled and soft looking. It falls past his shoulders and ends in a straight line, like the edge of a rug. Seph imagines that petting it would be like setting his hand on the sheepskin in front of his mother's bedroom fire.

Though his back is mostly covered by draping cloth, his form also does not disappoint. Even his ankles are perfectly sculpted, like they belong to a marble statue. His sandals look better because his feet are in them.

And the shape of his backside?

The set of his hips, how they slant from one leg to the other with his walking gait?

Why...

Frowning, Seph ducks. That is his *father*. But it is true what they say. He *looks* beautiful. And Seph remembers another thing his mother said to him once.

If he were to see you, he would want you, and you would want him. *There is nothing I can do to stop that. You wouldn't discover his true nature until it was too late, my sweet boy.*

Seph believes her. And so it is a good thing his eyes lower just as that head is turning back to speak to his mother. He is curious. But it is not worth it.

"Marry him, Demeter. Do it yourself or I will choose for you. Everyone who sees him says he's the reflection of me. And a quarrel is starting over him. I won't let this go on much longer."

"Go back to Mount Olympus. I am the Goddess of this Earth!"

"You're the goddess of the things that grow in it," he corrects. "And that is my son. I have the right to marry him. And I will."

"Get out!"

"I will, Demeter. That is your last warning."

Two

Seph crawls back to his closet as quickly as he can, knowing the first place his mother will return is to where her boy is hidden. His father has tried to visit before, when he was small. He only just gets the closet door swung into position, and Hibus in his lap, when his bedroom door bursts open and heavy gigantic footsteps test the strength of the floor.

"Persephone, get out of there. I know you weren't hiding."

"Y-yes, Mother."

Cringing, he sets Hibus aside. But not before lifting one pink ear and whispering, "Stay here."

It is a normal rabbit, who cannot understand him. His mother has reminded him many times. Yet Seph would swear Hibus is smarter and friendlier than all other rabbits.

He crawls out of the closet, and his mother is enormous. Towering. But small enough to keep her head high under the ceiling still. Seph *hates* being in trouble. To visibly watch his mother's anger transform her from the normal, kind-looking woman into an angry giant is upsetting. But she has never whipped him. It is only her voice he winces from as he stands in her shadow, his head only coming up to her elbow.

"What did you think you were doing, coming outside dangerously like that? Do you know what could have happened to you? Do you?"

Her hand is larger than his head and grabs his arm suddenly, tightly. Thanks to god magic, her bangle bracelets have grown with her, and they rattle, large enough to be crowns on his head.

"Do you know what Zeus would have done if he had seen you?"

He is called Zeus. Or dirty dog. Not father.

"H-he would have kept me," Seph answers. He is taller than his mother in her normal form. He has been quite proud of this fact, and he is taller than all the boys in the mortal village too. But now he is like a toddler again looking up at his mother, and in god terms, that's exactly what he is, no matter how his physical form appears.

Gods can be fully formed when they're born. If they detect a need of it. Seph has wished he could physically change his age or grow taller with emotion. But he is a very weak god, barely having more power than a nymph.

He was born a baby and he grows as a mortal would.

"He would have kept you, and he would have raped you, Persephone."

Seph *hates* when she uses that word. He knows what comes next...

"Just like he raped me. All those years ago. I'm grateful for you, my baby boy..." She pets his hair and leans close like she's cooing at a mouse trapped in her hand. "But your father—no, he isn't your father. Zeus is a dirty dog. A rapist. A pillager. Baby boy, he would have had you on the end of his cock, because the man has no morals—"

"Mom!" Seph yells and pulls at her hand. He doesn't want to hear words like that, not from *her*. And what she's talking about is disgusting.

"No, you need to hear this! He would want you, baby boy, and he would have you. And then Hera—"

"Stop! Stop!" She finally lets him go. She *lets* him go, as he fights for it, because she *lets* him feel like a fully formed god. Not her equal, but someone who could have power.

"And don't call me *baby* anymore! Ugh. You know I don't like that!"

Seph moves away from her, but there's not very far to go in this room she's occupying.

She yells at him, her hands on her hips. And Seph's neck shrinks into his shoulders, wincing like he used to when he was very little.

"My sister Hera would murder you, Persephone! Or curse you, if she thought Zeus actually *cared* a shred. If not for her, I might let him have you!" She gestures wildly, her voice taking on that perilous tone of a mother on a piteous rampage. "If that's the worst that could happen to you, and you wanted it, I wouldn't care! I'd let you find out what a monster he is, like I did. The man is nothing but the life and legs for a dick and testicles!"

"Ughhhh. *Mother.*"

Make it stop.

But alas, when she gets like this, the only thing he can do is wait and listen. Running will only make her catch him, make her angrier, and make her yell a lot more.

But if I was a real god...

He loves his mother. Most of the time, on a normal day, Seph would say his life is as perfect as it could be. There are only some times, like now, he wishes he had the power to get away from her. And to stay away. And to only come back when he wanted, as equals.

"But it's our sister Hera..." Now she shakes her finger at him. It's enormous, like a heavy stick, and her sharp nail is bigger than his eye. "It's what he does to her, you see. He's turned her into a monster! He makes her drunk on his love, which he only *pretends* to have, and then he leaves her without the drink. To go crazy for months. And she gets crazier the longer she's without him. Both of those two are dangerous."

She grabs him by the shoulders. The weight of it is like walking into a door frame.

But this will be the end of her yelling. It was a short lecture, thank the gods.

"Do not let him see you. Do not come out of your closet if he comes back. Understand?"

Seph nods. Speaking usually makes it worse.

"My boy, you can't imagine..." She clutches him close. Seph's face transforms with repulsion, trying not to think of where his face is and what's very near. Her breasts are practically atop his head! But she holds him tightly as if he were still a little boy and not a growing man.

"Our family is dangerous. Do not think gods have sweet, caring families like mortals. They are short-lived, child. And they age. So the temptation is not there, you see. Their virility fades. A god, however, is frozen in development. And Zeus is only an adolescent man. That's why he grew the beard, you know. To seem older and more kingly. He is a panting, thoughtless, selfish teen boy, but with the intelligence and power of a man. And he does not have emotions. Not since Kronos died."

Kronos is his grandfather. All the main gods are the descendants of Kronos, who swallowed his own children until Zeus freed them.

To say that gods don't have loving families like mortals is a bit of an understatement. Zeus cut Kronos apart with his own scythe, and now the old god's children are looking after the world, letting the mortals learn and grow.

"You would be his pet, child. His sexual slave. And only until

Hera found you and put an end to it."

He can't take it anymore. He has to talk.

"Mother, I know, I'm sorry. Okay? I-I just wanted to look at him. Just once. I didn't let him see me. I knew it was a bad idea. I just wanted to see... who Zeus was. I'm sorry."

She pats his back. It feels exactly like it did when he was nine. Back then, he looked forward to growing up and getting bigger. He didn't realize he would never age into a man, not in his mother's terms.

Sometimes he hates it here.

But she does protect him, and Seph would be lost without his mother.

"Alright then. Pack up your things. We're going."

She lets him go.

"What? Going where?"

"To the villa out in the country. You like it there, yes? You can race the horses. Or go hunting in the woods if you like."

"I hate hunting." Seph makes a face.

"Only since you got that rabbit," his mother says with a sigh. "Where is he anyway? I haven't stepped on him, have I?"

Once Seph had a cat napping in the yard when one of his 'incestuous cousins' showed up. And *that* is a memory they never talk about, for Seph will never forgive her. But it wasn't on purpose, and she still feels bad.

"No, he's in the closet."

"Good. Well, put him in his little carrier then, and I'll have the slaves pack our things. Come down for dinner, and we'll be off."

"Mother, uh, wait!"

Though he'd rather let her rant and pace in peace, as she often does when her temper rises, he has to call her back.

It's time.

He's not her little boy anymore.

"I don't want to leave."

She looks confused. "Why not?"

"I like it here."

"Pff." She waves her hand and turns, ducking to get outside the door safely.

"No, Mom! I like it here! I'm not going, okay? I'm staying right here."

She doesn't grow any bigger. If anything, she's shrinking but gradually. She regards him with stern eyes, and Seph finds himself regretting this action. Just like how he regretted that day he asked her to call him Seph from now on, and she laughed like he was telling a joke.

"Oh? Why is that, Persephone?"

"Teysus," Seph answers. "I love him."

She scoffs, tossing her head. He knew she would. But this is serious.

"No, Mother, I love him. I'm not going anywhere. We're... we're going to get a house together. His father and uncles have already provided it. I've just been waiting for the right moment to tell you, and for his cousins to leave, and then I'm going to move in."

"Oh my." She touches her head with her wrist. "Sweet boy. Sweet, sweet boy."

She's shrinking at a greater rate. Zeus, her better, made her inflate like a cat hissing at a large dog. But her son standing up to her doesn't cause any riled emotion. Besides... what? Pity?

Seph isn't sure. It's love, but not as equals. He's always a boy to her.

"Mother, I'm not backing down about this."

"Come on," she says and steps into the room again. She's almost her normal size.

"No."

"Come on, we're going to have the talk again."

"No, that's not about this," Seph says, and more firmly. He tries to take on that powerful tone he heard from his father. To speak from deeper within his chest, to have that mysterious element of unbreakable will. But he only sounds like a big boy starting a tantrum.

She takes him by the arm and forces him to sit on the bed with her. Resisting would only make him look more puny and petulant.

"Persephone. Please." She has that tired tone of a tutor explaining the same simple concept over and over. "You are a god. Not a mortal. You can live with a mortal, you can play with a mortal, you can *make love* to a mortal... But you cannot truly love a mortal. We've been over this."

"I do love him, Mother. We're going to live together."

"Well, maybe I'd let you if we could stay, but we can't."

"Mother—"

"No, son." Her voice is final. "You cannot love a mortal. You will love him a few decades, and then what? His body will get weak, you know."

Seph groans. "I've heard all this before. It doesn't change my mind."

"Yeah? Well listen to it again. He's going to get old and ugly and weak, and you're going to be just you. Just as you are." She takes on an airy, mocking tone, dismissing his love with a simple hand sweep. "And then what? What will you have in common, baby boy? Do you think he'll want to race horses with you? When he has bad knees and low energy? Do you think he'll still want to make love the same? Can you imagine what it will be like? You—mounting some old, stinky, *hairy* butt—"

"Mom!"

They wear equal expressions of disgust, but hers is for emphasis and Seph's is visceral.

"If you can't stand me talking about it, you're certainly not ready to live it! Persephone—this boy, uh, what's his name?"

Seph sighs. "Teysus, Mom. He's only been delivering apples every spring and summer we've ever lived here. And we used to play together as boys. You said he was handsome back then. Fourteen years ago, but I remember it."

"Yes, well, I remember his father now, and he's not that handsome, is he? That pot-bellied, furry old man? You could shave him to make a rug! All except for his head, of course! You really want to see *him* with his clothes off?" Her eyes widen with imagined horror. "Well, you go ahead, son. Because that's what you'll be walking hand in hand with, just ten years from now. Twenty, if he ages handsomely. But son, you will still be exactly the same."

He's prepared for this. He's lost this argument before and thus has the correct response.

"I'll love Teysus exactly the same too. I won't forget him, Mom. It's more than that. I love his personality. I love his smile. I want to spend every day with him for the rest of his life, even if I have to watch him die."

Her mouth gapes.

I've cornered her, he thinks, as she grasps her dress material over her lap.

But her lips lift with a bemused smile.

"Well, listen to you! Such a romantic!" She messes up his hair like she used to do when he was a small boy and did something funny. "My sweet boy! My baby child!"

"Mother, *stop.*"

"Oh. I trained you right, didn't I? Now listen—" She stands. Her face is serious again. "We don't have time, my love. You will have to pine away for your boy from afar. Because if I—"

Seph tries to speak.

"Listen! Even if I let you find out for yourself what it's like and let you discover your love is not nearly as deep as you think it is, Zeus—the dirty dog—is going to marry you. Not I, Persephone. Don't hate me for this. For goodness sakes, I'm the one fighting for your right to live with a little mortal boy, or whomever you choose. Why, I'd look forward to the day you came back to my doorstep and I'd say, 'I told you so.' That would be fine by me. But Zeus is another matter."

Three

The villa is nice. It's several smaller houses connected by a large court, with four decorative pillars rising high into the sky. And then the main house, where they stay, is not so plain either. Though, smaller on the inside than their mansion. The villa's beauty, his mother says, is not meant to compete with the nature around it, and that is attested by the fact that it is only one story high and the trees grow thickly all around.

This was his favorite place to hunt before he met Hibus, a young rabbit some mortal girls were playing with. They had several of them hopping around in a flower bed, the girls laughing to watch the young bunnies play and chew flowers. Hibus broke free of their herding efforts, darting across the courtyard to Seph's shadow. He must have thought the god was a friendly tree. He did not run when Seph bent to pick him up. And Seph has not killed a rabbit or prey creature since.

Though, admittedly, he does enjoy the occasional venison on his table still.

He used to feel guilty for this action, but alas, admitted that it was foolish to avoid meat entirely, like his mother said. Now he only eats much, much less. And that is because of his friendship with the white bunny.

He pets Hibus' ears and sets him in a small flower pot. The bunny sits up on his back legs, sniffing, and cautiously tastes the closest flower. Seph sits on the bench beside him, eating an apple. From the last basket Teysus delivered. It was over a week ago. He did not get to say goodbye.

And Seph misses him. He asked one of the slaves to give him a note. He hopes it was delivered correctly. He has been crying for days, swearing his heart will never heal.

But the ache is a little less today.

And watching Hibus helps.

'Pets only die and make you sad,' his mother said, those several years ago. Hibus is an old rabbit now, and Seph worries about his health constantly.

'They do when you *step* on them,' he had retorted, and Hibus was allowed to stay.

But it does get lonely being reminded that your friends and pets and everyone around you except for *your mother* are going to die soon and leave you lonely.

Seph offers a little piece of apple to the curious bunny. And he hears his mother's heavy footsteps behind him.

"Persephone, you're going to follow the nymphs into the fields. And follow them home. You can work if you want, or don't. It's their job, not yours."

She says this often, because Seph likes to help and learn what others do around the house.

"Where are you going?" When he turns, he sees the large empty basket carried on one arm. Slaves make a procession behind her, carrying pitchers, crates, and more baskets, all empty.

"Collecting tribute," she says. "When we were here last, I ordered the mortals to make me a temple and commanded the priests to respect me instead of the forest spirits. We shall see how the message was kept. I expect some fine things for the house, some new clothes for us both, and perhaps a little more livestock to give fresh blood to the herd. Is there anything specific you'd like? I'm getting new pillows for my bed. The ones we had already are way too flat."

"No," Seph answers, shaking his head. Though he's relieved to hear she'll be gone. It might not be fair to hate her for what Zeus says, but Seph was looking forward to living in the village. With mortals. And trying things on his own for a time.

"Alright."

She stands there. And Seph faces forward again. He can *feel* her standing there, looking at him.

"Go on then, Persephone. With the field nymphs. Look, they're waiting for you."

Now he notices the girls gathered at a far house, waiting to go to the fields. A nymph looks just like a young girl, except they live a lot longer, they don't age until they die, and they can converse with spirits and things.

This used to be their home. But when Demeter arrived, she built *her* home on top of it.

The nymphs do not resent his family for this, even if they should. Nymphs have an almost heartless understanding of nature, and they do not spare the small animals the deaths that provide their meat. Nor do they expect themselves to deny a goddess of her right to everyone's property.

Nymphs are at peace with the natural place of everything.

They are also entirely female, and Seph does not understand where they come from. His mother said they're born out of the woods. As adults, just as they are. Many mortal men, gods, and creatures fall in love with them, but that won't be so for Seph.

With a great sigh, he collects Hibus and starts walking that way.

Yet another reason he wishes they hadn't gone to the villa. Besides the slaves his mother brought from the house, the residents of this villa are all nymphs.

This is going to be a long, terrible summer.

But at least he will be safe from Zeus.

Who would Zeus choose to make me marry?

Seph has some time to think about it as he sets Hibus down under a tree and ties his back foot to a peg in the ground. He is a tame, loyal bunny, but a bunny can find trouble if a dog far away barks, or a shadow moves too suddenly. And then he will be lost in the forest forever if Seph can't find him. Hawks are a concern too, but the skies are clear.

Thimena, the leader of these nymphs, is quite amused when he asks for a scythe. But he works quickly, without asking how, for he has already had practice from when he befriended Fimus, a young slave boy. Oh, he had a crush on him. Such a pretty face. But as a young teen, Seph learned about the social castes and how his affection for Fimus meant that the young boy couldn't say no.

And he did say no. After Seph explained over and over again that it was okay and he wanted an honest answer. He didn't want the slave's body only. He wanted a kiss. He wanted to *be* kissed.

But he said no.

Teysus was the first boy who said yes.

They were going to live together.

And they would have done more than feel each other up under their clothes, in the dark, while his mother thought they were sleeping.

The rhythmic motion of the scythe helps with his thinking. His emotions are worked through his muscles and drift out of his mind instead of staying inside to fester. But he does not sweat with exhaustion, nor from the heat of the sun, which is bright on a windy summer day.

When the nymphs break for lunch, they offer him bread and cheese, impressed with how well he's worked. He turns down the meal and continues to cut the wheat with his scythe.

It is so relaxing.

A god, even a puny one, never feels his muscles ache or his skin burn.

The nymphs happily take a long lunch, benefiting from his labor. They feed and pet little Hibus, giggling at his cuteness. A cautious glance that way is certainly warranted. The nymphs are not *girls* no matter what they look like, and they would not feel guilty about slaughtering the pleasant rabbit to provide meat for their cheese and bread.

But they don't seem to be starting a fire pit, and they do know that the little bunny is claimed by a god. So he is safe. And Seph keeps working.

Until a flash of white appears under his blade as it sweeps past. Underneath the thickly growing wheat seems to be an unusual flower.

A beautiful flower. Tall, with a yellow center, angled directly at him, and somehow it missed the blade. Even though it grows higher than the wheat cut all around it.

Seph sets the scythe down rather than making the next cut. He bends to one knee, wondering how it could grow here. How did it get enough sun among the wheat? And just a single flower? Are there others, and he has been cutting them down this whole time?

His heart aches for Teysus and the life he wanted, but this seems to be a comfort offered from the Earth. As if Mother Gaia took notice of him herself.

He cradles the flower and draws in its scent. His desire to work dissipates. And so does his sadness, in a way. Though it is really just the acceptance that this is how things are. He is a god. And his mother is right. He does not want to see Teysus' father naked. So how can he be sure he would still love his friend as he grew old?

He can't. And his mother is so much older and wiser than him.

Oh, it would have been fun pretending to be a mortal young man. For several years, sure.

But he would have seen the truth of his mother's words eventually.

Then who? he thinks, letting the flower go. *One of my cousins, I suppose. Maybe it will be a good thing if Zeus marries me after all.*

It is better than being alone all the time and your closest friend being a bunny.

"Child, get away from there!" calls Thimena, and she runs at him with quick girlish steps, gathering her dress above her knees. Three more girls follow like a gaggle after their mother. They look weak and too pretty to know hard work, but Thimena's hands seizing him are nearly as strong as his mother's. The four nymphs grab him around his arms and waist as solidly as though he'd fallen off a ledge, and they pull him back with no wait for protest.

"Why? What is it? Is it poisonous?" It must be. "Thimena," he says in a stronger tone again, mimicking his father. "What is wrong?"

"It is a narcissus flower," she replies hurriedly. "It is a flower made by the gods."

They have only walked halfway back to the tree where the other nymphs wait with their arms crossed and their expressions worried, when a young girl points to the sky and yells, "Look!"

Above the tree and beyond the field, there are gray clouds forming where none were before.

The danger is real.

"Is that Zeus? My father?"

Thimena worries her lip, her eyes searching.

"Let's get him to the house," she says, speaking to the girls and disregarding him completely. "His mother will have put up protection. Come on, let's hurry."

"Wait! If we're going home, let me take the flower first." He recognizes the danger, but it is a very pretty flower, and he has had a very bad week. The flower is the only thing good that's happened lately. "It will only take a second. And I need to bring Hibus, too."

"There is no time—Master, please!"

Fortunately, the nymphs are *not* his mother, and Seph is both male and a god. Though, fighting off the four of them is difficult. They are like the children who come to swarm him with hugs and tiny fists whenever he walks through the village. Small and insignificant, but capable of slowing him down in a pack.

"We need to get going now!" Thimena says loudly in his ear as he reaches the flower.

And then an unusual sensation comes over him. An awareness. There is something wrong with this place. The wheat...

Visually, it seems fine. All is normal. Seph shades his eyes and looks up at the bright sun, which isn't disturbed by Zeus in the slightest. Yet.

Zeus certainly isn't rushing toward him in any great hurry. Though he is present for some reason.

So what is it?

Just the flower. Then I will leave.

But now the flower seems to be glowing. The wheat all around him—the *world* seems different somehow.

The wind. What happened to the wind?

Trees all around the field shake and wave their branches like an audience clamoring for his attention, trying to give him the answer. But the wheat grass itself?

Still.

Standing eerily silent and unmoving.

Even the nymphs have frozen for now, hanging off his arms and waist. While the flower seems to be *looking* at him, beckoning him to come closer and take it.

"Let's go." He's been foolish. There is terrible danger here! And he starts to make for the lone tree, urging the girls with him this time, for they seem to be stuck with fear. Thimena only looks at the flower with wide, terrified eyes. And then he hears the sound of distant horses' hooves.

He stops, though whatever it is will be awful. He's afraid to turn around, but he does, if only to dodge the coming attack.

There is nothing here. So where…?

"Come on, we have to go."

But not even he can make his feet move because he can't figure out *where* the horses are. They are not in the field, they are not in the *sky*, they are not anywhere, though they seem to be rushing upon him, diving on this very spot.

And then he has a new sensation. The ground wobbles. But not as in an earthquake, which would rattle and rumble. It wobbles as though the soil has become water. What he thought was a solid surface, the field, is actually the flimsy barrier to something deeper.

The horses are rushing at him from underneath. And there is nowhere to go. The distance to the tree does not feel calculable and real anymore. It is as if everything is floating and it's a miracle he hasn't sunk into the depths already.

He should run. Even if the ground isn't real anymore, he should struggle to get as far away as his legs can take him. But like Hibus, he is too scared. He and the girls huddle where they are instead.

Until, from a rising steam out of the ground, a dark figure

emerges.

Four

Four horses snort and toss their heads against the reins, their trot antsy but subdued, their master holding them back. They are solid black like the night, so that their legs and bodies seem to blend in with one another, making a wicked creature with many heads and frenzied eyes. They are harnessed to a golden chariot, which is elegant and bright and not at all foreboding. The complete opposite of the creatures. It would look right at an emperor's palace, perhaps carrying him to a race.

The man inside the chariot, however, wears robes that match the creatures. He seems to be one with them, though his skin is so pale. Moon white. And he is almost boyish, too young to be an emperor, though certainly tall and regal and manly formed. His eyes are wise though, making Seph take back her assessment. The god is old. Very old, older than Zeus.

The chariot turns rather than approaching them directly, and the god steps off the back once the horses have stopped. They look like they could take off at any moment. They don't seem to be comfortable here, dancing like the sunlight spurns them.

The god, on the other hand, approaches slowly, relaxed. Almost bored. He looks down at his flower as he passes it, but there's no emotion on his face. Seph huddles with the girls, and the god's eyes fix on him.

Why is he here?
What does he want with me?

Then his gaze shifts. To Thimena, who is bravely the first of them to rise, her fists clenched.

"The goddess is not here!" she shouts in a tremulous voice. It does not seem to travel far over the air. And the god does not seem to hear her as he continues his approach.

"You go back!" she shouts, and then quickly, quietly over her shoulder, "Take him now, girls. Go!"

To the god again, she says, "This is Demeter's son. And you have no right over this realm."

"Move, nymph," says a toneless voice. "His father has given him to me."

The girls start to take Seph away, whispering "*Run!*" and pushing on his back, but Seph feels bad about leaving Thimena. A nymph has a long life and spiritual sensitivities, but the girls are not magical. Physically, they are barely stronger than a mortal. And a god as powerful as this?

Seph knows who it is, but he isn't brave enough to think his name.

This god will not like to be disobeyed.

"It is best if I stay," he whispers back. And the girls don't have the strength to move him. They begin to cower behind him as the god comes very near, and only Thimena stands to face the great power, her knees trembling under her dress.

It's not right. Seph forces himself to stand also and not to run, as the nymphs who were helping him scuttle back to the others at the lone tree.

The god regards him with a hint of a smile. And this expression stays as he returns his eyes to Thimena.

He only sets a hand on her shoulder. She whimpers and stumbles as if she was hit. Her steps carry her to the side so that she does not stand in the way anymore.

Seph physically forces himself to breathe as the god comes closer. His crown makes him look terrible. It is black and spiked and rises up in a broken, frayed manner, like a tree that was snapped and burned. And froze in the winter. It shines like glass, and it is sharp, though it is not any precious metal Seph has ever seen.

His clothes are strange. Foreign. He's dressed like someone from the north, his arms and legs covered, and the robe Seph thought he had is actually a cloak tied around his shoulders. He would be very warm indeed for a regular Greek man here on a summer's day.

Neither his clothes nor his features look Greek. He does not look like he belongs here. Seph has only seen a face so smooth and perfect on a woman.

When he arrives, Seph expects to be grabbed. That is how this marriage ritual works. In the mortal world, the girl's family would throw a party for the bride, and the husband would carry her off over his shoulder, with the family in tow making a mock show of outrage. Of course, these are fun and games from the very real, very dark claimings of old times past. Times that a god still remembers, and this is the real thing.

"I-I've been married," Seph utters, facing the god now. They are the same height.

He is not angry, but he could be... if Seph runs.

"You will be. Our ceremony is waiting at home," says the formidable being, and he lifts his elbow from his side.

Seph takes it, setting his hand lightly around his arm. He doesn't want to, but he does. He even looks helplessly back at the nymphs, who have disappeared, and then at Thimena, who's finally collapsed to the ground. But none of these smaller people have the power to save him, and his mother is nowhere around. So he starts to leave. The god leads him in the same bored, unhurried manner.

Then he remembers.

"Wait!" Whispering, he asks in a more appropriate tone, "Wait please. I have to bring something."

The god only stops and gives no indication of yes or no. Since it is so very important, Seph lets go anyway and races back to the tree. Hibus has hopped as far as he can go on his lead, and still struggles against it as Seph closes in on him.

"Girls!" Thimena yells from far away. "We can't let this happen! Demeter will punish us! Get the boy! Get him back to the house!"

Their slender forms appear in the shadows of the rustling trees beyond the wheat grass. They had retreated back to where the world is real.

"Hurry!" Thimena yells, and they rush forward like warriors taking a battlefield.

Seph recognizes that he doesn't have much time, so he gathers Hibus into his arms and yanks the peg free by the lead. He runs to the basket, which will make do as a carrier, and dumping the bread and cheese on the ground, he covers Hibus tightly with the small blanket. He begins to stand when the girls are on him, pulling at him again, urging him toward the house.

"Young nymph," says the dark god to Thimena. "Do not do this."

"I have to," she says, sobbing. "Spare us, please! His mother will kill us if we don't give our lives to protect him."

He presses his lips together, thinking. Then he turns, his black cloak billowing out from his feet. His horses toss their heads and move toward him as he approaches. His hand trails along one of the reins as he walks around to the back of the chariot, where he steps in and takes control. Seph feels himself giving in to the overwhelming instinct telling him he should run.

Absolutely, he must.

Because the dark god Hades is after him.

The girls scream and shriek in his ears, fueling his panic, and finally, as the god snaps the reins and the horses bound forward toward him, Seph runs with all that he has. He leaves the girls behind. He clutches the basket with Hibus to his chest and sets his eyes on the rooftops of the villa in the close distance.

As a god, he can be there quickly, and he focuses all his meager power into his legs. But in moments, the path in front of him becomes dark and shaded. The many-legged beasts overtake him and run beside, huffing and neighing shrilly. Their master actually has to draw them in so they won't leave him behind at their pace, and they toss their heads with reluctant obedience, their hooves stamping the earth.

Hades gives them just enough lead to let the chariot pull up alongside Seph. His long silver hair blows back in the wind, and his brow is lowered over a pointed gaze of concentration, focusing on the horses.

Seph is nearly at the villa, but Hades will be there first. The chariot almost leaves him behind, but then the god turns his head at last as he ties off the reins. He jumps to the chariot's edge, balanced with his arms out, holding a perch that no mortal man could. And he grabs Seph with both arms, like a hawk snatching him out of the sky.

Seph is enveloped in that dark cloak. It smells like winter. Like snow and frozen cold.

Then he falls against sturdy planks, grunting, and making sure the basket is cradled safely against his chest.

He is inside the chariot now. At the dark god's feet.

Five

The chariot goes down, down, so far vertical and so fast that it seems he is free-falling and the chariot only happens to be going with him in this manner, not like he is riding in it. The dark god looks at him at one point, as Seph is curled around Hibus and trying not to scream. He switches the reins over to one hand and squats down to grab Seph's shoulder.

Perhaps the gesture is meant to be comforting, but his expression is almost cruel. Impassive.

And then he takes up the reins again because the horses are charging at full speed and their direction must be manned.

It is better as the chariot levels out. The world is complete gloom. The gray sky has no stars. But at last forms appear, and looking out the back of the chariot, Seph sees a winding river, very wide, snaking through a dim forest. He sees a pier and a large crowd of people gathered on the shore, but they quickly pass that.

The trees are like tiny toys because they are so far up. And the people are only like meager blades of grass. He sees a little ferryboat bobbing down there, somewhere, and then they are gone. It is just wilderness again for a long time. And then a road of dim white and gray stones. Houses appear next, in colors of white, blue, a tinge of yellow or pink, and silver. These grow larger and larger as they descend, and Seph begins to fear the impact of the chariot against the ground.

He will be okay, but what about Hibus?

He holds the blanket top down over the basket with the hopping rabbit inside. Hibus squeaks and scratches and claws. Then his little sniffing nose appears out of one corner, and Seph squishes him down, sealing the edges as tightly as he can.

The dark god is staring at him. Seph meets his eyes, wondering what he's thinking. Wondering where they're going. And then the elegant man stares forward again and snaps the reins, urging the horses to go faster, of all things.

Seph winces as he prepares to feel the road. He hopes Hibus won't jump out. There are many dazzling trees and a big lake nearby, but the scenery is moving so fast he can hardly take it in.

Then they are slowing. Not crashing, not colliding, just slowing, and it seems that the wheels are on solid ground. There are minor bumps and jostles from the cobblestone road. They slow down enough to spend a little time passing each of the houses, and villagers of wherever this is begin to step out of their homes and crowd onto the streets.

It seems his fear of landing was not warranted. And Seph has been looking like an idiot hunkered down in the chariot like this.

I should stand.

He tries, but the blood and balance haven't returned to his legs yet.

Hades slows the horses down all the way to a walk. The villagers are starting to jog to catch up and follow alongside them, behind them too, filling the streets. The horses don't pull at the reins or shake their heads more than once, occasionally. The wild, mad beasts seem to be at ease while they're at home, and their hooves make the regular clip-clop of a lazy, unbothered state.

The villagers, Seph sees as he climbs shakily to his feet, even walk in *front* of the horses. They have no fear of being trampled, even the small children, of which there are many. If this were a mortal village and Hades a mortal emperor, mothers would be shouting and dragging their children back by their arms.

These ones freely approach with their hands outstretched, petting the sides of the horses and even quickly feeling up their noses as they pass. A mortal horse would not be comfortable with this. These are very tame beasts.

And the dark world is nothing like he imagined. There are no crows staring down at him from the rooftops. There are no walking skeletons or ambling hordes of lepers. There is no three-headed dog, Cerberus, and Seph is at least certain *that* monstrous creature exists somewhere.

There are only beautiful, immaculate houses, all of them equally sized and generous, like the middle-class homes where he's from. There are many pale colors, like pastel pinks, blues, and yellows. The children's faces are fair and perfect, their innocent eyes wide with wonder.

"King!" calls a little boy over the chatter, walking near the chariot on the dark god's side.

For the first time, Hades' expression changes from an impassive scowl to a smile, and he bends to notice the boy, who only waves with childlike eagerness.

"Where are all the women and men?" Seph asks, just loudly enough to be heard. He's not sure if he's supposed to speak, or *allowed* to speak, or anything at all about how this works. This will be the first male-only marriage amongst the gods, which was put forth when his cousin Hephaestus caught him kissing Teysus.

"Where are their elders?"

The oldest villager here cannot be near thirty, and there are far too many children and no parents.

"This is Elysium," says the pale god, returning to his impassive expression. "Their parents are dead. And most of their children are dead. These are very old souls, and only the best, most gracious kind. When villagers are new, they will look exactly like they did in the upperworld. There—see those two?"

On the steps of one of the houses, a frail, withered man and woman hold each other's hands, watching Hades pass with timid fright.

"They were led here only months ago. The other souls are looking after them. In time, they will begin to heal from their mortal lives, and their physical form will simply be a reflection of who they feel like they are. Most mortals are still just children inside."

"What is your name?" asks a cute little girl by Seph, barely taller than the wheel axle. She grabs the turning spokes as they pass—an extremely dangerous act in the mortal world. Seph almost wants to scoop her up and save her from the danger. It is not so uncommon to lose a child under a wagon wheel.

But instead, he stutters, "I-I am Seph. Persephone."

"Well, you are very beautiful," she says matter-of-factly.

"T-thank you. You are as well."

Her voice unfortunately loud, she states, "I think you're more beautiful than our other king!"

Internally, Seph can feel himself shrivel in terror for the child. Hades is known for his merciless, eternal punishments.

But in this case, he only snorts like one of his horses, and his lips lift in a smirk on one side.

"Are you cold?" asks another girl, this one looking to be eleven or twelve, just before her teen years. She looks smart like Thimena, with straight dark hair.

"Uh, no, I'm fine."

She nods, then explains her interest. "Most people say the underworld is cold."

"Well I—I suppose it is. But coldness doesn't bother me. It never has."

Seph's powers are annoying in that they are small and too intuitive to be controlled, but his power to keep warm was tested once when he slipped into an icy creek. And now it has been tested by an unearthly cold even the king of the underworld feels. Seph eyes the dark god again, understanding his need of thick, full-covering clothes and the cloak.

The children wear all kinds of things. The girls wear dresses mostly, but of many strange fashions, and a very few only wear a grass skirt. They are all shades of pale, occasionally a few having lightly golden skin and some just a tinge of almond. They dress themselves in varying colors, all light pastels, and white or gray is the most common color of all.

In fact, Seph realizes there is not a shade of green to be found anywhere. The trees are mostly gray with brighter leaves. A very few are tinged blue or pink.

"Your home is gorgeous," Seph whispers to Hades. He doesn't know anything about the man, but they are married now. He will start with compliments and hope for the best. "And your people are..."

He tries to find the right word. Something besides *gorgeous*, though yes, they are. He wants to say that they are generous and good and they seem to be well looked after, which hopefully means Seph will be as well.

But all he comes up with is: "Enchanting. They are lovely. This place is... amazing."

The dark god shifts the reins to one hand again and puts an arm around him, bringing Seph close and putting him under his cloak. It is such a strange feeling, but not unpleasant. He expected it to feel as if he was falling into that icy creek again. Or as if grabbed by cold, hard talons. But if anything, Seph is warmer for the embrace. And Seph has no complaints about the male form beside him, which is muscular but not as thick and sturdy as Seph himself.

Hades has a far more pleasant face than the youthful-but-always-sly-looking Apollo. The god of the underworld, thankfully, doesn't seem to be into long beards to make him seem like an older man. And his slender, muscular frame is far more preferable than the

burly, squat Hephaestus, the smithing god.
I can be all right. This won't be such a bad thing.
Then Hades tells him, smiling slightly, "I am happy you like it here. It solves many things. You won't return to the upperworld ever again."

Six

They steadily, slowly travel toward a dull silver palace in the distance. When Seph first noticed it, he thought it was a mountain or a very large rock. But actually it is a palace that seems to grow out of the cobblestone road itself, made of the same texture and color, shaped with sharp angles and tall spires that mimic Hades' crown.

Thankfully, the palace isn't black. Seph would probably die of depression after a few years if it was black.

Gray marble isn't so bad though, and many tall narrow windows are lit up blue from the inside. There is no bridge or moat, and strangely, there are no guards anywhere to be found. The huge double doors are wide open, and the children-seeming souls ahead of them continue in a line up the broad steps and inside.

Several children are playing instruments before the doors, strumming on lyres, blowing into pan flutes, and a few are mildly pounding on large drums. Some children stall at the doors and begin dancing. Their chatter is loud and excited, and Seph stands corrected on his first assessment. He initially longed for the yellow-lit homes of the upperworld, constantly thinking of all the things he will never see again.

But the 'cold fortress' is unguarded and full of happy children. No other king's home, not even Zeus's on Mount Olympus, has ever contained so much playfulness and security inside its walls. The chariot pulls up alongside the bottom steps, and Hades exits first, providing a supporting hand as if Seph is a woman.

Seph accepts, carrying Hibus on one arm, who has thankfully calmed down. But Seph makes sure the blanket stays on with one hand as they are surrounded by many curious children now, who might squeal and act excited if they see the small bunny.

Or would they not?

The boy who comes to lead them makes a formal bow and seems well-behaved.

The children part for their king and do not grab at either Seph or Hades. Nor do they shriek or call out or get in the way. They are more orderly than mortal children would ever be, and the boy who leads them only taps and nudges to get the attention of those who need to step aside.

A mortal king would need many guards and possibly a town crier to pass through a crowd like this.

So many differences run through Seph's mind. From the assortment of the children's clothes to the very way the steps are carved. There are no blocks or bricks or seams in the stone. It's like the palace was carved out from one mountain-sized boulder as a single piece.

Even minute differences are important to him now because he's never going home. There are so many things he will never see again.

But maybe I will grow to like it here. Maybe. I suppose I must.

And maybe Hades won't turn out to be too bad. He's Zeus's older brother. He spent many centuries in the stomach of Kronos, Seph's cannibalistic grandfather. So maybe he's worse than the great thunder god? Maybe he's more damaged?

Seph hopes not.

My mother was swallowed too, he reminds himself. *She doesn't talk about it, but she wasn't damaged by it. So hopefully...*

He takes a big breath and reminds himself not to freak out. He climbs the many steps uphill to the great palace, looking back once to see the horses and chariot being led around the palace to where there must be a barn.

"Veil or no veil?" his dark god husband asks.

"Uh, w-what?" Seph asks. They are arriving at the musicians now, who take on a lively tune, and many villager children begin to clap with the rhythm.

"For your wedding," says Hades, only looking forward, not smiling or showing anything at the moment. "A woman usually wears a veil. But you don't have to, of course. I—would like it if you carried flowers."

Did Seph imagine that pause? It was so brief it could have been caused by an accidental inhale of breath.

The dark god does not show any hint of nervousness, shyness, or awkwardness. Nothing like Seph, who must look like the sacrificial calf being brought to the altar.

"I tend some flowers here. I would like you to carry them in a bouquet. As—" A definite pause, but he continues as calmly as before. "A symbol."

"Okay." *Seph, this is your husband. You can do better than that!* "Yes, I would like that."

He expected another smile or a *thank you*, or even a nod of the head would've been nice. There is no change at all from the dark god, and they pass through those enormous doors and into a hall lit with blue torches. The flames are only blue, dark blue on the bottom and bright aqua on top. They flicker and put out light just like real flames. No heat, though. There is no temperature difference from going outside to in, like there would be at home.

The voices, mostly children, are louder inside but not rambunctiously so. The villager children do not have parents to mind them and don't seem to need chastising for a quieter voice.

One more strange thing is how they wander anywhere and everywhere, as if this is their home. Up the stairs or crossing from another hall, they drift off and through various archways, knowing the palace.

"This is it," Hades tells him, stopping. Beyond is a great dining room, with couches set up to make many island squares, and food is already being carried around on platters to the guests.

Here, at least, the souls are exactly like mortal children. They eat with their fingers and crowd together on couches, having none of the formal manners that Seph learned.

Hades' pale fingers reach up and begin to organize Seph's hair. Seph recoils—just at first. This is all so new and frightening and strange. But not *necessarily* bad.

It's Hades himself who causes him the most fear. That and the prospect of never going home again.

"Veil or no veil?" Hades asks, and his tone gives no expression of which he would like. He seems to be looking directly at Seph's hair and not into his face.

"Um." Seph tries to picture himself wearing a wedding veil and winces. "No veil, I guess."

Hades nods once.

Then, "I would like to marry you just as you are. In these clothes, if it's all right. It is good, I think, to show the contrast of who you were then to who you will become. After the ceremony, I would like you to don the fabrics I prepared. A servant will help you dress. And then we will recline and eat as normal. Husband and husband."

There is a *small* smile then. Perhaps an inkling of happiness?

Or the pride of ownership?

Well, whatever, it's his call. Either emotion would be correct.
"That sounds nice." Seph bravely fakes a smile for him.

One nod, and Hades is back to looking impassive again.

They step out of the archway, and the villagers take notice, sitting up on their couches, clearing the middle of the floor to stand around the outer edges instead. They start clapping as Hades and Seph go to the center of the dining room. There is a small table here set up with a pitcher of wine, one large chalice, and a fruit cut in half that Seph has never seen before, but he has heard of it. Both the wine and the pomegranate are similar colors of red, and it is the most vivid color Seph has noticed since coming to the underworld.

The chalice and the table are gold, and come to think of it, many ordinary things are completely gold. Such as the serving platters themselves and the couch legs, and even the brackets to hold the torches on the wall.

His mother told him Hades was richer than Zeus. And this, it seems, is true.

She must have been wrong about him being gaudy though. Hades removes his cloak, giving it to a helpful young man Seph's age, one of the few. And Seph eyes his now-husband for the oversized jewels and gaudy rings his mother claims the god has.

He has large sapphire earrings. That is true. They're a deep vivid blue, very different from the faded pastel colors all around. And around his neck, over his shirt, he wears an enormous crystal stone on a gold chain.

So that rumor, he supposes, is true. And on his right hand there is indeed an enormous 'gaudy' ring of the same glittering stone, in an oval shape and covering most of his finger. It's rather beautiful though, and in Seph's opinion, it looks perfect on the dark god's hand.

That hand lifts and points with two fingers in a direction that Seph isn't looking. It takes him a moment to realize and react. He blushes, aware the dark god knows he stared, and turns to accept a large bouquet of the same flower he had been admiring earlier today.

They look just the same down here as they did up there, except that the stems are grayish blue instead of green.

Seph holds them in front of himself properly and bends his head a little to sniff. They smell lovely. Maybe he will get to keep them on a windowsill after all. Just a different windowsill than the one he imagined.

Hades lifts one arm and the room falls silent.

"People of Elysium! I would like you to meet... my mate. My husband. This is Persephone. God of the End of the Harvest. Son of Demeter, Goddess of the Fields. And son of Zeus, God of the Skies."

That arm lowers, and Hades lets the backs of his fingers rest on Seph's cheek. A shiver runs through his body. *Now* the dark god smiles. And it is a soft smile. And they are looking at each other like lovers, the way a husband and wife—or whatever the case—should.

"With this ceremony, you will be the second king of Elysium. Your home will be here. My table will be your table, and my children will be your children. I will provide for you. Extensively."

His touch disappears, and Hades pours the wine pitcher over the chalice, filling it up with the maroon liquid.

"Neither you nor our children will ever be hungry. You will never know poverty. And we will be prosperous and better for our union."

He lifts the chalice with both hands, holding it before Seph.

"From you, I only ask for your companionship and compliance. I ask that you make this your home and serve in your position as selflessly and faithfully as I do. Do you accept?"

There is a little gasp from some girls watching in a pile on a nearby couch, their fingers pressed over their mouths. They look like sisters, though a longer glance reveals that they come from different parts of the world. They could never have met before they died.

Do I accept?

What a strange question! Especially to be asked so long after his ceremonial abduction. These lines are not rehearsed nor common. They sound like they come from a few places actually, since the part about 'table being your table' is practiced throughout the Mediterranean, as well as varying promises to feed the bride and her future children.

Nobody ever asks the bride a question though. She usually just listens. The dowry payments will have already changed hands, after all, and there are many gifts to receive.

What sort of father or husband would give her the chance to possibly say no so late in the agreement?

But Seph supposes that he worded it this way since they are two men, and there are no official wedding vows for two husbands joining together.

Silently, as a bride would do, he lowers his lips to the edge of the chalice, and Hades obligingly, gradually lifts and tilts it into his mouth.

Fortune-tellers have various interpretations for how the bride accepts the drink and what that portends for the couple's future. It is generally bad to choke or spit. To drink too much, too heartily, means you will be unfaithful.

Somehow, there is just the right amount to drink, and Seph watches the god's eyes for some indication of how much that is.

When he is almost out of breath, the chalice straightens. And Seph sucks in his lips a little bit to clean them of the wine. Wiping your mouth with your hand might mean something bad, as might a spill or a dribble.

Did I do it right?

It's impossible to tell with the chalice tilted now to provide Hades the drink. Only his gray eyes watch Seph over the rim of the cup. He licks his lips openly when the drink comes down.

Seph knows what *that* means. He will be a heavy wine drinker. Possibly a drunk in mortal terms, though a god never gets more than a little tipsy.

"Our first meal, my mate," he says, lifting the fruit. It has so many seeds inside. "Every meal of your days onward will be provided by my hand. You will never need provisions from your father again."

They say something like that in the wild northern tribes who sometimes trade with the townspeople near his mother's country villa.

But instead of cutting the fruit into wedges, he plucks a ruby red seed from the white inside. He sets it to Seph's mouth and says, with his fingers still attached, "Bite and swallow the juice."

Seph must let the elegant fingers go inside his mouth slightly, and then he must bite down carefully with the fingertips behind his lips. Obedience, chastity, and demureness are desirable traits in a bride. So he keeps his eyes lowered and lets the dark god feed him the next one and the next one.

The juice is good. Different, exotic, and thankfully delicious too.

A little messy though, and Seph has to lick his lips or wipe his mouth or else let the juice stay on his chin. His tongue accidentally slightly slides against the god king's fingertips, and there is a reaction.

Seph can't say whether it is positive or negative, but it does seem there's a twitch in the god's expression.

Cheers and applause break out, and the formal part of the

ceremony is finished. Seph takes a big breath of relief. He lets the dark god feed him several more seeds from the exotic fruit, but they are done with the wedding rites. It is over.

There is only one part left. The wedding night.

And then the rest of my life.

Seven

All he can think about from the moment they finish the wedding ceremony is the impending act to take place in the bedroom, but the dark god is not in any hurry to get there, it seems.

First, Seph is led away from the enormous dining hall to put on new clothes and discard all the things his mother provided for him. The helpful servants are even adamant that he gives away his braided belt, which was a gift from Teysus. Seph regrets wearing it today. And they eye the blanket atop his basket as though they'd like to ask for that as well, but Seph says firmly, "This is mine. Hades said I could keep it." And while a teen-looking boy appears particularly doubtful, he doesn't say anything against it.

Seph is at a loss of what to do to keep his rabbit safe, and worries about him jumping out and shooting through the palace, getting lost for good. Then the servants present the new clothing he will wear per Hades' instruction. Seph almost tells them it's a mistake. This must be a throw blanket from one of the chairs! Or perhaps another picnic cloth like the one that covers Hibus.

But the servants efficiently wrap him in it, a new solid gold belt going around his waist, and there is just enough material to cover his front and back. Just enough. The hems end far too soon, not even halfway to touching his knees. If Seph was to bend over very far, the bottom of his ass would be seen by all.

This is not an uncommon way to wear a robe, but it is usually done by younger, growing boys who have merely sprouted up in their childhood clothing. And sometimes men wear boys' garments on purpose to show off their form. Athletes are especially well known for wearing next to nothing or literally nothing. But Seph usually wears the longer robes of older men, which reach his ankles.

His new outfit only attaches on one shoulder, so half his chest is bared as well. He almost wants to cover his exposed pec shyly, like a growing girl.

The only good thing he can say about his new clothes is that the fabric is unbelievably soft, shimmering, and has pleasant patterns around the edge in gold. The main material is the deepest black, just like the dark god's current outfit. The symbolism Hades seeks is blatant. Now they match and Seph clearly belongs to him.

Finally, at last, servants present him with a circlet on a purple pillow. It is made of the same glossy black stone as the dark god's crown, but instead of jagged spikes and spires, it is a carved laurel wreath. The servants help him fix his hair so that several narcissus flowers from his bouquet become part of his new crown.

Seph likes it fine, though it does make his head a lot bigger. His clothing though...

The entire kingdom is going to see me practically naked!

This is certainly not traditional wear for a bride on her wedding day!

But Seph supposes Hades chose to dress him more like an athlete since he is a man and not a virginal young girl.

He *feels* like a virginal young girl as he reenters the dining room, carrying Hibus' basket in one hand and quickly sneaking one more tug in the back to cover his assets. His new belt jangles a little when he walks, and he quickly learns that he had better straighten his head or else his circlet and flowers are going to tumble right off.

By the time he reaches his couch beside the dark god where he will dine, Seph has abandoned his natural state and moves with more balance and care. Even sitting and assuming a lounging position is done tactfully, or else the revealing chiton will expose his butt and balls.

Which, of course, is exactly what an athlete would want, to get more coin from admirers.

The dark god, on the other hand, is entirely covered by his northerners' garb. Only his hands, face, and neck are visible. He even reclines with his boots on, which would earn Seph a sharp scolding from his mother if he ever tried the same in his sandals. His form, however, is pleasantly apparent by the shape the clothes take over him. And after a while, tasting a small portion of roasted pig, Seph realizes he and his new husband have been staring at each other for long silent moments since he sat down.

Their couches are positioned perpendicular to each other, their heads at the meeting ends. For the rest of the night, Seph is aware of every movement the god makes, particularly of the interest displayed in his expressions and sometimes the distance of himself to those hands.

Glancing at his new husband is done with an assassin's care to not get caught. Yet somehow, at the same time, Seph is always watching, never taking his eyes away.

Seph decides to rest on his back, thus saving the diners behind him the view of his rear end. He props one leg folded up. Then stretched out. Then crossed at his ankles, to see how he's most comfortable. And what affords him the most modesty.

There is a moment during this that Hades eyes the vicinity of his legs and definitely wears a promising smirk. But then his mouth disappears behind the rim of a tilted wine goblet. And he drinks for a while, leisurely, leaving Seph to wonder...

Does he like what he sees? Did he put me in this revealing outfit on purpose? Or perhaps he truly thought this was fitting—athletic wear for marrying a man? Or perhaps he thought this chiton was appropriate for a man my age?

Seph is extremely young for a god. Perhaps Hades saw what other adolescents were wearing as he prepared this outfit.

Is he smiling for the satisfying taste of the wine?

Or for me?

And when he licks his lips—just once, as the goblet goes down and gets refilled—*does that mean anything?*

Quietly in Seph's mind there is a constant state of analysis and emergency. The merest thing, like a twitch of an eyebrow, or especially a slight smile, will send Seph into a hopeless maze of possibilities. And meanwhile, he tries very hard not to show too much of himself to the many friendly children. Dancing and celebrating and chattering goes on all around.

The dining hall is enormous, like a complete palace in itself, with rows of pillars extending far beyond where they sit, open archways all around, and floor-to-ceiling windows beyond that.

Seph suffers through many meal courses. At a wealthy man's party, the dinner may be so elaborate and continuous that the guests have to puke to keep feasting. Seph eats little and slowly, for a long time. And the only thing Hades says to him, sitting so close nearby, is, "Did you like the wine?"

"Y-yes. I loved it." Seph does not remember the wine very well. He was too nervous during the ceremony. But it was sweet, without the strong bitter flavor he expected.

"Have some more. Have as much as you like." With the wave of two fingers, a serving boy comes and pours a pitcher over Seph's empty goblet. "It is the finest, most delicious wine in all the realms. And I only allow it to be enjoyed by the permanent residents of Elysium. Zeus has been after it for ages, you know. He's completely jealous. My wine is the only kind in existence that can make a god drunk. Though, it does require many hours of drinking."

That is strange. Seph has tasted many strong liquors with Teysus and his uncles, and a lot of them made him gag outright. But they didn't get him drunk. Not even a little. The maroon wine tastes more like one of the weaker, gentler drinks. Except... It settles. From one sip, pleasant tingles warm up his insides and spread gradually into his limbs. It is the best wine he's ever tasted, and it has just enough lingering warmth to make him want the next sip, soon.

"It is amazing. I love it," Seph says, meaning this honestly but not having the wordful skill to describe his appreciation of the wine any better.

He expects Hades to say, *I'm glad you like it. Because you will never have any upperworld wine ever again.*

But instead his new husband is distracted by the performance put on by the underworld citizens. They wear animal costumes and dramatic masks, and a singing chorus tells him the story of a great hunter who comes to worship his prey, a magnificent white bird who transforms into a woman.

It is a long night. And Seph spends the last portion admiring how the teardrop sapphires dangle from his husband's ear, lying upon his neck when he angles his head right. And then there is his hair, of course, which is impressive as every god's mane should be. But it is not curly, nor overly thick. It is not fashionable by current Greek trends, and Seph feels a little ashamed for the man-made curls in his own hair, achieved by sleeping in rollers twice a week. His mother ordered her cosmetic slave to start tending his appearance when he was twelve. Sometimes for a party Seph will even let his brows be connected with a dark line, as is fashionable to the Greek mortals.

He's glad Hades didn't snatch him up from a party, where all those trends would look silly and overstated next to such natural beauty. His hair is especially fascinating. It is silvery white, straight, and falls to his elbows with the manner in which he is currently propped. The more Seph drinks the wine, the more he thinks the pale white god in black attire couldn't be any prettier. Especially not in Greek fashion. That wouldn't suit him at all.

He must be drifting off. He blinks, opening his eyes to his own

name spoken in a gentle and authoritative voice.
"Persephone."
His husband's hand waits to lead him to bed.

Eight

If this were a mortal Greek wedding, they would be followed by many rowdy and drunken guests, congratulating the groom on his newly acquired bounty. They might shout things like, *Give it to her good!* Or, as Teysus' father said to his older brother when he got married, *Plow the fields well, son.*

Helpful lewd tips are offered up, of course. As well as congratulations for the large belly the bride will soon have. The perfect bride should be 'fat full of seed' according to the bride's grandmother, who was the lewdest of all at her granddaughter's wedding.

The dead souls do not have that nature, thankfully, though several sway and catch themselves on tables and walls as they follow their king toward his personal chambers. The potent liquor does not only get gods drunk, it seems. And yes, while the small children-appearing souls stick to innocent activities, the few adolescents and young adults are seen openly engaging in sexual acts as they leave the dining hall.

This would also be common at a mortal Greek wedding, since it is good fortune for the bride and groom if their guests celebrate with a physical union as well. Public or private and how far it goes is a personal choice.

Their procession stops at two enormous golden doors. The area before the doors opens up to a small courtyard of sorts, covered by a ceiling of glass, with a large marble statue of Cerberus, the three-headed dog that must indeed be really exactly as his mother described. His marble likeness poses regally at the center of a pool of water, narcissus flowers growing all around the water's banks, as though at a natural pond, though this sight of nature and beauty is contained in marble planter boxes. And the pool is an impressive fountain.

Seph has never seen such a thing indoors before. It is a

courtyard under a roof, and none of the plants contained here are slowly dying in a vase. They live amongst the tiled floor and stone walls! And those are covered in rugs, tapestries, and art. Benches are all around, with pillows atop them for long sitting, as well as a small table here and there.

It looks like a beautiful room for reading or just relaxing, and Seph looks forward to being here alone sometime, with hours to spend.

Beyond the doors to the personal chamber, there is a large den as Seph would expect, with an enormous curved desk and many shelves containing a personal library of scrolls and a few oddities. Such as a wild mask of feathers and paint like Seph has never seen before. And large, raw, unfaceted gem rocks. Any one of these is probably worth as much as his mother's estate. He doubts the entire weight of his mother's jewels equals the weight of a single precious boulder that Hades displays like a simple vase.

And through a smaller door of many intricate carvings, the three-headed dog appearing again up top, they enter, at last, the personal bed chambers. Only four servant souls follow them this far.

Two begin to help Hades out of his clothes, the adolescent boy from earlier kneeling to grab his boots as he steps out.

And two begin to work on Seph. The first, another child, kneels to take him out of his sandals. The other, a teen girl with uncovered breasts and hair cut close to her head, tugs on his basket, twice, insistently.

"N-no, I will take care of it," Seph says, holding Hibus close. He can feel the rabbit hop inside.

Her voice is rather deep and pleasant, and her Greek is imperfect. "You must put it down to undress you, my king."

His husband watches with sharp eyes, and Seph feels as though he's protecting Hibus from a circling hawk. Although he must show Hades what's in the basket eventually, he feels like his husband will call it a silly pet. Maybe he will make Seph get rid of it. Maybe Hibus will end up in the kitchen, or hopping around the gardens, fending for himself. It took a long argument and a heap of immature stubbornness to convince his mother to let him keep a box of straw in his room, that he cleaned of rabbit urine and feces every day.

He does not want to face the same dilemma with his dominant husband just now.

"What be it?" asks the servant girl, and Seph does not answer, merely stepping away from the boy removing his sandals. He bends to set the basket under the bed.

He's acutely aware of how he is presenting his backside. And how unusual it is to be secretive over a silly basket. He prepares feeble excuses in his mind, expecting the dark god's curious gaze to turn into questions, while he quickly ties the rabbit's lead to the basket handle and pushes him far under the bed. Then he removes the picnic blanket and sets it aside.

Hibus looks curiously at him from the dark, one ear gradually lifting up, his nose twitching over the rim. He has lettuce and leaves and fresh things to eat that Seph snuck him throughout the meal. He will be mildly unhappy without his safe cage to sleep in, but he is a very smart rabbit, and Seph can trust him to stay under the bed for now. For urination, he will probably use the blanket, and Seph hopes dearly that it won't smell before he gets to throw it out in the morning.

Hibus cannot stay a secret for very long.

You are still my bestfriend, he thinks at the bunny, stroking him a few times, though the others must think he's weird and he had better stand up now. *And now you are the only thing I have from home.*

Hopefully, when Hibus dies, he will just become a spirit in this underworld. That is a small bright side to this place that Seph can accept.

Another one is the sight of his husband's unclothed backside as Seph straightens and finds Hades finishing the undressing process, inclining forward so that the adolescent boy can reach to take off his crown. A strand of hair is caught in one of the spires, and Hades untangles it himself, making a subtly displeased expression.

Seph's servant says nothing, but Seph gets the idea that she's exasperated. Her hands are on his belt at once, working in an efficient businesslike manner. She gives the belt to another servant and pulls his clothing away roughly, like removing a towel.

There was not very much to take off anyway. Seph's fingers curl into his palms, and he looks at the floor.

"Wine for you, king?" asks the girl, bundling Seph's clothes in her arms. "Kind of food?"

"Leave the pitcher. That will be all, Verah."

She nods once, and they are gone.

The dark god pivots and strides toward him. Seph sucks in a breath and thinks of what to say—fast!—and prepares to be kissed. Or touched. Or pushed onto the bed for the final act of the evening.

But he passes Seph and crosses to the vanity along a wall. Naked, he sits on a cushioned stool and picks up a brush. A few passes get the already perfect hair immaculate again, and then he poses one ear at the mirror, and then the other, removing the large, heavy sapphires.

They are so beautiful.

Seph opens his mouth for a moment, wishing to tell him to keep them on. He's admired them so much tonight. He looked forward to seeing them in bed, perhaps dangling from the dark god's lobes as he propped himself above Seph.

But soon they are off. Along with his dazzling large ring and two small ones on the other hand. The gold and crystal necklace comes off last, set atop a headless bust that has an assortment of jeweled pendant necklaces stacked carelessly like plates in a wash bin.

The god regards his fine face in the mirror, frowning and picking at an imperfection only he can see. Unwatched, Seph's examination strays to lower assets. The curve of his thigh, presented in how he crosses his legs. The plush, pale roundness parked on the stool cushion. The little Y crevice, teasing.

And then Hades turns to him, and Seph picks up his eyes like a guard snapping to attention.

"You can go to bed or do whatever you wish. The latrine is through there." He nods at one of the doors. "And that way goes downstairs, to my private bathhouse. Which is *your* private bathhouse now." He smiles at this, in that very calm way that he does. "They are always heated and full. You might like them sometimes before bed, if the day has been stressful. I do."

Seph nods stiffly. He cannot imagine Hades wearing one of the beaming smiles that he and his mother are used to.

Will that change for me? Will I start to look and act like him?

"We will live together for some time. Until I am used to you and you are used to me. It will be years probably, maybe ages. But eventually, when we are trusting and adapted to each other, I may construct your own private quarters in the palace. If you wish."

"Oh. No... it's fine." Of course, Seph realizes immediately after he finishes speaking that the dark god didn't ask him anything. He merely *informed* Seph.

Hades turns back to the mirror and dips a cloth into a nearby washbowl. He runs it over his neck and works upward onto his cheeks. Then he finds a round glass container among many on the vanity and dips a finger inside. Some type of thin oil is spread along his jaw.

Seph sits on the bed, a nervous tension vanishing out of him. But also... disappointment. He looks at his own body and crosses one arm, rubbing his shoulder.

No matter how humble he's trained to be, he could never actually believe he's *ugly*. Though Seph doesn't think about his features usually. He's used to his mother doing that for him, caring about his hair and his clothes, and even his shoes. Seph might forget he needs clothes and shoes if his mother didn't keep replacing the old ones with new items when they become worn. And if his chamber slave didn't keep setting out something fresh for him, he would probably wear the same thing for days.

As a late teenager, Seph refused the slave's help to dress. He began to care for himself more and more as he became an adult. He even learned how to set his own hair in rollers because he felt like his mother's doll.

Now he looks at his new husband and wonders...

Does he think I'm a boy too?

Is that why he'll 'stay up and read'?

He wants me to go to the baths alone?

For all he knows, Hades plans to seek the final act of pleasure and union from someone else!

"Ahem," he says loudly, standing up as Hades is nearly gone, leaving for the den. Seph doesn't know what to do with his hands. If he keeps them in front of himself, he will fidget like a shy boy. Or they might shake.

"Yes? What is it?" asks the god, naked and comfortable. His cock is a pinker color than the rest of him, and a simple, elegant form. His eyes are his imposing feature. His physical strength is sculpted and apparent, but that is nothing to the sense of old age and wisdom held in his calm eyes.

Seph does feel like a boy to him. That makes this request the hardest thing in the world. Far scarier than asking his mother to stop treating him like a baby.

"W-we are married." He swallows and resolves that this will be the last stutter in front of Hades. "So—so you must have asked for me. My father—Zeus—you asked for me, didn't you?"

Hades returns to the room and stands before Seph.

"Yes."

Seph nods, forcing himself with extreme will to focus on those powerful eyes. And not on his own feet.

"And why did you ask for me?"

Hades wears the small smile again. "I explained to him that you are a son of the earth. And I am the god of all things belonging inside the earth. The jewels, the souls, the very rocks that make the continents and the mountains. Everything that comes down into the earth is mine. And you, Persephone, are the God of the End of the Harvest. A time of life for the mortals, yes, but a time when leaves fall, and a phase of death for the things that grow in *my* earth."

Nothing changes except the light of his eyes, which are beaming with glee, as he finishes, "I explained to Zeus that I have more claim over you than anyone. And he's not smart enough to come up with his own logic against me. So here you are."

This is his new master. His new parent, his new *everything*.

Seph's stomach turns as he realizes he doesn't have free will anymore. There will be no rebellion to go live in a mortal town. And no silly pets kept against his master's wishes.

He might as well call Hades *my king*, the same as the servants.

But regardless of that, he has no intention of living out his immortal life as an unclaimed virgin. This was supposed to be a transformative summer.

"That is *how* you asked for me. Not why."

The dark god's brow ticks. His smile becomes a perplexed frown. He has probably not been corrected in millennia. Seph speaks quickly, hoping his intention will earn him forgiveness for this mistake.

"You asked to marry me, right? And you prepared our wedding. And... you hunted me. You took me. And here I am. I-I'm naked before you." He closes his eyes briefly, disappointed in himself for the stuttering slip. He had better finish saying this, or the god will think he's married an infant.

He finds the right tone at last, and glares at his new husband. The opposite of fear is *anger*.

"I am Persephone. Son of Demeter. Son of Zeus. If you want a pretty face in your bed, anyone can lay with you. There are enough beautiful souls here. You can find someone interesting. I am here to be your husband! We are a union, a pair. And you cannot just... go to read! On our wedding night!"

Slowly, the smile Seph did not imagine could exist on such an impassive face spreads across the dark god's lips, and it looks as natural and beautiful as the rest of him. Except... wicked. Devilishly intelligent, like a demon was asleep and now Seph has prodded it awake. It's as though the person behind the dark god's features notices Seph for the first time.

This wickedness fades very fast. It was fleeting, mischievous pride. As Hades sits, oh so naked, and puts an arm around Seph, his expression is kind.

"Persephone. You are not livestock that was sold to me. Rather, you shouldn't be. You, like so many girls, were given away like a burden, without a thought. But you are more than that. And I detest a man who rapes his bride."

Seph blinks several times, processing so many sensations from having the naked man's body next to him, and then his words to go along with it. Hades is slightly cool to the touch, but not unpleasantly so. Seph is always warm. And his arm around Seph feels heavy and strong. He smells slightly of a narcissus flower.

Or maybe that is from Seph's own head? He blushes hotly, realizing the servants took the circlet but not the flowers. He's been sitting here, naked the entire time except for the flowers!

He takes them out of his hair quickly, no matter how out of place and stupid he seems, feeling like his chest is collapsing in on him. He had these flowers in his hair the entire time he said all that 'I am Persephone' stuff!

Determined to control the conversation before Hades says anything to humiliate him, Seph mentions hurriedly, "You cannot rape your own wife. Or your own husband for that matter."

Hades turns away from him. Seph can't see what he's doing, but he hears the ceramic clink of the pitcher spout against a goblet rim.

"Is that what you think?" Hades says quietly. And then leans back, tilting wine into his mouth.

"I..." The answer is *yes*, but Seph thinks he might disappoint his new husband if he said that. "I've never thought about it, I guess."

"A scared young bride thinks about it constantly."

"Well..." *I failed him in some way. I failed his test.* Though Seph can't figure out when that was or how they started talking about young girls getting raped. This was not the *take me to bed* conversation he hoped to be having.

"I-I am not that."

Stutter be damned!

"No. You are not. It seems you want me to be assertive, though. I can do that. But before we go any further, Persephone, you have to know that you have no personal duties towards me. Your vows are just as they are. Companionship was not a euphemism for sex. Not in *our* wedding ceremony, anyway."

"I know that. Now I do. I still..." His own bashfulness irritates him. He shouldn't be afraid of sex! This is his *husband*. They have lawful rights to each other, no matter how Hades may personally choose to interpret it.

"I don't want to be a virgin on my wedding night. You married me. So I want you to take me."

There. Finally saying the words makes him feel better. Exposed, yes, but he's going to get what he asks for. He has the feeling Hades does not play well into coyness. Straightforward asking might work better.

"And you would say this to anyone? Your own personal feelings have such little value to you?"

"*You* married *me*," Seph says.

"Alright, sweet colt. Lie across the bed. I won't disappoint you."

Nine

Pleased is an understatement.

Hades takes another long satisfying swig of his own wine, one that bests even the finest creation of the wine god, Dionysius. Oh, his siblings are terribly jealous and threatened by him, for good reason. And now he has Zeus's own son sprawled out naked for him on the bed, obediently rolled onto his stomach.

Sweet Persephone makes this too easy. He knows his place in the world, poor man, and he doesn't know anything of Hades. He doesn't know that Hades despises his siblings. Any one of them would have treated the young god as chattel. Either to be acquired for physical purposes, or in Zeus's case, to be given away quickly, without thought, to avoid a pointless squabble.

Hades has been lucky, of course. Lucky to see Persephone speaking to his slave one day, telling him it was alright to refuse his advances and the boy would not be in trouble. Lucky that Persephone stayed out of Zeus's eye, for while Zeus is not as smart as Hades, he is every bit as driven to acquire rare things. A rivalry which Hades is currently winning with his divine wine.

Carefully spoken words would not have worked if Zeus had spied his own son. Hades was instrumental in protecting Persephone from that day on, making sure Hermes, his messenger, had an ear in the Mount Olympus court, listening for the latest gossip of Zeus. (Which is not at all a hard job.) Hermes would deliver a warning to Demeter if the boy's father was to arrive, which he did more often as the colt grew up and became a potential stallion in the herd. One that caused other stallions to fight.

Hades himself did not watch over the boy, nor did he go back since spying him that one moment. But he thought about him consistently, and as the topic of the young god's marriage became a subject of Hermes' reports, Hades was not surprised to find himself seeking out Zeus to stake his claim. The words, while not rehearsed, seemed as though they were already thought of. And he only waited long enough for the mother goddess to leave so he could take his new 'bride' home.

Demeter. She is not as detestable as his other siblings, and he usually wouldn't mind her, but it is her tiny selfish desires that add up and overwhelm her good qualities in number. Particularly her desire to be worshiped by the mortals and seen as the giver of life. Because of this, she's lost her own son.

Hades has never hated her especially, but he suspects yet another sibling will despise him forever now. Zeus has his reasons. Hades loved their father too much to kill him, and thus doomed all the others born after him to suffer the acid inside their father's stomach.

But such thoughts of the very long, very cruel feud among the immortal god family are not appropriate for his wedding night. Only, what is important is that the feuding is not over. Their lives are not calm. And this act tonight could become another stone the siblings hurl at each other, if Hades is not careful.

The golden body before him was squabbled over for a reason. The young man's beauty is too much. And his innocence isn't found in any of the other gods, ever. He is like Zeus before he ever knew violence, and Hades has this opportunity to step in and protect him from that final maturity. That doom. To see that his innocence is not torn apart by his family's cruelty.

He takes a final long swig from his wine cup.

This is Hades' first and only wedding night, after all, and he's not entirely certain how to go about it. The baby stallion is curious. But is he ready? Does he even play with himself in the manner in which Hades is supposed to take him?

Probably not.

They will stick to safer activities then, which is not at all a hardship.

"Roll onto your back, Persephone. I will straddle on top."

"But how will you—erm—reach?"

He fills the wine goblet again, and this time passes it to his young stallion.

"Oh, trust me, I could find it facing you as a man does with a woman. But that is not why you'll be on your back." He smiles teasingly. He likes this. Since a god lives forever (well, almost forever, until they are, say, cut to pieces by a scythe wielded by their own son), Persephone's innocence will be a treasured but fleeting moment in their marriage. "You said you wanted me to take you, my new bride. So I shall take you. I shall take *all* of you."

He is much like a baby stallion as he waits nervously, holding the goblet atop the center of his chest, looking at the ceiling with a worried expression, almost like he expects a scolding. But his eyes darken as his gaze shifts to roam over Hades' form instead. His innocence ebbs away. Seph presses his lips together, then lifts his head off the pillow to take several hearty gulps of wine. His uncertainty is still there, but his desire is palpable. Nearly visible too, by his growing meat.

It is tempting to start there, the wine's effect making him impulsive, but Hades orders himself to proceed in a civilized manner. Too many virgin spouses are taken much too fast on their wedding night. Little do the girls know, the men are spurred into it and have much reputation to lose if their friends and family find out they didn't complete the act.

There is one thing they should get over with. Hades crawls over the young stallion as he finishes his drink, helpfully taking the goblet from him to set it aside, and then resting his bare butt on the young man's knees. He sets his hands on Seph's shoulders and leans in. Of all the wedding rites he combined for his guests, he forgot the one where they kiss.

The stallion is not good at it. Much too frozen, like a colt about to dash back to its mother. That is why Hades will warm him up.

"Would you like to touch me?" he asks, and does not wait, guiding Persephone's hands onto his body. Onto his chest first, and then down, near his naval, and then further back around the curve of his ass.

"You can touch me. You can watch me. You can kiss me and taste me and play with me. What do you want to do, stallion?"

Already those hands find a bit of courage. Those fingers become stronger on his backside, his grip sinking in, kneading him carefully, and the young god looks at him a bit like a boy given a birthday gift that he can't believe is his.

"I take orders too." Hades looks him up and down, his tongue poking inside his cheek with devious excitement, the emotion overriding the laziness wine usually brings in the evening. "Tell me, my king, how can I serve? I am an eager, loyal servant, and I know many tricks with my mouth and hands."

Now the young man snorts as though he made a joke.

"I am not your king. It's the other way around!"

"I am pretty sure I am the only king who has married another man. And I'm certainly not going to call you my *queen*, am I? I suppose I could call you my 'prince', but since I am the only king down here, and for the souls who have been here long enough, I am the only king they remember—it would feel as if I was calling you my son."

Hades winces and frowns. Does Persephone know how close he came to being another body taken by Zeus? And then destroyed by Hera. This would not even be the first time that's happened.

"While the thought of that doesn't disgust me, obviously, I did not bring you here to be my son. I am not your replacement father." Hades leans closer until their noses almost touch. He raises his hands and lets his fingers card through the young god's hair.

Finally.

That has been a damn near irresistible itch since the poor stallion was captured and frightened in his chariot.

"You are a King of the Underworld, my God of the End of the Harvest. There are two now. And as far as I know, a king and a king are equal, are they not? Especially if they are kings of the same kingdom."

"That won't work," the young man says, and he lowers his eyes bashfully. But then he smiles. His first smile. Hades holds his breath for this moment.

"Ask me to kiss you again, my king," he whispers.

"I suppose, since you are my king as well, I have to do as you ask!" They both smile playfully. "Kiss me again."

It is much better this time. Persephone angles his lips for him, and licks against him, and their tongues slide hotly together. Blood begins to awaken his groin. His thighs flex. And as his tongue retreats back into his own mouth, the colt follows, hinting for the first time that he might actually, in fact, be a grown stallion.

Persephone picks his head up off the pillow. And then his hands go to the back of Hades' hair. They keep each other in the same dominant, wild hold, except Hades is more gentle and passive, his fingers merely resting and lightly stroking inside the soft, thick locks. The stallion's hands in his hair are a completely different experience, grabbing, holding, tugging, controlling.

He has such big hands. Hades has always thought of him as a puppy, pretty much. Or a colt or a calf or any kind of baby animal. But he has domineering hands, and Hades makes a little whimpering sound into his mouth. He likes to be held. So securely, so firmly. He folds into it.

When the kiss finally ends, both of them panting heavily, he finds himself clutching Persephone's shoulders like the scared little virgin his new king is supposed to be.

"What else can I do for you?" Hades asks, thinking frantically. There are so many options. They seem more hassle than pleasure at the moment, though he never intended to rush his virgin mate.

One more little game. Then he will have his stallion the way he wants. He rides his hips on him, imagining it already.

He's so empty inside.

"Perhaps you'd like to be inside me?"

Curse his tongue! Curse his impatience! The pleasure will, of course, be worth it, but a first time is likely to be short with a virgin.

He wants more of this intimacy before he ends it.

"I-I want to lick you."

There's that cute little stutter. It won't be long before that's gone too, along with his nervousness. It may not even last the night. Perhaps in the far away future he will ask the grown stallion to roleplay.

"Of course you may. What would you like to lick? My king."

"Um..."

Then the stallion is on him, licking him, his hands traveling down to eventually settle and grip at his waist. Again, they are strong. Hades could probably let himself fall back or forward, and those hands would position him just the way they want and keep him sitting up.

His new husband licks high on his rib cage first. It is pretty clear what he wants. But he doesn't go for it, licking and kissing toward the center of his chest instead, his nose coming near the desired target, but stopping just shy of taking it. His eyes flash upward once, perhaps checking to see if it's alright.

"Would you like to lick me here, my king?"

He presents his nipple between two fingers. And at once, like a stallion given lead, he lunges for the prize, enclosing his mouth over Hades' flesh.

"Ahh."

There is not much sensitivity for him here, but watching it is another matter. Persephone is curious, he can tell. His nose squishes cutely into Hades' chest. He sucks the nipple into his mouth and rolls and licks it behind his teeth. He even pulls on it a little, glancing up again to see what Hades will do.

Hades watches with a patient and indulgent smile. He can find pleasure in other ways while his cub explores. He reaches behind and underneath himself, which also requires him to bend backward and present more of his body to that curious mouth.

The angle is not quite right. Usually, if he's going to do this to himself, he would have a toy and he would reach down from the front. But his fingers do find himself and push inside a little. There is resistance. He has been alone and working so much that he can't remember the last time he played.

He can't remember exactly where he put his bottle of slicking oil. The bottom drawer of the nightstand, maybe? Leaning over to check it is too much inconvenience for him. He doesn't want Persephone's hands or mouth to leave for even a moment.

He brings his fingers out and up to spit on them.

"What are you doing?" Persephone asks, lifting his head.

"Getting ready for you, my king."

"Shouldn't it be the other way around?"

A bit breathless now, Hades replies, "I said I would take you. What did you think I meant?"

Of course, this is a game. Anyone can see what Persephone thought, and the young man is not foolish for thinking it.

"Um, I've never... You know, I've never—" Those large hands go straight to his backside now, but they've lost their grabby, domineering quality. They pet as gently as if Hades was a meek chick.

"Rest assured, my king, I have heard your complaint about the bed chambers, and I will personally *rectify* the situation."

The young man looks astonished. Then gives a nervous laugh.

Then he asks, "What if I'm bad at it? What if I hurt you, or—I don't know. What if it doesn't feel right? What if I'm not..." He shrugs apologetically. "...good?"

"Shh. Sit back, my king." Hades gently pushes him to the pillows, kissing him along the way. He decides at last to lean over the side of the bed and reach that bottom drawer. He comes back with a corked vial, and holds it up in the torchlight. The substance needs to be refilled again, but he has just enough.

"This will ease the way," he says, tapping it impatiently against his palm until enough slides to the end. He rubs his palms together briefly and then looks down for that sensitive flesh he's been ignoring. That's because Hades doesn't want to cross too many boundaries too fast.

But all of that thinking flies out the window as he starts his palms at the base of the thick cock and spreads them slowly upward, slicking the shaft and touching the tip last. First with his thumb. Then rolling it between his palms like a ball of dough.

I am a chef preparing a feast.

And oh, he wants to taste. Just a lick. Just to get the flavor, to test the seasoning.

But I shouldn't. Or he will be too quick. He might be close already.

And it would be a shame to spoil the meal.

But only two seconds later his will reserves run empty.

"My king. May I... lick?" He swallows. His mouth salivates. He wants it very much.

Persephone nods, frantically. And Hades dips down for his treat, inhaling deeply at first, and thinking, *It might not be the young one who has to worry about finishing early.*

He sticks his tongue out to taste the slit. But of course, a quick little taste *only* is not something he's capable of. His mouth opens and swallows the head. He slobbers and guzzles and slurps onto it. He only stops because he's licking off the lubrication too, so he can't clean and nurse the cock to completion the way that he wants.

He picks up his head with a frustrated pout.

Next time.

Then he lifts himself up and positions his body over the hard cock. Persephone grabs on to his waist again. And while he does nothing to control Hades, such as shoving him down on his cock (that would be nice), the grip is strong and insistent. Hades is certain he could get a rise out of his stallion with enough teasing. Fortunately, he is not that patient.

Ten

Seph has never seen anyone more graceful and elegant than the pale god straddling him, playing with him, smiling seductively and gathering his long silver hair to one side so that it doesn't get in the way as he lowers his mouth and sucks on Seph's cock.

It is not Seph's first time for that, thank the gods, or he would be done already. It is not necessarily the skill of the tongue that makes Teysus not even a nudge of guilt-laced memory at the moment. It is the image of the dark god *enjoying* himself over Seph, *with* Seph, that makes him feel like he hasn't had a sexual experience until now.

He's glad he didn't move into the mortal town.

He's glad Hades found him when his mother left.

Staying here forever and ever and never seeing the upperworld again gets no complaints from him anymore. This new life is all he has, all he looks forward to, and all he will ever need.

The god's legs are so long. So shapely. As he picks himself up, reaching behind himself again, parting one cheek to nestle Seph's cock inside, Seph runs his hands over Hades' knees. Up his thighs, right up to his waist, where he lets his fingers spread and take hold.

His husband gives him a playful smile. In the dining hall, the god might have been as impassive as stone, but here every little pleasure shows on his face. When he widens his eyes, that smile spreading, Seph knows he's doing something right.

He likes to be caressed. He seems to like Seph's hands best when they hold tight and squeeze. Hades rolls his hips downward with a pleasurable, girlish little gasp. Seph's cock pushes against the tight, warm space. It's small. But Seph is slick.

Still, *Too wide*, he thinks.

This is why Teysus was reluctant with him. Seph agreed to play the submissive role, but Teysus wouldn't take the chance with the goddess nearby at the temple or in Seph's home.

Hades balances himself on Seph's shoulders. He goes up and

down, nudging Seph's cock inside him, and then holding it there, his muscles trying to push him out.

Seph holds tight to his waist, preventing his husband from sinking down any further.

"It's too big."

Hades erupts in a breathy laugh, but Seph doesn't feel humiliated.

"You'll hurt yourself. Give it more time. Or, let me... you know. Let us switch. I don't mind."

"Stallion, I haven't even started to feel you inside me."

He's probably correct. The gods withstand pain a thousand times what can be experienced by a mortal. That doesn't mean Seph wants to split this body, or even stretch him past the point of comfort.

"I want you to go slow. I want you to feel pleasure."

"I will feel pleasure as soon as you are inside me."

He tries to lower himself again, and is partially successful, but Seph strengthens his grip on Hades' waist enough to keep him up. The dark god and he look each other in the eyes. And then, there seems to almost be a connection between them. Besides the physical one, of course.

Hades lowers himself slightly, experimentally. And Seph allows it for a short ways. When it seems too much, too tight, too small, then his fingers dig into his husband's waist as hard as he can, to keep him from going lower. And when he impatiently tries to resist, Seph refuses to compromise. He won't let Hades hurt himself.

In a way, Seph is in charge just now. Like he's never been before.

And while he certainly wants to be buried in that tight heat, to open it up and rut until it's loose and wet with cum, the absolute safety and comfort of the slender god is more important to him.

"I'm not the virgin here," Hades says, clearly prodding to get his way.

"Almost there. Why are you so impatient?"

Hades chuckles again. It's such a good sound. Seph gives him a little more while he's answering. "I haven't had the real thing—*ahhh*—the real thing in a long time."

He continues, like a cat purring, "Oh, that's it, love, all the way. Now let me move."

There is no further to go, but Seph restrains him, shutting his eyes with concentration because the muscles are so tight and pulsing on him, up and down, his entire length. Hades keeps rocking, pushing the head even further, and his ass sits atop Seph's balls.

He has such a cute ass. What would he say if Seph told him that? Seph marvels at the fact that he's buried inside it.

"I'm getting a little upset, stallion," Hades growls, and then they are kissing again. Hotly. Deeply. His husband coaxes Seph's tongue into his mouth and swallows it.

Without really meaning to, Seph's grip loosens, and the dark god gets his way, moving on him. It feels amazing. It takes all of Seph's concentration not to cum already, and he tries to focus on his tongue instead, how it's deep inside his lover at the same time that his cock is.

Hades moans into his mouth. The bed creaks. Hades pushes down on his shoulders, bringing himself high for every thrust, and slams back down, his thighs flexing, his feet arched into the bed like a runner.

Seph gives up on the kiss. He throws his head back and just tries to breathe. To focus. Not to let loose, not yet.

His climax comes close, and he grabs behind the god's cute ass to stop him. This is a far easier way of controlling him. He holds the god high, lets the tension ease out of his balls and cock a bit, and then sets his own pace with his hands. A slower pace.

"I want to enjoy this a while."

By which he really means, *I want to watch you on top of me.*

Hades stays obedient, letting Seph dictate the pace. He whimpers often though, his eyes closing, his body rolling like a cat. He breathes with his mouth open, and his tongue makes a frequent appearance, licking his lips, curling behind his teeth, and sometimes he mouths a silent curse word.

And then there is his hair. Seph hopes there's another night soon in the future and he will get to do this and play with the god's hair.

"You picked me," Seph says, not making an accusation. Just stating the facts.

"*Uhh.* Yes."

"You wanted me like this."

"Yes. Yes, stallion, *yes.*"

"Forever?"

Pale hands come and spread through his hair.

"You're mine now, stallion. Nothing can take you away from me. Not Zeus. Not Apollo. Not any of those idiots."

"Then I want to do this forever. With you. Only you. I don't want to play the games the other gods do. I don't want you to have an affair—" Seph bites his lip. He nearly came. But he's not quite ready yet, and he's not done talking. "Don't take another lover besides me, please. Or I'm going to be—"

A squeeze almost finishes him. He'll have to cum soon before he starts to hurt. "—*ah*—the messed-up boy version of Hera."

"Ugh. Don't say her name." Hades pets up and down his arms. "Do not worry, my mate. I am not popular enough to take other lovers. If you are not available, then I will have nothing."

"I will always be available."

"Then I expect we will get along quite well."

"Can I have you on your back?"

Perhaps this is too greedy. He should've waited for another night, when they could've tried something else. Hades certainly seems to like this position.

It's okay, Seph is about to say, and pick up pace to finish, but then Hades gives a breathy laugh.

"Yes, of course."

Pulling out of him is quick, but not easy. The muscles try to pull him back inside as he leaves. Fortunately, it is not for long. Hades looks much better against the pillows, silver hair spilled everywhere, and Seph hikes his legs up high. Hades grabs both his knees to help, holding them high to expose himself, and Seph kisses the top of his head. Then there is only the sensation of a hot, slick hole pulling on his cock, sucking Seph back inside like it missed him, and those pale, muscled limbs all around. Seph bends an arm under his head, cradling him, and drives as fast as his hot cock begs him to.

Hades finishes first, his mouth open, a deep manly moan coming out of him for several moments. And Seph ruts with the mess of his seed smearing their stomachs, not giving a damn how unusual and slightly gross this is. This is not exactly how he pictured it. But in a lot of ways, it's better.

As well as he can since he's cradling his head, Seph strokes the dark god's hair with one hand, comparing him to a cat again for his softness and that super pink tongue, and then the flood rushes out of him. He buries himself deep and stays there, feeling his cum gush deeply into his husband. Whose inner muscles squeeze and caress and hold him.

That hole is wider now. Seph bets the next time they do this it will be easier.

He finds himself without a thing to say, parked as he is and not ready to leave quite yet.

"I-I think the situation has been rectified."

He hates himself and his stupid brain.

"Oh, Persephone!" Hades kisses his nose.

"Call me Seph, please."

And then he pulls out and away, wondering what the dark god will say. He does not feel so controlling and confident now, and he can't believe some of the ridiculous things he's done. The things he's *thought*. Where he put his mouth. Putting Hades on his back like this, for gods' sake.

Hades is smiling though. And sprawled without shame.

"All right. Seph."

Eleven

Hades wakes up feeling refreshed. He was exhausted, he slept deeply, and now he's rejuvenated. It is not such an abnormal feeling for a mortal or even a normal god, but for decades now it has seemed that Hades was quietly dying inside his own head.

It would be easy to blame the underworld for this. There is not so much color down here, and that includes the spectrum of emotion as well. There is not a lot of drama and misfortune and mishap amongst the old souls of Elysium, all of them only the best of their mortal kind.

It is a happy place. A peaceful place.

A *boring* place.

Far less disruptive than the beautiful, vivid, chaotic world above.

More and more, as the centuries roll by, Hades ventures there less than ever. That was the purpose of appointing the three judges at the Fields of Asphodel, and the various ferrymen, and assigning souls with leadership qualities to look after their individual neighborhoods in Elysium. He made a kingdom that runs itself without a king, technically. So he could leave sometimes.

Though nowadays he finds too many things to do down here, expanding the kingdom and making sure the other gods don't bring their trouble and cruelty into this place. This is his domain. And always, he is planning with his architects for the constant expansion of Elysium into the infinite underworld wilderness.

It is a point of pride with him that every new area of Elysium is crafted with uniqueness and care, and that the neighborhoods do not make a lifeless pattern that repeats itself.

The souls must live here forever, after all. Someday the underworld will be the *only* world, and he wants exploration and wonderment to be the final state of all mortal beings who cross the threshold into Elysium.

But lately, it's seemed that he might not make it to such a vision.

The mortal world is still in its infancy, that final death billions of years away, and Hades is already quiet in his mind. Having no strong emotion. No passionate thoughts. Just the calm completion of everyday tasks, like a plow horse of this vast infinite world, trenching one house at a time.

And now he has Persephone.

Seph, as he likes to be called.

The dark god has not been surprised in forever. Seph has surprised him several times in a *day*. And Hades does very much appreciate the physical aspects of the young god. He eyes Seph's figure as he sits up and yawns and stretches—physical activities that he hasn't done lately. And he's looking forward to doing more, particularly in his private bathhouse, where the home tour he intends to give Seph today should end.

He explores his dark bedroom naked for a bit, appreciating the minor discomforts of his physical body. Things he hasn't noticed in a while. Like the cool marble floor and the difference in texture from that to the rug. And the feeling of the wine goblet in his hand. The weight of the liquid shifting inside the pitcher as he tips it over the golden cup.

He only pours a third of what he usually would for his morning drink. Lately, he has been drinking it so much to feel alive. He won't need that today.

Then, of course, it is time to start the business of the day. He opens the bedroom door and finds his three personal chamber servants sitting cross-legged in his study, chatting and laughing lightly. They all beam at him. For the first time in a long time, the dark god smiles back.

He supposes his slight upturn in the corners of his lips doesn't count as a smile, but for him this is the most cheerful he's awoken in eons.

The servants know him well enough to count it. They rise to their feet joyfully, bowing with respectful remarks made with mischievous intent.

"Sleep well, my king?"

"Shall I change the sheets, sir?"

"Still pretty by the day as in the night?"

Verah is bold. She is also the oldest-appearing chamber servant, around the age of an adult, maybe in her late teens.

It is the littlest one, Alfric, who was born with a cleft palate that his soul figure still maintains, who gives him the bad news.

"New ones runned off, sir. Gorgos and Jaffrès can't find them. Need you to chase 'em down."

"Thank you, Alfric," says Hades, with a sigh after.

Perhaps the kingdom does not *quite* run itself. Yet. Half of his job is overseeing the design and expansion of this place, making sure that it is an interesting world. The other half is maintaining his border, a job he gave to his very loyal pet, Cerberus. But Cerberus was shut in one of the stables yesterday, to keep him away for the wedding.

While Cerberus is everything a perfect dog should be, he is perhaps too ugly (to others) to meet the frightened, demure young god Hades expected to bring home. The feature that made each once-separate dog chosen as his hounds—the extreme love and protection of their family combined with fearlessness and a wary regard for strangers—led them to become the abomination they are today.

Cerberus was once three dog souls, who became so attached to each other they *literally* became attached to each other when their essence reached its ideal form. Remembering how they slept in a heap and clambered together on top of him, Hades has thought that they are not much different than they were before. He is an unsettling creature to meet though, for newcomers. And an additional god in the underworld will be met with a warning growl and vigilant stares for a few days.

"I'll go get them then," Hades says, following Verah back into his room. He whispers, "Do not wake him."

The chamber servants nod and go about their chores, bringing Hades his layers of clothes, even selecting his personal items.

Hades used to brush his own hair and select his own jewels, but when Verah noticed that he had stopped taking an interest in himself, she began to do more things for him. Today he lets her jump in and look after him simply because it's efficient. And because, while lifting the occasional foot for a boot or holding his arms out so someone can reach a button or buckle, he can watch the bed where Seph sleeps.

The stallion does look as pretty in the morning as he did last night with all those flowers and the dark circlet in his hair. Now, however, his hair is wild and tangled and spread all across his pillow. A tempting piece of it touches his nose, and Seph twitches like a rabbit. Then he huffs like the snort of a horse.

Whichever animal he is in Hades' mind, he's a cute one. And

gloriously male as well.

"No thank you, Verah," he says as she approaches him with diamond earrings today. The diamonds are actually his favorite, but after noticing Seph's interest, he may have a new favorite now. "I'd like the teardrop sapphire earrings again today."

She glances toward the bed and rolls her lips inward, hiding a smile. She nods once and comes back with the appropriate stones.

"Necklace for you today?"

"You choose."

She brings him an aquamarine necklace, heavy with several rough-cut pebbles attached and layered around a diamond rope chain. This one is her favorite. Hades loves it too, especially when he goes to visit Poseidon, who doesn't have anything nearly as nice. The god of the deep ocean tries to make *seashells* look like jewelry...

"You in a good mood today," Verah says, lifting it over his head.

"Shh," he tells her, tilting his head toward the bed, though he does smile extra just for her.

She acknowledges this and comes back with some rings. She shows him the first one silently to see if he has any objections, then pushes them onto his fingers.

Hades spends a moment admiring crystal encased in silver. For a long time now, he has not noticed any of the stones she decks onto him.

The crown is the final piece, made of obsidian. Gleaming, yes, but otherwise humble compared to the rest of him. While Hades did not relish the underworld at first, he has grown to love every aspect of it, and he thought the god of the underworld should start to look like one. The crown seems to imbue somber power into whoever wears it.

"You ready, sir," says Alfric, and he stands on tiptoe to fetch Hades' wine off the nightstand. He clutches the pitcher to his chest, sets the goblet on the floor, and prepares with two hands to carefully pour it in.

"Not today, Alfric," Hades says, flexing his hands inside his gloves. So soft. And he moves his toes too, which are already warm inside his boots.

"In fact, you may take that back to the kitchen."

"Is something wrong with the wine, my king?" asks Sefkh, who called him pharaoh for many years.

The dark god thinks of Seph's hands and gives an unhelpful answer.

"It isn't strong enough."

The chamber servants look at each other, uncertain.

"Shall I bring you some more?"

"Some fresh," Verah says with a nod to send him off, but the dark god interjects.

"No, I'm heading to the stables now. Verah, bring me breakfast there. Alfric, run ahead so the stable hands can get one of my horses ready."

With bows, they disperse.

Twelve

Seph wouldn't even be awake if he didn't have to piss so bad. He swings his legs over the side of the bed, yawns, stands, and shuffles across the room. He doesn't realize he's not where he's supposed to be until he stops, blinking sleepily, looking at a table of his mother's jewels and wondering why.

Then he remembers and looks back at the bed.

It's empty.

He's disappointed by that somehow, and rubs the back of his neck, eventually yawning again.

Then he hears a soft little clink and notices Hibus against a different wall at the large window, standing on his hind legs to paw and sniff at the curtain. If he had his straw box, that is where it would be.

Seph goes to the bed and crawls underneath it, bringing out the basket and slightly soiled picnic blanket. He wipes up the rest of the urine puddle under there and wads the blanket into the basket, careful to keep his hands clean. He presents this new straw box to the confused bunny.

"This is all you get for now. Okay?" He lifts Hibus inside and pets over his ears. Seph has several vegetable pieces in hand, the leftovers from last night, and feeds a little piece of broccoli to the white bunny. Who only nibbles once and stops, scrunching his nose, then turns in a circle to scratch at the blanket.

Hibus knows these aren't fresh treats.

The rabbit also bundles the blanket up underneath him, turns around and keeps turning, ending on the edge closest to Seph, stretching over the side on his front two legs as though to leave. The state of his straw box upsets him.

"Me too, buddy. Me too."

Though, Seph's elimination experience is nothing to complain about. He almost feels bad for the fine marble and artistic skill that went into *his* 'straw box'. So much beauty for a simple shitter. Then when he's done he wonders where the bucket of water is to toss in. The hole is angled instead of going straight down, so there must be a pipe in the wall going outside. And he needs to clean up after himself somehow.

He notices a lever in the wall, near the trickling fountain for his hands.

He pulls it down and water gushes into the pot, making it clean again.

He then spends some time flushing the pot over and over, discovering that the water takes a few minutes to be ready, but it never seems to stop flowing, somewhere.

His mother's latrine in the villa is considered state-of-the-art. The nymphs were very excited when the construction of it was finished. Water continuously pouring from a fountain is divided into two channels. One at the front of their feet to wash dirtied rocks or sponges in. And one that runs under the seats to carry waste away without human intervention.

This is far more modern.

He does not quite get tired of pulling the lever over and over again, since the sound of water flowing in the walls is interesting and the lever makes a rattling, ticking sound as it gradually climbs up on its own to its top resting place.

Then he hears the bedroom door opening and rushes back to Hibus.

A nymph—no, just an unusual soul—carries a bronze bowl suspended on chains. Blue fire burns within, and this unusual person is scooping it out with a ladle, pouring it gingerly over a torch mounted on the wall. As though the flame is a liquid. The glowing blue ember still alive on the torch brightens considerably as the ladle feeds it. Initially, the new flame seems to sag like the boughs of an old bent tree. Then life springs into it, and the blue flame flickers and glows like a real flame would.

As before, the flame does not seem to put out heat in this cold place. It doesn't seem to burn the bronze container it's in or heat the chains.

Out of curiosity, Seph puts his hand over the embers of a dying torch next to him. He feels nothing. He taps a finger there first, and then covers the charred stick with his palm.

"Ow!"

This new person, with strangely ice blue hair and soft perfect features, looks at him in surprise and puzzlement and comes over, setting the ladle in the bowl.

"Why would you do that?"

He?—for he looks very female but he has no breasts, so he must be a he—hikes the chains onto his shoulder, having no concern for the dangerous bowl contained by them, which could spill and burn the palace down. He opens Seph's palm with two hands.

Seph's hot, burning hands. But burning differently. The initial sensation is *cold*.

"Oh. You are healing quickly," says this new person, gingerly poking around the large red burn. "It should fade back to normal in a few hours."

"What is that? How could it burn me if it doesn't put off any heat?"

This person blinks. By the blankness of his face, Seph can guess that what he's about to say is common knowledge.

"The flame is not fire. It is ice. You can be burned by ice, young master—uh, I'm sorry—my king! I am used to there being only one king here." He sounds slightly annoyed by that fact.

"It's all right. I've only been a king for a day. Yesterday I was cutting wheat in my mother's fields."

This person frowns. "You were a slave? A slave *god*?"

"No. My mother is the Goddess Demeter, the Goddess of the Fields. I was helping her nymphs. They are not slaves, but they might as well be. They tend her fields and she claims the bounty. She claims everything from them."

Even their forest, their homes, and their land.

Seph's brow furrows as he examines this person closely. This is not an ordinary mortal soul. It is his face. The doll-like eyes. The smallish mouth with full pink lips. Not to mention the petite size of this person. He is a man, dressed simply in a chiton of loose, thin fabric, but not tied around his waist by a belt or string. The manner of his clothing is exactly like a slave in the mortal world.

And then there is his blue hair. Blue is a trendy color in one fair-haired village he knows about. But the dye is expensive to make and requires a cosmetic slave or two to apply.

"What are you?"

"Ah. Good eye, my king." The person lets go of his hand and grabs the chains instead, as casually as if the bowl of ice flame was a shoulder bag. He demonstrates a small bow that doesn't topple the bowl. "I am Minthe, a nymph of the underworld. I handle the blue flame, which only burns down here. Only an underworld nymph can make it. There are many nymphs down here, but only a few in the palace. We mostly walk the roads of Elysium and keep the street lamps lit."

"There are no male nymphs," Seph says with confusion. But then he feels stupid because one is obviously standing right in front of him. "At least, that's what my mother told me." He looks the male nymph up and down. "And a goddess as old as her is never wrong about anything."

She is not even wrong about him. His love for Teysus was not as deep as he thought. This new love though... Maybe.

The male nymph gives him a friendly smile and holds the chains off his shoulder again, picking up the ladle to resume work.

"She is not wrong. I am technically not a boy. I'm a hermaphrodite. That means I have both, though I am mostly impotent as far as male attributes are concerned. The underworld nymphs can appear as male or female, but we are all hermaphrodites."

"Oh. Umm. Hm. I see." What is the correct way to say *Thank you for that information* and also *Sorry I am so rude*? And also *I can't control my eyes*? Because while he acknowledges that asking someone to explain their gender might not be the most appropriate small talk between two respectable strangers, he also eyes the groin area of Minthe's chiton and wonders... how... that... works.

"You want to see," says the nymph, and he sets the ladle back into the bronze bowl. The torch near Seph's head burns brightly again, though not as bright as an orange flame would.

"No." Seph holds up his hands. "No, I'm sorry. This is, uh, just new to me. I've never heard of a hermaphrodite before. Well, I sort of have. But... it's very rare, isn't it?"

He wants to steer this conversation onto anything else, but Minthe grabs the bottom of his chiton like it's a dress and seems posed to lift it up.

"It's okay to look. It is only your curiosity, and I can understand. There is nothing to be ashamed of, my king."

It is not servitude or enslavement that causes Minthe to say this. Along with a deep understanding of nature and the violence and death of things, nymphs are also quite comfortable with their natural state, and it is not uncommon to see naked nymphs doing ordinary things around his mother's villa.

Seph catches Minthe's wrists before the chiton goes any higher.

He winces for the painful burn on his hand.

"No. It's alright, Minthe. You don't have to show your body to me. Thank you for explaining. I was confused, and now I am satisfied."

Minthe looks a bit stunned to be grabbed in such a way, but then he shrugs, not caring.

"Gods and mortals can be strange. Even the dead ones. Next, I suppose you will ask me which I liked to be called by. A man or a woman?"

"Erm. Yes, actually." He's clearly had this conversation a few times.

"We have no preference, my king. We find it quite funny that you other types want to label us by your terms. We are merely as we are. And you can call us what you like."

"Okay. Minthe it is, then," Seph answers, letting go. He's glad to have this conversation out of the way. And he's found yet another reason to like the underworld. Sort-of-male nymphs! If his mother had told him that, he would have been excited to see this place.

Gods and men fall in love with nymphs for a reason. Their faces are lovely and their understanding of the world is alluring for how wise and peaceful it is. When you talk to a nymph, you feel like you could tell them *anything*. Your deepest, darkest desire would seem normal to them. It is impossible for a nymph to be embarrassed or shy about themselves, and this personality can make a man bold.

But I have something better now.

What a late discovery, unfortunately.

"You are beautiful," Seph says with a stiff nod, wishing to apologize but knowing that this would only confuse the nymph. They find flattery to be funny, though. Beauty is not understood by a nymph, but they love that it gives them power over the silly mortals who happen upon them.

Saying *You are beautiful* is like telling a joke.

It works. Minthe gives him a small chuckle and scoops another wriggling, dancing glob of flame into his ladle.

Then Hibus scratches madly against the floor, trying to dig a hole in the rug, and he stops to taste the tassels.

Everything here is a thousand times nicer than the goods made by mortal hands in his mother's homes. Seph rushes around Minthe to the bunny and scoops him up as he falls to his knees.

"What is *that* doing here?" Minthe asks, and his ladle clangs in the bowl.

Seph cradles and pets the bunny, who kicks his back legs twice because he wants to keep exploring.

"This is Hibus, my rabbit. He is a *pet* rabbit, which means we can't eat him. That's important, okay? Erm, my word as King is that this rabbit—" Seph holds him up. "—is not to be killed or harmed for any reason."

Nymphs don't understand pets, but they do understand the authority of kings, and especially gods.

"That can't stay here," Minthe says in a stern tone. "How did you get it here?"

"Well... I am a god," Seph reminds him. "And I brought him here in a basket."

"Ah. A basket. So our other king doesn't know that it's here. Am I correct?"

"Yeah."

Minthe moves to the next torch and resumes lamp lighting as before.

That is that, then. Though Seph decides not to set down the bunny until the lamplighter is finished. He doesn't trust his new authority as a king. Who's to say how a nymph interprets the presence of *two* kings? Seph is willing to bet the youngest, newest king might not have to be obeyed as strictly as the older one. And he called the rabbit an *it*.

"I take it you don't have rabbits here."

"Not alive ones, anyway," he says, his voice drifting. He seems to be thinking about something. Probably the rabbit.

"Are you going to tell Hades?"

"Hm? I'm not sure," he answers. "I might." A nymph is also terribly honest.

"Well, you don't have to. I'm going to tell him myself today. Hibus needs a straw box and a cage to sleep in." Seph pauses for a moment, then asks, "Do you think Hades will be okay with that? Or will he make me keep Hibus outside? Maybe I could keep him in another room. A room just for Hibus. Do you think he'd approve that?"

"No." Minthe laughs. "No, not at all."

The last wall torch is lit, and Minthe puts the ladle away, turning to face him. "If our other king sees that rabbit, he will take it away from you. It will go right back to the upperworld where it belongs."

"He let me bring him..." Seph says uncertainly, stroking the rabbit's ears. Hibus kicks twice again, but Seph won't let him down.

"Perhaps he did," Minthe says with amusement. "But I already knew Hades didn't know about the rabbit before you said anything! Do you know why that is?"

Seph shakes his head. He has the feeling he won't like this answer. And he can't imagine abandoning Hibus after taking care of him and raising him for so long.

"It is because the things that belong in the upperworld stay in the upperworld. And the things that belong in the underworld stay in the underworld. Our king is *obsessive* about this."

"Maybe if I ask him nicely? Maybe if I plead? Hibus is the only thing I want to bring with me from the upperworld."

Seph feels like he will do it for him. Hades *likes* him. He thinks.

In the morning, the emotions he felt last night are only a memory, and they feel so far away. Who knows how today will go when the king comes back. And who knows when they will do *that* next. But Seph thinks the dark god will be kind. That he will smile a little more when Seph is around, and he might even make another soft, pleasing laugh.

It's different than the laugh Minthe makes now, which seems to mock him.

"Oh, that won't matter! Let me tell you something now, young god, and don't you forget it! Hades does not answer to *pleading*."

Minthe climbs on top of a couch and hangs his bronze bowl from a curtain rod. The blue substance sloshes to one side exactly like water. A bit falls out and drops to the floor. It seeps into the stone like rain on dry sand and doesn't ruin anything.

Minthe steps past him and hops onto the bed, sitting on the edge with his legs hanging down. He pats the space next to him.

Seph decides Hibus might be a bit safer on the floor. He sets him free and sits where instructed.

Minthe speaks to him like an old friend.

"Now, young king, let me explain so you can understand. The god of this place..." Minthe makes a sweeping gesture. "...has heard every plea. Every cry, every wail, and every sob. He has heard the immense grief of mothers and grandmothers. He has listened to every deserving excuse of every murderer and warrior and sinner and all manner of things you cannot comprehend."

He leans over his knees and props his chin on his hand.

"So whenever you want to appeal to the dark god's sensibilities, you had better try something besides *pleading*. He does not have emotions like that. Not like you or I."

"That sounds a lot like how my mother described Zeus," Seph says sadly, wondering if he's misinterpreting everything. His mother said Seph wouldn't see the truth until it was too late. Could the same thing be happening here?

"Well, they are brothers," Minthe says simply. "Though, I have never met Zeus. He sends a spy here sometimes to try and steal our king's wine or get the recipe. But he knows better than to come down here himself. Hades would gut him."

"No he—" *wouldn't, they're brothers.*

But of course, in Seph's family, that doesn't mean anything.

"So what should I do about my rabbit?" Seph asks, realizing that Minthe would know best. If he works in the palace, he must know Hades well.

"I don't know," Minthe says with a little shrug, straightening up again. "But things stay where they are. Where they belong. It's the only rule here that Hades enforces himself. Otherwise, he lets the village leaders run things. Do you know what he's doing right now?"

Seph shakes his head.

"Two young souls—though they look old—the new ones usually look *ancient*—well, they decided to use your wedding as an opportunity. They saw that Hades was distracted, by you of course. And they found out that Cerberus, the big hound dog, was kept in the stable so that you could get married without getting bit or something. These two young souls are trying to escape back into the upperworld now. They're running for their lives, trying to find a place to cross the River Styx."

"Does that happen often?"

"Yes. It happens as often as a mother or father or son feels a purpose that they need to return to in the upperworld. Even at the cost of angering the most merciless god."

"And what happens to them? What if they do cross into the upperworld?"

"If they can get there, they will go to Tartarus. A place of eternal punishment."

Seph frowns. He does know about Tartarus, of course. Everyone does. Hades is infamous for the eternal punishments he's given the giants, Tantalus, and others. The ones in Tartarus are mostly mortal or creature souls, but they are sent there by Zeus, and everyone remembers that Zeus (and Hades) can keep a god tortured in Tartarus forever. The stories are enough to make sure that the rulers are obeyed among the other gods, and challenges do not happen often.

"It makes him that angry? That somebody would try to leave?"

Seph hasn't directly thought about escaping yet, but the gravity of this question pulls on his soul.

"Yes, young king. So don't you do it. These young souls are stupid in my opinion. What Hades will do to them if he catches them before they escape is not that bad compared to Tartarus."

"What is that?" Seph asks, wondering who it was really that he made love to last night. "What does he do to them?"

Thirteen

"Cerberus, my good boy! How are you?" Hades says excitedly, unlocking the stall where his large hound is kept. The animal stands on two legs with its front paws sticking out of the gate bars, three muzzles pushing through to lick him up.

The middle one gives a frustrated bark and howl, the sound sorrowful.

"Oh, I know, boy. I know, I know." He has to swing the door open slowly, and the big dog walks with it, not understanding the physics of his imprisonment right away. Until the door is out far enough, and then the hefty beast drops to the straw-covered floor with a *whump*. He barges at the open space, and the door slams out the rest of the way. Hades only has time to put his hands up before he's downed by the happy, impetuous beast.

And though he'd rather not be picking straw out of his hair, it's only a matter of seconds until he's on his back on the dusty barn floor, guarding his face from three slobbery tongues and awful breath, while also trying to pet the hound in reciprocation.

"I missed you too, boy. Aah! I'm sorry I had to keep you in here!"

The hound paws his guarding arm away and snaps a bark at him.

"I only had to do it because you're such a bad dog! You're such a mean good boy, aren't you?"

The hound hops off at last and turns a circle beside him, indicating he would like his rump scratched, which his master does for him as he sits up.

Hades would look a lot more kingly and regal if it weren't for his hound, who seems to be convinced the god is just as rowdy and common as he is.

"We've got to go on a hunt today, boy," Hades says to the ear of the left one. It is difficult to scratch all three heads at once, and they demand equal attention.

The word *hunt* does not trigger the dog immediately, though usually he would run to the horse and start looking back, as if to say, *Hurry up!*

He is too distracted by the appearance of his master, and no doubt wonders why he was locked up in the first place. Cerberus will usually sleep in the room with him, curled up to the right of the bed. And since Hades has ended his relationship with Minthe, he usually wakes up to the hound 'sneaking' into bed with him, his paws on the mattress, inching his snouts closer and closer to give Hades sneaky, playful good-morning licks.

"You'll be in the stable for a while, boy. I've got romance in my life now. Do you smell him on me?"

Perhaps, perhaps not. The dog does have a preoccupation with his clothes, but that's likely because he wants to learn everything that Hades was up to while he was imprisoned.

"He's going to be your new master, boy. You're not going to like him, I know. He's not going to like you either. But pretty soon you'll be back in the palace where you belong, yeah? If we have to... maybe we will stick Seph out here in the stall instead, eh?"

Not really, of course.

But possibly. If he finds out that Seph doesn't like dogs and isn't willing to change his mind, well then...

Easy problems first.

Hades stands and starts to brush himself off, but there's just no way to get all the straw and dirt off of places.

"Hunt now, boy. We're going on a hunt!"

The dog turns in a circle, whines, and yaps. He rears up to two legs again, holds briefly, tongues lolling out adorably, and then bounds in a circle around Hades' legs.

"Yeah, we better go get them, huh?" Hades says in his dog voice, bending over to pet him again. "Let's go bring them home! Come on!"

He trots toward the open doors, where Alfric and a stable hand are waiting. The stable hand holds the horse, one of his black steeds who sits with a back leg cocked and her ears back like she's grumpy to be kept out of the pasture this morning. She tosses her head to remind the stable hand that she's inconvenienced.

And Alfric waits with two sets of manacles, the long chains tangled and drooping from his arms.

Despite his small size, Alfric is only truly happy when he's being helpful.

"Thank you, Alfric," Hades says, bending to take the heavy, rattling burden from him. He winds them up in his hands and slings the loop across the front of the saddle. One ear flicks forward on the horse. She knows that sound. She knows what they're doing now, and she shuffles her feet.

She's going to get to run.

Cerberus bounces toward the gate, growls, and looks back. *Hurry up!*

"On the day after my wedding, too," Hades says with a groan and pulls himself up onto the horse.

"Sorry, my king," says the stable hand Taushev. He is a quiet boy who still to this day only says *yes* or *sorry* and *my king*. He looks at the manacles with fear.

He was a runner once himself.

With a nod to him, Hades kicks the horse to trot toward the paddock gate, which another stable hand is already opening. They gallop through and gain speed as they follow a path around the palace that leads to the banks of the River Styx. Cerberus bolts like mad with his ears back, streaking toward the trees.

Hades chuckles to himself for how silly and excited the dog looks. He likes to work, his loyal dog. Like Alfric, he likes to help his master. For that reason, he is always excited to go on a hunt, and Hades usually gets the news that someone has run off by his excited dog yapping and turning in circles in front of him.

The horse huffs steadily, her neck bobbing with her gait, and easily takes the narrowed, curving path into the trees. They've done this enough times that she could follow it blind. Soon the path will meander out, sticks and debris appearing in the way, but his horse has most of the forest memorized too, especially the riverbank, where she can hop over every errant rock and root.

Hades loves his broad, winding river. The River Styx. It's as deep as the ocean possibly, and all manner of things reside within. Enormous creatures who haven't existed in the mortal world since longer ago than when the giants were around. They are older than he is.

And sometimes there is the Goddess Styx herself, of course, who the river is named after. A quiet, compassionate type, she is a great animal keeper and looks after the aquatic beasts. She is also sometimes helpful in pointing the way to one of his strayed citizens.

He doesn't sense her in this area of the woods today. He shall have to rely on Cerberus and the speed of his horse, who has a harder time keeping up the further they get into the rocky, untamed woods.

Then he hears the joyful howl of his hound catching the scent.

The two souls are the same ones he pointed out to Seph as they traveled to their wedding. A man and a woman. Not a couple, but they are from the same part of the Earth, a place Greeks haven't discovered yet. They're quite overwhelmed by everything, but their village leaders know their culture, and their village has others from that continent in it.

This is not a huge comfort. The souls come from different times. When the citizens of Elysium run off, it is because they feel alone. Some purpose pulls them back. Usually it is the love of some family member who needs them. Or sometimes they are just not happy here.

But they drank from the River Lethe, and they swore the oath to be his citizens. They swore to forget and renounce their earthly life. Hades made it very clear that they are his.

He hears a frightened scream up ahead and urges the horse to pick up speed. There are only moments now. He hears the dog howl happily. And then there is a growling, yapping roar in the trees as Cerberus catches the prey.

What condition his errant souls are in when he gets to them will depend on how quickly he gets there.

His horse bounds into a small clearing amongst the trees, and Cerberus has the woman underneath him, his three heads biting, shaking, and tearing her flesh off the bone. Blood flies off his jaws and teeth as the woman, appearing elderly, raises a weak arm to stop him. She beats on him with a frail fist. This only causes Cerberus to tear at her arm, two heads wrestling for dominance of the limb like they're squabbling over a bone.

Her blood is ink black and pools all around her. Blood is imagined by the souls, who don't actually have physical bodies. Those rotted in the upperworld shortly after their death. But his errant citizen can certainly feel herself bleed. She can feel the dog's teeth in her flesh and his claws digging rends against her struggles.

Old souls are much harder to catch. They can be wandering in the forest for days by the time Hades catches up to them. And they greet Cerberus' violent vigor with an amused smile.

An old soul of Elysium cannot be caged in by their king. That is why the hunt is so important. A new soul is like a new babe, but one who is destined to be absolutely free of anything you say or do. Their training must be harsh and realistic. If Hades were to jump off of his horse, shoo Cerberus away, and act like a doting father, she would not be afraid enough to never run off again.

He made mistakes in the early days.

Now he pulls in the horse, doing a half circle around where she shrieks and screams, wailing to get away as vividly as if she were a live woman attacked by a real dog.

"Shh, woah, there now," Hades tells the horse and pats her neck. She turns her ears back distastefully from the screams.

"Please! War chief, please! Mercy! Call off the dog!"

She reaches for him, and Cerberus claws into her back, biting her neck and clamping down on it hard. In the upperworld, he would hold her like this a few minutes until she died. In this world, she only continues to wail and bleed, trying to fight off the dog. But she is handicapped by her own memory of her elderly feeble strength.

The other two heads bite her arm and shoulder.

Hades walks the horse up close to her and then dismounts. He takes one set of manacles with him and does not call off the dog as he approaches.

"Stop him, please! I will die! It hurts! He's killing me!"

Hades lost many sweet children who didn't fear him in the early days. Those were his mistakes. He hates himself just thinking about it. Of course they wandered! What sort of child behaves with a father who doesn't punish them?

Fatherhood took hundreds of years to learn and hundreds more to perfect. Now Hades is an expert, and he has no reaction to her cries.

Going to one knee, he captures each wrist in the manacles.

"Let go, boy!" he says, standing with the chains in hand. "We've got another to catch! Go on!"

Cerberus puts her down, stares a moment with a happy, ink-dripping grin, then bounds off.

The man, wherever he is, will suffer the dog's attack for longer, until Hades can be there.

So be it.

"Get up," he tells the woman, pulling on the chains.

"I can't walk!" she sobs at him in her language. Hades knows all the tongues of men, including the ones they've forgotten. "P-please, chief! Leave me! I'm maimed! He crippled me! Just leave me!"

All of this is said around a lot of wailing and gasping. She's in so much pain, she can hardly speak.

Hades drags her. His horse snorts and takes a few reluctant steps forward to meet him.

"I can't walk! Chief! I'm of no value! The dogs broke my back! They tore my leg!"

Indeed, her soul body is bent and maimed in several places. But he doesn't answer. Hades lets the new souls believe that their bodies are healed and the memories taken by drinking from the River Lethe. When the truth is, it is their own mind that cures such things. This is not a secret he wants getting out.

With her on the ground, he mounts the horse. He nudges her into a walk, and the wailing old woman is dragged, broken and bleeding, her screams rising in fresh pain. It is easy here, for now, in the clearing. Going over the rocks and roots, all the way back to the palace they ran all night to flee, will be a long journey of agony. And they will take it slow. One step at a time.

Neither she nor any of the younger souls in Elysium will be inclined to run again. The newest babes, of course, will always need the lesson.

Fourteen

Seph only pretends to be asleep as he hears the door to the den open and close. A soft, almost imperceptible voice says, "Undress me here. So we don't wake him."

And an answering female voice says, "Yes, king. Wine for you?"

"Yes. A lot of wine, Verah. Thank you."

"I will get it for you, sir," says a child's voice, the loudest of the three.

"Go with him, Sefkh. Help him carry."

Then there is only time to wait. Hades stays in the den for some time, while a figure quietly enters the bedroom and places objects that clink on the opposite nightstand, where Hades will sleep. He hears the sound of pouring liquid, and then the figure leaves.

Seph opens his eyes just enough to see an adolescent young man carrying the wine goblet back. Hades can be seen through the open door, his shirt being removed, his hand reaching for the wine goblet as soon as his arm is free of a sleeve. He tilts his head back, taking a hearty gulp.

Seph wonders about the events he heard from Minthe. They must be true. A nymph doesn't have any reason to lie about this. And Seph knows the rumors of Hades. Neither the mortals nor the gods speak of him often, and if they do, they'll try to avoid saying his name. Yet, somehow, everyone knows the name Hades. That isn't an accident.

And everyone was entirely too pleasant and too vague all day, as Seph inquired, *Where was his husband? When would he be back? What was he doing?*

Minthe gave him the straightest answer. Even another lamp lighting nymph in the palace only said, 'He is doing what a king must be doing, my king. And he will be back when he is done, my king.' Repeating titles of respect is something his mother's nymphs do also when they must give the goddess some news that will upset her.

This nymph also added, 'He wants to return to you quickly, for his task is necessary but unpleasant. He will be with you as soon as he can, my king.'

The nymph was probably just telling him the same thing in a different way, trying to say something closer to what Seph wanted to hear because he wouldn't stop pressing for details. But that little phrase has stuck in his mind, and Seph wonders whether or not the nymph bent the truth a little? Or if this was genuine information.

He wants to return to you quickly.

And then, *Don't wake him.*

It seems he's being foolish at first, watching the pale god let Verah take him out of his pants. Seph's breath deepens, and he thinks that surely a god who wanted to spend time with him would ask for Seph's help with that? Seph would do it gladly.

He's been missing Hades. Even hearing about the hunt and how Hades drags souls injured by his dog back to the palace to heal, their walk being their punishment, has not dampened this emotion that yearns for the dark god.

He would not call it love. Rather, for now, it is a mixture of fascination, fear, and hoping to be loved.

Fear because the longer he is away from Hades, the more his mind has analyzed and twisted the memory of their lovemaking. He wants the dark god in bed again. Just to be close and be in private, not necessarily for physical pleasure.

He feels like he didn't truly meet Hades until they were both naked in this room. He would like to meet his husband again and decide for himself which interpretation is correct. The unfeeling monster that Minthe described? Or the slightly playful, alluring god that Seph remembers?

Something in between?

Seph shuts his eyes and makes sure his breath continues steady and slow as the naked god turns to the door. He hears footsteps, and then the door closes. When he peeks out of his lashes because he can't help himself, his husband's face is hidden by the bottom end of the wine goblet.

Then he crosses to his side of the bed, sits, and Seph hears the wine pitcher pouring again.

"Three pitchers. Smart, Sefkh," Hades mumbles to himself. And every glass downed is followed by the sound of pouring.

Seph realizes the fault in his plan of stealth. Pretending to be asleep might let him observe the dark god unknowingly for a few moments, but those moments will only be spent drinking, and Hades may soon use the aid of the wine to pass out.

So he sits up and mimes a yawn. "Oh, you're back."

Hades looks at him over his shoulder. "I did not mean to wake you."

"No, it's okay. I, uh, wasn't sleeping that deeply anyway. Obviously. Uhh. Where have you been?" He shrugs as if he doesn't care. But he really, really wants to hear this. And he wants his husband in bed with him again.

He gets his wish quickly. Hades puts his feet up and scoots back into the pillows, drinking from the wine goblet, then holding it on his chest.

"No one told you yet? I was fetching some souls who ran out during our wedding. They are new souls. The very ones I pointed out to you, in fact. The new ones have to be brought in periodically. And..." He drinks, but this time it is only a sip. "They have to be taught not to try and cross the River Styx. Not to try and cross me either."

"What happens if they cross the River Styx?" Seph asks, propping his head on his hand. Hades finishes two more sips of wine. He seems to be thinking of what to say. Then he lies on his side and faces Seph in the same manner.

His hair is like liquid silver spilling on the sheets, and every highlight of muscle from the dimming torches calls to Seph's hands. Even in this merest second before Hades speaks, Seph's free hand idly travels a little closer than it was before.

And then his husband answers him.

"What have they told you already?"

Seph pets the sheets instead. He wishes they were closer.

"They said you didn't want to leave me but you had to. They said that the souls are hurt by your dog Cerberus, and that you bring them back in chains like slaves. And they said that if the souls manage to escape, you get angry and send them to Tartarus to be punished forever."

His hand lies flat.

Yes, it is difficult to get over that last fact. That is the part that frightens him the most. What if Seph was ever to decide that he missed his mother so much he wanted to cross the River Styx? What would Hades do to him?

His husband is well into his third glass of wine already and still seems to be thinking about what to say. This is not a good sign. Seph might have been hoping he would say, *That's not true at all!*

"Why do you get so mad at them when they try to leave?"

Finally Hades' lips let go of that wine goblet and he mumbles when he speaks.

"It is not anger. It is fear. Fear sometimes looks like anger though. And kindness is sometimes punishment."

"Tell me more," Seph says, settling comfortably into the pillows. "I want to hear your side of it." Feeling brave and a touch shivering scared, Seph reaches across the bed and catches his elbow. "Before you get drunk. Please. My king."

This is to remind him of their little game that Seph hopes will be repeated someday. Also, the nymphs might be onto something about mentioning titles to deflect offense.

Hades frowns, stares, and frowns a little deeper. But then he turns and the wine goblet goes back on the nightstand, where two pitchers are waiting on the flat surface and one more is parked on the floor.

When Hades returns he scoots closer than ever, to the middle of the bed, and he sets an arm across Seph's waist. Their knees touch. Hades leans in with his eyes closing, and Seph gets two seconds to panic, realizing they're about to kiss and he suddenly forgot how. Hades does it differently than Teysus, who would usually kiss his neck and very rarely his mouth. And even then, their tongues only met once.

Hades goes straight for his lips. His tongue licks against him at once. Seph's cock twitches, and he opens his mouth to receive the slick, delving muscle. It is sort of like having the dark god enter him the other way. Seph is looking forward to that someday. He hopes it will feel as good as this.

Or better?

Maybe.

He tries to tilt his head right and be passive for him.

It is a lot more difficult with both their heads being sideways.

Hades tastes exactly like a cup of wine.

Then he is away and breathing on Seph's lips, his eyes lowered.

"I had to get that out of the way before we go into the gruesome details."

"We can get a lot more out of the way too," Seph offers, hoping to be kissed again. He doesn't let his hand lie idle anymore. He sneaks it under the covers and onto that tempting body, massaging heavy, slender muscle—not bulky like Seph's own form. Perfect.

Made for my hands.

"Mmm." The god rolls onto his stomach and crosses his arms under his head, letting Seph rub up and down his back. And even to go lower. As low as he dares. He squeezes one cheek firmly, spreading the crevice and imagining what he can do inside...

But that fire dies when Hades says, "I'm not in the mood for it today, my king. We shall have to stick to simple petting."

And Seph's hand travels north to less heated places. He's disappointed, but respectful of his husband's wish.

"Of course, my king. Um. It must be hard. For you. To punish your people like that. I can see how happy they are. And how much they don't fear you, usually. So it must be difficult to bring them in when they try to run away like that."

But why punish them in Tartarus?

His mother is right. He is youthful and naïve. Easily distracted and easily fooled.

"Actually, it isn't that hard. I have been through the grief of losing them permanently, so this is very little pain for me at all. Every soul is unique, Seph. No two children are alike. So to lose one permanently across the River Styx is a great loss this world can never recover."

"That is why they go to Tartarus? So the others will be so afraid they never do it?"

"Almost," Hades says with one of his slight smiles. Seph's exploring hand reaches the back of his neck, and that soft hair is in his fingers at last. Hades tilts his head for him so Seph will go behind his ear.

"That is what bringing them back is for. The hunt is their deterrent. The dog cannot truly harm them, but they don't know that, and their imagined pain is as true as real pain, fortunately.

"No, Tartarus is because once the souls cross the River Styx back into the upperworld, their life is drained out of them. They become wandering, empty shells. Physically, they can't tell it's happening, but emotionally they are filled with great terror, panic, and grief.

"It is the realization that they are dying—truly dying, not just crossing into another world. They are being eaten alive, by life that needs to be fed. One interesting thing about mortals—in all their many myths about us gods and this place, and all their many theories and great imaginings, they never realize that the simplest equation is right in front of them. Life consumes life. It always has. It always must."

Seph does not know when he stopped petting. He resumes strokes with his fingers now, but they are small compared to before.

"But not so in this place."

"That's right. Not here. Here they are unique and beautiful and perfectly formed by their own mind. This is the end of the equation, Seph. That's what we're trying to make it. The gods can create life. We can get it going. We can watch our many beautiful things and unique children prosper, but we cannot keep them alive forever. The physical world doesn't allow it, and the lovely, innocent mortals cannot be gods. Not in that realm. Here, however... we can get close."

Being a god is a very lonely existence, his mother told him over and over. Sometimes it was while Seph was pining for some boy or wishing Fimus loved him for real. Sometimes it was about herself and the lack of trust she has for her siblings. And sometimes it was observing the town that grew from poverty to a thriving community, thanks to his mother's presence.

"I see. So returning to the upperworld is death. True death."

"That's right."

"So you punish them instead. You make them afraid to cross. And then it is not so bad."

He nods. "Tomorrow I will show you around this place. I wanted to do it today, but I had to return those two. There is usually a hunt twice a year or so—though once we went three years without one. The blood of it will scare off any rebellious young souls. But there are always newcomers. There are always those who need to experience before they believe."

He stretches. And then he faces away from Seph, rolling to his side. Seph lays his hand on his hip, wondering if what he wants is okay, but finally he decides that Hades wants Seph to touch him. He must, or he would ask Seph not to.

So Seph inches forward and closes the space between them, sliding an arm over Hades' waist. His husband's form against his entire naked body makes him exhale into Hades' hair. Which still reminds him of cold mornings for some reason. How a smell can be cold, he can't quite describe. But it is frost and sweet, and Seph has his lips in the god's hair, breathing in its flavor, pressing a kiss behind his husband's ear.

Hades takes his hand and intertwines their fingers.

"Tomorrow we will spend the day together. I will show you

more about this place. And then you will begin to understand."

"Yes," Seph agrees, and nuzzles him.

I think I might be falling in love.

But he also worries that it's too easy. He hardly thinks of Teysus anymore, and it's only been a matter of days. He's so distracted by the god's physical form when he shows up, how can he know if what he feels is real or not?

I wish I could ask my mom.

He wants to talk to her very badly at the moment. With her age and knowledge, she could advise him about everything that Hades has said. She loves him. He trusts her.

Here, falling asleep with his husband, he's still alone.

"Why not tell them what happens across the River Styx?" Seph asks in a murmur, not sure if he will get an answer or if his husband is already asleep.

"They know. They're told of it when they drink from the River Lethe, and they agree to make this their permanent home. The young souls are foolish enough to try to reach their families at the cost of their own annihilation."

Fifteen

Seph grips the edge of the golden chariot, his knuckles white.

"There, below us, you see?" Hades says, shifting the reins to one hand and pointing down—far, far down—to where a bluish tinged river meanders calmly toward the city of Elysium.

"That is the River Lethe, which the souls drink from and then swear the oath to become a citizen of Elysium. Once the ceremony is complete, their residence is permanent. They cannot be taken from Elysium, and they cannot leave. If they do commit a crime of some kind, which almost never happens, they can only be punished for their transgression, not executed or exiled, obviously.

"And trying to leave is a crime that only I punish. My rules are laid out plainly in every single language spoken in the world. See those houses on the pier? That is where my oath criers are kept, one for every language, and the souls are sworn in individually. It is explained that they can refuse and go back to the Fields of Asphodel for a different path, but once they drink from the river, they are mine to keep and look after."

"Uh-huh." Seph gulps, bracing himself against the front of the carriage rigidly with all the strength in his arms. In order to stay in the air, the horses have to keep moving. They cannot be still. So whenever Hades wants to explain something to him over some monument, or a river in this case, they will keep trotting and minding themselves, usually opting to take a downward angle that brings them closer to the trees and grass and things they enjoy.

So every time Hades stops to speak and show him something, all the piss in his bladder rushes to be released, making his fear even more difficult by putting him at risk of wetting himself.

Going up is not as bad. As long as he holds to the chariot like a ship in a storm about to throw him over. And being level is a brief respite from the terror that grips him constantly. But level movement does not seem to be something the horses are good at.

They only accomplish it when Hades is mastering the reins, constantly tugging on one horse or another. As soon as he gives them lead, even the tiniest bit, the horses will sneak their way downward, where they seem to want to be.

Seph agrees with them. But they could not have covered all this distance on the ground. The palace is quite small in the distance, and the city of Elysium is bigger than he ever imagined. Grander, too. The awe of it helps abate his fear a bit. Or, it did at first, until they climbed so high Seph thought he would die of fear.

"Next I will show you Acheron!"

Hades snaps the reins and the horses level out, running at a gallop. He seems to be following the river upstream and in a straight line, covering a massive amount of distance that passes underneath them slowly due to how high they are.

"Why do their hooves make noise?" Seph shouts over the clatter of the horses running. "We're in the air! Their hooves aren't striking anything!"

"Oh!" Hades smiles. He's been doing that a bit more today. Showing Seph the world he's created seems to bring the dark god happiness. "It is fake! The sound must be there for the horses to be calm and mannered. When I brought them off the ground for the first time, they panicked and threw the chariot. I broke my neck and a lot of other bones."

"They can do that?!" Seph yells, wishing he hadn't asked.

"If they're frightened enough, of course. But these have had many millennia of training and flying, so don't worry!"

"Okay..."

Yeah right.

Seph is trying to look brave for his husband. And all he wants to do is cower on the chariot floor by Hades' knees and wait for this to be over. He has remained standing upright to seem fearless and manly and like the sort of mate the King of the Underworld should have. All this time, gritting his teeth, he has thought about their game of *my king*, realizing that he can't be a timid young man if Hades is going to fall in love with him.

But that can go to hell.

Which is down here somewhere. Hades will show it to me.

Seph goes to his knees, only his eyes looking out over the chariot's edge, and both hands holding on so tightly that it hurts. They are not going up or down anymore, but they are going very, very fast. And every snort from one of the horses, which is frequent, makes him wonder if they are getting riled enough to have a small spat against their master's orders, which happens often enough with horses. Even well trained ones.

"Are you afraid? Why didn't you say anything?"

Hades takes his eyes off the horses as he bends down to lift Seph to his feet. Seph almost whines, but contains himself. Cowering will not be allowed then. He can tell.

He allows Hades to help him up while his stomach wishes otherwise.

"Get in front of me here. It is not so bad. I promise."

Hades positions Seph in front of him, and his arms wrap around him to take the reins.

Seph firmly disagrees. Being upright and at the center, behind the horses' bobbing necks and streaming tails, is not any better. In fact, there are only two steps of difference between this and where he was before. How is this any better?

But then his husband speaks in his ear, and Seph does not quite have to wet himself as much anymore.

"This is how I wanted to bring you when we first climbed in. Here, hold these." He passes the reins to Seph's hand, which Seph wants to refuse, but he forces his fingers to comply. The tension on the reins is slack, the horses guiding themselves.

"I don't know where we're going!" Seph says, still wishing he could curl up on the floor. The small pleasure of having Hades all around him is not worth it.

But Hades continues to speak directly against him, his lips touching Seph's earlobe. His hands run up and down Seph's arms.

"The horses know the way. They heard me say Acheron, and they know I want to follow the river by the direction we're going. They are just horses, but they are the smartest and best of their kind."

It is more difficult to hold the chariot's edge and the horses' reins at the same time.

"Lean back into me, Seph. It's all right. Let go of the chariot when you're ready. You will see that I am stable. You're not going to fall."

"We're going down! We're falling already!" It is a small angle, but Seph thinks the horses might be eager to swoop to the river. And such a thing will frighten him so badly, he will probably fall out and drop all the way to the ground. Where he will not die, since he is a god. But he will feel everything that happens to his body.

Mother, find me. Save me!

Seph has never been in pain like that. He's never even broken a bone! His mother has always protected him.

"How is this?" Hades wraps both arms around his waist and holds tight. Very tight. One arm goes a little higher and holds him around his abdomen. The grip is as though Hades is restraining him. "Now lean into me."

Seph allows himself to go back a little farther, though it is like he's pushing himself rather than leaning because his arms are so taut.

"When you're ready... let go."

Never going to happen, Seph thinks, but what if his husband never respects him? What if he thinks Seph is too cowardly to go anywhere in the chariot again, so Seph is not taken to the upperworld, not even for a visit?

He means to ask Hades about what he said about never returning to the upperworld. Surely he can't mean *never*. For Seph did not drink from the River Lethe. And he can't remember his wedding vows exactly as they were worded, but he doesn't think he promised to never see the upperworld again.

That discussion, for another day, will first rely on Hades believing he is at least brave enough to stand in his chariot. To hopefully have some respect and affection for him too.

I am a god also. Not as powerful as him, but I do not want to be treated like a meek little bride.

And so, while Seph hates himself for making himself do this, he masters all of his screaming instincts and eases back into Hades.

The god told the truth. He's as steady as a wall.

And Seph takes one grip off the chariot's edge, bringing the reins closer to his chest.

The final hand is a lot harder. It takes a lot more mastery and determination. Seph even for a moment returns his second hand fearfully, his instincts overriding him.

But in the end he manages it. Both hands let go. And then there are only his feet on the slightly forward-sloping floor of the chariot, and his husband's strong arms keeping him from plummeting forward to horrible disfigurement far below.

"I don't want to do this," he says, trembling.

"You're doing well. I have you, Seph. I'm not letting you go."

Well, that answers that, then.

But for now, isn't it a good thing?

Seph certainly doesn't want to fall to his death. And also, didn't he plan to leave his mother this summer anyway? To stay away for years so he could enter adulthood?

Not forever, of course, but a god has forever, so his departure could even be many mortal lifespans. And he was happy with that. He thought it was time to start his own life and stop being looked after like a toddler.

Seph is suddenly quite proud to be standing mostly on his own.

Well, it feels like it's on his own, even if he has the support of a husband and a friend. Just like he always wanted.

"You are smiling. Are you discovering thrill-seeker tendencies about yourself?"

The god still sounds like this is a regular day, and not like they are careening perilously through the air at the height of a mountain.

"No! Fuck no!" Seph says back, speaking louder. Hades can only get away with talking so quietly because everything he says is directly in Seph's ear. "I'm just feeling... so free is all!"

"I'm glad, my king."

He kisses Seph's neck. It would feel a lot better if they were on the ground and safe, and Seph is sure that he would like to do a lot more than that as well. Maybe they will take a picnic someday in one of the parks they passed over.

But maybe that would not be so good because Seph would quickly be trying to hide an erection under his unfortunately short chiton. He is not an exhibitionist.

"We're going to descend now. You won't like this part, so turn and face me."

They exchange the reins again, the horses returning to their master's hand, and Seph does as he asks.

"Can I just curl up on the floor?"

He's only half joking.

"Hold on to my body. As tight as you wish. Look at me. Into my eyes."

Seph thinks his eyes are more amazing for the dark sapphire earrings hanging from each lobe. The dark god's gray irises do not catch color or light, but they seem less gray, less cruel, by the glimmering beauty around his face.

His jewels make him a man with desires. Whereas without them, he would seem like nothing. Unhuman and unfeeling.

"You are not falling, Seph. It is just sensations. Hold tight to me, and you are as safe as you are on the ground."

He shifts the reins to one hand again and pets Seph's back. But only briefly. They must be getting near the trees again, for Hades is soon looking out past him and his hands are busy controlling the horses. They neigh and snort and toss their heads occasionally. The blood pounds through Seph's frayed nerves.

But he only focuses on his husband's face and finds himself testing his newfound trust by letting his arms loosen, just a bit. Just enough to see if he will start to fall.

He doesn't. And soon the trees are taller than him again.

Sixteen

The horses walk slowly through the black marsh, water splashing up around their hooves. The chariot wheels leave two treads rippling out through the water behind them. This is the most entrancing thing Seph has ever seen, and now, despite all the fear to get here, Seph is grateful to have such a unique husband and to be riding in a flying chariot.

The horses are technically still suspended in the air, but they are level on the water's surface, reeds passing around them and scraping the underbelly of the chariot like grass. The only terrible thing about the Acheron Marsh so far is how dark it is. There is no sun, moon, or stars in the underworld like there is on Earth.

There is only one small light in the sky, which Hades tells him is the open gate other gods come through when they arrive here. It's hard to find the blended barrier between the upperworld and the underworld if you are not dead, but a gate in the sky is plain to a god.

There are many tall trees here with giant outreaching branches, so Seph can't see that light up above except in a few places.

"Are there any monsters here?" he asks, because he has seen a thing move along the tree boughs or under the water several times now.

"Monsters, no. But there are many Earth creatures that the Goddess Styx looks after. The waters are bottomless, as far as I know, and Styx has filled them up with all manner of things. She loves aquatic creatures. She was one of the oceanic gods before Poseidon staked out his domain, you know."

Seph did not know. His mother does not mention the very old gods much, who would have been her cousins or possibly her aunts and uncles. The family tree is twisted up beyond logic now. His mother's siblings took their claims fresh, resetting the world and discarding many old things.

"There. Up ahead is the Fields of Asphodel. It's an island, actually, but also a giant meadow of a flower I made to grow like a weed."

Seph had wandered away from Hades' arms and his protective hold to gawk over the side and look at things. Now he returns his attention to the front and steps alongside his husband. It does not alarm him so much anymore to bump against Hades or brush past him. Hades sets an arm around Seph's waist, and while this touch is still new, it's starting to feel very natural.

"This is probably the most important part of my world here. It's certainly the busiest. Look there! Hang on." Hades snaps the reins lightly and the horses pick up the pace to a trot, splashing water everywhere. They pass several trees—he seems to be chasing a boat up ahead—and then he urges the horses into a gallop, only to pull them to a stop shortly after.

They cannot really stop, but they can walk slowly.

"It will catch up to us now. See the ferryman and the barge?"

"Barely." The figure he points to is a skinny old man in dark, loose robes, and every time he passes under the shadow of a tree he becomes invisible. Seph can only find him because the souls behind him on the barge are wispy white. But even they seem to vanish and shrink under every old tree.

"We cannot pass too closely. If they see us, we will scare them. But those are the new souls destined for Elysium. Only one barge comes every few days, when it is full. It takes a while for the barge to fill up and make it worth the journey. That is Irus, my ferryman who is unknown to the mortals of the world."

"Ah, yes. I know of Charon."

Hades might be the only god whose servants' names are known by mortals. That is the significance he takes on in their lives, as they wonder where they are going. Nobody can name one of his mother's slaves, and very few can list all of Zeus's consorts.

"Charon has the busiest job of all," Hades says. "He is a man who does not rest, not even when he was alive. Now, look closely as they pass us. I will do my best to keep the horses still. See how they are deformed? And old. That man, holding his neck like that? Executed, perhaps. Or killed in battle."

Another soul Hades does not mention is a young girl standing on a twisted leg. Another is an old man with sunken pockets in his face and a missing nose. Leprosy. Yet another has so many wounds and flesh missing that it looks like he was chewed on by animals.

When he turns his face, a grisly skull makes half of his expression. His eye is in place, but large and round, the bulb exposed.

Only a third of the souls seem to simply be old and have nothing wrong with them. Even the old ones have bent backs, bent necks, and some of them cough with diseases. One is naked, and many of them only wear a loincloth or a tattered gown.

"I love to see them when they come in," Hades says, almost breathless. "I love to watch them heal and transform into their true, perfect selves. That is why all new souls live closest to the palace. When they are well-adjusted, they may choose to wander to less populated areas."

The man with so much flesh missing bothers Seph. He can't take his eyes off him! But what's left of his face to make an expression is terrified as he looks in their direction through the trees.

"These are going to be your new children," Seph says, understanding.

"Yes. They look ugly or old or maimed, but remember—these are the youngest and most innocent souls. They are the newborn babes here. And the long-lived citizens of Elysium take great happiness in looking after them. Myself included, though I am not involved directly, unless it is for a hunt. I have to keep my distance."

"What about the souls who aren't in graves?" Seph asks, knowing he might not like the answer. This might be another dark part of Hades' rule in the underworld. Every mortal knows that Hades will not accept a soul without a grave, nor a soul without coins over his or her eyes. "And what about the coins? Is it true that souls have to pay the ferryman Charon?"

The barge passes on, and Hades guides the horses to walk in the opposite direction, continuing into the marsh.

"That is a combination of true and false. The coins-over-the-eyes ritual was invented by greedy undertakers. Also, the eyes of the dead are unpleasant to look at, so it serves two things. The importance of burying or burning bodies and funeral rites, however—there's some truth to that.

"You see, a soul is very attached to their body. They will try to stay with the corpse and sit with it for as long as they can. When a soul has a proper funeral, however, they are put at ease. The grieving of their loved ones is a comfort, and they're likely to soon realize they need to move on. They will feel the call of the underworld. And they will begin their journey in time, before they're consumed by the upperworld forces.

"But a soul without a funeral is like a lost babe in the woods who cannot find their home. They sit where they are dead for ages, crying out. Often they try to pester the living to notice them and get some kind of help. They hear my call, but they are afraid. Or resistant. They sit all alone, grieving for themselves, not realizing that permanent death is imminent.

"That's why Hermes is so important to me. He collects as many of these babes as he can find. Ones who have been murdered. Ones who have been forgotten. Sitting by corpses that are picked apart by birds and dogs. They must be rescued quickly, or they will be lost forever."

While he speaks of all this and Seph absorbs every word, the horses begin to wind their way through the trees as if they know where they're going, and a glow appears. There is an island ahead—the Fields of Asphodel, Seph presumes—and lanterns are lit, hanging from tree boughs. The blue flame does not emit light as well in this extremely dark area, but it helps. Seph sees many figures up ahead. Like a gathering or a festival. And the murmur of talking voices—sometimes of crying, maybe someone begging—begins to drift through the trees. It's more voices at one time than Seph has ever heard.

"We will rise up again so I can show you," Hades says, and Seph nods.

He grabs the chariot's edge with one hand and his husband's elbow with the other. He holds tight as his stomach seems to crawl inside his body, but he manages to stay standing without wanting to curl up and whimper this time.

Just so long as he doesn't look down or back.

Hades levels them out before they rise into the sky at the same dizzying distance as before. Now they are more like a huge bird hovering over the treetops, only with clattering hooves and a gleaming gold chariot spinning wheels on nothing.

Voices below rise in alarm. There are terrified screams and souls scatter, a patch of the island emptying.

Seph is more bothered by three figures on giant pillars, erected to the height of a house. The top of each pillar is crafted into a throne, and the figures sit in regal robes, their enormous feet in expensive sandals. They're the size of giants! And the face of each one is monstrous. Many eyes, many noses, many mouths. All shifting, moving over one another.

It seems as though the heads of each are shaking back and forth vigorously. Though the ears are still and the hair does not turn.

"Those are my judges," Hades says, holding him around the waist again. "Do not be afraid. I know they are not comforting to look at. But they are wise and just souls, all of them. Any time a new soul is presented to them who would make a good judge, that soul is offered a chance to join them and become one of the many faces and voices and minds who weigh the decisions of a mortal's life and decide whether they are fit for Elysium."

"Why do they look like that?" It is painful to stare at any one of them. The features vanish and appear and twitch all over themselves. They are like a deformed animal, and looking at them fills Seph with dread.

"It is the only way to fit them on the island, of course!" Hades answers. "They have to share a body, or else I would need a city like Elysium just to hold them. And the judging would be an insanely complicated process. Here, each judge will appear as one face to the souls on the island. That will be the judge that they are assigned. And when they are ready to leave this place, the souls will approach the judges and ask for their life to be weighed."

"A-are there scales? Like in the myths?"

"No, that's only a metaphor."

"O-okay," Seph says, with a fearful chuckle.

The crowd gathering to the base of the three pillars is a lot smaller than the crowd gathered everywhere else. The trees hide many of the people from view, but from what Seph can see, they are packed shoulder to shoulder.

And another barge, which must be led by Charon, is very long and has so many souls packed onto the deck that Seph can't see the bottom of the boat. Only its sides and the dark-robed ferryman at the front.

"You said there is only one barge bound for Elysium every few days."

"Yes." Hades nods, the sapphires dangling. "I've been waiting for you to ask me that. Very few souls are good for Elysium. And it is not that they are *good enough* necessarily, but that they are a good *fit*. Some souls are not happy if they aren't competing for power. If they are not achieving something over others. So even though their accomplishments may be good and their intentions may even be selfless, they will become restless in Elysium.

"Elysium is a world with nothing to gain. Nothing to earn. Nothing to desire and nothing to achieve. It is a world for people who are done with earthly pleasures and will be content to leave those things behind for good. Not very many people go to Elysium."

"So where do they go?"

"To Tartarus. Those boats there."

The barges can hardly be seen because the trees grow so thickly in the area where he points. But a continuous line seems to be leaving the island, and a continuous line of empty barges are returning.

"So that must be the River Phlegethon. My mother told me about that one."

While he can only catch glimpses of water through the trees at this angle, it seems that this river is three times wider than Lethe and runs less crooked. In the distance, the boughs and foliage are so thick that he can't see a river at all. Or a building or a city or anything that Tartarus might have. Seph bets it's the place where the trees grow taller and thicker than all others. From here, it just looks like a dense forest.

"We will explore it on another day." Hades snaps the reins and the horses pick up speed, crossing the island toward Elysium. They pass over the heads of the judges, which look fairly normal from up here except for three or four noses shifting around.

"But wait! What happens to most of the souls? Where does everyone go? Why Tartarus? Isn't that where people are punished for being bad?"

"Very few are bad enough to be punished. Even the cruelest humans are usually victims of some mistreatment. Most souls are reborn, and that happens in Tartarus." Hades puts an arm around Seph, guiding him to stand in front again. "Now we have to go fast. So fast that you may feel as if you are slipping backwards, but you don't have to worry. I am right here holding on to you."

"Okay," Seph says with a nod, though he has more questions. "We will go to Tartarus another time? I-I would like to see the souls being reborn."

"Yes, my king." It's still strange that he says that in normal conversation when they aren't playing. He even did it in front of the servants once.

Hades continues, "I'm not opposed to revealing it to you now, if you absolutely insist, but Tartarus has many unpleasant aspects, some of which you already know about. And I would like my tour today to be of the places I am most proud of. The wonderful spots. That's what I want to show you first."

Seph grabs on to his arm—they are going very fast now—and strokes in an affectionate way. He loves that he can do that, like they are normal lovers. His weight slides backward just like Hades said, the air around the horses' heads blurring, the trees below rushing underneath them, and he feels nothing but trust for his new husband.

Even so, he asks, "Where are we going?"

"To Cocytus!" Hades says loudly in his ear. "It is the furthest river I know about that breaks off from the River Styx! Elysium will not reach it for several millennia, so I consider it the farthest border of my kingdom for now."

Seventeen

When they find the Cocytus River, the trees are so thick he can't see the ground, and the palace is only visible as a speck if he stares in the right direction for a very long time. From here, the tallest spires look only like tiny gray spikes poking out of an endless gray lawn. The white-leafed trees, sometimes tinged with pink or blue, do not seem to grow naturally in the underworld wilderness.

Seph wants to ask him things, but the wind is too loud, and even the fake clattering of the horses' hooves is faint at the speed they're traveling. Seph continues to hold on to the front of the chariot, just in case, but Hades' feet haven't slipped once against the barrage of wind.

Sometimes his nose moves through Seph's hair. Perhaps smelling him?

Or perhaps because his nose itches and his hands have to hold the reins. At this speed, turning has to be done with precise care or the entire chariot will upset and flip. Seph checks on Hades when a sway disrupts his balance. But his husband seems as impassive as he did on the day they first met.

But not when his nose is in Seph's hair again, and Seph turns to get a look at him. Then he has his almost happy expression. And it does not disappear when their eyes meet. Seph wants to kiss him.

But he also wants to land safely, very much so, and their balance begins to tilt as Hades guides the horses into a wide downward spiral. The river below looks more like a creek. The River Styx is wide and coils endlessly onward, never narrowing nor ebbing away in its depth.

Cocytus, on the other hand, is small and spriggy, running through and over rocks, breaking off into creeks and making trees into islands, their roots bare and reaching out through the water.

"Duck down now," Hades says. "All the way to the floor, in front of my knees. This will be too scary for you."

"I can handle it," Seph says bravely, but a moment later the horses swoop downward, the chariot dives forward, and the ground rushes up at him. A sensation of weightlessness and terror comes over him, his heart thudding, the wind rushing past his body with nothing to catch him. His grip on the chariot's front, while solid and white-knuckled, seems insubstantial as he is falling with it.

But Hades is not falling forward. Not the way Seph is. If so, he would be pressing against Seph's back, and Seph would be the only barrier keeping them inside. They would be flung over the front, and all would be lost.

Seph closes his eyes, makes sure he continues to breathe, and the terror...

It doesn't leave him, but it becomes manageable.

As long as he closes his eyes and Hades is still there, his stance unaffected.

He would not let me crash. If it was going to happen, he would prevent it. He would hit the ground before I would.

Seph doesn't know if that's true or not. But imagining the sentiment helps.

Again, there is no clash of the chariot wheels striking the earth. Or in this case, the water. He notices that the wind has lessened, a shadow passes over his eyelids, and then he hears the hooves of the horses splashing in water.

Hades presses on the back of his head, and they both duck to squeeze under the bough of a tree that is bent far forward in the current, its roots barely hanging on. The water here, however, is calm, shallow, and widens to a sandy beach on both sides. A lovely place to wade. If only the sun would show brightly here and warm the sand.

Hades guides the horses onto the beach, the chariot wheels allowed to make deep treads into the sand, and they step off, the horses completing a half circle to wet their noses in the river. Seph kneels to the sand at once, gathering it in one hand and letting it fall slowly. It is dry and softly fine, but cold. Cold like stinging snowflakes that don't melt, not even in his warm hands.

"Grateful to be on the ground again?" Hades asks in a friendly manner, fumbling with the ties of his cloak.

"I was not afraid," Seph says playfully over his shoulder. The cold, while not as pleasant as sun-warmed sand, does not bother him much. He wishes he could stretch out in it, but...

"My chiton is too short to sit. I'll get sand in my ass."

"Never fear, my stallion. Your ass shall be free of coarse sediment in my kingdom. *Our* kingdom. Forgive me for misspeaking, my king."

Ah. He is playful, then. Or at least mildly happy, which seems to be the most optimal setting his face can achieve. Seph grins at him, thinking that smirks and smiles might be easier for the dark god in the future, with a little practice. This playful personality is a surprise, and one that he loves.

He is doing more than making the best of a bad situation. This marriage to Hades might not have been his free choice, but it does seem to be one that he wants.

Hades puts his cloak down on the sand, the fur and everything unfortunately touching the dirt. He takes his boots off one by one while standing, toeing out of them from the heel, and Seph wonders how rare it is for the dark god to perform any act of dressing himself. It is endearing to see a somber man in that wicked black crown wobble for balance on one foot.

Seph removes his own sandals quickly and easily. He feels bad for sitting on the cloak though.

...Though he does like the soft material against his thighs. He has not asked Hades for longer chitons yet.

"Tell me about the narcissus flower," Seph says, watching the water rush around the bent tree. "You had something to do with that, didn't you? I heard the story from my mother, but I have never seen one until... until you abducted me."

"Ah, yes. That reminds me, I would like to plant some here. They are quite hardy and should spread naturally all along these banks."

Hades does not continue right away, settling on the cloak beside him instead.

"You don't want to answer?" Seph asks after a few moments, when it seems the dark god has forgotten.

"You want to know the morbid parts of me. The parts I'm holding back," Hades counters, though not angrily. He speaks as though stating facts, and not particularly interesting ones.

"I know that you have good qualities as well. I have already seen them. Your subjects are not afraid of you. Not even the way that I am afraid of Zeus, my father. Which I find rather confusing since you punish them so harshly. So your good qualities must outweigh the bad."

"Not necessarily," he says, brushing off his knee. "The souls know that running off is one of few crimes I personally punish.

Everything else is handled by their village leaders. There is not much I need to do since everyone in Elysium is a gentle kind of soul. So there is no reason to fear me. That does not mean I am as gentle and sweet as them."

"So you would say you are the opposite?" Seph is careful not to look at him. He is careful to keep his tone neutral as well.

Perhaps I should stop this line of questioning.

Offending the dark god will not go well. Especially in this faraway, private place.

Though, Seph suspects that it wouldn't matter.

"I am sorry. We can talk about something else."

"No, it's okay. Eventually you need to know these things about Tartarus... and Sisyphus, Tantalus, and so many others. I do not..." He seems to search for words. "...judge others. Officially. I do not pursue the act of torture. But there are some souls that I recognize can only be punished by me, and who *should* be punished.

"In the case of Narcissus, a mortal boy with the fair face of a god, his beauty prevented him from suffering the consequences of his actions. The young man was destined to become a king or emperor for how people worshipped him so. For nothing other than looking beautiful.

"Did you know that men committed suicide when he rejected them? That's how much they fell in love with him! And even these terrible acts did not cause sympathy in his heart. He was a little mortal Zeus but without the justification and Hera keeping him on a chain."

Hades removes his crown, looking into it as he speaks.

"I came close to observe the boy. A mountain nymph who had fallen in love with him lured Narcissus away to protect him. I hardly wanted to scour the upperworld for him for very long. My beasts do not do well up there.

"So I sent Hermes, my messenger, to Artemis, and she trapped my quarry with a puddle of water from the River Styx. It is true that I named my flower after him. His namesake was given as an honor, for it seems unfortunate that something so fair should be lost forever."

He looks up at the river.

"However, Narcissus was not turned *into* a flower. That part of the story is wrong. He is still in Tartarus, gazing at himself and eternally starving to death." He lets the crown dangle from his fingers and looks over. "So that's it, my king. You've heard one of the terrible stories about me. And you've seen our kingdom. Four-fifths of it, anyway. What do you think? Are you miserable in your new home?"

Seph feels like he's falling again, his breath held in his chest as though to scream, but he faces his fear head-on like he did with the chariot's descent.

"If I run, will you hunt me?"

"Most certainly, yes. But not with Cerberus, not with my dog. And I'll try not to bring you back in chains unless I have to."

"*Why* would you have to?" Seph faces him unflinchingly at last, in the direction of the dark god's knees. Getting to his eyes requires more determination and passing seconds. He's relieved that Hades seems to be as relaxed as ever and is not becoming angry or stern at this unexpected questioning.

"I have to keep you here for your protection. There are two gods to protect you from—well, six if you include your rowdy cousins, who will not entirely be dissuaded from stealing you for a romp or two until I catch up. Oh, they probably won't rape you outright, but they may succeed in tempting you. Your mother will become a villain against me, if she ever sees you again. She's never going to let you come back to me. Not willingly.

"And your father, Zeus, is not known for his respect of marriage. In fact, none of the gods are. Thus, the still existing danger despite our marriage.

"The best place for you is the underworld. There's one entrance and one exit for gods. I have other dogs guarding the gate, and no god is allowed to linger down here without a purpose. I'm picky about who I let in my kingdom. That is how I keep you safe."

"It doesn't make any sense," Seph says, squeezing the bridge of his nose. "Why all this trouble? Over *me*? I am nobody. My mother appointed me the God of the End of the Harvest, but *she* makes all the things grow. She's the goddess who brings the spring, when important conditions have to happen. I just... help reap the wheat sometimes. That's it! With an ordinary fucking scythe. I don't have magical powers or anything!"

"Ah, Seph." The dark god reaches over and puts his crown on Seph. It's heavy, like balancing a pot on his head, and it sits slightly lopsided on his thick wavy tresses. "You are what Narcissus should have been. If he was perfect."

Eighteen

They have an early dinner at the palace—at *home*, since this is where Seph's home is now. Hades' cloak is given to the servants for cleaning, and his crown is also removed for the meal. He looks more like the man he is with Seph in bed, and today he wears a chiseled orange stone around his neck that seems to glow from within. His sapphire earrings are deeply hued and beautiful, and Seph stares at them almost as much as he stares into Hades' eyes.

After they finish the meal, Hades takes him to his indoor courtyard, which Seph learns is called a *solarium*. He talks a lot about the plants, with some words that Seph doesn't understand, like 'germinating'. Seph learns that the base of a plant is called a crown, which must not be buried, and Hades goes on to say something about *phosphorus*, a nutrient required to keep the plant growing.

He doesn't really follow and just nods politely. He is more concerned about keeping his arm positioned so that Hades won't see the little bulge of cooked vegetables he's keeping in the folds of his chiton, above his belt.

He is especially worried that Hibus won't be under the bed when they finally make it back to their private quarters. After speaking with Minthe yesterday, Seph hunted around the palace until he found a little vase that he filled with stones from an outside garden. It is rather heavy for a rabbit to drag around, and it's anchoring Hibus at the center underneath the bed. But that doesn't mean the little rabbit didn't find a way to knock it over and make it roll. Seph made it as sturdy as he could.

But he also worries that his fresh straw, acquired with the help of Minthe, will start to kick up a smell. Now there are rotting vegetables from his wedding night that need to be replaced and thrown out.

Seph begins to wonder, *How long can I not tell him?*

Minthe was very firm in saying that Hades would no way, no how approve the bunny. Every time Seph started to doubt or offer a solution, Minthe would remind him, *No way, it's not a possibility.*

But neither is keeping a secret pet under the bed forever. If Hades doesn't find him, the servants eventually will. And when Hades' dog returns to the palace, which he mentioned once today, being relieved that Seph doesn't mind dogs—well, Seph had better have a new home for the bunny by then.

"Are you tired?" Hades says suddenly, looking at him instead of the flowers. "I'm sorry. I think to myself by talking aloud sometimes. None of this information is supposed to be part of the tour. I hope you didn't start to think of me as your dusty old tutor or something. Botany is fascinating to me, but I don't expect us to share the same hobbies."

"No! That's not it. I like listening to you. Um, I don't understand very much, and I'm not really the reading type... My mother just makes plants grow naturally with her powers, I think. She doesn't have to know all this stuff."

"Ah. Well, that works too, but the difference is that plants grown and cultured in the natural way can continue to proliferate. I am making improvements on my narcissus flower to make it quite hardy. My hope is that someday this beauty will spread across my world and the upperworld both. I have nearly reached a strain that could make my flower quite common, like a beautiful weed. But not so invasive."

"I'm sorry," Seph says, since he would really like to listen to Hades talk about his flowers and his interests—all day, in fact—but he's also really worried about Hibus. "I have to use the latrine. If it's all right, would you excuse me?"

Understanding lights in Hades' eyes, and he smiles and nods toward the large door leading to their private chambers. Unfortunately for Seph and Hibus though, he also follows after Seph, and even gets the door for him.

"Thank you," Seph says and tries to hurry forward without looking like he's hurrying anywhere.

"Do not make yourself uncomfortable just because I am lost in one of my speeches," Hades says in a friendly manner, and then thankfully gets distracted at his desk, opening a drawer.

Seph moves on alone and calculates how weird it would be to close the bedroom door completely after him. He decides half closing it is not too strange, and then he rushes on the side where he's covered, going to his knees by the bed and fetching the vegetables at once.

He can pretend to just be looking for his sandal or something if the god follows him a few seconds after. So the new vegetables join the old ones, and Hibus hops toward him hopefully, like he's happy to see him. Only to greedily take the first radish and start munching on the top.

That should keep him from exploring for a while. Cleaning up shall have to happen later. And yes, his basket of straw does have a detectable smell already. He hopes the bed blanket hanging low over the edges will help contain the odor for a little while. Just until morning. Seph will find a moment away from Hades to fix it. Somehow.

He doesn't come up with any ideas or clever plans as he goes through the motions of using the latrine. When he is done and returning to Hades, he stops at the vanity, looking in the mirror.

His cousins were squabbling over him, sure, but that had more to do with masculine rivalry than anything about Seph. His cousins are infantile, trying to best each other for no reason other than competition, and Seph was not flattered by their attention.

Nor does he see anything special about his face. Tan skin and a few darkened sun specks across the bridge of his nose, lightly scattered into his cheeks. He looks like an ordinary Greek. And a young one, since he doesn't have a beard.

Fimus resisted his charms just fine. And certainly no one has ever committed suicide over him! Seph can't imagine such a thing.

I am nothing like Narcissus. Nor am I what Narcissus should have been. Whatever Hades sees in my face comes from his eyes alone.

Certainly Teysus never composed any poems for his features, as some writers are still doing for Narcissus, his beauty, and his punishment.

"Are you perusing for jewels?" Hades asks from the doorway, watching him with his arms crossed.

Seph jumps. He's been caught doing something extremely silly. Looking at himself in a mirror is vain foolishness.

"No! I was just thinking about Narcissus. That's all. The mortals don't know what really happened. They think he turned into one of your flowers."

"Of course. That is because I gave it his name." Hades crosses to him, touches Seph's jaw, and points his face back at the mirror. "I wonder what would look best on you. Something red, do you think?"

His scrutiny makes Seph feel like uncarved marble that's just arrived at an artist's shop. "Or a diamond, perhaps? Those are my favorite."

He opens a drawer and many rings are set in rolls of velvet cushion. He picks up one as big as Seph's own thumb and holds it up by his ear. Then under his throat.

"Hm. So beautiful. But anyone who sees you in diamonds will know you were dressed by me and not of your own choices. Here, why don't you pick a stone." He opens more drawers, revealing more rings and bracelets and earrings and necklaces. He picks a thing or two out of each and sets them atop the vanity in a row.

Seph doesn't know the names of any of these. He can only describe them by their shininess and color. None of the gems appeal to him greatly. He is not a gem-wearing kind of guy, nor would he care to set his own hair in rollers if his mother didn't insist on it. Curly hair is fashionable with the Greeks, and being fashionable is the basic grooming standard for the son of a goddess.

He supposes being the husband of a god amounts to the same thing.

"There. Pick something. What do you like?"

There are two and a half rows of jewelry on the vanity now, in no particular order. Seph looks them up and down, back and forth, and does not feel drawn to any particular one. Some of them are so close in color that Seph would say they're exactly the same. Though he knows by their distance from each other that Hades would disagree vehemently.

"They are all amazing," he says with a shrug, realizing he's about to offend his rich and fashionable husband. His mother made keeping up with the trends a downright decree when he complained again and again about the tightness of hair rollers.

"Take your time. A favorite stone is like a part of your identity. It will choose you, in a way."

After another moment, he says, "They're not going to break. They're rocks, mostly, not glass. Pick them up! Try them on. Otherwise, how can you find the one you like?"

"Alright."

He picks one. The plainest looking one he can find, which is a shade of brown.

"Topaz," Hades says, sitting on the corner of the vanity with one leg propped and the other stretched to the ground. "It might complement your skin, don't you think?"

No, Seph does not think. In fact, the earth-toned stone looks fine until he sets it over his own hand, and then it is like his skin makes the jewel uglier. He puts it back quickly and regards the rows of sparkling colors and smooth, deeply hued surfaces, holding in a sigh of frustration.

Not all of them are a solid tone. He picks one that looks interesting. Like the shadows in a forest, kind of, over a hue of blue fading to green.

"Labradorite," Hades says. "A more common stone, but I should have guessed. It fits you perfectly."

He takes the earring from Seph's hand before he's even finished lifting it, and turns Seph toward him, holding the gem up to his ear. When his eyes regard Seph, again it is like being molded inside an artist's vision, a fine piece existing only in imagination for now. Seph himself is still the untouched hunk of marble. And he finds, as the god starts talking about piercing his ears and Seph realizes he's going to do it *right now*, that he is resistant to change.

He catches Hades' wrist, making sure that little silver point doesn't come too close.

"Oh. It doesn't hurt or anything. Not enough to bother a god anyway. Are you worried?"

"No. I just don't like earrings."

Hades does not touch his sapphires, but one hand reaches sort of high, resting on his collarbone.

"I don't like earrings on *me*," Seph elaborates. He hates that he has to do this. He acknowledges that he can't always get his way about his appearance on account of being a god and now a king. But he really, really doesn't want to wear the damn earrings.

If he had known Hades would want to pierce his ears right away, he would've made sure to pick a necklace or bracelet or maybe a regular ring. All the earrings, incidentally, would not 'choose him'.

"I will wear something else. Anything else. Here—" He fetches a pendant that is clear and shiny. "This one speaks to me. This one is my favorite. Look, a diamond like you suggested. We will be matching husbands. That is nice."

"That is colorless zircon," says Hades, looking befuddled.

"Oh. Well, it looks diamond-y, doesn't it?" Seph looks from this stone to all the sparkly clear things on the table. It's all the same to him. How can Hades tell the difference? "What about this one?"

Maybe he got the diamonds confused. Maybe they're white and not clear. He never paid enough attention to his mother's jewelry and the offerings she would receive. Of course, she never asked him to wear them, which was nice.

"That's moonstone!" Hades answers, sounding horrified. "Ehhh. You don't have to wear the labradorite if you don't like it, my stallion. I just thought since you've been admiring my earrings all day that you might like some of your own. I... I haven't misjudged you, have I? Are you wishing I'd take the earrings off?"

Now he reaches up and touches them, toying with removing the hooks from his lobes. "Do you hate them? It is okay to answer honestly. I have to know."

"No! No, no, no." Seph regrets getting into this ridiculous conversation. He must be as frank as he can with Hades, for the god is drawing all the wrong assumptions.

"No, I love your earrings. On you. I-I'm hoping you'll wear them to bed tonight, actually. I was planning to ask. But I don't want to wear these things. I just want to look at them on you. I do like these earrings."

He takes them from Hades' fingers. "But I would rather see them on you."

He holds the moonstone up in front of the sapphire. "How could I even admire the jewelry if it was hanging off my own ear all the time? I'd have to stare at myself in a mirror! Or... just... drink from shiny cups all the time!"

He waves a hand with exasperation and it drops at his side. "How else am I supposed to see it?"

"Oh. Okay. Hm... Rings, then. And bracelets. How do you feel about necklaces?" Hades stands, looking prepared to go on a gem hunt for him in the drawers of the vanity.

"Honestly, I would rather just see all of these things on you."

Hades nods, once. Seph could leave his words there, certain that the god is flattered and hopefully won't want to put earrings on him anymore. But this boldness with his husband feels important.

Hades does not respond to pleading, Minthe said. Seph is certain he does not respond well to shyness and timid requests either.

It is difficult to speak so plainly to one who is so intimidating. And Seph wants Hades to like him so much, he can hardly speak. He's usually not shy. But this union has to be good. He wants to impress his husband.

"I want you to wear pretty stones when I make love to you. I've imagined it, and—and it is nice."

His husband's eyes widened. He glances at the bed, and Seph is hopeful.

But then he says, "Come. There is one more place I want to show you." He smirks. "Don't be disappointed, stallion. You will like this. We're going to take your clothes off."

Nineteen

Behind the door in their bedroom, one Seph hasn't opened yet, there lies a tight hallway with a staircase leading down in a spiral. Seph hears a steady rippling splash of water before he's inside the room. Now he remembers that Hades pointed out a private bathhouse on their wedding night.

It is magnificent. As big as one of the two public pools at the town near his mother's mansion. While it is not the biggest bath he's ever seen, he has never had so much water all to himself, and steam rises off the top, signaling that it's freshly heated.

Or so he thinks. When he goes to one knee at the pool's edge and puts his hand in the water, he discovers that it's no warmer than a bath at home that's been sitting for a long while. The steam is due to the frigid nature of the underworld, which he can mostly forget about. It is not the cold he notices, but the absence of warmth.

Regardless, he is still eager to climb in. His chiton is so short, all he has to do is remove his sandals and he can start to wade in.

Hades goes to a wall of double doors made of slats, opening each one and exposing a small private courtyard with couches laid out for lounging. Of course, here there is no heat from the sun, and the courtyard still has to be lit by torches even though this currently passes in the underworld as daytime.

Hades' white narcissus flowers grow in clumps around bushes with small pink blooms. And three marble animals decorate the courtyard. A deer, a bird on a flat-topped pillar, and a white bunny in the bushes.

Seph's eyes grow with hope.

I have found a place for Hibus!

Then, *He will be lonely.*

Left out in the cold. At least in the room, Hibus knows that everyone in the house lives at this temperature and he is not being neglected.

He can almost see his mother sigh and prop her hand on her hip. He misses her. But that longing disappears as Hades turns around, a promising glint in his eye, and approaches a wardrobe that must be filled with towels. He begins to work on the laces and buttons on his clothing.

"Tell me, in these fantasies of yours, do I ever wear the crown?" He looks over his shoulder as the shirt drops down, exposing layers and layers of fine muscle and a scar Seph hadn't noticed on his arm. "It's okay to say yes," he says with that mischievous smirk still in place.

"No," Seph answers honestly, shaking his head. "Mostly, it's just the sapphires. They speak to me, like you said. Maybe that is my stone, but only when they're on you."

"How about the rings?" He shows him the back of his hand and wiggles his fingers in a backward wave. "Or the necklace? Shall I wear these into the pool?"

"Just the sapphires, I think," Seph answers, and decides that his lust for Hades is greater than his desire to bathe. He leaves the pool and comes up behind his husband, as he's unlacing his pants. He brushes Hades' hair away from his ear and kisses all the sensitive skin he finds, his hands grabbing on to his hips next, his groin pushing into the man.

"I like your body. Your earrings are... I don't know. Just sexy as fuck, I think."

"Stallion, you are more grown than I realized."

Seph grins to hear that nickname again. It is proof. Hades does not respond well to meekness. But if Seph is bold and adult and everything he's wanted to be for so long... they may be a perfect match.

They may have something.

"I want to fuck you against the vanity," he whispers against Hades' skin. Partially because it's sexier to do it that way. Partially because his bold spirit flees and hides in the courtyard with the marble rabbit, so he can't say it in his regular voice.

He never talked to Teysus like this, and certainly not Fimus. He's never said anything like this before, and his heart is pounding inside his chest. Surely Hades will feel it.

Surely Hades will laugh.

But his big smile is not outright guffaws yet, and Seph once again feels a newfound thrilling freedom, like he's soaring in Hades' chariot.

"I'd like you to lay out some pretty stones again, I think. And then I can bend you over them and take you from the back. We both can watch in the mirror." Seph lets go of his hip so one hand can come up and gently grab around the front of his throat, his thumb stroking near his earlobe, those sapphires rolling over his joints. "And you can wear a pair of pretty earrings like these. I want to watch them swing back and forth while I'm fucking you."

"Oh." Hades inhales a shaky breath, his head tilting back. "We can go back upstairs," he suggests quickly, and Seph shakes his head.

"It'll be something to look forward to. I haven't seen your hair when it's wet. I would like that. Also..." With so many desires cramming into his head, so many fantasies and possibilities and the freedom to speak any one of them, it is now hard to choose what should come first. They are all so tempting.

"Do you think you'd like to fuck me? Now? Or ever?"

I would like to experience both.

"I am fucking you, stallion," Hades says and turns in his arms, his mouth opening for a kiss.

It is their best one in Seph's opinion. Surprisingly, he takes the lead on it easily, naturally, and Hades lifts his arms to rest atop Seph's shoulders in such an enamored way. Seph feels more manly and grown than he ever has, and his cock points high, pushing against Hades' lower belly now. His husband's pants are just barely hanging on.

"We best get you in the water," Seph says, hating that he has to break the kiss. Hating that he has to stop. And quickly, he retakes that mouth because he wants him so bad. And in so many different ways. And so many frequent, repeating times.

What a relief to know that he will not have to be shy and patient with his desires!

Could he—?

No. No, of course not.

No, that's insanity!

Seph gulps. He is in Hades' chariot again, after climbing high to such an impossible, lethal altitude, higher than any mountain—and now he's facing the downward rush. The falling! And Hades is asking—will you stand front and center?

Or will you curl up on the floorboards?

I may die tonight. He might send me to Tartarus.

But how can he have freedom if he doesn't take a risk?

The action is not as bold and fearless as it is in his mind, as his initial impulse willed it to be. Still, he opens himself to the threat of execution. He swings his hand back and arcs it forward, landing it firmly against Hades' cute ass with a little pat sound and a quick (very quick because he practically wants to run) follow-up squeeze.

It is how the men grabbed the girls at the tavern sometimes. And for that reason, Seph immediately pivots and walks to the pool's edge, waiting to hear an eruption of rage behind him. His hands fumble and mess up as he tries taking off his belt.

It's only a simple knot. For some reason though, he can only find one end or three, an illogical predicament.

"What was that?" he hears behind him, and all his fears are confirmed. He rubs his nose and doesn't answer, truly complexed by his belt and deciding to give it all of his attention.

I hope Tartarus is nice...

"Stallion. Did you just... smack my ass?"

Currently, the dark god seems to be in shock.

Seph makes a murmuring noise. It could be yes or no, but it's really just him mimicking sounds like an animal. He won't add ignoring the dark king to the charges.

"No one has—smacked my ass—ever."

He seems to have a hard time getting the words out.

Seph shrugs. And then frowns deeply because that is definitely not the right response.

I have to make up for this. I was stupid. I was rude!

"I'm sorry," he says behind him, looking at the floor. "I don't know what—or why—I-I wanted to. And I did. But I'm sorry."

He holds his breath while footsteps approach. He can't bring himself to look Hades in the eye, but his naked knees and his pert, pink-tipped cock remind Seph of what he could be losing. Why he shouldn't have taken the risk. Why his impulse was selfish and stupid, and why he should be saying all of this right now before he finds himself eternally starving to death in Tartarus with a flower named after him.

He looks at the water again. Hades' hands touch his shoulders and smooth across his back.

"I hope you plan to do it again," the dark god whispers, and his tongue laps inside Seph's ear, a ticklish sensation that makes Seph shirk.

"I—can I?"

Seph looks at him finally, and Hades is smiling broadly enough to show teeth, and it makes his face beautiful in such an unexpected way. Youthful, almost, though that aged look never disappears from his eyes. The dark sapphires are lovely, though, adorning such a happy, peaceful expression.

Seph finds himself turning again and petting his husband's cheek with his thumb.

I wonder if he's ever looked like this for anyone else before?

By the stories everyone tells... he thinks not. At the very least an expression like this must be extremely rare.

I have done something right.

"Why are you still dressed?"

"I can't figure out this knot Verah put on me."

"Ah. She has a different custom. Here, let me see."

They are already kissing again by the time the chiton drops to the floor. Today, much to Verah's exasperation, he wears a loincloth for his genitals. He did not want any accidents while meeting the people of Hades' kingdom, especially those souls who look like children.

"Ugh. What is this thing?" Hades asks, tugging on it. He was already awake and in the study when Seph got dressed.

"You made my chiton too short," Seph says with a chuckle, undoing the wrap.

"Well... it looks good, doesn't it?"

He sounds exactly like Demeter just then. Perhaps fashion ability is a trait Kronos passed down.

"Of course it does. If I was an athlete. Or a young man seeking attention. Or, you know—a prostitute."

"There's nothing wrong with showing a little form." Hades is his frowning, stern-looking self as Seph leads him down the steps descending into the pool, and they wade out to the middle together.

"I don't like you to be so covered up," Hades says.

"Like a concubine? Or a prostitute?" Seph grins. He's only teasing him.

"Like a stallion, my mate. Pretty assets are supposed to be worn. Presented. Shown to others. I don't like my acquisition to be so hard to reach when I want it."

Seph laughs openly, pulling the god into his arms.

Now how shall I dunk him?

He would rather keep the naked body against him for now. He moves against his husband's groin, loving that he can do whatever he wants to Hades with his hands. He can hold him steady. He can grind against him. He can bend him over...

So why shouldn't the god, in return, be able to do what he wants with his eyes?

Yes, but all those children...

"Let me wear the chiton a little longer. And I will go without an undergarment just for you. You can reach for your assets whenever you wish."

"Hmph. A *compromise*..." Hades says, looking dissatisfied.

"How long can you hold your breath?" Seph asks.

"Why—oh."

Seph does not push forcefully. He only sets a hand atop Hades' head and guides him down. Of course, a god can hold his breath indefinitely. They can survive being drowned, crushed, burned, and many other things. But for this, Seph tries to keep a count in his head. He doesn't want Hades to hold his breath long enough for it to hurt. Sexual acts should not hurt.

What he does want is to see his husband come out of the water soaking wet. Wearing those earrings still. Maybe his eyes narrowed with purpose and water trickling down his chest.

Hades' mouth wrapping around him is a fabulous sensation. Taking Seph's cock deep inside him. His gentle, slow thrust is matched with the pace of his mouth, the tongue sliding against him, his throat muscles closing up tightly on his head...

But he pulls him up before they get very far with it. He *likes* that Hades is not a young girl flirting in the public bath, posing an arm to cover her breasts. Nor is he like Teysus, who basically equated bath time with wrestle time, and bathing was a sport of catch and tackle. This was to 'innocently' put his hands all over the young men their age at the pool.

Hades is too serious for that. But happy. And peaceful. And wet.

His hair sticks flatly to his head and clings to his skin, the ends reaching his nipples. Seph freely palms the well-formed pec. Smaller than his own, but strong. Curvy. Heavy. And he thumbs the nipple up, tilting Hades' jaw with the other hand for another kiss.

That is about all the romance he has patience left for. If he doesn't get off soon, this bath is probably going to kill him. Godly status and all—*poof.*

Hades calls him a stallion, so Seph pretends to be. He turns his mate around and grabs his cute butt with both hands. He kneads firmly with several gratifying, squishy digs and finally parts him to find that tight heat he desires.

His awareness for Hades' comfort and safety slows him down a bit.

"Where's that oil? Did you bring any with you?"

He almost wants to whine, realizing that Hades can't have it in the bath with him. How annoying!

"Don't need it," Hades says. He reaches backwards and smacks Seph's ass with a slap. "In you go."

This seems ill-advised. But Seph is too greedy to argue. He prods Hades with his thumb, testing him. He is resistant, tight, but the digit goes in easily. All the way up to the last joint, and he can move it in and out, fucking him.

He does this for a bit, keeping Hades close, putting a hand on his neck again so he can tilt his head and keep his throat exposed for kisses. The god's pulse beats like crazy under his palm. Hades swallows and gasps, and the knob in his throat bobs against Seph's hand.

"You smell amazing. Like ice. I think. I can't describe it."

Hades smiles again. "That is one of my plants. A potent herb that smells strongly. I named it Minthe."

Minthe...? Like the lamp lighting nymph? Why...?

Maybe it is a coincidence.

Maybe Minthe is named after the herb.

I will find out later.

He is much too hungry to question his mate now. So he rams his cock against the crevice of his ass, not going in. Only because it is rather difficult to fit and he doesn't want to force his way inside. He delays, thrusting against him instead, pushing with the tip sometimes, but pulling it back. Until finally he can't take it anymore. Hades is still so tight as he nudges inside. He pushes. He's forceful with it, but slow, hoping he's not hurting Hades too much.

The hole sucks him in, inch by inch, and tries to punish him. It squeezes and pressures and almost seems to twist. A shudder runs through his husband, all the way down his legs, his thighs shivering. He makes a helpless sound, his head thrown back.

Seph remembers to kiss him. On a corner of his jaw, which is all he cares to reach.

He wants this to be romantic. He wants to have more with Hades.

But he also really wants to feel this space widen for his size and become soft and welcoming. The way to do that is to teach it.

He begins to thrust, pulling himself out and in. And gradually it gets easier. Hades clamps down on him so tight, but Seph feels like he can shove as far as he wants to. His husband will always take him in.

His mate is made for this.

Hades gasps, and Seph brushes a strand of silver hair out of his husband's face. He wants something to say. *I love you* is tempting. Seph wants that. But just now he is not as compelled to say it as he was to smack his ass earlier.

Seph feels like he is still discovering too much of himself, who he is without his babying mother, to truly say whether he loves someone or not.

But he wants to be loyal to Hades. He wants his husband to like him, all over and all through. To like his hands, to like his cock. He wants Hades to show more of himself too. Even the bad parts, like Tartarus. And Seph knows that their relationship should be one of total freedom with each other.

No shyness. No manipulation. No secrets.

Nothing like what the other gods and goddesses have in their marriages.

I like that we are alone. I like that I never have to see my cousins again.

And yes, he might even like that he never gets to see his mother.

Though, he does love her.

It is just that she belongs to that other world. The underworld is quiet and private and personal.

That is what he wants with Hades. If only he could find a way to say it.

The answer does not come before his primal needs finally turn him into a man of purely selfish desire. Hades is snug but accepting, his ass letting Seph push however fast and hard he wants. He's warm too, and pulling him in. The god arches his back and so much strength is displayed in his muscles.

The occasional faint scar here and there, stories that Seph will find out someday, makes Seph drive harder. He wants to be felt when this is done. He wants Hades' body to get used to wearing him the way he wears these other marks.

This isn't just about fulfilling sexual pleasure, which is still quite new for him. This is about taking a man and making him his.

He should feel my cock inside him for days.

He should feel empty when I'm not doing this to him.

He should come back for me like he's hungry. Like a kitten after milk.

That cute butt against his groin makes delicious slapping sounds in the sloshing water.

I want him like this again. In our bed. I want to make the walls shake.

The sapphires, dangling back and forth, beat against the hand on Hades' shoulder, by his neck.

And finally—*finally*—Seph cums, pushing Hades forward slightly with his other hand, making him sink his back and present himself for it, while a high wave rushes over and out of him. Little frequent spurts follow, lasting a long time.

"I like being your stallion."

Hades does not seem capable of words through his heavy breathing. But he pats Seph's hand on his shoulder. Twice, quickly. Like, Good boy. And Seph doesn't leave yet. He knows he has his husband close, but he hasn't finished him yet.

He dips his hand into the water, reaching around the front. His Hades has himself in hand, but Seph takes over, bumping him out of the way.

He fists the cock and pumps it diligently, letting Hades take his time. His thighs flex. His feet slip a little and his stance becomes wider. Seph gets an idea and doesn't see why he shouldn't try it. The arm in front supports Hades around his waist. The other leaves his neck and picks his leg up from behind a thigh instead, lifting the knee out of the water, exposing him fully while he's still on Seph's cock.

Hades becomes very loud then. Whispering a curse and then sounding a bit like he's under attack, making squeaky pants and a rising sound like, "Ah! Ah!"

He finishes at last, his cock spitting cum like a fountain, far across the water. Seed gushes into the pool. Which Seph is only now wondering how in the hell it's ever going to come out. The public pools have to be emptied and refilled quite often. That must be the case here, though he does wonder about the grates in the pool walls and the lion-head spigots that are continuously pouring fresh water into their bath.

He shall have to ask Hades about the plumbing sometime. Which is an amusing thought considering how he's holding his lover at the moment, still inside him. Seph kisses the pale god's neck, feeling romantic again.

"What do we do now? Just regular bathing, I guess?"

Hades groans. "Take me to the steps. To sit. So I don't drown."

Seph puts his leg down so they can walk, but yet another impulse teases him. He grabs Hades around the waist and lifts him up by the knees, carrying him the way a studly man might do for a girl.

Hades is dripping and beautiful against his chest, and cooperatively puts an arm around his neck. Then he rests his head against Seph's beating heart. And Seph has never felt more different than the coddled, pampered son he used to be.

Twenty

It isn't just botany that Hades experiments with. While they're bathing, he reveals a cabinet of soaps that he designs and manufactures for himself in an apothecary. He sets out a dozen bottles in a row along the pool's edge, while Seph watches from the water with his arms folded on the edge tiles, realizing that perhaps Hades is beyond his sophistication.

He is like a simple farmer an aristocrat has taken a liking to.

Hades tries to tell him about the various chemical properties of the soaps. The Minthe herb, which shares a name with the lamp lighting nymph, has a pleasant, strong taste and a lasting fragrant smell, but the asphodel flower will be better for his skin. This Seph can understand. But everything else about the chemicals and the process used to extract herbal elements is just a bunch of confusing noise to him.

"So which one do you like?" Hades asks when he sets the final bottle down. The liquid inside is dark, whereas some are clear, some are white, and some are pink.

"Umm, do I just… pick a color?" Seph has been listening, but Hades rattles on so fast, he lost track of which bottle was which. He didn't describe them one by one as he laid them down. Rather, he started with the first one, then a middle one, and then the second one, and then back to the middle one again…

He has to take all the facts and sort them out himself if he wants to figure out what is in which container and all the helpful properties of the plants used. There is even a pomegranate soap for goodness' sake, and Seph assumes that's the pink one but he doesn't know for sure.

He feels like he is back at the vanity staring at a bunch of stones. Hades knows an awful lot about everything. He's very particular about the specifics.

Seph, meanwhile, is the kind of guy who says, *Color blue good.*

Color clear not so much.

His tutor never said anything mean to him, but his mother would sometimes smile and make a comment about him being dense.

Seph would much rather be riding a horse than learning about philosophy and politics or any of these science-y things. Though, he is becoming curious just because Hades is so animated and enthusiastic about his creations. Also, his science knowledge so far seems to be applicable. Astronomers, mathematicians, and all the smartsy scroll readers in the city don't seem to actually *do* very much in Seph's opinion.

"What would the color have to do with anything?" Hades says with a snort, sitting on the pool's edge, and Seph loves to see his form naked, doing normal things. He wades to his lover's knees, intending to lick and kiss them until Hades forgets he married a dingus.

He loves to see his tan hands on Hades' pale thighs. He loves to move those knees apart (though he is truly sated for now) just because he can and he likes to see Hades respond to his touch.

"We have to wash this hair sometime," Hades says, running a big handful of Seph's wet, messy locks through his fingers. "Ack!" His thighs close around his head as Seph experiments with a bite. Then he licks the pinking spot and sucks it into his mouth.

Not for long. He would never want to see a bruise on this lovely skin, but he does like to see what other ticklish ways he can surprise his usually somber mate.

Hades points at the bottles and speaks like he's ordering a dog.

"Get over there and sniff some soaps. Choose which one you like best. We can touch and play and romp some more when you've made some progress. We have to apply several of them, you know. And rinse them out of your hair. It's going to take some time."

"Several?" Seph echoes, his eyes widening. "Why several? I'm not that dirty!"

"Well, there is the oil-penetrating layer, and then the restorative layer, and then possibly a finishing restorative treatment, and then most certainly an oil to be applied for luster. I don't think you'll need a thickening balm like I do. You have so *much* hair."

And Hades ruffles his top like a good dog.

Seph can't even recite the list of 'necessary' soaps, but he realizes that this is going to be a *process*, so he moves sideways to the row of uncorked potions and starts sniffing. He picks one that he likes on bottle number three, but Hades scolds him.

"You haven't even smelled all of them yet!"

"But I like this one."

"How do you know if that's your favorite if you haven't smelled all of them?"

So Seph continues the smelling, and honestly, all the flower scents mix in his nose until he really can't tell the difference between one or the other unless he moves his nose back and forth several times.

However, he does discover that bottle number six is his favorite one. He feels like he recognizes the smell, and when Hades speaks he knows why.

"Ah. My narcissus flower. Yes, that is a good one. And I like that this shall reinforce the scent when I put the flowers in your hair. If it's all right, I would like you to wear my flowers more often." He gets a little quiet and looks over the side of his left knee. Being unusually bashful. "I would like to add the flowers to your hair when you do. Maybe for dinner. If you don't mind."

"I will wear every flower you wish," Seph says, kissing his knee and watching his expression. There is not much change. Noticing how Hades is feeling is becoming a science of its own, and Seph is finding himself to be a diligent student.

In this case, he believes Hades is more pleased than he's letting on. He draws this conclusion from the fact that Hades is *too* passive. When there is not much to express, his face is much more animated. And now Seph does not get even so much as one of his little smiles as a reward for agreeing to his request.

He must be as giddy as a girl!

Seph hopes so.

Perhaps he is reading his husband wrong since they have only been married a few days, but he shall be watching him closely and learning as much as he can. He thinks there is much the god suppresses.

"We should get started then," Hades says with a sniff, slipping into the water in front of him, and then moving toward the bottles.

For the next several minutes, Seph is like a stallion being groomed for the chariot races. He does not touch his hair once as Hades applies his treatments. And yes, several bottles go in. Ones from different shelves of his cabinet. And he continues applying serums of things even after telling Seph to get out of the bath!

"Why?" he asks, bewildered, still slightly disagreeable to the fact that Hades insists some soaps have to be left 'to sit'. Getting clean was never this complicated at home or in the public pool.

"We don't want the new shine of your hair to wash out, do we?" Hades responds, with the same bewildered attitude.

Seph does feel a bit like he's arguing with his mother again over the hair rollers and other ridiculous things.

He mutters, climbing out of the pool, "Do we have to curl my hair? I hate that."

"Goodness, no," Hades says, leaning way back to rinse the last of his treatment out of his own tresses. It is a good sight from up here, and again Seph wonders what happens to all the soap they've put in the pool. Water becomes rancid if it's not changed often enough.

Suds are drifting toward a nearby grate instead of traveling to the water spigots to gather and froth. There seems to be a current drawing old water out of the pool.

"Curls would only make you look like your father," Hades says, walking up the steps toward him. He's an alluring animal, walking with grace and glistening with the muscles of a predator. "While Zeus does look classically handsome, I never understood why Demeter was displeased with your naturally wavy style. Hair should not be tortured to achieve a look. All things are equally beautiful in their own right."

He dries his hair with a towel and then brings it for Seph, fluffing and scrubbing it over his head, after Seph has already dripped a sizable puddle.

Hades goes through his soap cabinet again, pulling a selection of smaller bottles from the top shelves, touching a finger to his bottom lip sometimes while he thinks—when the sound of heavy, swift footsteps makes them both look toward the staircase.

Seph is a little shy and immediately uses the towel to cover his waist. Hades only draws his brows inward, looking mildly perplexed and upset at the same time. He takes a few steps toward the base of the staircase, awaiting their visitor.

It is Verah. She shoots a nervous gaze across the pool room, seeking them, as she finishes the spiral and comes off the stairs. Her mouth opens to speak—and stays there, her words caught the moment she meets eyes with Seph. She looks at the dark king again, mouth moving with no sound for now, and Seph gets a bad feeling that he knows what this is about.

Something of his has been found.

But Hades says, "No. They ran again?"

Does that happen often? Seph wonders with alarm. What kind of pain are some souls willing to endure for the chance to see their loved ones again?

"N-no, king," she answers, and then bows deeply, her hands clasped in front of her skirt. "I am sorry. For interruption. It may be nothing. You may already know, my king. But…"

She looks at Seph again. There is no doubt. She found Hibus, the illegal upperworld bunny.

Why didn't he stay under the bed, munching his radish?

That should have lasted him awhile.

Seph does nothing, because there is nothing to do. He has thought about how to explain Hibus' existence to Hades, who apparently hates upperworld rabbits, possibly because of his fondness for his monstrous hound dog. And now Seph only knows he will be having this conversation very soon. As best he can.

"There is a *thing*," Verah says. "I do not know the word. There is a *thing* upstairs. That needs you now." She points at the ceiling, and she does look apologetically at Seph. But it's not necessary. He knows she's only doing her job. Mortals have no fractures in loyalty when their king is also a god.

"I will look at it, Verah," Hades says calmly. "Where is it?"

"The bedroom," Verah says, reluctantly moving her sorrowful eyes away from Seph. "The bed, my king."

Now Hades looks confused and he glances toward Seph also.

Seph is stoic. Not mad, not yet, but starting to be.

He wanted this to work out. So, so badly. He thought he would get to know Hades a few more days, maybe a couple weeks, and then he would find him in a *very* good mood and have a discussion about his rabbit. It would be a calm adult discussion. Nothing like the whiny tantrum he threw as a teen.

Now he feels more like that teen, about to have another tantrum. One that might cause him to cry.

What will he do if Hibus shows up on a plate? His stomach turns just thinking about it! His mother put rabbit on the dinner table often for several months after. She even ate Hibus' siblings! All to remind him the manor requires the sacrifice of many little animal lives to feed everyone and keep the mortals going.

"Verah, go," Hades says with a small tilt of his head. She bows again and scuttles away, taking the stairs up two at a time, practically running to avoid trouble.

Minthe warned him, 'Hades will dispose of the rabbit when he finds it.'

'So he could stay here as a spirit?'

Minthe shook his head. 'It doesn't work like that. We do have animal spirits, but only certain ones of their kind. Most of them are just gone. Very few of them can make it. Hibus will likely be one of those who just disappears.'

I don't want to find out yet. Seph's hands tighten into fists, imagining the worst possible outcome. Hades faces him.

I won't let you or your dog hurt him.

"Seph..." Hades starts, his voice passionless. "What am I likely to find upstairs in my bed?"

"A rabbit."

Though, how could he get on the bed?

Verah must have misspoken.

"Oh." Hades makes a small laugh, but is it relieved? Friendly? Seph wishes he had more time to get to know the man. "Shall we go attend the emergency then?"

His reaction is good... right?

Was Minthe wrong?

The nymph seemed knowledgeable about Hades, having known him many years. But... maybe he's different with Seph?

Twenty-One

Up the long stairs and back inside the bedroom, Seph discovers that Verah was quite correct about the rabbit being *on* the bed. He is there in the middle with his new radish and today's broccoli, and Seph hopes dearly that he hasn't soiled anything yet.

Hades is an orderly man. Even if he's all right with letting Seph keep the rabbit as a pet in the palace somewhere, he will likely not be happy to find out about the dirty basket under the bed. Which Seph assumes Verah has thrown out, though he quickly checks anyway. That slight smell of pee has to come from somewhere, and there are no wet spots on the bed. If there's a puddle to be cleaned up, he will do it before they start arguing.

But the basket is still there. Verah did find it, but she didn't move it. Perhaps because she's not sure whether she had permission to?

Great. So now a box of feces and urine can be used against me.

Seph leaves it under there for now. The smell is not very noticeable, if the blankets are kept down, and Hades sits on the bed on the other side, reaching slowly toward the middle to pick up Seph's rabbit.

Seph watches protectively, ready to intervene physically if necessary, if the god becomes cruel.

Instead, Hades croons.

"There, there, cute friend," he says, scooping up the rabbit's front just as it tries to jump away toward Seph. His back legs kick in the air as the god lifts him up. "Who do we have here?" He holds him with two hands for inspection. "A boy, I think. Does he have a name?"

He sets the rabbit on his lap and pets his ears.

Maybe I'm worried for nothing.

But Seph does not know how this is going to work out with the dog he's supposed to meet one day.

"Hibus," he answers. And since more questions will likely be coming, he adds, "I kept him under the bed. I don't know how he got out."

The lead and weighted vase are intact down there. His bunny must have slipped it off his foot somehow. Perhaps when Verah was cleaning, or whatever she was doing, the rabbit panicked and tried to run.

But he has never slipped his lead before.

This was just bad luck.

"I was going to tell you. He's my pet. I brought him from the upperworld. I just... I just didn't know when was a good time. Not everybody likes rabbits." Seph reaches across the bed, carrying Hibus' radish for him to munch on, since that's probably what he wants and he's not straining for Seph's protection at all.

The rabbit stops trying to flee and starts munching.

He was correct.

"Well, I think he's a beauty. A fine pet." Hades continues stroking him while he eats, and he seems to have a genuine smile. Seph starts to relax, sitting and scooting toward the middle of the bed where he can be close to them both. He puts an arm around Hades, and he thinks they make almost the perfect family in this moment. Only instead of a little gurgling babe, they have the grinding crunch of a chewing rabbit.

"We don't get many small animals down here. We don't get many animals at all. It is hard enough to rescue the abandoned humans who don't come to my call without a funeral or a grave. No god is powerful enough to catch all the animal souls, and then I would have to create additional processes to sort them and pick out the best. The strongest."

He sighs and leans into Seph.

"I did consider it briefly when I was new here. But it is too much. How am I supposed to keep the souls of rabbits and dogs and cats from crossing over the River Styx, back into the upperworld? And an animal is always true to its nature. They're never done with the ambitions and satisfactions of physical life, like an intellectual human soul can be. The life of a soul animal has to be exactly the same as the life of a real animal."

"So there are no animals in the underworld? What about your dog, Cerberus?"

"Dogs are pretty easy to keep as long as they are obedient. We keep all the ones who come in. Mostly, they are aquatic animals.

They do not leave the waters we put them in, so that is easy. I keep some deer and horses and things in my parks. The parks are really where we keep the animal souls who make it through. But they have to be specially crafted so that every animal is content and allowed to follow its normal routine. I am not building my underworld to be a miserable zoo."

"That is noble," Seph says, wondering why Minthe didn't mention that. The nymph was absolutely certain that Hades was a danger to the bunny. He said Hades would destroy the rabbit, or the rabbit would go back to the upperworld without Seph, and Seph would never see him again.

Why was the nymph so wrong?

Why would he lie like that?

"I really want to see your parks someday. All of them."

Hades scratches under the rabbit's chin, and Hibus stops eating long enough to yawn and tilt his head back.

"We were supposed to see one of them today," he says with a smile. "One that I filled with tame deer and every kind of bird I could find that wouldn't fly away. But I was impatient to get you into the bathhouse."

"Oh," Seph says, very pleased. He's grinning like a boy, and if he had to describe this feeling, he would call it *giggling*, even though he doesn't laugh outright. "Another day though. Maybe tomorrow? We can take Hibus to hop around the grass. He's very calm around children, you know. They love him."

"He would give them a fright," Hades says quietly. "They know how I am about where things belong."

"Oh." A different kind of *oh*. The bad kind of *oh*. He senses he is not in the clear yet.

"Uhm. We could keep him next to the bathhouse, in that courtyard area? I already thought it might be perfect. Heh, he has a little statue friend down there already."

I would just have to visit him every morning and make sure he knows he hasn't been abandoned. Poor Hibus. He'll miss being kept inside. And I won't get to see him as much. But he'll be safe.

And I'll ask Hades to put another door right before the stairs. A gate. Just to make sure his hound dog doesn't get down there.

Seph didn't see any other ways into or out of the private bathhouse.

"No, Seph. I'm afraid not. I can't allow that." Hades straightens up and pulls away from Seph's embrace, passing the rabbit to him.

Seph frowns, wondering why everyone in all the world has such a problem with this one sweet, mild rabbit. "Why not?"

Hibus peacefully settles himself on Seph's lap, even though he's without his radish, trusting and unaware.

"Look at his eyes, my king," Hades says softly. "Do you see how different they are? Look inside his ears. Look at the veins. Look at the pinkness of his flesh and the red of his blood. He does not belong here. He is a physical being."

"But what does that matter?" Seph asks angrily, though he stays quiet for Hibus' sake for now. "So he's *one* upperworld bunny. It's not a big deal. I'll find somewhere else. We'll keep him where no one can see him, and then no one will think you're hypocritical about your... upperworld laws."

"Hmm." Hades rolls his lips together. Seph knows he hasn't won. The argument is just starting. Why do gods have to be so stupid and stubborn about keeping a little fuzzy prey animal safe from the dinner table? Just one? What does it matter?

"H-he's my friend, Hades. Please. He's not just a pet to me. I-I can't be happy here without him." He feels like an infant again. The thrilling freedom he experienced with Hades is gone.

"I know," Hades says with a sigh, looking downward. "That is why I am thinking. But the beings of the upperworld belong in the upperworld, Seph. I'm trying to put it in words. So you can understand. He is made of *things*."

"So am I."

"You are a god. You were born into this world a soul already. All right, you know what? I'm going to explain it to you. As best I can. So don't get mad, and be patient with me. I am not a very good teacher."

"Okay," Seph says, reminding himself that he can breathe again. Hades does not seem to be angry or horrified by the bunny like his mother was. He doesn't seem cruel, and he didn't madly rush the bunny to the upperworld to drop him on the ground like Minthe said he would.

Minthe made it seem like this bunny was a catastrophe.

But Hades starts explaining himself calmly.

"A mortal soul does not come into the world fully formed. It is a thing. An awareness, perhaps. But not a full awareness, not at first. Also, souls get better the longer they live. The more they are reborn. They change over time. They are not static. It is like..."

His hands move in the air like he's holding dinner plates. "The soul and the body are symbiotic. They learn from one another. They grow with one another. Through rebirths and physical revision, they get better. They develop over eons. The humans I brought here the first time were not as developed as the humans I bring here now. And these will not be as wise or strong as the ones I bring here in a millennium or two. Of course, they will all adapt into their true selves over time, and that will change, so it doesn't matter."

"What does this have to do with my bunny?" Seph asks. He whispers because he realizes he's not being very patient, but he doesn't see how this relates to one little bunny.

"Well, I was going to explain how souls need their body. It is the most precious and personal thing. It's a home you've always had, and the love of their old physical forms is partially why souls long to return to the upperworld, no matter how good they have it here. A body is like a mother. Your rabbit's soul does not want to leave his body. That would be the cruelest thing you could do to him. Just in case you were thinking of slaughtering your rabbit here, if I would agree to it."

"I had roasted pig at my wedding ceremony," Seph says, unconvinced. Though, he had not realistically considered Hibus dying unless it was from old age. He can't even think about hurting his bunny.

"Yes, and the animal from the upperworld was slaughtered specifically for that feast. I have to routinely bring in meat and things for myself to eat, or this body will starve just as a human body would. But Seph..." He picks up the broccoli. "Most of our food? Including this piece? It's different down here in the underworld. There is no sun to grow crops. Did you know that sunlight is a necessary nutrient for mortal health? If the crops do not absorb sunlight, they do not create the same fulfilling nutrients that a physical body needs.

"This piece, and this radish, might fill your rabbit's stomach and keep him from being hungry, but his body will shrivel away. These vegetables hold nothing inside them that your rabbit needs. The simplest thing to call it is essence. The upperworld consumes essence to create essence. Since there is no essence from the sun and no essence from the soil, there is none of it in this thing that only looks like broccoli."

"Why do the souls eat at all then?"

Hades shrugs. "Most of the souls here get used to not eating and never do so again. They usually only come to the palace when they want to eat, and it is for some celebration or just a special night with friends. Those who live too far away from the palace have a dining hall in their neighborhood where they can eat and celebrate. Humans like to eat. The same way the birds in my park like to hunt fruit and bugs that they will never need again. And the deer will keep the grass short even though none of it will ever come out as droppings. It is just consumed. It is... not quite physical material."

"Alright." Hibus leaves his lap, peering over the edge of the bed. "So we will bring him crops from the upperworld. Just like you do for us." Hibus stretches his front paws downward, preparing for a big hop. Seph scoops him up quickly and gives him a ride down, letting the bunny wander on his own while he and Hades figure this out.

Hades shakes his head. "I can't do that. He needs sunlight, like I said. And air. And water. The entire upperworld is made of essence, Seph. It is fulfilling for a physical being to be up there. Even if we did feed him upperworld broccoli and radishes, he would become sickly without the rest of it. He would wither slowly and die a painful death."

"All right, so death then," Seph says with a sigh. He is not seriously considering it, but he shall have to hear Hades the Pig Eater give him a valid reason why slaughtering the bunny is not an option. "You slaughtered pigs for your table. Why not put this bunny on the table? He will not wander away because he is already here, and we will keep the doors shut."

Hades puts a hand on his back. Seph already knows he won't win this. He's out of options. And he begins to feel very sad, realizing that Hades has already considered all this. Hades wants to give him the rabbit. He thinks. He just can't. For underworld reasons.

"When souls grow with the body, they become strong. They form the ego. The idea of a self. Many animals, especially small ones, cannot form an ego. Only the wisest and most unique of their kind can. Your rabbit will likely just disappear if we slaughter him for the table. He will be here for a moment or two, possibly as some twisted, odd thing. Remember, souls become what they think they are. What they should be. A thing without an ego just vanishes into the air."

Seph sniffs and rubs his nose.

I am losing Hibus today.

And meanwhile his sweet bunny sniffs the rug tassels and paws at them. He must think they look something like grass. He nibbles on a thread, one ear perking up, which means he's thinking, considering this new food.

Maybe. Or maybe he is not at all as smart as he seems and both Hades and his mother are correct. He is just a simple rabbit. Something of no consequence.

"It doesn't seem right that most things in the upperworld do not get to come down here and live in Elysium."

"Believe me, I agree."

Twenty-Two

Hades did know about the basket, which Seph clutched protectively against his chest while huddled inside his chariot. And then he noticed that Seph kept the basket under his couch and would often reach for something on the floor whenever Hades was deep in his drink.

What could a young god keep so secretively under the covering cloth?

He didn't *wonder* necessarily. Gods are funny like that, especially when they get as old as him.

Humans are impatient for a great many things, and rightly so. It is how they accomplish so much in their little lives. They are always curious, always inventing, and often surprising the gods. They are pleasant children to have when they are being good.

An old god's perspective, on the other hand, is quite undramatic and dull. Whatever was in the basket would be revealed to him at some point, either through accidental discovery or the boy would tell him himself. Maybe it would manifest as an attack of some kind, a poison. Maybe Demeter *somehow* knew he was coming and equipped her boy with a weapon.

Whatever it was, it would reveal itself. In time. There was no need to interrogate an already terrified young man and possibly postpone his wedding for something as insignificant as a basket.

But now he is glad the basket appeared within a short time. Seph would have begun to wonder why his rabbit got sick. Why it chewed on furniture so earnestly. (Now it is trying to eat a pillowcase, and Seph is curled around him, trying not to cry.)

Hibus, as the beloved pet is called, is already starving to death. He is technically full, but his body is starving for nutrients. There is such little physical substance in the vegetables he's been eating that the food dissolves quickly in the stomach, to nearly nothing. He will get hungry again and again, growing more ravenous no matter what he consumes.

And now Seph is sad. It is hard to see. Hades frowns, checking his pitcher for wine.

Good, loyal Sefkh.

"Here," he says, splashing some into a cup.

Seph drinks heartily, sniffing, and resting back by the rabbit. He pets him continuously.

"S-so you think he will just disappear? He won't become a spirit?"

Hades delivers the facts.

"Technically, he will live. All essence lives and grows and lives again. The essence... divides. That is how life on Earth works. Division creates and grows more life. It is the same with plants and everything else. But yes, your rabbit will cease to exist upon death. Only an ego can shape essence without a body, and that shape is not held for very long without powerful belief."

His own cup disappears before and after this speech, with a few simple gulps. He has been meaning to tell Verah that the wine goblets on his nightstand need to be deeper.

"So the cat my mom stepped on? The pony I had when I was a kid? They're all just... air now. Just gone now."

Maybe he should put the wine down. Seph needs him. But Hades doesn't know how to soften this truth any more than he can do it for the mortals.

Since it is cruel to make Seph feel guilty and ungrateful, he doesn't say:

It is worse for the souls. You are losing a bunny, but they lose everything. Loved ones. Daughters. Little babies and siblings they were hoping to be reunited with.

And they are so loyal. So loving. They feel great pain when they learn the truth of this place.

My souls learn to make new families here in Elysium just to cope.

That is why they go back across the River Styx at the cost of themselves. To warn others. To tell them, when choosing between rebirth back into the world they love or living forever in Elysium, what rebirth *actually* entails. How the ego is stripped away and reformed. Only odd little traits, branded into the essence from all the things that essence once was, can live on in the ego of a new person. Not every stain and glitter comes out in the wash.

And that's what Tartarus is. A place to process. And wring and rinse and destroy.

He calls it the thresher.

And it is vitally important.

But that is not a thing to tell Seph or even hint at.

If he feels this bad for a bunny...

It shall be a long time before Seph is ready for the full tour of the underworld.

He thinks all of this while continuing to drink and hearing Seph try not to sniffle. This might be easier if he was gone, but he can't decide. He wants to be loving with Seph. He does not want to be his cold, usual self around the young man. Leaving would let him cry in private. But it is too much of a *him* thing to do.

If he's ever going to have a love, this will be it. Hades certainly doesn't have any cousins or nephews arguing over *him*.

He gags in his drink imagining it. And sets the goblet aside for now.

He looks at Seph and sighs. His destiny is to be a villain, even though his intentions are to act so differently than he must.

"Let me take him."

He reaches for the bunny.

"No!"

As expected, Seph curls around the rabbit with his entire body, guarding him like a mother wolf over her cubs.

"He doesn't have to go right away just because you found him! He can stay for a bit. A couple days. That's all. I promise he can go when... when he needs to. But not right away."

Great. Now how to argue with him without being an asshole?

"Hibus has been starving for days already. He's without the sunlight and the nutrients he needs. Also, it is cold. Even for a thickly furred bunny. Don't you think he would like to be hopping up there in the sun? In a green field? Full of butterflies and birds?"

That might be pushing it on the imagery, but it is summer.

Seph snorts. "He won't be hopping in the sun. He'll be in a tiny cage in the shade somewhere. Until it's time to eat him."

"I will find him a nice field."

Hades touches Seph. He expects to be rejected, the lovely face turning away, but surprisingly, Seph scoots a little closer.

"He'll get eaten by a dog."

Probably, yes. But it is a cage or a field for a bunny. There are not many options.

"Nobody wants to keep a rabbit as a pet," Seph says, having the same thought. "No one will be as good to him as I am."

"I will put him somewhere pleasant."

Where exactly? he challenges himself. Though Hades does want Seph to feel better, soft words are not something any god is good at. His family, especially, has been pummeled with reality harsher than this. Worse than Seph or the mortals can imagine.

Zeus was mad at him for not killing their father when he could. When it should have been his responsibility as the oldest.

But Hades was eaten first. And it was him alone in there, his flesh continuously melted by acid, feeling love and betrayal for his father. Then the agony when his sister Hera joined him. His sister would not exist if he had acted responsibly, but she also wouldn't be the unstable monster she is today. *He* is the strongest god now and was the second strongest when Kronos was alive. *He* probably could have killed their mad father.

Their mother could not. Nor any of the others. Kronos was the most powerful god any had ever known. Zeus barely managed to trick him, and it required the cooperation of Gaia and Rhea, who faced annihilation if they were caught.

"Why are you crying?" Seph asks, and these thoughts stop.

"What?" Hades checks his cheeks quickly and around his eyes. "I'm not." *Am I?* "No, I'm not." He takes a big breath. "Why would you say that?"

"Well, you're looking at yourself in the mirror over there. And you look so sad." Seph isn't focused on the pet anymore, reaching over to grab his shoulder. "It's alright. I don't blame you. I know if you could do something for Hibus, you would. But... wouldn't it be nice if I could go to the upperworld for a little while? Just a little while! So Hibus could grow old with me and live a good life. Please, it's the one thing I ask. Hibus is old already, and a few years are nothing for an immortal god."

"You are right," Hades says, patting that hand touching him. He longs for yet another drink, but he lies down instead, getting close, with Hibus the hungry rabbit between them. He gives the rabbit a pet and forces his features into a mild smile.

He has not cried since leaving his father's stomach.

"And I would give you your wish. Except, like I said, Zeus is curious about you and will not let you return to me once he lays eyes on you. He is mad, Seph. Almost as mad as our father was. And Demeter, knowing this and hating *me*, would not let you return either. Not for any reason. My guess is she'll stash you in some sea cave.

"Seph... you are not powerful enough to resist her. You are *her* rabbit, don't you see?"

And now you are mine.

But Hades has enough tact not to say that. All the things that are not powerful enough to face a god are sort of rabbits in a way.

"I'm her son. And—ugh—and you're right. She wouldn't let me come back."

Hades expected stubbornness. Illogical arguments going in circles for hours. Like the begging of a mother asking to go back to the babe she just gave birth to. These things do not sway him anymore. Hades does not flinch from responsibility.

Seph has surprised him again. One this young should not be so sensible. When Hades married Seph, he did not expect to have anything in common with the man for a millennium. If at all.

"That is correct." He doesn't know what to say.

"And he has to go back soon. I get it." Seph sighs and pets the little creature, who scratches inside his ear with a big foot. He shakes his head and twitches. He sniffs around Hades' hand to see if he's hiding any treats there.

He's extremely tame for a rabbit. There must be a little child in the upperworld somewhere with doting parents.

"I will find him a good place. I promise. I will do my best."

Seph nods. "But can I keep him one more night? Can he go in the morning?"

No, is what the usual him would say. Though the days may seem long and endlessly repeating, Hades has a great responsibility down here in the underworld. It's his job to make sure the creations on Earth do not vanish forever into nothing. That is what happens when life has divided so many times and the essence grown so much, spread so thin, that it can no longer sustain itself.

The days are long. The underworld is forever. But Hades is actually in a *hurry*, and work cannot be postponed. It is one of his policies.

But for Seph...

Maybe just once.

"Alright. Another night. I'll take him back after breakfast in the morning."

It is worth it to see Seph nod, his eyes wet with tears. Hades strokes a thumb underneath one and finds his touch wandering to his cheek. They kiss. And it is sad. And sweet.

Hades feels...

Remorse.
Genuine remorse.
About a *rabbit*.

Twenty-Three

Hades frowns at the bunny the entire night—in his manner, which means his expression is one of quiet, slightly displeased concentration. What does it say about him that the fate of one animal should suddenly become so important? Why should this small thing's pain matter at *all* in the grand scheme of a larger world?

Of course, it is his new husband's sorrowful face that makes it so. And *that* is just as confounding. As troublesome. As worrying.

Yes, Hades did not intend to be cruel to his sweet young bride. Of course not!

That does not mean he intended to be treating Seph's things as precious objects, and for the sake of comparison, Seph's desires count as objects. He did not intend to *court* his young husband. He did not think they would have very much in common at all. He still thinks that—for if he asks Seph a small question after a long-winded explanation of botany, he gets a shrug and a clueless expression.

But the young man is very polite, smiling and paying attention throughout. He just doesn't seem to retain anything that's been said.

Regardless. This *being nice* to each other should not have formed a genuine attachment from him. Hades is nice to a lot of people. A lot of creatures, too.

He did not bring Seph here because he loved him. It has weighed on his mind for many centuries now that he is alone here. He has no equal, no true companion. And he began to wonder...

How long can I keep this up?

A god lives forever, but *forever*? Designing neighborhoods? Playing with his dog? Sometimes bringing back an errant citizen?

He forced himself at times to stray out of the underworld. Just to be where there are other gods and drama and life. To cure himself of the deepening gray of this place, which seemed to have faded him as well.

He brought Seph here to be his equal in most respects. For as much as the young god can be trusted with. And then he assumes the natural course of two equal beings will be to challenge each other. That will bring him back to life, he hopes.

He did not account for this first spark of emotion to be for a *rabbit*. When the screams of your own beloved children do not sway you from punishing them, you can safely assume you are empty of all compassionate emotion.

Not today, however. Seph fusses over his rabbit in the morning, and Hades lets him, frowning at himself in the vanity mirror. His sapphire earrings go on again today.

Or maybe he should opt for the rubies?

Would Seph like that?

The fact that he cares at all is astounding.

And then from his stool, applying an ointment to protect his pale skin from the piercing sun rays in the upperworld, he says, "Say your goodbyes."

He feels like the passive tone is an act. A practice. After Hades has ordered many mothers to forget their own babes they left behind.

"Wait! Can I just..."

He's searching for any reason. Any excuse to delay the inevitable.

Hades should not tolerate this.

"Can I show him your solarium? Please? It's nice in there. I'll make sure he doesn't eat your flowers."

"Yes," Hades replies, and without much hesitation. And the corners of his lips draw downward on his face, to the point where he can feel them. He is not used to such strong emotion.

Was bringing Seph here a mistake? Will Hades now start to feel the remorse and burden of his actions?

He has a difficult responsibility here. It is his alone, and he doesn't pine away in acid anymore, moaning in self-pity and agony.

So what is this?

This... *humanity* inside him?

They go to the solarium, which is open to any of his subjects so long as they respect the plants. It is empty this morning, for once. Seph places the bunny, untethered, on the floor. And while Hades did not think a rabbit could bond with a person very much, the two of them are soon exploring together. Seph is like a father with his infant son, showing the rabbit things and lifting him up to a bench seat or planter.

The rabbit seems intelligent enough to comprehend a simple game of hide and chase.

And of course, it chews *a lot*.

He tells Seph not to mind. "Don't worry about the leaves. They grow back."

But what would he do to a soul if he found one running through his solarium and plucking leaves?

None would dare.

This is a dangerous emotion. I must watch it and be wary.

And *why* does it exist? What is it about Seph that rekindled something in him?

"You've had enough time. I'm sorry, Seph, but it's nearly noon in the upperworld where I will take him, and I think he will fare better if he's discovered before the cooks have started heating their pots for stew."

Seph bundles the rabbit close. What has Demeter done to him to make him so attached to this ball of fur?

Hades expected tears for the people Seph would leave behind. But come to think of it, he has not said anything about the friends he left in the upperworld. There is just this rabbit and his mother. That is all Hades knows.

I will discover more when I return. Maybe over dinner. On another day, when he is not sad.

Surprisingly, Seph approaches with the rabbit cradled in his arms, needing no threats or further cajoling. And after a last pet and a loving kiss, he holds Hibus out to him. Hades expected to take it from him forcefully by the end. And he knows he would have hesitated more before completing the task.

It is not comforting. These emotions are inexcusable. A king should act once the correct decision has been made.

Fortunately, such an ignoble hesitation is avoided by Seph's own willingness to part with his pet in the end.

"Where will you put him?"

"I will find a good place. I'll check your mother's home first—"

"Not the villa!" Seph exclaims, his eyes wide.

Hades nods. "No, of course not. I promise I will not set him near any nymphs. No, I think... a healthy town is the best place for him. In a household with little daughters, cared after by a somewhat wealthy man. A friendly rabbit like Hibus should be safe there."

"Alright. Nobody mean, okay?"

Ah, but none of the souls are mean. Not usually. They are injured and imperfect, yes, sometimes fractured within their essence. But they are not cruel in the willing way that only gods can be.

"He will go to a sweet household. I promise."

"Okay," Seph says with a sigh. He touches Hibus' foot with a finger. "Bye, little one."

Hades' own eyes are blinking more than they should be. Strangely. Is there dust?

And then he almost speaks. *I do not want to take him from you.*

Odd.

He shifts the rabbit to one arm and embraces Seph with the other. He kisses the top of his head, as if he is a son, and then makes a promise.

"It will not be long. I will give him to a happy home, and he will be well looked after until his life ends. He might come here and he might not. But if he does... I will find him. I can watch his soul from here and tell you how he is at all times."

All of this—for a *rabbit*.

"Thank you," Seph says with a nod and hugs him back.

The rabbit kicks impatiently. He wants to eat Hades' entire garden and then will wonder why he's so hungry at the end.

"This is truly what's best for him."

With those words, he leaves. Away from Seph, not looking back at him, he feels like a man prodding his own chest and wondering why he's bleeding around a large knife. *He* put the knife in himself. He brought Seph here. And now this.

What is this?

Twenty-Four

The rabbit goes into a small chest with a latching lid, his smelly blanket lining the bottom and a few substance-empty treats added to satisfy his constant gnawing urges. Hades carries him through the palace, which has noticeably fewer faces and quiet conversation throughout the halls. Despite the distance he keeps from his subjects emotionally, he always welcomes the proximity of their presence, and the doors to his palace are open to the public.

Was the hunt truly so terrible this time?

"Sefkh," he calls, seeing his servant cross from one room to another. "Where is everyone?"

Sefkh pauses, bowing over his broom. "They heard you had trouble, my king. They are keeping away so no one gets hurt while gods fight."

"There is no fighting," Hades says, confused. Why would they think that? Do they think he's furious about the bunny being where it doesn't belong?

Actually... that might make sense.

"May I ask, my king—what is in the box?"

"It is Hibus, a living rabbit. The source of the 'trouble.' He was Seph's pet, and my mate smuggled him here in a basket. Would you like to see?"

Blinking, Sefkh nods once and sets his broom against a table to come close. Hades undoes the latch and brings the lid up slowly. Without Seph here, he can't be sure that the rabbit won't try to hop away. It sits still inside, its nose twitching quickly, watchful for danger. But it doesn't seem scared.

Not like Sefkh, whose eyes widen considerably. He curls his hands in front of his chest like a scared boy. Sefkh is sweet, appearing around the age of fourteen, but he was ancient when he came to Elysium. Barely four feet tall, for humans were smaller when Egypt was new, and he was so wrinkled, without a tooth in his mouth. He had lived a long life and had approximately fifty sons and grandsons by then.

He longed for the upperworld greatly when he arrived.

"It has so many... different... *parts*," he says, knitting his brows, seeming confused or wondrous or both. His hands twist over themselves nervously. "It is not one piece, like I remember. It is not a *rabbit*. It has all these... parts."

"Yes. All the pieces of its body are living. Together, combined, to make a whole. Some parts of him, like his fur and claws, grow without consciousness, like... like a plant on top of your head. Or moss on a rock. They are separate, living off of the body, growing out of the spirit with roots in the soul. Do you want to touch?"

Only one finger goes down into the box, cautiously.

"I used to hunt these with my brothers," Sefkh says. "And then with my sons. We used rocks and a slingshot. We—we pummeled them. We thought it was fun. They used to eat our vegetables and dig holes in the fields." He rubs his eye with his other hand.

"You did not know," Hades says comfortingly. It is not a rabbit's death that he mourns, for death is quite normal and the sadness is unavoidable. A soul as old as Sefkh knows that. But he hurts for the damage he inflicted on another physical being. Having a body is a short and cherished memory for a soul.

Everyone cries over this rabbit, Hades thinks unkindly, but his mood is one of admiration for Sefkh, one of his sons.

"I am not touching him," Sefkh says, continuing to stroke with one finger only. "This is only his fur. This is only his ear. These things are just parts. But together they make all of him. His soul is inside."

"I have to go now, Sefkh."

His son nods and takes his hand away, returning to the broom.

"Tell the others it's okay to come here. Seph and I did not fight. No one is angry. The rabbit simply doesn't belong, and Seph didn't know that he couldn't bring him. I have explained things."

Did the others think I would punish Seph the way I punish my children with the dog?

He considers asking, but the question is inconsequential. The hunt must repeat as many times as it is necessary. And it works. Hades has not lost a soul in almost a millennium.

He moves on toward the stables, and is nearly out of the house, when a bit of blue disappearing into another room alarms him.

"Minthe!" Hades strides quickly to the staircase leading to the kitchens, and there is Minthe, glaring at him with an angry little pout. "What are you doing here? You're not supposed to be here."

"Many things are in the palace that are not supposed to be—"

He grabs the nymph's arm, and Minthe falls silent with a small scared gasp.

It is true, Hades gets alarmed eyes and cautious avoidance for days after a hunt, though he does not think he has a violent temperament. Rather, the hunt is a reminder to the children (and a bluff) that the father who doesn't hurt them *can* hurt them.

But Minthe is not a child, nor a soul. Just an unruly subject, one who he suspects is not right in the mind.

Minthe was an attractive friend at first. One who cared for him physically and emotionally when Hades himself could not. It became more than a physical arrangement very quickly. Hades looked forward to returning to his rooms every day.

Minthe has a devilish way of smiling. He made Hades feel young and zestful again. For a time. And only in the bedroom.

But then he began to notice the sickness. Minthe's attachment goes beyond love. He has a fractured essence, Hades suspects, something that is constantly yearning. Something that feeds like a parasite. Hades was the new food source, and Minthe began to play deceptive games to make the god vulnerable to him.

It did not work. The little lies of so-and-so did this and so-and-so should not be trusted were exceptionally easy to see through.

"What are you doing in my palace? And why are you running from me?"

Minthe puts his chin up, a stubborn, hateful glare creasing his pretty features. "I heard there was a thing here that did not belong. And so I thought the palace had become a place for all the cast out, wicked things. Including me."

A snare for pity is another one of Minthe's games. Hades does not feel the emotion very often, but Minthe *craves* it.

He is sad for his ex-lover. He would keep him in Elysium if he was able to. Jealousy is just another form of suffering, in this case from the consequence of feeling inadequate. Minthe's soul would heal from this fracture in the afterlife, if it was able. But the price of a nymph being so connected to the Earth and the primal understanding of all things is that their souls are claimed very quickly. Instantly. Even down here, in the underworld.

But unlike humans, nymphs do not fear or harbor remorse for their own deaths.

For that reason, Hades is sorry for Minthe. But giving in to such an emotion would not be healthy for his past lover. Minthe's best option is to find peace before he dies, and for that, Hades banished him to light the street lamps in parts of Elysium that are far, far from the palace.

"Do you think your presence will affect my new union? Are you hoping that my seeing you again will bring back what we had? Minthe... don't you realize your wounds are self-inflicted? This pity you feel for yourself would not be so palpable if you had not returned here."

He steers Minthe back into the hall and they continue toward the stable. Once he reaches his horse, he will make sure Minthe is escorted far away. Verah and several other peacekeepers around the palace will be notified again to keep an eye out for Minthe.

"I had to come here," Minthe says with a sniff. "You weren't supposed to find me. I just wanted to make sure you are happy without me. That's all. I was just checking. And I'm already going now, so you don't have to do anything."

Again, that self-piteous snare. Hades can sense it like diagnosing a man with a giant head wound, blood seeping everywhere. It is the same affliction that Hera suffers, but hers can actually heal. Hers has a source.

She mistook Zeus's jovial laugh for love aimed at her. Love that she craved.

Closing the wound is the start to the healing process. Hades did the best that he could for Minthe. He went without his physical needs being sated, even on the nights that it got very bad. Even when he craved closeness with someone so much that he wondered if he was dying inside.

He did not act as Zeus does and just used Minthe's body and affections when he personally desired.

But he is rather cold with the nymph to sever their ties. There is no other way Hades can think of to help him. Pity and affection only make the parasite worse.

"Whether I am happy without you or miserable, you cannot come back into my life. We are over, Minthe. And your presence is forbidden near the palace."

If only there were more souls here today. He would've passed Minthe off already. He feels like one of his own servants, carrying all these unwanted things out of the place. How did Minthe even get in?

Ah. He must've taken advantage of fewer eyes after the hunt.

"Why am I forbidden?" Minthe asks in that bratty way he does.

"Is it because you don't want your new lover to see me? You don't want me to tell him about all the cruel things I know about your heart? Or you don't want him to be jealous of me? Are you afraid he'll lock you out of the bedroom if he finds me?"

"It is bad manners to keep an ex-lover under the roof when you've only just been married. I don't need to tell you that. But that is not why. I have moved on, Minthe. You need to do the same."

Minthe tries to slow him down by turning and stopping to talk, but Hades only grabs him harshly and pushes him forward. They continue at an efficient pace outside, and Hades makes for the stables.

His dog being locked up also gave Minthe an opportunity to sneak into his palace. Cerberus is extremely smart, and he would have sniffed out the unwanted guest immediately. Hades likes to think it is the smell of Minthe that makes his dog bark and scratch viciously at the stable door. But of course, at this distance from the barn, he can likely make out Hades' footsteps from all the others.

"You will make for the trees now. You will cut through the forest from here to the neighborhood of Corythia, where you should be. Do not let me catch you here again, Minthe, or I will have to banish you to the upperworld, where you will miss your ice flame and the shaded things."

Cerberus howls. Hades hears a frantic scraping inside the chest. He lifts the box a little higher and a little closer, though there's nothing he can do to reassure the bunny.

"Is your lover going to forgive you about the rabbit?"

Hades stops. "How do you know?"

Minthe crosses his arms. His eyes glance to the side, then he focuses on Hades and says, "Well, everyone's talking about it—*the upperworld bunny.*" He shrugs one shoulder. "Can I see it?"

"No. It's time for you to go now. And Minthe, your banishment is permanent. I am wondering if I should send Cerberus after you *now*. I do not usually let someone go unharmed when they have broken one of my rules."

"Unless it is your new lover, I see!"

"You are making me doubt my decision."

Minthe evaluates him. It is a short moment. Hades has told him the truth, and as part of fatherhood, he has learned that idle threats cannot be made as punishment. The things he says have to be intended or else he will find himself pleading for the subjects to behave, and a king cannot be so powerless.

Minthe sniffs and rubs one elbow with his hand, his lips lifting with a hateful sneer. Then he pivots and heads for the trees at a different angle than the barn. Hades waits with the rabbit, wondering what he should do.

He does not look forward to the hunt. Minthe is a physical being. He has never had to punish any of the underworld nymphs, and he's not sure that he would do so with his dog.

But getting angry at Minthe, or even imprisoning him, would only feed that wound of self-sorrow in his heart. Minthe has an obsession. *Hades.* His parasite wants to both feed and destroy.

His ex looks back once. Hades has not moved. His expression must hold something (maybe it is the steadiness of his eyes) because Minthe picks up pace toward the trees, running.

Taushev comes out of the barn with one of his horses on a lead. He looks in Hades' direction, probably wondering why he's stopped, and then continues around the side of the barn where they will have the chariot waiting.

Hades still doubts. Minthe is tenacious. He cannot have come all this way for a little talk and a pout.

The fact that he showed up here once should be proof enough that punishment is needed. He clearly does not fear Hades as well as he should.

But I do not want to hurt him.

Yes, that is true.

Surely the hunt and taking away Seph's favorite pet is enough damage and sadness caused by his hand for now.

"Tell Verah and everyone else to keep an eye out for Minthe," he tells Taushev when he arrives, tucking the chest into a bag strapped on his shoulder, then walking around his horses with a trailing hand. He checks the harnesses every time out of habit, tugging on a strap here and there. "Do this immediately. Minthe is not allowed anywhere near the palace."

"Yes, my king."

I may have to punish him anyway, when I get back, he thinks as he steps into the chariot, taking up the reins. *He can't be allowed near Seph.*

I should hurry then.

Twenty-Five

Seph sits on the bed feeling miserable. Feeling like he's abandoned a promise. Or a friend.

And also feeling confused about himself, because it is true that Hibus is just a rabbit. Hibus probably can't become attached to him the way a dog becomes attached to its owner, or even a horse. Hibus is a little prey animal, mostly afraid of everything, not really knowing anything.

But when he scooped up Hibus out of his shadow that first day they met, he felt like he had found something special. Something he would always take care of.

And when he insisted on keeping Hibus in the house, despite what his mother had said, that was the first time he stood up to her and won. That was when he started noticing boys more lustfully. That was when things started changing for him, and he felt more like a man, choosing his own name—Seph.

But it is just a rabbit.

Seph sniffs and rubs his eyes. He takes a big breath and stands up from the bed, walking a pointless circle around the room.

He purposely didn't follow Hades to his chariot for that one last goodbye to the rabbit in the box because he knew the tears would well up like this. He doesn't want to openly cry in front of his new husband yet.

And that is another source of confusion. As much as Seph wishes the rabbit could stay here, losing Hibus is an acceptable cost to deepening the relationship in his marriage. He likes Hades. A lot.

Maybe his looks have something to do with it. Maybe it's the power that he's drawn to. When he had Hades in his hands yesterday in the bathhouse, he felt like a god. A *real* god. Not a puny *baby boy*.

So there is a great deal of guilt in knowing that he has willingly given Hibus up. And the little rabbit, loyal or not, will not have any idea why he was abandoned.

Seph has no foolish hope that Hades will find a family that cherishes rabbits. He can find one that's well-off and not cruel, but Hibus will likely go into a small cage outside and stay there until he dies.

And then he will truly be gone forever.

It is not a thing a god should be upset about, he tells himself, because his mother is not here to do it for him. *I will last a lot longer than a rabbit. In a millennium, what will I even care about a rabbit I had when I was a kid?*

Still upset, he paces some more. He wanders into the study and picks up one of the heavy enormous gems Hades keeps as ornaments. Just to have something to look at, to distract himself.

It's time to grow up, Seph. You're not a baby boy anymore. Rabbits don't love, obviously. And you're being stupid.

Still, it was a promise. When he held Hibus close and told him not to worry, intending to keep him, that promise should have been forever. He made Hibus his.

A door slams in the bedroom, making Seph frown and put down the stone. He returns to the bedroom, perplexed, and sees a figure standing before the bed with clenched fists and ice blue hair.

"Minthe?"

The nymph whirls, his mouth open. Then he looks delighted.

"It's you! Good. Come on, we have to go!" He takes Seph's hand with two of his and pulls, but Seph does not allow himself to be led yet.

"Where are we going? And what's the rush?" He takes two slow steps as Minthe pulls with all his strength. "Did something happen?"

"Yes, something happened! The dark god—Hades—he's got your bunny. Don't you know that?!"

Does the nymph think Hades stole Hibus?

"Wait, Minthe, it's okay. I know, I—why are you out of breath?"

Minthe is frantically struggling to take him to the bathhouse door, Seph's footsteps slow and reluctant, and now he's noticing that the nymph breathes like he's been running. Like he's panicked.

"Minthe, I know Hades has Hibus. It's okay. I mean—it's *not* okay because he's taking Hibus to the upperworld, like you said. He got out from under the bed somehow. The weighted vase we made him worked very well, but I think Verah—"

"No, Seph," Minthe says with wide eyes, pausing the tugging for a moment. He glances toward the den nervously and continues,

"He's not taking the bunny to the upperworld. That's not what I said."

Seph's brow furrows. Did Hades lie?

Why would he?

"He's taking him to Tartarus," Minthe says in a horrified voice. "He's going to kill the bunny because—because it's just easier that way! Don't you see? We have to go save your rabbit!"

Now Seph's feet move willingly, but his emotions grow heavy with betrayal.

To Tartarus? No, he wouldn't.

"Why would he?" Seph asks sternly, unsure. But if Hibus is going straight to Tartarus, assumedly to die, he has to do something right away! He no longer tries to stay in place and lets Minthe lead him into the narrow hall with a spiral staircase.

Minthe moves around him quickly to shut the door after them, and then takes his hand to guide the way down.

"Because it's just easier that way!" he says, his voice loud among the stone walls. "Things that don't belong go to Tartarus! Where the truly wicked are punished, or the unwanted souls are put to death! Permanently. Come, I'll show you. You'll see what I mean."

"Why would he lie?" Seph asks. He's not sure what Minthe is saying is true. Why go through so much trouble to assure him that—

Well, actually, no. It makes more sense that Hades wouldn't give a crap about a rabbit, doesn't it? This is a king who runs down his children with a dog. Also, long-lived gods barely care about the short-lived animals in the world. They care a bit more about humans, since they're so personable and smarter than an animal, but a rabbit might as well be a bug as far as a god is concerned.

And while all of this runs through his mind, his cheeks heating as he realizes he has not only been foolish, he's been acting like an absolute baby in god's eyes... Minthe explains it all for him, allowing his ears to hear as well.

"Because he doesn't care about a bunny, young king. Not any more than he cares about a slipper or dirt under his nail. He only wanted you to feel better about losing your pet. So he told you he would take Hibus to the upperworld and give him a good home and all that—but really he's just going on the chopping block. And you would've never known if I hadn't come and told you. I want to help you save Hibus."

They jog alongside the pool, to the opposite end of the bathhouse, where Minthe grabs one of the gold torch holders on the wall and reveals a sliding door. A little narrow set of stairs goes upward and turns.

"Wait," Seph says, his instincts still unsure. "Aren't you a nymph? I thought nymphs didn't keep pets. I-I thought you didn't understand them."

According to everything that Seph knows about nymphs, which he learned from his mother, it actually makes more sense for Hades to care about Hibus than it does for Minthe to do the same.

Minthe stops and turns around on the narrow stairs, Seph's hand falling out of his grasp since the god does not follow. He looks a bit astounded, and he's quiet a moment as he puts his thoughts together.

"Every second we stand here, your rabbit is getting closer and closer to death," he says in a scolding-yet-subdued tone. "And I only care about the rabbit because you do. I like you. We nymphs are not all the same."

"Oh. Of course not," Seph says, and starts up the narrow steps after him. He's right. Why is Seph even arguing anyway?

But...

"Didn't you tell me that you were going to tell Hades about the rabbit?" He has to call upward, since Minthe still moves so much faster than him. Like he's in a panic. "Weren't you thinking about it?"

"That was before I liked you!"

And that's a simple enough answer to make sense. Minthe did help Seph make the weighted vase, after all. He did warn several times that Hades absolutely must not find the rabbit on his own. Of course, he made it sound like the dark king would be furious at him. But maybe Hades tempered his actions. Maybe Hades thought it would be easier to let Seph stupidly believe he would scout for and place Hibus in a good home.

Honestly, don't you think the dark god has something better to do with his time?!

Seph's shame in himself burns deeply. His mother, who knows Hades better, would have corrected him and protected Hibus if she was here. Seph is helpless and stupid on his own.

He does not hesitate anymore, urging his feet faster to catch up with Minthe as they climb the stairs. It seems there's a maze inside the walls, narrow hallways branching off, more steps going up or down. These must be the servant passages, Seph assumes, though his knowledge of palaces is slight. It makes sense that the servants who look after the bathhouse would not be allowed to tromp through the king's bedroom whenever they wish.

"Wait!" Minthe hisses, stopping, and Seph hears footsteps that aren't theirs. "Back! Back!" he urges quietly, and they retreat to the last corner, huddling unseen.

"Why are we hiding?" Seph has enough sense to whisper. Also, his eyes are leaking and his voice is hoarse with new tears. He wipes his cheeks dry and sniffs.

Minthe waits until whoever it is disappears, a creak like a door sounding before the footsteps are gone.

"We don't want him to know we're coming." He tugs Seph along. "All the ghosts here are loyal to Hades. They're afraid of him. Come on!"

Seph thinks about his first day here and how impressed he was that the young-seeming souls were happy and unafraid. Unfortunately, he was wrong to have hope. Hades is the generous ruler, but only when his word is obeyed. How stupid of Seph to start feeling free and daring! And to start wondering if their games of *my king* meant anything about being equals.

He doesn't know enough about Hades. He should have been more cautious, more alert. And more protective of Hibus, like Minthe urged him to be.

They come to a door. It has a barred peeping window that Minthe peers through, checking left and right before pushing it open. It leads to the outside.

"Alright. We have to move even faster now, and we can't talk. Nor more questions, okay? I know the alleys and back streets to keep us hidden—hopefully. But you have to keep up. We have a long way to go, very fast."

Seph nods, taking a deep breath to calm himself, wondering what he will even say to Hades when he sees the dark god again and calls him out on his lie.

I will make him take Hibus to the upperworld and make good on his promise. I will go with him, which I should have done in the first place, and make sure that Hibus is looked after. And then—

And then...

Then he will come home. Where everything is ruined.

Twenty-Six

They run for so long, for such a distance, that Seph feels like he has no hope of getting to Hibus in time while he's alive. He tries to say as much to Minthe, while they are crouched inside a building and waiting for some idle souls to turn another way. But Minthe only shushes him harshly, focused on the task of always moving ahead, always as fast as they can go without being seen.

It is not an easy thing to do in a city, and Seph is a tall bronze man in a world of small pale children. There is no need for underground tunnels like a real city might have, for here no one dies a second time and is in need of a grave, nor do they have latrines or kitchens or any of the practical necessities that would take up space and give Minthe and Seph more room to hide.

Elysium is a place of open doors, open spaces, and plush pillows on benches. There are a lot of trees though, which help. And a lot of shrubbery and fountains too.

There is also painting, playing, climbing, singing, and all manner of activities that only well-off children get to afford in the living world. There are many ghost cats, which Seph did not notice before, and they are all some shade in the spectrum of black to white. He sees one small flock of chickens, looking exotic and beautiful in their light golden tone, but they are only six, and they seem to be doted on by a large pleased crowd of children.

Seph does not have to ask. By how pleased the children are, and how the street is literally covered in seed by their spoiling efforts, Seph can guess that these might be the only chickens in all of Elysium. The smartest ones who formed an ego and made it to the afterlife.

Surely if there were more, they would all flock together.

He sees one goose, looking rather lonely and not chasing anyone.

And throughout the city, dogs are a common appearance, but

not nearly as common as in the town where he grew up. There are no puppies, nor can ribs be seen on the animals. Every single pet is well looked after and seems to wander without following any one person.

The dogs do not bark when they happen upon Seph and Minthe sneaking through the city. Indeed, they do not seem to be aware of the concept of danger at all. A shepherd's breed ambles up to them while they are sneaking along a row of wine barrels. Seph speaks soft words to calm the coming eruption, but she only sits, scratches her ear for a moment, and then looks at him peacefully with her tongue hanging out.

Everyone in Elysium leads calm, untroubled lives. She collects a pat on the head from Seph as casually as acquaintances saying hello, and then she wanders on. The lack of fences and stone walls makes traveling easier. And hiding harder.

The woods are completely empty, and here at last they pick up their speed.

Minthe only says, "Keep up with me," and then they are off.

Keeping up is not hard. Seph does not even have to pant for breath. But nymphs do move faster than mortals generally do, and they can weave through the trees like wolves. Miles pass quickly under their feet, and soon Seph begins to wonder if he can find his way back. He looks over his shoulder and can only see the same-looking trees.

Not being in Hades' chariot, the towering palace is invisible to him.

So I may have to climb as I find my way back.

He does not know why the ever-increasing distance from the palace into the woods bothers him. Like he's getting lost. Like he's not where he is supposed to be.

The underworld might be dangerous maybe. Everything is new. There are things I don't understand.

I should not be doing this perhaps.

Hades might be mad that I left.

But then, he does have Minthe to look after him. Nymphs have such subservience to kings and gods and things that are greater than them. Seph doesn't have to worry. Minthe will see that he's returned to the palace safely. Even if Hades might not want him anymore after this confrontation.

Ah. Is that what this is about?

He holds the thought until Minthe naturally slows down. They've come to a riverbank, though this is not the River Lethe. The water is shallow and spread far, and trees grow out of it. This must be the Acheron Marsh. He and Hades crossed an expanse of it before they were hovering over the Fields of Asphodel.

"Minthe! Wait! I have to ask you something!"

Minthe rushes ahead to where a boat is resting on its side amongst tall grass. He starts dragging this a short distance to where the bank becomes river mud.

Seph catches up to help, though he quietly suspects he will be staying.

"Why does Hades have a plant named after you?"

He can see Minthe pause. He did not expect Seph to know this. Though he continues trudging with the boat through mud as the water comes up to his ankles. He does not seem to mind that some of it splashes and gets the bottom of his chiton wet.

"He names his flowers after a lot of random people." He does not look at Seph while he speaks. "The narcissus is named after one of the people he tortures in Tartarus. The asphodel is named after a friend—I've never met her. I think she was just a random soul. So I am not the only random normal person to have a plant named after me. I think he's just bad at choosing names himself, so he borrows whoever's close by."

There is enough water here for the boat to float on its own. Minthe steadies himself and steps in. Seph does the same, though he recognizes that Minthe is not telling the whole truth.

Probably.

"Minthe..." He sits on the second seat as Minthe picks up the oars and moves them off into the water. Seph is not alarmed since a god can swim a long way back.

"Were you and Hades lovers? Is that why you were in my room the morning after our wedding? Are you planning to start a feud between us over this rabbit so that you can come back to his bed?"

The fact that Minthe does not have much of a reaction is telling. Seph's accusations sound almost ludicrous to his own ears, but he knows well how gods and nymphs have a habit of tangling with each other. They are such lovely beings, alluring to all. In fact, Seph can imagine that Hades might have taken several nymphs as lovers here in the underworld. He is their king, so it would be incredibly easy.

"Why would you say that?" Minthe says and tries to look nonchalant, checking over his shoulder as he guides the boat. "What gave you such a dumb idea?"

Seph sets an elbow on his knee and props his chin in his hand. The water is growing darker as it deepens, and the trees grow thicker and taller in the marsh, their branches reaching impossibly far on thick, gnarled boughs.

"I just don't think he would name a plant after *anybody*. He puts so much work into them. I don't know why he named a flower after Narcissus... Perhaps because the flower was so beautiful, it reminded him of the man. But I think to have a flower named after you, you must be very significant in Hades' life."

There is a moment when Minthe's eyes widen and it seems like he might look happy. Like he wants to hide a smile. Or maybe a relieved expression. Like that is what he wanted to hear.

"It must be hard for you to have me in his bed while you have to keep looking after the palace."

He means it sympathetically, though he does not say it in any particular tone or another. Just as a statement of fact. And the following is said casually too:

"Hibus is just a rabbit though. Even if he's already dead... it's not like I'm going to run away or anything. If that's what you're hoping. I'm not going to punch him or get in a fight. Hibus would have died soon anyway. He's an old rabbit. And I accepted that I would never see him again when Hades took him."

Minthe is still avoiding looking at him, and he rows with continuous effort, not slowing down.

"Well, you're wrong. About me and Hades. We're just sort of friends is all. And you might change your mind about hating him when we get to Tartarus. You will wish your rabbit had just died the normal way instead of being sent there."

"Why is that?"

"Some things are better left seen than said," he answers.

A creature moves close by, coming toward them, only the curl of its back to be seen, and the monster is huge!

Seph jumps to his feet fearfully, but Minthe says, unconcerned, "It is only one of Styx's creatures. Do not worry. They are awfully ugly and were dangerous when they were alive, but they've been dead for a long time now, so they are peaceful. It does not even know what we are. There were no nymphs or humans when it was in the world."

"Oh," Seph says with a breath of relief, though he is timid at the thought of sitting. He has come a long way from the palace where he's supposed to be... with a nymph who acts very strangely over a

160

rabbit. He's glad Minthe's plan is not to tip the boat and watch him be terrified in the water with monsters.

And having that thought, he has to admit that what he said to Minthe is probably cruel and baseless. Perhaps he is wrong. Perhaps it's not the rabbit that causes Minthe to feel merciful and feel like helping him with this bunny. Perhaps Tartarus itself is what prompted Minthe to help.

Is the place so awful that it's worse than death? That it's the utmost terrible fate to happen, even to a rabbit, from a nymph's perspective?

"So you're taking me to Tartarus to save Hibus? This does not really have anything to do with Hades and why one of his creations is your namesake?"

Minthe nods and keeps rowing. "When we get to Tartarus, you'll understand."

Twenty-Seven

They row a long time. Seph keeps his eye out for the Fields of Asphodel, but it never appears. Wherever they're going, he has no reference to anchor himself with, and soon through all their gentle turns and meandering, he cannot say in which direction Elysium is for certain. And that is troubling. But Minthe seems to know exactly which way they are going. As they travel, Seph notices a lone narcissus flower growing here and there, at the base of a tree, or on a pocket of land crammed with tall grasses and weeds. The flowers grow in such places that they could only have been placed there, where their appearance will not be diminished by the surrounding plants.

So there is a path, it seems. And one he bets was not cultivated by Hades himself, for why would a man with a flying chariot slink around his swamp in a boat?

Seph suppresses his fears and worries. Whatever Minthe wants to show him, it clearly has to do with Tartarus, and he is very curious about that place.

Hades told him he only wanted to show the places he was most proud of. He hinted that Tartarus might cause horror or sadness. But Seph still wants to see, if only to know the entire truth of the man he's wed to. He knows some of that truth will be unpleasant.

Will this destroy his burgeoning feelings of affection?

They make their way slowly to where the shadows grow deeper, darker, and longer, until they are trapped in a continuous night of shade. The trees don't rustle overhead. Nothing creaks except the rhythmic knocking of the oars, followed by the smooth rush of water over the paddles.

The truth is only the truth. The facts will not change if I chose not to go to Tartarus with Minthe. Besides, Hades never planned to hide it from me permanently. He said we would go on a different day.

So going to Tartarus without Hades' command, without his

knowledge, does not feel like a betrayal. The only thing he doubts is Minthe. Did he form a friendship with a nymph strong enough to overcome their disregard for pets? Last time when Minthe helped him secure the rabbit, it seemed the nymph was just obeying an order and not really displaying compassion for a small creature that is insignificant and defenseless. He continued to say that their measures would not work and that Hades would find the rabbit eventually. He hinted that Hades would destroy the rabbit and be angry...

Which might have happened already without Seph being aware of it.

He sighs after a while and stops mulling over the possibilities. He just hopes Hades won't be mad *now*, to discover Seph going to this terrible place without his permission. But he does say *my king* sometimes, so...

He imagines his mother telling him, *You know it is just a stupid game. You are not his equal. Persephone, you are barely more than a nymph!*

She never said that to him, but the words are true.

He has enough god in him that he doesn't have to worry about a knife across his throat or a very hungry sea serpent deciding to snack on him. Seph will find a way out of it. Somehow.

There is nothing to do but wait for a very long time. To stare off into the shadows and notice how lifeless everything is. There are no birds flitting in the branches. No insects *anywhere*, ever, and that's a bit of a blessing. Seph hasn't had to shoo a fly off his shoulder since he arrived.

It is very cold though, and Minthe pauses rowing to take a cloak out from underneath the seat. It is dark and ragged, and the nymph's delicate face stands out starkly under the hood. His features are so gentle. Tresses of his long blue hair fall out of the hood in a messy, pretty manner.

Seph can feel himself developing a crush for Minthe.

How is it different?

Well, with Hades it is like... He owns me. And I own him. When I see him, it's like... he is the most fascinating person there. I can't stop staring at him.

But it is more. I love to study him. And I feel like I know him well, even though it has only been a few days.

When I am playful with him, I never feel like I am overstepping my bounds or behaving stupidly. Though I am still fearful around him sometimes. It is like... what we have is new. But it is not perilous.

And with Minthe it is different. He is just a pretty face. I cannot know anything about the person inside. I don't feel that way about him.

And Teysus? Seph's once good friend, the *love of his life*, as he told his mother?

Well, Seph already feels like Hades knows him better than Teysus ever did. Teysus knew the *man* Seph was trying to become—the mortal human he pretended to be. Hades treats him as an equal (so far). He treats Seph like a god. A young one, but not in the coddling manner of his mother.

He concludes at the end of these long, ever-spiraling thoughts that what he and Hades have is real. Hades is the first love of his life, besides his mother and Hibus, and he's the most important kind.

Minthe steers them into a place with tall grasses, where the reeds rustle as they part and run under the boat. The marsh must be shallow, though the water is as dark as ever in this light. Some of the cattails grow as tall as he sits. Then there's a short mild scrape. They've run into mud.

"We're here," Minthe says, pulling the oars into the boat. Seaweed clings and slides off them, back into the water. The land ahead slopes upward into a long hill, and the tree at the top grows with a little speck of white at its base. That must have been Minthe's signal.

Minthe prepares by gathering up the bottom of his cloak, but since it is very cold, Seph hops out quickly and performs the chore of pulling the boat to the shore himself. He is stronger, so Minthe's extra weight is no strain. And he will not mind the freezing wet water.

There are no frogs here. No bugs as he noted before, no flying things.

The land is dead.

Seph wonders if it has always been like this, or if it was even *more* dead until Hades came and started planting things. Are these trees his creations as well?

I will ask him when I get back.

Hades might not only be the King of the Underworld. He might be its entire creator.

They get to solid ground, the boat nestled in some untouched, unbent grass, and Minthe hops out, the cloak dramatically billowing with his movements. Traveling in the boat was slow and aimless, but now the nymph's natural grace and speed make him like a dark mouse scurrying off for the high tree.

After a sigh, Seph follows at a small run, noting how there's an absence of rocks under his feet. An absence of stray sticks too. The ground is easier to walk on than his mother's well-groomed fields back home.

They reach the top of the hill, Minthe stopping and putting his hood back, and Seph takes in the scene.

"There is Tartarus," Minthe says, pointing.

Seph scans and squints, finding it difficult to pick up details in this light, and with the many tree trunks blotting most of his vision. What he sees is in fractions, but it's another palace. Sort of. More like a fortress, really, or just a very big, very somber building. There are no pillars, no statues, no normal things you would find on a Greek government building. And there are no walls. There are none needed.

It takes some examination, Seph only able to view strips and peeks through the many broad trees, but Tartarus is an island. The land cuts off suddenly, as do the trees on the side where he is. The water... Well, it is very strange for a moat. It must either be shallow or dry, for Seph can see the rock underneath the soil of the island. The grassy lawn cuts off to a cliff.

"Be very quiet, okay? You are about to see the most upsetting thing. We are on the wrong part of it now. This is the back end. But when we circle around Tartarus' front, you will see why I brought you here."

"Okay."

And I have the feeling it has nothing to do with Hibus.

Or does it?

Am I about to see my bunny dead, hanging upside down, with his throat slit and his entrails emptied from his carcass?

The thought of it makes his stomach clamp down and his intestines shrivel. Perhaps he is not so forgiving of Hades as he thought. If Hibus did end up here...

What will I do? Can I really say I am in love with my husband if he's betrayed me like this?

No. No, of course not, Hibus meant too much to him.

So perhaps Minthe's plan, if Seph has guessed it, has actually been working all along. But at this moment, that doesn't even slightly convince him to turn back. Tartarus will reveal a truth about Hades, even if it is a truth Seph does not like. He has to see it, or his love for

Hades will not be any more significant than his love for Teysus was.

They move away from Tartarus a few paces, going back down the hill the way they came, and Minthe leads him, racing, in a long gradual arc through the forest. The land to their right, towards Tartarus, becomes rocky and jagged, the trees more scarce, but the hill keeps the fortress mostly hidden from view. Only the top, a corner and a plain tower, are visible now and again.

Seph begins to hear... something.

Not much.

The rush of water. And an on-and-off-again hiss, like steam let out of a pot.

Or...

A bird?

The sound becomes more high-pitched and shrieking, like a wild cat's warning.

But distant. Louder at first, when he can hear it best, and falling off into nothing. There is quite a pause between the noise ending and starting up again. They can run past six or so spread-out trees, but then it will start suddenly again.

"What is that?" Seph asks, calling ahead though Minthe told him to be quiet, for he is very curious.

It's a beast, he thinks. He already knows how Hades seems to like utilizing ugly creatures to maintain borders. So that's what it will be.

But he can't imagine what kind of beast it is.

Minthe looks back at him with a grin.

"That is the thing better left unsaid. You will see!"

He sounds gleeful about it and rushes ahead.

Seph pauses, frowning, acknowledging again that he might not want to be here. He might not want to see. And what reason could Minthe have to show him this?

What does this have to do with Hibus?

But alas, all the answers lie ahead, and all the reasons to keep moving are the same. Ahead is the *truth*. Seph cannot turn back now and pretend that he still loves Hades completely and deeply after refusing to learn this secret.

He also has the terrible feeling that his love is about to come to an end on its own anyway.

But Minthe was wrong about Hades' reaction to the bunny. He was not mad or cruel. Perhaps Minthe is a jealous ex-lover, or simply not a nice person, and he doesn't know Hades well at all.

Then why does he have a flower named after him?

Again, all Seph can do is continue forward. He'll confront this disaster and hopefully be able to withstand the terrible secrets of a place that even gods are afraid of. Even Zeus would not come here.

What if it is just a very big dog? he thinks in a joking tone, to give his legs courage. But then, *What if it is a very big dog whose job is to eat souls, the way Cerberus harms the souls who run?*

He pictures a dog as big as his mother when she's angry, terrorizing a village, eating women and children. Yes, that would be very Tartarus-like.

It is something like that.

And so he continues.

Minthe crouches behind a tree, stopping again with heaving breath. He puts a finger to his lips, then speaks.

"We have to be very quiet now. The grindstone is ahead. It's an enormous crank, turned by the most dutiful and strongest slaves ever born to humans. Ones who are peaceful with their position. Hades calls them his gentle giants. They're a lot bigger than regular humans, since their form requires it. And once Hades found out that some souls are sneaking here for a peek against his wishes, his slaves grew really big ears. So they could serve better."

"Weird," Seph murmurs, incredulous, but it is not the strangest thing he's heard. Gods make everything weird, especially the ones related to him.

"We have to sneak close, but don't worry. If you stay by me you won't be seen. Their job is tedious, and they are not very good guards. They only listen well. They won't turn their heads unless they hear something.

"I know you will have questions, so I might as well tell you. The chains run underground. What they are attached to, you will see in a moment. The boats to Tartarus don't have ferrymen. I don't know if you noticed that. Soon you will see why. They are all attached to this crank."

Seph is tired of hearing about all the things he will see and understand in a moment. So he nods quickly, twice, and twice more again when Minthe puts a finger to his lips, reminding him to be quiet. That is no challenge. There is no forest litter, like dead leaves, to make noise. The grass grows as if from freshly tilled earth, and only the occasional tree root must be stepped over. Staying silent is easy.

There are fewer trees here overall, and the downward slope becomes a wide open meadow. At the bottom where it is flat, Seph sees the gentle giants working, even from a great distance. They are big for humans, certainly. Twice as big. But still not as big as some of the Titans' children. Before humans, they made creatures enormous so they could protect themselves against other creations, which were all large and deadly at the time.

Nobody knows where the humans came from exactly. It is believed they are Gaia's children, and that the nymphs are an earlier version of them. The first humans were small and ugly, timid little creatures, his mother told him. Prometheus saw that they were smart though, and he began to speak to early humans and teach them things. He gave them fire and made them stand upright, like the gods, and so began a feud with Zeus that he lost.

Prometheus is still on a mountain somewhere, having his liver eaten out by an eagle every day.

'It was not about the humans, it was about respecting Zeus's rule and conceding to power back then,' his mother said. 'A god of gods was a new thing. Back then all the gods ruled themselves, and thus there was no one to punish your grandfather, Kronos, for what he'd done to us. There were no laws. Zeus was an even greater tyrant back then, for a man who puts on a crown is a fool unless he can see to it that he's obeyed. He could not have done it without Hades' involvement, and Poseidon conquered the many powerful sea gods, bringing them to heel. The three of them made the world what it is today. Peaceful, with less catastrophe among gods and mortals both.'

Then she added, with a heavy sigh and a sneer, rolling her eyes, 'If only Hera was never born and your father's cock was cut off. The world might be a paradise then.'

As he remembers all of this, they get closer and closer to the large slaves working in the meadow below. There are no more trees on their end of the hill to cast long and comforting shadows. Instead, he and Minthe dart from boulder to boulder, which are frequent here. The occasional fall of dust here and there worries Seph, and he begins to take extra care where he places his feet, traveling more carefully.

At their closest point, he ducks beside a rock with Minthe and examines the slaves.

The crank they turn is a massive wheel on its side, the middle wrapped in chains. Six giants keep the wheel turning by spokes sticking out, and the chains disappear and reappear in two places, into holes in the platform they work on, going into the earth.

There is no end to it. Seph feels sorry for the giants. The crank seems heavy. But there is no slave master here, nor a dog to nip at their ankles and keep the giants in line. They are doing this on their own.

And the ears they've grown to serve Hades are massive as well. Like bat ears on a human head, but with lobes. They have small eyes compared to the rest of their face. It seems like their eyes are always closed, covered by enormous bushy brows.

When one giant turns to him, Seph ducks quickly behind their rock, certain he's been seen. The giant crinkles his nose in their direction, which is huge even for his face. Seph wonders if they enhanced their sense of smell for Hades as well?

But why not their eyes?

Perhaps because they like to look down, which this giant soon does. The slaves look at their feet, and the crank keeps turning. The chains rattle and clink, but their noise is quickly lost by the emptiness of the world all around.

That beast in the distance calls a bit louder.

It reminds Seph of hunting and the squeal a boar makes as it's speared. He helped kill a big wolf once, and he was very proud of that hunt. Though the animal snarled and fought until its death, he did not feel bad because human children were disappearing from their yards where the houses thinned out towards the country, and they had already found the remains of one in the woods.

He was celebrated by the humans and his mother both. That was a couple years before he met Hibus, and he thought he would be a great hunter at the time.

They leave the giants behind and continue. He can see the other side of the tower at the fortress now. There are only small windows like slits. The top of it is flat. Unlike Hades' home and all of Elysium, there could not be any less effort put into the building's design.

"We're here," Minthe tells him, looking up the hill. A large rock sticks out over the cliff. They have left the giants far behind. Seph feels like they have traveled far enough to have come from his mother's mansion to her villa in the mountains, and all of it by foot or by boat. He's not exhausted by physical effort, but he can sense that it's late in the day.

"I'm going to have a look first to make sure it's safe, okay? Hades is probably searching already."

Seph nods, and Minthe goes up the rock alone, looking out at the fortress. And then to one side.

The screeching sound bothers him. It's so familiar. Yet too rhythmic and predictable to be from a cat or any animal. He frowns, puzzling it out, and then realizes Minthe said something confusing.

What is Hades searching for? For *him*? And why out here?

For the last time—*what* does Hibus have to do with all this?

He determines to ask Minthe immediately, and he's already approaching the rock when Minthe turns.

"Alright!" the nymph calls. "We're here! Come see for yourself. *This* is Tartarus."

Twenty-Eight

Hades parks his horses and chariot in a cave, where the beasts won't be so tortured by the piercing sunlight. But they are still bothered by all the small sounds in this world, including the constant mild wind which makes the leaves shake and rattle. The horses are not used to it. And a fly around their heads, near their eyes, landing on their ears, is nearly enough to make them panic.

They've forgotten the discomforts of being alive. But with some crooning and petting and apple slices from his travel pouch (they don't need to eat, but the apples will still taste good) the mares finally calm down.

Then the only matter is to find a suitable home for the *bunny*.

Frowning with dislike, Hades opens the top and peeks at the bunny. It is safe and as lazy as ever, only sitting up because its lid was opened. Why so much trouble for a rabbit? Why is this *allowed*?

Of course, it is for a sweet young face that will be sad in the coming days. And Hades wants him to feel better.

As Hibus becomes curious about the outside world, perhaps wondering why his box was opened, perhaps sensing that he is back in a real, physical place, he pokes his head up over the side and Hades gently shuts him in again.

Sure, it would be easy to tilt the box onto the ground and be done with this.

Does he think about it?

Oh yes. Extensively.

As he's removing his crown and setting it on a nearby rock like a common item. As he retrieves the helmet kept in a simple bag, another one of the great perks of being Hades, King of Underworld, and someone all gods are a little jealous of. And astounded by. His helm is unpolished bronze, hammered and shaped into an overly simplistic Greek warrior's battle helm.

He fits it over his head and mist envelopes the lower half of his body, spreading thickly around his feet, which vanish at the ground. He is essentially a ghost. He's turned invisible.

And why has he done this? Why has the Evil God Hades come out of his realm, donned the Helm of Hades, one of his great weapons, and now ventures down a mountainside to the mortal city below?

Why, the mortals would shudder in terror if they knew!

He is here to deliver a pet bunny to a happy household.

Has love made him sick? Is he as foolish as Hera now, only instead of chasing after his cold lover, he's simpering over the sweet boy instead? Working for smiles and strokes down his back like his dog Cerberus?

Yes, he thinks sourly. But only for his foolishness. Seph does not mean to use Hades' affection against him frivolously, and Hades cannot return and lie to the pretty face. He does not particularly care what happens to this rather unexceptional rabbit. But he does care about Seph. Deeply.

He will not harbor lies in this relationship, and he told Seph he would deliver the bunny to a well-off household with happy children. He will do just that.

With the helm's magic, he has legs but no feet, only mist, and he travels swiftly like a wraith, through the grasses and the trees. He rushes down the mountainside like a cold wind, sweeping through trees and gliding over rocks. It is easiest to pass in the shadows. Here, Hades is so airy thin, his form can wrap around and through physical objects. He feels it only as bark scraping against his skin if he is passing a tree.

In direct light, he is still invisible to others but solid enough that he should avoid bumping into them. Fortunately, a wealthy town like this has a covered space, a roof held up by many pillars, a building which they call the *agora*. Its shade will make his search easier.

He enters the busiest place of mortals, especially packed on this late noon day, and slows down, passing them leisurely as if he was really here. Feeling the brush of their clothing and occasionally the smell of their sweat as he goes by.

It is strange to see humans like this. To see so many of them *aged*. To Hades, the wrinkled faces and missing teeth are a sign of innocence and naivety. That is why he comes. To wander a while, gaze on this youth, and wonder if any will come home to him when they are ready.

The time is close for several, including a skeletal girl clinging to her mother, both of them to be sold as slaves. He touches her, though she cannot feel him, and her cheek is blazing hot, flies circling nearby. The occasional one crawls on her shoulder, others taking turns landing in her hair.

Her mother kisses her and bounces the young girl, only a babe in Hades' eyes.

He is sad. He would take her now, if life was balanced that way.

Again, he looks at the box in his hands and wonders how a rabbit's life can be so important. Shouldn't the slaves all go to well-looked-after homes as well?

What about the poor children?

But alas, it is not the nature of life to occur without pain, and the humans are very young still. They will get better. They are the smartest creations to ever happen on Earth. Everything else has just been a slightly smarter version of an animal. A mortal's mind is equal to a god's, and they must have free will in order to grow. They will become wise. The things they make already have surprised the gods. No other creation has been inspired to make art. To sing and make music, or even to govern themselves in some manner.

The nymphs just hunt, love, and sleep. Only one or two of them are born exceptional, whereas with humans, *all* of them are.

Hades moves on. There is no need to mark her. If she is a good fit, he will meet her shortly—probably this winter if she survives the early weeks of fall. And having heard the slave seller's prices, he wanders not far to where they sell raw fish, eggs, and bread. He listens to the prices called and hears the egg seller haggle.

Their stock is normal. Many baskets of eggs, many hanging fish. But a young woman is turned away, unable to buy anything at reasonable prices. The women selling weaves are doing so without a profit. Their time is not accounted for, nor the materials, and feet are shuffling past them, ignoring their offers.

It will be a bad winter then, and Hades is sorry to hear it. But it happens all the time.

He considers traveling to another town, wasting *more* time, but at least he might find one not about to be hungry.

Looking across the open space at the slave girl, he decides this is ridiculous.

And he notices that the egg seller has a young son, here to learn his father's trade. Perhaps he has young daughters as well. And since they are selling food, they likely have enough to share it.

He whispers in the family dog's ear. "Go home." And the mutt quickly takes off with purpose, ignoring the call of the merchant's boy. They are perplexed, but not bothered enough to leave the stall, and Hades follows him to a house at the elevated part of town, much nicer than the hovels below, with a clean well nearby too.

There are many girls here, all slaves or the shopkeeper's children. It's hard to tell on this common day. The slaves look after the masters' young ones like their own for a while, and all the babes wear the same gowns or loin clothes. The toddlers are simply naked on a hot day like this, and all the children not old enough to help are looked after in the courtyard.

Here Hibus is released, under a rose bush. Soon the rabbit is swarmed by screeching children, and he takes off to escape. The fleeing bunny surprises a young slave mother carrying pots, who does not want a creature dashing for her feet, under her dress. But she rescues the poor rabbit as he's trapped in a storage room with only one exit. As she smiles widely, she reminds Hades of Verah and he thinks that her eyes are kind.

Hibus will go to the slave mother then. She carries him like a pet cat and pets down his back. Her oldest girl is a curious teen who looks motherly and wants to hold the rabbit.

So Hades leaves. He's done well enough. But knowing as much of the world as he does, he does not feel like he's done a good thing.

The other slave girl at the agora will not be sold tonight. In this market, masters will not be looking for more mouths to feed, but they might be looking for fresh workers to replenish the stock in the spring. It is a bad winter coming, and Hibus may not survive it. And he will not be the only one.

Seph will need to come to understand all of this. He is young still, so his affection for Hibus can be forgiven. But Hades cannot continue to give him the impression that the world is *kind*.

Twenty-Nine

"Hurry up!" Minthe yells at him, pulling on Seph's hand, taking him up the rock's ledge to where it juts out over the open space. "The next one is coming! You have to see it go over the edge!"

Seph is reluctant to approach what he now sees is a very steep drop-off. Tartarus is just as ugly in full view as it was through glimpses. It's plain, stone-colored, and square, one tower sticking up at the corner closest to him. The architect apparently did not care for symmetry or form, only function.

And Seph was wrong about it being contained by a shallow moat. The river runs here and just… drops. A little further along this round unending pit, there is a massive waterfall like he's never seen before. But no lake below, no river, no end that he can see.

Instead, beneath the island that holds Tartarus, there is an enormous turning machine of wind sails fashioned like paddles. The rock Tartarus is on looks like an apple core, the building on top. The 'trunk' holding the island up is a series of turning pillar blocks, twisting at different speeds, sails as big as houses driving the wind.

It shoots up in a blast, so much so that Minthe's hair is only contained by his hood. Seph's rushes all around his head, and his chiton is almost impossible to hold on to. He twists it tightly to one side and does not particularly care if he flashes Minthe or something private hangs out.

He is simply awed. The sheer amount of water dropping into this pit is picked up by the sails and water rushes in a spiral downward, crashing against the rock walls, like he's standing over a turbulent ocean. He understands now why the river sounded so loud, though it was so far away. Everything beneath him is splashing and frothing.

It is dangerous. Seph takes two steps backward, afraid that he might be falling. Minthe grips him too tightly to go any further without a struggle. He sees…

An arm! Someone reaches out of the water for him, calling for help but his cries are choked by liquid.

"Minthe!" he calls and tugs urgently, stepping close to the edge again, meaning to urge his friend to help. But first to make sure that his eyes didn't trick him, because the face is lost to water and it's just rushing foam again.

"There they are," says Minthe. He's smiling, and his face is beautiful, but he looks... off. "I wanted you to see. So you can understand this place."

He steps behind Seph and pushes him forward. Not too close to the edge, but this keeps Seph from falling back to the safe land behind him. Minthe's grip is the only thing that keeps him standing as an enormous barge approaches the drop, tiny figures already clinging to the furthest end, and the boat approaches faster as it gets closer.

There is nothing to stop it.

There is nothing to slow down time so that Seph's eyes can appropriately process what he sees, and then he can figure out how to help.

Instead, he only watches, the events happening too fast, and his legs not doing more than trembling.

The boat goes over the edge. Several figures have already jumped, trying to beat the swift current and get to the shore. The faint calling sound has started—the screaming. It must be loud to be heard so clearly over the rushing water. He and Minthe have to shout to speak to each other.

But their cries are heard, sharply at first. The ones who jumped ship are the first to go over. And then the boat is in free fall, and the screams are very loud.

They end.

Little figures fall, flailing.

Seph breathes so fast it is like he's run a race.

The boat doesn't fall far. It hangs from its bottom end, the water smashing down onto it. Those who managed to cling to the edge now fight the pummeling of the water from above and the waves crashing from the sides as well, driven by the sails. The boat drifts in the current like a leaf on a branch, attached on one end.

Then it is drawn upward. Seph can barely see the enormous metal hook on the bottom of the boat, a contraption made of heavy steel, which should not be on any ordinary boat. Somehow as it is dragged up, the chain shortens. Seph notices two other crank wheels on one side of the waterfall, turning in opposite directions, manned by other giants.

The boat goes under the water, moving up river, empty of its passengers. The river is so deep, the boat is swallowed, invisible if you were standing on the shore.

"I-I don't understand." He's leaning entirely on Minthe now, clinging to him like he's his mother.

Minthe pets his hair, but does not speak comfortingly.

"This is Tartarus. It's like... a granary. For souls. People get ground up and made into more people. This is the great secret Hades doesn't want getting out. It makes his souls want to escape and warn the others—"

"There's another one coming!" Seph shouts, pushing away to stand, but he is lucky Minthe is here. The nymph catches him and grabs him close before his misplaced weight topples him over the edge.

Seph looks into the water again, searching for faces.

He can see... parts. Just barely, just swiftly, before they are swept deep and under. A sandal drifts atop the waves for a time.

"We have to go get them! We have to go—"

It's too far. He can see that already, and somehow he has to sneak past two sets of those giants. This ship will be lost. And several more if they are arriving so fast.

"There is no time!" he yells at Minthe, who does not want to move.

The nymph has a funny half smile on his face.

Seph sniffs. He already senses what the matter is. And he looks again in the direction of the oncoming boat.

It is packed tightly with no room to sit, the souls crowded in shoulder to shoulder. And no belongings, cargo, or crates reduce the number of passengers. Each barge carries *hundreds* of passengers— enough for a whole village! And this one approaches the waterfall at swift speed.

Several men begin to jump and swim for the shore, realizing the river ends. The others just wait. The river moves too fast and is too wide for the quick thinkers anyway.

And down it goes.

They scream very loud, but with the sound of crashing waves everywhere, they cannot be loud enough to disturb the next arriving boat. It does not sound like screaming. Just... a whistle over the wind. A faint screech, like a cat. And Seph realizes why it felt so familiar. Many animals reach that high screaming note as they die.

"I can't be here. I'm going to be sick."

Hades is a butcher.

Seph can see that plainly.

Tartarus is worse than he ever imagined.

"Are we going to go save them?" he asks, bent over his knees, heaving.

They ought to get moving. He hates that Minthe even paused long enough to show him one, let alone two! They need to save as many people as possible!

Has Hades gone mad?

"Save who? What? And why?" asks Minthe. He gives Seph a pat, but he does not sound troubled. "They are already dead, dear king. They needed saving in the upperworld. Not this one."

"Why is this happening to them? I thought Tartarus was—" A *place to serve out punishment.* Well, this is certainly more efficient, though it doesn't account for any one person's crimes. His lips say something else, his mind reeling from one memory to another of *anything* Hades ever said about this place.

"He said they were reborn. The unwanted souls. He said they came to Tartarus to be sent back into the world as babes."

Minthe's chuckle is like a pleased child. "That's what this is!" He gestures to the open pit, his cloak billowing. He's chewing his tongue and smiling, badly hiding how much this pleases him. He's happy Seph is upset.

"To make baby humans, you grind up a bunch of *other* humans! They all get mixed in here. And killed. This is permanent death, the same thing that happens in the upperworld! Only here there is not so much essence wasted. A lot of it, when a soul rots, just disappears into the ether.

"Hades found a way to drill into the very heart of Gaia—who gave up her form to create the Earth. It's Gaia's essence that has been bleeding and building and giving life to all of you. She was too selfless for her own good. And now her essence returns to her—all these human souls—so that she can keep bleeding and birthing. Everything becomes something. Everyone becomes *someone.* It makes you wish to appreciate the time you had on Earth, doesn't it?"

Minthe carelessly walks close to the chasm, his arms spread as he speaks, like he is revealing a great magnificence, and he does not watch the next ferryboat arrive. He is looking at Seph instead.

"This is the great truth that humans do not understand. Part of it. Life feeds life. It is how it will always be. Your life is precious, given, not to be wasted, and not to be spent suffering either. We all return to Gaia and become her creatures again. Whatever you are, whatever you become, is not up to you. But humans come up with such fanciful notions. Things about *having a purpose* or serving a divine being."

"Minthe, come away from there," Seph says, his voice hoarse. Minthe has only two more steps before possibly falling into the rushing water. It feels especially dangerous because the wind is so strong.

The screaming is at its loudest as Minthe grins at him, his hood falling down, his hair flying everywhere. The whistling shriek fades quickly, the boat hanging in the waves.

"Hades understands, you know. He's more nymph than god. He's... brilliant. *Powerful*, yet not silly like your stupid father, Zeus. Hades and I belong together. That is what I brought you to see."

"I figured that out," Seph says dryly, approaching only to make sure the nymph doesn't do something stupid. Like jump. He might have been brought here to witness the nymph's suicide, though he does not believe nymphs ever attempt such things.

They are a strange people. Death is no tragedy to them, even when it is as terrible as this. Nymphs do mourn their own kind, but only for a day or so, and not to the level that humans do.

"Come away from the edge, Minthe."

He has so many problems. His chest is so heavy he feels like he can't breathe.

He suspects a great many things have died for him today. His love for Hades. His love for the world and *himself*. He can't be happy again knowing that *this* is going on. He will fight and beg and cry when Hades is available—of course he will—and already he knows it won't change anything.

This is where souls go to be reborn. Hades did not lie, exactly. Seph is too small and powerless to change anything.

But he suspects he's about to lose Minthe to the pit. The nymph is mad! Or Seph simply can't understand his nature. Nymphs often seem heartless and weird. But now his heel is such a small distance to the ledge that it is clear he intends to go over.

"Nymph, your king demands that you come here. You will not kill yourself today. I'm not allowing it."

His visage of strength and authority vanishes as yet *another* barge approaches the waterfall. This has a greater exodus of hopeful survivors than normal, and they all, screaming, rush toward the pit.

His knees threaten to buckle, and he finds himself doubled over, his balance barely holding, his stomach threatening to undo him.

If I go down, I won't get back up. That'll be it for me.

He might need to catch Minthe very soon.

Psychotic bastard.

"Your bunny is down here," Minthe says, one foot sliding back until the heel is cocked over the edge. There is no other place to go. He's intending to walk backward and fall. "Come see. Come reach over and rescue him."

"What? That doesn't make any sense."

Now Seph definitely doesn't want to approach. *Should I just let him die?*

"Minthe, get the fuck over here. I'm leaving. I'll let you jump if I have to."

I'm not getting any closer.

But Minthe only grins at him.

And then he is gone.

Seph's eyes widen a moment, the space before him *empty*, and he carries himself forward, crawling as he gets to the edge, wondering, *Why?!*

And what would make the nymph go in such a manner?!

On his knees, sobbing, that faraway barge now being lifted and the chain shortened so it will be kept underwater, Seph clings to the rock and looks over the edge, looking for Minthe.

He sees the cloak. It takes off like a lost kite, swirling past and around the turning sails, changing shape and twisting over itself. A messy drop of saliva falls from his mouth and tears also from his cheeks, as he gazes down, knowing it's too late. Minthe brought him here and left him.

Did he just want someone to know what happens before he died himself? Did he not like that Hades was keeping it a secret?

He looks for that pale form anywhere and only sees water. A face comes around from the ferryboat, but the person is too submerged to see clearly, and way too far to reach.

Then he notices fingers clutched to the rock right below him. Minthe made it! He's here!

Seph is reaching down to help, when an arm shoots up over the edge of the rock like an underwater serpent to snap at him, and Seph is unprepared to fight. Minthe takes a hard grip of his hair and yanks down. Seph's arms reaching to assist put him at a disadvantage, too much of his weight pitched forward already. His balance topples. And the next ferryboat approaches the drop as Seph opens his mouth and screams with them.

Thirty

Hades urges the horses faster. His task has taken too long already, and he's ashamed of himself for it. This has gone against his very nature and is insulting to the souls more deserving. Somehow, he's going to have to make Seph realize that he can't request things like this. That he is not a *good* god, he is a *fair* one. He is who the underworld needs him to be.

And while he won't mention the rabbit specifically as being a problem, since that would drive a wedge between them, he has to devise a way to share his real self with his husband. To make him see the beauty and horror of the nature in which all things exist. The balance.

Tartarus. The great truth.

Then maybe he will understand.

But Hades would like to do so in such a way that he doesn't lose the young god's affection because of it.

That makes him selfish, he supposes. Does this mean he will do another foolish thing by avoiding his responsibility to tell Seph properly?

He will have to analyze it later and make sure he is not doing a disservice to his kingdom or anyone in delaying telling him. But what harm could there be?

Hades can think of nothing.

Still, he urges the horses onward, at their fastest, having the notion that he must tell him soon. Seeing the little slave girl in the market was a stern lecture from a disapproving parent. There is more cruelty in the world than the mistreatment of some undeserving bunny.

He passes over the Fields of Asphodel, looking down at the ferry destined for Elysium. The poor frightened children cling to the boat and shout, frightened by the chariot and the appearance of Hades. He has never tried to appear kind to *them*, so this *love* he feels toward Seph is causing him to lie.

It is a foolish, dangerous emotion that must be watched and culled with honesty.

He notes that the boat is only a third full at the moment, but in eight weeks there will be nearly daily deliveries from the ferry. And many, many, *many* more deliveries to the Falls of Tartarus. The great mill grinder. The spring of life (and death).

Soon he will put extra boats in the assembly line. One extra for the river bound for Elysium. Daily deliveries of *two* ferries of young souls would make his kingdom very happy. They have empty homes and parks for his children waiting already, prepared for a famine or a plague to fill them up. Every home near his palace might have a 'child' to look after, and the dining halls will be full and loud. That will be nice.

And the ferries destined for Tartarus will need to be doubled. They will have to pack the souls on until there is barely room to stand. But they will make it work. He will run a continuous line of boats if he has to, if there is some great war, and the ones who jump early will never make it to the shore. The current is too strong and the river too wide. But he doesn't like to terrify them so much so early.

The giants especially don't like to hear the constant tears and screams.

But they can double the amount with minimal panic, he thinks. The extra boats will have to be attached to the track before the influx of souls is to arrive.

They can ship the barges half full until then, though this will increase the amount of fear and early swimmers. Humans are actually easier to control in a crowd than they are as small groups.

He lands the horses outside the paddock and guides them in through the opening gates, their hooves kicking up dust.

"Welcome back, sir!" Alfric calls. The little soul is delivering lunch to Taushev, his friend, because if there are no chores to do for Hades, Alfric will start serving the people around him. Even if those people technically don't need to eat or dress. Alfric was shunned in life for the disfigurement of his face, and is too happy to be useful to the ones who love and accept him now.

He is a good sight to see so frequently in his palace, so Hades smiles.

"Where is young Persephone, sir?" asks Alfric as Hades approaches the stable, letting Taushev take control of the horses.

"Up in our room, I imagine," Hades answers, removing his gloves. "Why do you ask?"

"Well, he is not in the room, sir, and I wanted to show him the new clothes we got him. He asked that we lengthen his chitons, but we kept a style you'll find quite nice."

Hades lets a smirk creep onto his face, forgetting his recent dilemma of perhaps loving Seph too much. Perhaps such things can wait until tomorrow, or another month. Their marriage is still young. Seph will be forgiving to hear how his rabbit ended up. And Hades would suddenly *very* much like to see him in a new chiton. And then to kneel and put his head underneath it.

He still has not finished the young god in his mouth, and he's looking forward to it.

"I will find him and dress him, Alfric," he says, tucking the gloves into a pocket.

So perhaps this new *niceness* is not going to leave him quickly after all.

What is happening to me?

Perhaps it is like a virus, and I just have to let it play out.

Will I ever grow bored of my husband like all the other gods do in their marriages?

No. He can't see himself being disloyal to Seph. He was never disloyal to Minthe or any of the lovers who came before, even if they were not serious. He just doesn't usually like so many people, so finding someone to have an affair with would be a huge chore to take up his time. And then how would he get so much done in his studies?

Life is better simple. Boring to others, perhaps, and maybe he bored himself when he was alone for so many years. But Seph is all he needs.

If only I can stop acting so foolish!

Seph is still not in the room, he discovers, nor is he in the private bathhouse, nor is he in the courtyard or in the private den. These would be the common areas to find him. Hades expected to find him weeping on the bed, or close by.

But there's also the public garden.

He is not there.

And there is also the public library, which the scholarly souls add to all the time, writing down magnificent tales from all the cultures of the Earth, some already told and most of them new creations that will never materialize in the upperworld.

He is not there. Nor is anyone but a group of wine-sipping creatives, for even the most ghastly hunt won't keep the true artists and craftsmen from their work.

"Have you seen my husband?" he asks.

They are all small children, barely old enough to hold an ink-dipped brush in the upperworld, yet they are pouring over several pages of refined, complicated work, coauthoring a great masterpiece.

"Never seen him here, my king," answers Bion in his newly young voice. Another plague sufferer from his time. There are so many of those.

"Hm. Send him to the rooms, if you see him. Tell him I've requested him. If any of the servants pass through, make sure my orders are heard."

"Yes, my king," Bion answers, and starts a chorus among the others.

Hades leaves them.

Perhaps... the kitchen?

One of a hundred sitting rooms?

What else is there?

While there are many interesting places in the palace for his children to wander into when they visit, this place was not built with the young handsome god in mind. There are no spectacles to attract him.

Where might a young man wander, if he is sad and looking for comfort?

The city parks, perhaps. Or just out. Maybe he wanted to converse, and there are not many here.

He's relieved to find Verah. She and several others she's rounded up are watering plants throughout his enormous home.

"Verah, have you seen Seph?"

"Seph? Oh, the new one? No. He is missing," she says, and Hades eyebrows shoot up.

"*Missing?* And no one is looking for him? No one told me about this?"

"No, no, no!" she puts her watering pitcher down and waves her hands, her eyes wide. "Mis—misunderstanding, my king. I am saying—he is with you, no? Or with others? He is not here."

"Oh." For a moment, Hades thought wildly of Minthe and concocted a purpose to find and destroy the nymph at once. That was a quick assumption on his part. But... Seph is still missing. And

Minthe is an unbalanced little thing, like a wine cup wobbling on a table next to a fire.

"Verah, take these girls and have everyone searching for Seph—and for Minthe—at once."

Now she looks confused. "The mean one? I not seen him many years."

"Yes. He was here today, and I want to make sure he's gone." *I saw him run into the woods. It was the right direction. Perhaps I'm paranoid?*

The watchful souls of his palace already know Minthe is not allowed. It would be difficult for his ex-lover to return. But... there are so few in the halls now. And Hades already saw him in his palace.

Could he...?

But what could he do to Seph? Even a weak god is more than a nymph can handle.

He could lead him away.

"King?" Verah calls as Hades leaves. "Anything else to do?"

"No!" he says back over his shoulder, not stopping his strides. "Find my husband for me! Make sure *no one* is in this palace who shouldn't be!"

He returns to the stable. A short way into the journey, he decides he is not above running, which he will almost always avoid since it makes his subjects fearful and prone to gossip. But there are not too many of them to worry about anyway, and Verah will soon inform the entire palace that they are looking for Seph and Minthe. This news will spread around the city too, and his lovely people will not stop searching until the god is found. They do not need to sleep or perform maintenance rituals like living humans do.

They will do a thorough job, making a game out of the young god's disappearance. But Hades has something better.

He ignores the welcomes of Alfric and the stable hands, going straight to Cerberus' stall and unlatching the door.

"It's me again, boy. Yes, you're free." His dog is very excited to meet him, and Hades bends over for a proper, but rushed, greeting. "Yes, you're a good boy! Of course you are! My favorite hound. But now we have work again to do."

He takes his short lead, a thick chain with a leather-covered handle, off a hook in the stall and attaches it to his dog's collar. While well-trained, Cerberus can get excited, and Hades doesn't have time for him to greet every servant they pass as they go back into the palace.

When the lead is clipped, Cerberus loses his excited demeanor, two of his three heads closing their mouths with their tongues inside. The other one, the left one, has always been a little slower on the uptake.

They proceed back to the palace at a fast jog, the dog keeping pace. They do not stop to greet the girls who have abandoned the water pitchers and are now searching room by room, opening every closet and looking underneath tablecloths.

Cerberus takes the steps up to the private wing confidently, his tail wagging. And in the solarium, the left head tries to make an extended sniff at the flowers growing by the fountain. The place where Hibus spent a lot of his time. While the right head sniffs suspiciously at the door and the middle, his always serious guardian, only looks at it with impatience and duty.

They go in. The left and right heads seem to want to pull in opposite directions, but the middle guides them directly into the bedroom. Where even he is finally distracted by the new smells, and he noses underneath the bed, growling.

"Not now, boy. Verah will mop the scent away for you later. I need you to find this."

Cerberus paws and pulls on the chain briefly, wanting to crawl under the bed. But he is obedient as soon as he notices the pillow Hades drops in front of him. All three heads sniff eagerly, taking in the scent, the left one slurping the fabric twice.

Hades gathers the face of the middle one in his two hands.

"*Find him.*"

He speaks slowly and clearly. *Find* is not as often a command as *hunt* is. Usually the citizens of the underworld are well looked after and accounted for! Only since Seph has arrived and Hades has apparently become *nice* has so much chaos happened in the space of a few days.

Hopefully he is just at a park or something.

And hopefully Cerberus doesn't immediately switch into hunting mode once he discovers that Seph is a new someone who does not belong. Hades has trained the dog to sniff out and attack Zeus's trespassers.

But he will try to keep command of him to prevent that.

And then, when all of this is settled and Hades accepts that he's probably overreacted, he is going to find Minthe and put an end to him anyway. Probably. An exile to the upperworld will do.

That is what a god of the underworld should have done in the first place, since kindness leads to faulty judgment and foolish mistakes.

Thirty-One

Seph clings to the rock, far below where Minthe was perched, only able to avoid falling into the never-ending pit thanks to the wind that pushes everything, including himself and the water, up against the walls. He is bruised. Bones might be broken. But thanks to his strength, he manages to secure a hold in the grooves of the wall.

He clings there, helpless, wave after wave of water pelting him mercilessly, slamming against his back. It is like being beaten by a slave master's whip and paddle—relentlessly until his death.

"Minthe!" he calls up, his voice surely too weak to be heard over the sound of rushing water. Still, he calls desperately, "Help me!" And then, sobbing because he knows Minthe lured him into the pit in the first place, "*Please!*"

He hugs the wall, withstanding tremendous pain, a pebble falling loose from the trembling grasp of his fingers. He claws for a new hold, water slamming against his arms and against the back of his head, some of it coming at an angle as though the slave master is trying to pry him off.

He looks up, but he can only see water, the sky sometimes, and that distant, so far away ledge sticking out where Minthe is.

And then a speck of bright blue hair, wispy like a flame.

Echoing in the giant pit, coming to his ears like a whisper over the sound of crashing water, Seph hears a high-pitched, childlike giggle.

"You are quite stupid, you know!" says that distant voice. He must be shouting into the pit as loud as he can. Even Seph's own terrible sobs and gasps are physical sensations to him, unable to be heard unless he shouts.

"You are not a thing that belongs! You are nothing like him! Saving a bunny… What were you thinking?! Break its neck and spit it over the fire if you must! Rabbits are not useful or loyal like dogs."

This is all over Hibus?!

No, it can't be.

Another massive wave rushes after him, spinning through the pit, beating against the rocks like a charging bull.

Seph shouts with all his strength, before the giant wave overtakes him.

"Why?!"

It hits him, and he ducks his head, praying that the water won't sweep him off the wall. If he loses his grip now, he will be lost. He has to do something, he has to crawl out, but every attempt to move up only makes his grip more precarious, and there's nothing but slick, smooth granite above him.

He can barely hear Minthe answer until the giant wave moves on.

"Because I love him, stupid! And you're not meant for him. You're not even meant for this world! You're doing bad things to him, you know? I thought when he discovered the bunny, he would put you out of the rooms for good, realizing his mistake. But then he didn't! Oh well."

Above him, two pale feet dangle off the ledge and kick in the air. Minthe has sat down.

Bastard.

He's crazy.

I can't stay like this forever.

"You wouldn't have loved him anyway," the deranged nymph shouts at him. Somewhere a barge is being dangled over the waterfall again, and souls are screaming, dropping in.

I'm going to become one of them.

He can feel this horrible... scraping. This prying, this abrasive scouring. It's inside him, and Seph feels himself weakening. Soon he will lose his grip. And not because he lost his strength—he has plenty of that, due to his lineage. But because more and more he and his body seem to become two separate things. The connections he uses to control his muscles and his grip...

Well, they feel far away. Thin.

He feels like he's spiritually stretching.

I have to make this count. Do this one last thing, Seph, or you're going to be torn away.

He has this image of himself swept away from the rocks at last, swirling in the current, and then watching his own body, lifeless like a doll, drop away from the wall and be carried into the pit after him. A separate thing.

It is how he feels. It's what's going to happen.

So I have to make sure he hears me.

Summoning energy into those thin, breaking connections—imagining himself tied to his body like ropes to a ship in the harbor, and then those lines breaking away one by one, snapping loose—Seph shouts, "I am your king! Obey me, nymph! Make me a rope!"

A gasping woman gets her head above water. She is far from Seph, but close enough that he can see the wild terror in her eyes. And then he sees her fading. Quickly, like a light is snuffed out. At first it is only the color in her irises, gone in a second. All souls have expressive eyes in pale colors, usually brown or blue and no green.

Hers start out with a blue tint and then quickly fade to ash. Her pupils too, the black dulling, but slower, until she truly looks like a ghost. An aged corpse. Her voice fades as well, her mouth remaining open. But then, the eyes fade even further. Physically. They disappear into holes, her sockets empty, and her head flops forward lifelessly onto her chest. Like a puppet that's been set down.

She's gone. Though she didn't drown. She was above water, so she could have kept fighting the waves for a while. Her connections, the ropes to her ship, have been cut. And Seph eyes the frothy waves again with terror and new understanding.

Somewhere among the white waves are all the souls that have been 'reborn'. They've had their ego stripped away. The essence, Hades called it. It's swirling all around him, and when he dares to look further down into the darkening pit, he cannot see the water's shape anymore, but he can continuously see the swirl of white, glimmering, dizzying lines, which must be glowing as they spiral down and down into the pit.

Seph is a god. He can hold on longer than most. But Tartarus is a place where even gods die. Easily.

"Nymph! I command you to help me!" Surely that will work. His voice is deeper and rougher than he has ever heard it before.

He wants to add, *I am your king!* to ensure obedience, but his strength is spent. He manages to croak, "I am—" and then another massive charging wave, enough to cover his head and deprive him of breath, sweeps past.

His two fingers on his left hand don't work anymore. He's losing his grip.

Focus. Maintain. Those connections... don't lose them!

He keeps his head down, too weak to even look up, as Minthe begins to talk again. His words drift in and out, unimportant, as Seph just tries to hold on to his body. More and more it feels like a separate thing. Like a shell.

"You are not even a god with any powers! Do you know how insulting that is?" By the tone of Minthe's voice, Seph has failed to compel him, and the nymph speaks lazily, "Here you are, pretty and stupid—just some dumb lump of a thing calling yourself a god. Really, you're retarded, you know? And you're married to *my* Hades! Mine! Why—you aren't even as good as a human as far as I'm concerned!"

He hears a strange sound. A *plunk-plunk* that disappears into the waves. Seph looks up briefly and sees falling pebbles. He can barely make out Minthe above and beyond him, blurry from the water running over his eyes, and the figure is throwing rocks down.

"Hades deserves the best if he's going to end up with anyone except me! I love him too much to let him do otherwise. And a nymph is the most perfect match, in my opinion. If he's not going to choose me, he should choose another one. Only a nymph can understand Tartarus and love Hades more because of it!

"Admit it! You were horrified by what I showed you! You didn't understand at all. And you would have blamed him. You would have tried to make him change it!"

Rocks skitter down the walls above him but get swept up in the current. Seph went around twice before he was able to grab on and hold himself here, almost directly underneath where he was pulled over.

If he had dropped any further he would also be drowning right now.

"You're stupid! *Stupid!* And you know what?!" His tone becomes shrieking, wild, loud to its very limit and tearing like an animal's snarl. *"You aren't that pretty either!"*

I know, I know, Minthe.

Seph opens his mouth to speak. He doubts his ability to be loud enough for the nymph to hear, but they do have better senses than humans. And he has to do something. It's time to bargain.

I will leave Hades. Right now, right away. He'll never find me! I won't stop moving! I won't go back to Mother! I'm done with all of them. I will run so far on the Earth that I'll find the end of it and circle back around and keep running again.

Hades will have to chase me forever.

But what he tries to say is, *You can have him. You can have him!*

Only to find that the connections to his voice are severed. He can open his mouth but he can't move his tongue. He can only make this groaning yell, and it is weak-sounding.

He has lost the two smallest fingers on both of his hands, and he suspects the middle one on his left hand might be gone as well. His toes are merely flesh smashed into the wall by the strength in his legs.

But even the connections to his legs are fading and snapping free. His arms will be gone soon. Seph feels like a clinging torso. A doll without limbs. And his body is just a shape. A mold. On the inside, Seph is... something else.

There is nothing to do but wait and see what will happen to him. See what it will be like for a god to be reborn. But he will not be Seph anymore. Not even close. He won't even be reborn as one whole, complete person.

He does not feel himself leaving as though walking through a door. He is like water himself, being swept away by this incredible wind. He can feel droplets of his own essence running freely out of this mold, swirling away into the current with the rest of the souls.

He won't get them back. And he can't stop the leak.

I am dying.

The only thing to do is be sad. He is not even afraid anymore. He clings with all his strength still, but his will to fight is gone. There's nothing left, and his weak godly soul will join with Gaia, for whatever it's worth.

His mother never told him it worked like this—that Gaia has been bleeding out, giving life to all these things. But she did tell him that Gaia is the entire Earth and everything living in it, and that was confusing. All the other gods have forms like people, even the very old ones.

I should have asked more questions, he thinks and chuckles in his thoughts.

He has to force himself to breathe now. His body won't do it automatically. He feels like he's working a water pump at an empty well, and when the flow sputters out his body will be dead. It's amazing that he hasn't been swept off the wall already. He can't feel his arms or his legs anymore, so how he still clings here, he doesn't know.

At least Minthe isn't talking anymore.

Where is he?

But Seph doesn't have the strength to look up.

And then something covers him. It's dark. He can't see anything. And a male voice speaks in his ear.

"Let go, Seph. I've got you. Let go, love. Trust me, I've got you."

Thirty-Two

The world around them is chaos and Seph can only process a small part of it, details slipping to him through a filter like grains poured into a narrow funnel.

He is held by Hades, who doesn't feel like a man to him. He certainly doesn't feel like his husband, and Seph has forgotten how a person is also a physical form, like a doll. He does not register that he and Hades are the same sort of thing. That they are both contained in meat form, and Hades uses his to lift them up out of the water, floating, flying without the assistance of his horses, up to that overlooking ledge above.

The world is very large to him. Seph is dropped onto the rock, sputtering, and he can't feel the ache of his struggling breath nor the penetrating cold deep throughout his body. Indeed, it seems that his body is bigger than he is, and he is just a weak, trembling kitten cast upon the rock.

Hades' dark cloak flies over his form. Seph can see it covering him, but he can't feel the soft texture. Only the hard rock under his knees. Everything else is numb. Hades' voice seems to float all around him. Seph is not connected to his ears, and so the sound doesn't seem to have a source.

"You are not lost. Not yet, my love. Come back to me, okay?"

Hades kisses his forehead. Seph finds this rather odd. Why would he do that with a mouth and a face that are not his? The form is a mask—a doll, a glove. The real Hades is inside and underneath, making this puppet do things, like pet his hair and hold his face.

"Do not try to go anywhere. That is an order, Seph! Do you hear me?!"

Hades shouts at the form of his face, holding the head part tightly in his hands, and Seph sees himself in the reflection of the dark god's eyes.

It reconnects something. Something small, but something

important. He can see Hades as a person again and not a fleshly doll of odd shapes.

He can also see that the light is gone from his own eyes. They are a colorless, nothing gray, but the pupils are still black.

Green. They're supposed to be green. My eyes are the only fleck of green down here.

There are a few of Hades' stones. But nothing living except for Seph.

His memories feel tenuous, like they have been stripped away. Like he has awoken from a dream and now the vivid fake life is fading fast as Seph starts the real one.

This body does not belong to me. Does it?

Do I always feel this cold?

"Come back to me, love. Stay close to me. Here—" Hades kisses him. His lips are like fire. "Do you feel that? Do you feel me, love?"

He is speaking so quickly, it doesn't sound like Hades at all. Seph does not remember him sounding so urgent about anything, nor does he remember so much emotion showing on the dark god's face. His eyes are wide. He keeps blinking and searching, his nose and breath so close to Seph's face.

He can't feel him. But then... He starts to search for the sensations. Hades has sweet breath. Minthe breath, that herb he named after his...

After his lover!

Memories are coming back to him. Real, substantial memories. The moments right before this are the only ones that seem to belong to a person named Seph. The others are still part of the dream that came before but never happened.

He becomes aware of the muscles in his face—how he is staring lifelessly with his jaw hanging open like that woman he saw die in the waters.

He is so pale too, by the reflection in Hades' eyes. He doesn't look like the man he remembers.

He tries to close his mouth. And it works.

Hades breaks into a scared smile. He laughs—no, he *sobs*. Seph is not processing his facial features correctly. The smile is actually a grimace and the god is weeping.

"That's it, love. You're coming back to me. Can you feel it? Do you know I'm here now?"

And then, over his shoulder, he harshly shouts, "Shut up or I will hang you over the pit!"

Seph tries to figure out why. He reaches outward, but he's very careful because Hades told him not to move. He repeated it a few times, so it must be important. And now Seph can feel those newly regained connections weakening when he tries to spread out and discover his world. Several of them snap.

It's rather frustrating. He must stay here in this one contained little box, when he could be *everywhere*. He could be and know and experience *everything*. For a little while, at least. Seph senses that the last connection will be himself—his ego—and when it is gone, his awareness will vanish as well.

So he stays inside this box even though this box doesn't know anything. And he feels like he's putting his eye to cracks in the walls as he looks for the places that will tell him something.

He finds... a connection.

He was not truly hearing Hades before. They were speaking a different way. Now the first real sounds come in, and they come with a lot.

"Forgive me!" someone shrieks, and there is a loud rumbling over that.

There's a scrape, claw, and clip—a creature's hooves are striking the stone, followed by a fluttery sigh. And then there is the water! Seph forgot about that. It is still rushing all around, and he startles, trying to get away, his body lunging forward, but Hades holds on to him. The grip from his fingers hurts.

"You are safe, love." His voice seems to come from two sources. One all around and one from his breath. "I'm here with you, you see? I'm going to protect you. Don't worry about Minthe—he's already gone, love. You'll never see him again."

Hades kisses him several times, sometimes on his skin and sometimes in his hair. Seph looks for more connections. He wants to feel the kisses. And as these ropes are untangled and reattached to internal places he can't describe, he gets some sensations that won't go away. Things that he doesn't want, like the pain in his knees. He can feel his body start breathing on its own again—a different energy, something from Hades, was doing it for him.

"Oh, that's it, my love. Yes, come alive again. You're right here with me. Can you feel me? We didn't—" He gasps, wiping his face. "We didn't lose too much."

Seph has never seen anyone cry like this.

Not anyone real anyway.

He thinks. The faded memories are too difficult to find and

replay. The connections are easier, though they're coming all out of order, and he really wants to use his voice.

"K-k-kiss—k-kiss me again."

That is the last time I stutter in front of my husband!

What was that?

That voice didn't come from Hades, and it didn't come from this body either.

"Yes, Seph. Yes, of course I will, my king."

He is then kissed several times, some of the kisses covering his mouth and making it more difficult for his body to breathe. *But who is Seph?* he wonders. And it takes a moment to realize that name belongs to him.

It is a funny utterance of breath and voice moving over his tongue.

"S-S-Seph."

Persephone, your name has important meaning and announces to everyone who and what you are! Seph is—is what?! Is nothing, that's what! You are my son.

What a strange woman.

Yes, it was a woman, wasn't it? One of those people from his dream. Is this a memory? Or does this actually exist? Where is he hearing it from?

More voices flood in. The ropes are pulling the ship back into the harbor. A large piece that was drifting away—what he is—is now anchored and slowly being dragged back into place. The funnel through which he perceives things is widening, and the rate at which he makes new connections increases.

Seph feels like he is falling. And he clings to Hades because he is scared. But there is no end to this drop. He just keeps going and going, and soon he becomes aware that he is a wet, shivering, bedraggled thing. A being that does not freely move unless it can balance on its legs. Something that does not see or hear or experience unless it comes through one of the limited connections.

He sees less of the world now. But what his eyes can filter, he perceives better, and he is not in danger of spreading out too much and becoming one with everything.

"Hhh—help..." His mouth moves, his tongue flexing, trying to remember how to physically say the words. "I am... I am dying."

"No, you're not, love." Hades buries his face against Seph's chest. His breaths are ragged and heavy. When he looks up, his lashes gleam with tears. "You're right here with me. We're alive. Both of us.

Seph—can you remember who you are?"

He is a creature called Seph, but he knows that syllable should mean something more.

"Almost. It's coming back, I think. But I'm confused." He points at two dark shapes. His unused fingers curl slowly and his limb trembles. "What are those?"

There is a horse and a dog. But at the moment, he can't remember which is which.

"That is Nyctaeus, one of my horses. That is Cerberus, my faithful dog."

So *dog* is the shorter one. Seph expects a memory to come bubbling out of the abyss, but nothing does. The horse though—Seph has seen another one of these. It was brown and had stubby legs compared to this one.

"What is the dog doing?"

The horse is just standing there, its ears twitching and its sides heaving in and out with breath. The dog has another object though, and a bright red liquid spreads against the dim ground. Seph doesn't care for it. The quieter colors are better. This one feels loud and alarming.

"He is about to kill your assailant." Then Hades shouts, and Seph winces. "Cerberus! Down! Guard the quarry! Don't bite! Good boy."

The dog stops shaking and tearing the figure, but the other creature continues leaking red onto the ground and wailing. It drags one of its legs.

Oh! It is a person too. Splayed on the ground. And it is crying like Hades, looking back at them with wet eyes, strands of hair falling over its face.

"You love him more than me."

The thing coughs and scoots, bringing his legs underneath him.

Seph tries to do the same, looking at his own limbs. They are not as shapely and pale as the young man's across from him. They are more like... Like something he cannot think of... Like...

Like a man's legs.

Mother, I am a grown man! I do not need you fussing over me all the time!

Do not call me 'baby boy' out in public—ever—again!

Faintly, he remembers the woman's voice.

Well, how am I supposed to remember that?

Breath escapes his chest. It is puffy. Light. His body is responding to him, not just through purposeful mechanical

movements, but to his emotions as well. To his internal being.
It is happening. I am coming back.
But who am 'I'?
I am Seph.
Seph, I am Seph!

Thirty-Three

Few things have given Hades the jolt of fear and panic that he experiences now. Not even meeting Zeus for the first time, shivering, gasping, flesh melting still from the acid—and looking upon his brother's face, the one he didn't know existed.

He grasped Zeus to him, forgetting about his state, embracing the gleaming god before him. His savior.

Zeus, despite showing disgust and then a grimace of pain, did not reject him. Nor did he embrace him. But for Hades, who hadn't seen sunlight nor breathed air for so long?

It was love at first sight with Zeus and him. As it was for Hera and the rest of his siblings.

That was how it started. For a brief century, the lost siblings were reunited in love, going up against their father, all of them, together, with most of Rhea's creations as well.

And then the first chip. Hades stood up to the clever thunder god successfully on Hera's behalf. He hadn't liked that Zeus had such little respect for her affection and had an affair so soon.

Zeus was suspicious, but their love wasn't broken yet. Not until Hades had the opportunity to kill Kronos, having lured him away from the battle, but used it to speak with his father instead and seek forgiveness for being his son.

He told Kronos that love and the right to live were all that was important to any of them—they wouldn't destroy him like the prophet said! Only for Zeus to step in and steal his father's scythe, disemboweling him with it. His little brother knew to stay out of the fighting and watch Hades closely.

Hades hadn't realized what he'd done at first. He wept for Father. When he gathered his strength to stand, he asked Zeus, *Why?* and did not get a response. He insisted some things. That he was their father, he didn't deserve it. When he was ignored, he charged at Zeus's back, shouting in tearful rage, but Zeus turned and stopped him with his words. They spoke in many fragments, snarling at each other. But over decades of mulling, Hades pieced together everything he said in a wise, eloquent speech. So he wouldn't forget it.

You love him over us? The man that would eat your own siblings? Why?

I have loved you more than he ever did. Yet you accuse me of this murder? And you accuse me of being the evil one?

Hades, you sick, twisted fool. You are the one who should have defeated Kronos. You injured him and brought him here, after all. I watched. It was not very hard. You bested him like you were wrestling with Poseidon.

You are the most powerful god in creation, and you did nothing to stop this man, not only from torturing yourself, but from the torture and near deaths of our innocent sisters and brothers alongside you.

You have been responsible for our misery all along!

This is why I will take the throne and rule all the gods. I will stop men like him from hurting others. And I will act when other gods usually just look away. I will not let the weak be trampled on the way you have done!

You let the cruel tyrant rule.

Zeus did not understand how much Hades loved their father. He would have suffered much more for him. The other siblings heard, arriving some time during their quarrel, and a tearful reunion was reduced to mistrust and betrayal. They took their youngest brother's side.

How could Hades do that to them? When he had the power this whole time to burst out of his father's stomach and save them all?

It would have killed Father, he told them, crying. And they never loved him the same.

His self-reflection did not happen that day. Hades was in too much agony, grieving over the ruined corpse of the father he loved. But in time, the words finally gnawed through his blind adoration and let him see the truth. His family was put through enormous pain by his continued inaction.

Initially, Zeus was cruel as he convinced the gods that he was the new Kronos, only with an interest in controlling their lives and settling their disputes for them.

And though Hades apologized and even begged at their feet, no one but his mother could forgive him for truly being the most powerful god alive and doing nothing about Kronos.

Hades decided to get up and take on Zeus for a short period. That seemed to be the way to mend his errors and become his rightful self. He aspired to be the new Father and somehow make up for what he'd done. But then Zeus, with his words again, convinced Hades to take the underworld.

The everlasting underworld, the place in which gods existed before the Earth made a new physical realm, will be all that is left of Gaia's sacrifice once she is truly gone. And Hades decided this was more than a fair trade.

Eventually, Hades will be the god of all there is and ever was. His treasures will be the last physical things left in the realm. And the gods will have many spirit children to look after. The underworld will not be quiet and depressing when his siblings retire to the final realm.

But all of that will mean nothing—*nothing*—if Hades doesn't get Seph to recognize him again.

Don't let too much of him be gone. Please.

He had an opportunity here. He squandered it. Of all the scenarios to ever befall Seph, including an uncharacteristic plan of sabotage by the homely Demeter, losing Seph so young, so soon, is not something that should ever have happened. It's not something he has an excuse for.

And yes, thinking of going to Demeter and telling her that her only son has died is a terrifying prospect. Not only for her power, for Hades can handle her, but for the grief of losing someone they both held close. Then the shame of facing her, knowing that Hades has harmed her truly, cruelly, outside and in.

Again.

I can't face that.

I never want to.

"You have to come back to me, darling," he says, crying. "I can't exist without you. You're everything to me. You're all that I have."

"He's not!" shouts a petulant, shrieking voice. "He's nothing! Just some puny god you took a liking to."

"Don't go anywhere. Okay?" Hades cups Seph's cheek. He's past the danger. It's safe to leave him. But Hades doesn't think he can let him out of his sight for a long time. "I'm going to take care of something. Then I'm going to be right back."

Thirty-Four

Hades regrets his choice already. Minthe is such a wicked, insignificant little thing. Punishing him matters, of course. It has to be done. As cruelly and thoroughly as Hades punishes his own children. But Seph is far more important, and seeing to him is the critical issue right now. Not getting revenge.

Hades makes sure his cloak is tucked securely around Seph. He whispers blessings of protection. From cold, from abduction, from attacks. Since the cloak has been around Hades long enough for his essence to have left its residue, he can tack this magic atop the fabric like a quick patch. Temporary, but it'll do for an hour. Though, he does not expect to be gone long.

Minthe is a very rare kind of devil. One who is self-destructive and not afraid of him. But one who is harmless and weak.

He walks toward Minthe and toward his dog, holding out his hand and summoning his scepter to him. It is a magical shape-shifting weapon. And after a moment, Hades chooses its form. A long deadly sharp blade, almost as thin as glass.

The punishment is execution.

And should Minthe be spared the long torture he puts some of his other subjects through?

Shouldn't Hades at least drag Minthe home in chains first, experiencing the pain of his injuries like Hades inflicts on his own runaway children?

It wouldn't be fair to execute him quickly, would it?

He contemplates his feelings and his decision as he approaches the cretin, aiming his sword to stab.

Minthe, though scooting backward, narrows his eyes and lifts his chin up defiantly.

"Any god would have flown up the cliffs by himself. You know that. And the essence would not be pulled away so easily if he was not weak. Hades, he's barely more than a mortal. Do you know that?

He isn't better than me."

Hades is quiet. Seething. But not uncontrolled.

He doesn't know what to do with Minthe yet. He can't decide.

"He's always been better than you. Even when he was a babe."

"Yeah?" Minthe sniffs. "Get it over with then. Put me in one of your dungeons. Assign me a punishment. I'm not afraid of you, King Hades, and my fate is your bidding."

Hades tilts his head, considering. His dog growls faithfully but stands still for now. He understands that Hades wishes to handle this himself.

But how?

It is not clear.

Hades thinks aloud, "There is no purpose in punishing you, Minthe. The things wrong with you are not your fault. You were born with a crack. A deformity. You are not much different than the children who come in with shriveled limbs and blindness. Except that your deformity cannot be seen. It is why your own kind avoid you. It is why you're all alone."

"I wasn't alone when I had you!" Minthe shouts. "I wasn't alone... and then you didn't want me. And I didn't do anything wrong! You just banished me to nowhere! And I tried to fix it. I promised to get better. But you wouldn't let me prove it to you!"

"Oh, Minthe..."

Hades pinches the bridge of his nose. He's still reeling in the fear and fury of seeing Seph cling to the rocks, the water nearly sweeping the essence out of him.

Seph's head bent back, his mouth opening. That is when the spirit escapes. And Hades flew to him, levitating as Minthe pointed out. Most gods with any power can do it. But Seph has... well... a different kind of deformity. One with physical consequences.

Hades could sense the spirit pulling away. It tried to float at first. Gradually it spread and wisps of it disappeared into the ether like steam into air. That is why the Falls of Tartarus and the grinding sails are so important. The force of them takes the souls quickly, all the way down into the well from which the Earth draws her power. Gaia's beating heart.

Hades put his cloak around the young god to capture his spirit and save the essence from disappearing any more into the winds. Then he carried Seph's body carefully to the ledge.

His *body*. His spirit hovered above and around him, tethered by a few thin threads.

There was no guarantee he wouldn't lose Seph right there. Souls are free of anything Hades might do to contain them. Looking back at Seph now, Hades wonders how he can still feel compassion for the nymph. This same love is what doomed him every time he faced his father.

"You tried to take him from me. And that wasn't your right."

Minthe gasps. Murder is not much of a sin to a nymph like it is to a human, but they have a high sense of honor and goodness by their own definition.

Mouth open, searching for words, Minthe finally gets out, "I am your mate! I have your best interests at heart. Even when it hurts me. Even if you kill me! Hades—look at him! Look at the color of his skin! The spots on his face! From the *sun!* He doesn't belong here. He doesn't even look good standing next to you."

Hades resumes walking forward. Minthe will talk all day, most likely. Due to his deficiency—that parasite, that swirling sickness in his head—Minthe can't self-reflect or understand when he is wrong. The blame is always with others. Which by itself is mere ignorance, but Minthe's sickness is how he tries to pull innocents into his web.

First he is a friend. Then he sows seeds of doubt. Then, by the end, when he has you isolated and dependent on him, trusting only him, your truths warped by a wicked tongue of lies... Then he feeds. It is a dance to see how much he can toy with you.

Minthe scoots back faster, his lower lip trembling.

He shouts again, his voice taking on a desperate tone.

"He wasn't good for you! I'll prove it! You weren't ever going to show him Tartarus, were you?!"

Now Hades looks down at him over the blade's point, standing over him. His own eyes in the steel are solemn sadness. His hair has several out-of-place strands. His expression is pinched like he's in pain. He can see his mother's features in himself. He hurt her too with his forgiving love, letting her children be taken and eaten.

Death is the only way. You should have done it the first time, when you realized there was no cure for him.

Well...

Minthe's chances were slim. It was not likely. But he could technically, *maybe* have gotten better...

Hades was optimistic. Stupidly so.

Minthe talks in this pause, building up another false world. One where he is always right and he is always at the center.

"You didn't show him what you are because you knew he'd never accept you. He's not your true mate. You're lying to him, showing him pieces of yourself—only the good parts you think he'd accept. He won't go on a hunt with you! He won't help! He'll just sit around your palace and wait to be fucked. That's all he does, you know! Some mate! He wouldn't be like me!"

"Minthe... I..." Hades touches his forehead. This shouldn't be so difficult. Hades should have learned his lesson already. But Minthe's actions are not his own fault. He is not even truly self-aware. He is not here, in this world.

He is his own victim of the manipulative fantasies first and foremost. He wants to harm others. He wants to spread. But he has harmed himself most of all.

"I have not killed a lover before. I don't know if I can do this," Hades admits.

And doesn't that make him unworthy of the throne? Isn't he still the same flawed, irresponsible son of his father who has done unsurpassed harm to his family?

And aren't I more deserving of death than Minthe ever will be?

If he was the unbiased judge of these two souls, Minthe's and his own? Yes, probably.

"But you harmed my mate," he says aloud, while his thoughts twist themselves. "This cannot be forgiven."

I would not forgive myself if I let the traitor live after what he did to Seph. If he had succeeded, this wouldn't even be an issue.

So there is only one way. And no reason to stall any further.

"Go on, do it then." Minthe spits. "You're so *just*. So smart. So loyal, my king, to your stupid new lover with a thick cock. You're as dumb as your brother, you know that?! Both of you just look for the nearest ass. I would have been more than that, and you know it! I was... I was good too! And you didn't want me. You still don't, you stupid... stupid trash!"

His youth makes this painful as well. Hades' children are playful, but old and wise in spirit. A nymph never quite fully matures. If they did, they'd be interested in starting families and securing material things for their prosperity. A nymph's view is shortsighted and always rooted in the present. Free, wise to a very basic level of existence, but they are not humans.

The minds of humans are like the gods'.

"I will execute you, Minthe. There can be no other response to your attempt to kill my mate. But first... you must experience pain."

The blade shimmers and becomes a whip. Minthe stammers, but

Hades is through letting him speak.

"Your punishment has no fulfilling purpose. You cannot learn from your mistakes and suffering. But it's wrong to let you go from this world without experiencing the agony you would have inflicted on others."

What is the purpose?! his thoughts speak. *His essence will go into the pit, and either way, there is no awareness left behind to reflect on his crime. Or even to experience the long-lasting suffering his actions would have inflicted.*

But that is the gentle part of his soul. Minthe will suffer here and now. Hades will make the pain very great. And then he will go in the pit, and Hades will be done with him.

There are other matters to see to.

"Hades, stop! Wait! I love you! I'm sorry—"

The whip comes down with a crack and Minthe shrieks in pain. There is no pause to think, not anymore. All of this was a reaction to extreme emotion. Usually Hades would not think twice once he determined the correct way to rule. He's grown from the foolish, adoring boy he was.

The whip strikes. It strikes and it strikes. His lips pull back in a snarl, and he goes after Minthe like an angry slaver, paying no mind to his ex-lover's suffering.

Minthe sobs and gasps and tries to run away. He crawls, bleeding, and the whip opens a gash across his back.

"Stop! Please!"

He sounds like a woman with the harshness of his cry, and somewhere, Hades acknowledges that the slave girl he left in the upperworld may well come to the same fate. He is not a good god, not by any measure.

"You were foolish to harm what is mine."

He stops. Only because there is not much point in dragging out this agony. There was only a level of pain to be achieved, and he's reached the most he could inflict with a whip. Now it is time to drag him into Tartarus. He won't need a weapon for this. The most justified method of execution will be to toss him into the pit, the same as Minthe did to Seph.

From his knees, Minthe looks at him with huge eyes. Then gets his feet under him, running lowly a few steps and collapsing.

Hades does not rush.

"I am the perfect one for you." Minthe tries to back up, meeting his gaze. Hades' punishment did not break his spirit, and this hurts

Hades' heart. Before he detected Minthe's sickness, he admired many of his qualities.

He used to worry about the day Minthe would grow old and the grief it would cause.

Now he will be gone even sooner than that, and in a terrible way.

I won't regret anything. Inaction is the cruelest sin of all.

And yes, Hades has rejected many souls from Elysium for the things they *didn't* do. Kindness is a virtue. Timidness is not.

"I love you still!" Minthe shouts, kicking to scoot backward. Cerberus growls and steps forward, but does not charge.

Minthe throws a rock and it misses Hades, hitting the dog instead.

"I am the one who will help you build this place! I will take on the responsibilities! I am the one you want!"

Hades bends down to grab Minthe's foot. But suddenly the nymph is up and running! Hades stares after him, realizing the state of his injuries was a bluff. And a stupid one. If running was all it took, Hades would have lost every soul down here already.

Cerberus gives chase. With the prey running, he can't help himself. But it doesn't matter. He won't be first.

He calls on the scepter. It turns into a spear as Hades lifts it overhead, cocking his arm back and launching it through the air. It is not physical prowess alone that sends it at the target. Hades narrows his eyes at his prey, and it sails high and true to aim.

It hits with the whistle of wind, a strike, and a thud. Minthe goes down some ways away, and his dog skids aside, yelping, surprised.

Hades strides forward calmly. He tells himself that he does not feel anything at the moment except certainty that he must act. Minthe must be punished. And these moments of agony for the nymph? They are nothing compared to what could be experienced.

Why, if Hades chose to grow and swallow the nymph whole like his father did to him, he might get close to the soul-twisting agony Minthe would have inflicted on Demeter. Only for a few seconds though. Minthe would not survive the acid.

His ex-lover struggles to move, coughing blood. His body heaves with nausea and pain, making the spear move inside him and cause wrenching pain. He moans. He tries to make a scream.

He looks at Hades with blood coming down his chin and unintelligible words spitting from his lips.

"S-sorry—"

Hades' shadow falls over him. Somewhere, the gentle part of his soul screams. And he grabs Minthe by the hair.

His cry of agony is cut off to groans and choking. Slippery, blood-covered hands come to claw and fight his hold. Cerberus growls, lowering to lunge, and barks unhelpfully as Hades handles the nymph himself. He drags him toward the edge, choosing a spot a wide distance from Seph. He won't carry the traitor so close.

The spear awkwardly scrapes against the ground, drawing a jagged line in the dust. His horse shuffles a few steps, getting out of the way.

"Mercy! Please, my king! I know you won't listen—but I—I was your beloved!"

Hades only looks at the spot he picked. He must get this done so that he can see to—

Seph appears in front of him. Hades stops immediately, shocked.

His love is standing straight, though he should be too weak to move. His brow is low and he looks angry.

"Don't."

"What? Seph... He's—"

"*You* should go in the pit! Not him. Y-you do this to so many. He only did it to one. Y-*you* are the evil one. You are the monster!"

Thirty-Five

"Seph," Hades says gently, though his grip is tight on Minthe's hair as the nymph tries to pull away. "This has to be done. He is a murderer in my kingdom. He is a traitor against me." With his free hand, checking first for blood, he cups Seph's cheek. And when Seph grabs his wrist, it seems the young god is trying to pull him away, but he doesn't have the strength for that. Hades doesn't even know how he's standing. His knees tremble like a weak colt's.

"You kill more than him. Every day."

In the distance, there is a great wooden creak and crash as yet another ferryboat slips its cargo over the edge. The humans' screams from this distance might remind him of the cheers at Greek athletic games—if he did not know the true cause.

How to make Seph understand?

"They are not being murdered. It is a sacrifice, done with reverence and care, the way that mortals will cut the throat of livestock over an altar. A shepherd will choose the best animal in his flock. He will raise it, feed it, and when the time comes—"

"They are not—" His strength fails and Seph collapses forward. Hades lets go of Minthe to catch him, his other hand unfortunately covered in blood, and Hades winces for that fact.

He knows the violence Seph sees here today will have long-term effects. Hades hasn't had time to explain, and the death of another is always hard to watch when you're young. Even humans may cry for the first animal they see go to its fate.

But now is not the time for explanations and comforting, so he gives a sigh, watching Minthe struggle to get away.

He will not go far with that spear sticking out of his back. It was a good aim, the point traveling upward from the last rib and coming out in the front under his sternum. If anyone simply removes the spear, Minthe will be dead.

But he ought to go over the edge first. Alive. His essence

shouldn't be wasted anyway.

Hades evaluates the cost of having Seph fall to the ground to finish his task. It would only take a minute. It would be done. And then his attention would be entirely for Seph, and his only focus would be to secure his lover's health and forgiveness. In that order.

"They are not *animals!*" Seph finishes, glaring at him even though he is pale and weak. His eyes are not bright as they once were, and Hades' blood-smeared hand comes close to brushing his brow.

How much did I lose?

The essence can repair itself, slowly, but what if it's always less than what he was?

Hades will love him no matter what illnesses Seph might have. Will he be like Minthe now? Damaged internally?

Consumed by his inner thoughts, he's barely listening as Seph says, "They are mothers! And fathers and daughters and sons! They are all the people you're supposed to take care of! Everyone should go to Elysium! Unless they are wicked or cruel. And you are just dumping them over a cliff as if they mean *nothing!* For what? Because they have a little ambition! Because they like to compete! Or because they didn't choose you and your little city—they chose to be reborn! And look what you're doing to them!"

He grabs Hades' shirt, trying to shake him. He can't stand on his own, and his fists are trembling with weakness and fury. "You're lying to them! They chose to be reborn. Not *this!*"

Briefly, Hades checks on Minthe. His ex-lover leaves a long blood trail as he drags his body away, Cerberus following with a continuous growl. The heads of the dog take turns looking back. Sometimes the middle one snaps, not letting the left or right engage. His pet isn't sure what he should do.

Hades embraces Seph and speaks softly.

"I do not lie to them. They are reborn. But to be reborn, first you must be stripped. Think about it. The humans do not come into the world as some other person, right? They must pass on, Seph. They must be flayed of everything but their true essence. Tartarus is the quickest and most merciful way to do that."

Seph glares at him through tears, shaking with hate.

"You deserve to go in the pit. Not Minthe. Not them."

Ah. Seph's tugging on his clothes is not just an emotional reaction to his anger. He truly wants to drag Hades into the pit.

Hades rubs his back. His stallion is sweet and noble and Hades has nothing but admiration for him.

"I can explain my actions, and you can decide how to judge me. I will work very hard to win your favor back, my king. I never meant to hide this place from you forever. You would have seen it, but in the proper light."

He guides Seph to the ground. There's nothing the young god can do about it, his strength spent, but he twists his fists in the fabric of Hades' shirt and seems determined that the god won't get away.

Hades smooths back his hair. It is sopping wet, and Hades thinks it is not as lustrous as it once was. In Tartarus, the body decays quickly if there is one. It will die and wither, even before the soul has left in the case of a god. Seph is inhabiting a corpse that has only just found life again.

"You cannot understand. And I accept that. All I want is to take you home, Seph. There we will figure out your healing. But first, the creature must be dealt with. What kind of husband would I be to let a threat like that keep existing?"

Minthe has only been spared so far because Hades knows all too well how a single event can grow and fester into everlasting hate and feuding resentment.

He must soften the blow with Seph first.

"He is not just dangerous to us, you know. What if he harmed one of my little souls? What if he brought one of my children down here to teach me a lesson? Anyone who throws another into Tartarus, regardless if it was you or someone else important to me, would meet the same punishment I've dealt out. Do you see how that's fair?"

Unless that person was self-aware enough to experience guilt, repentance, and reformation. If someone can be healed from their crimes and Hades wants them in Elysium, like Narcissus, then they would be put inside the prison. The painful portion of their punishment might last many, many years. But he shall leave out that detail.

"You are a wicked king. If your souls knew, your children would never trust you again. They would never stay! I could tell them all, and we could bend you. Hades—you have to stop this. You can't do this to everyone."

There will be no explaining then. It'll be best to just get it done and soothe Seph in the aftermath.

"They already know, my love. Why do you think so many make

the sacrifice to run? Do you think it is selfish desire to see their babies again? When they're supposed to be dead? What a frightening experience.

"The parents leave to try to tell their good children a message—don't choose rebirth. Go to Elysium. They offer their life for the eternal life of their children. That is what motivates them."

Hades stands to leave, and Seph clings around his leg like a begging child. It would be simple to separate him, but Hades only watches a moment, stunned to see him fight while being so weak.

I could not even fight after something like this. Not for the murderer who caused my fall.

The fate of the reborn souls must be more harrowing to him than Hades can understand, and he wonders what he should do.

Should I take Seph home first and find Minthe after?

That is another risk. Letting Minthe out of his sight a *third* time would be highly irresponsible.

Inexcusable.

"He left you for dead, my love. Let me finish with Minthe. It shall not be long. And then we can discuss the fate of the souls in our palace. You can turn Elysium against me, if that is your wish. I promise, Seph, whatever you want to do is logical and fine. But surely you won't miss this rotten little murderer if I toss him over the edge?"

"Why? You abandoned him. You were lovers. And you left him for me. Why?"

Again, Hades checks on Minthe. Now is not the time for this. Minthe seems to be losing consciousness, and now is the time to throw him over.

"Later, my love." He reaches down to pry Seph's hands off and step away. *Your mother will thank me, even if you don't forgive me.* "We will talk at length. I will do everything in my power to make amends to you. But now—I must be a king."

He leaves. He notices but does not react to stepping in fluid to catch his victim. He gathers Minthe's arms by the elbows and carries him backward. Minthe kicks feebly and groans, crying. But he is much too weak to put up a fight now.

"I will not forgive you!" Seph shouts from the ground, barely in a better state than Minthe. "*You are nothing but a monster!* You hear me?! You have no soul! No kindness, no love, just like my mother said! You are like Zeus. All of you! *All the gods are just cruel, wicked beings!*"

Hades pauses. His accusations are not much. Hades has been called many things. It hurts the most when it comes from the children he has cherished. But it does not affect him beyond that, certainly not in a way to change his mind.

But in Seph he sees himself. Desperate. Pleading with a father who is insane.

The wrong should be punished.

A king should take action.

Inaction is worse than anything.

But is the loss of Seph's love worth it?

I brought Seph here to challenge me. Not necessarily to be his friend and romantic lover. But... in order to have an equal king, I must give him equal power. He can't stand up to me on his own.

My father ate his own children because he could not abide another being with equal power.

He puts Minthe down, while his instincts tell him he is wrong.

"All right, Seph. I'm listening. You are my king. How shall I punish your murderer?"

Seph can't hate Hades if he chooses the punishment himself.

"Just let him go! Heal him and let him go! I don't want anyone to go into the pit."

"That is unacceptable." Damn it, Minthe's eyes roll back and close. He should have felt the terror of flying over the edge. This inaction has cost him, but he must find a balance with Seph and decide a punishment as a couple. "He has done something terribly wrong, and as a king, it is my duty to punish the terribly wrong. Releasing him creates danger for others. We have a kingdom to protect. And Seph—I have let Minthe go before. Twice. This is the second time he's come back, and look what he's done."

Seph cries. He curls up on the ground where he is, and Hades wonders if this is too much.

That's it. I'm leaving with him. Cerberus will watch the murderer. Maybe he'll kill Minthe for me while I'm gone. It wouldn't matter.

"Never mind, Seph, we are going home."

"Banish him," Seph says, looking up from Hades' feet. "Just send him away. Not into Tartarus. He won't cause any trouble up there, right? So just send him to the upperworld. Don't kill him. Please."

Hades wants to growl the same as his dog.

Cerberus sniffs the ground, approaching, and Hades orders him to sit with a snap and point of his fingers. The dog slinks with submission and does as commanded.

Hades feels like the same is being done to him. And for what?! Juvenile feelings of kindness and mercy. The same youthful goodness that somehow convinced Hades to deliver a rabbit to the upperworld.

Not just to deliver it, but to make sure it ended up with a *happy family*.

What has this boy done to me?!

"Hm." He purses his lips before he speaks.

"Then you will come home with me. You will let me see to you and heal you and give me a chance to explain myself and everything about Tartarus. I know you are feeling scared and betrayed, but your unwillingness to listen is aggravating. Seph. I will listen to you. And you will listen to me. That is a fair deal. What do you think?"

Seph frowns miserably. Another wail picks up as a ferryboat goes over the edge. It will be silent very soon, but not for long. The souls on the incoming boats are nervous and suspicious, but not panicked initially. They don't start to scream until the end of the river is in sight, and Hades has planted the bank densely to make sure the forest is dark. Many will jump to swim ashore, but they will not make it. The current is strong, and the boats are only held at their steady pace by the chain and track they're attached to underneath.

"Tartarus is necessary," Seph mumbles, not looking at him. "I will... I will try to understand."

Thirty-Six

I can't believe I'm doing this.

Of all the people who have deserved mercy from him, Minthe is not one of them. Yes, Hades does feel some measure of guilt and sympathy for the being who did not choose to be born like this. But ultimately, that is Hades' own personal problem. Those feelings barely made him hesitate.

He would have done it and grieved about it later. Briefly. He would not have blamed himself (not for the execution anyway) because in the end Minthe's actions are his own. And Hades is the ruler of this place. He has to act in the appropriate fashion.

He will feel more guilty for the damage done to Seph. And in the following days, he will analyze his actions upon discovering Minthe and wonder if he should have done something different. Should he not have banished him the first time, but executed him instead?

What about the second time, when Minthe was sneaking around his palace?

That makes what he is about to do especially ironic. Bitter-tasting to his sense of justice. But he made Seph a promise, and it was for a good reason. As with the relocation of the silly bunny, Hades does not want Seph to hate him. Not in this place, where they'll be eternally bound to one another.

I've become... attached.

No. Looking at the boy now, just checking on him because it's hard to walk away—seeing him so weak and desperate—it's a lot more than attachment.

When Hades pulled the young man out of the pit, he felt like his heart had been ripped out of him. And now he feels like it was shoved back in the hole left in his chest and is struggling to beat.

With his magic, he dissolves the spear in Minthe's body and heals him at the same time. Some. Enough to keep him alive and keep him from hobbling. Many of the lashes from the whip will stay.

Hades stands over Minthe with his scepter, the weapon's true form. He holds a hand over him with his fingers spread out.

"Wake."

Minthe gasps at once, turning over, grabbing his abdomen where the spear poked through.

"I-I'm still here," he mumbles. "I thought I died."

"You most certainly will die," Hades says, frowning. He can feel his features being as impassive as stone. While he did not relish killing Minthe because of how they know each other, Hades has not changed his mind or altered his decisions in a long, long time.

"But it will not be by my hand, Minthe. You will die somewhere else. Not in this world."

"You are letting me go?"

If Minthe were a regular man, he'd be running already. But Minthe only looks confused.

"What is wrong with you?" he says, one arm raised up as if to protect from another lash.

It is tempting, in a way. Hades feels compelled to enact some form of justice, and Minthe's physical pain certainly would have been prolonged had he known he would be letting the nymph go instead of throwing him into Tartarus.

This is the worst thing I've done since coming here.

And by *worst*, he means unfair. Above all, Hades prides himself on being a fair ruler. A good king, though not in a nice sense. He strove to become the eternal ruler that the God of the Underworld should be, fairness above all else, including personal ties and grief.

But now that shall be put on hold for the sensitivity of a colt.

"Did you mean to kill yourself by my hand? That is the only thing that makes sense," he wonders aloud. "You cannot have expected me to spare you out of love."

Hades' eyes widen.

That's exactly what I'm doing! Sparing him out of love! Only it is for the love of a different person.

I hope I haven't destroyed what we could've had forever.

It might be too late.

"I didn't expect you to spare me," Minthe says. "You wouldn't be the man I love if you did. But I also needed to save you from yourself. From him. When I saw what he was like—saving rabbits!—I knew you had somehow become a fool."

He rubs his chest where the spear had been. He gives Hades a look that is both weary and mistrustful.

"Hades, what have you done?"

"I am not the man you love. I'm going to be the man *he* loves. Maybe. I hope."

And that is as much emotional sharing as he wants to do with Minthe. It is time to send him away. He has to see to Seph.

Minthe shakes his head. "Hades, you lovestruck fool. You've doomed the underworld if that is the case. Take me instead of him! I can be better!" He crawls toward Hades.

Again, Hades is reminded that Minthe is sick. He does not look right, his hair disheveled, his eyes enormous. He throws himself at Hades' feet, and the king sets a foot back.

"I am not a god, and I won't pretend to be! But I am better than that sun-kissed fool. I know your darkest places, my king. A nymph understands what you did for this place! Normal minds cannot comprehend—they're too naïve—"

"And it is my job to make sure he understands." Hades separates Minthe with the bottom end of his scepter. He is firm and does not go out of his way to cause more pain. Though the image of him beating Minthe one last time does cross his mind.

Punishment must be dealt.

It is what his instinct says.

His hands and spirit, however, seem to be shackled to whatever Seph wants.

"You have the sun-kissed fool to thank for being alive, Minthe. I know you don't appreciate that. But understand that your begging has no effect. If it weren't for him, you would already be in the pit. Vanished. Gone."

Minthe looks a bit like a snarling animal as he eyes Seph, who huddles miserably on the ground, still trembling. Hades can see what he thinks—*now is my last chance*—and if Minthe were to lunge right now he would discover that invisible shackles have come around his feet and hands.

They will dissolve soon, once Hades speaks his terms.

"My dog is coming after you, Minthe. I will leave you here, and you're free to do as you please. But once I've reached the palace with Cerberus, I will send him after you on a hunt. And I will not be following to call him off. You would be wise to travel to the gate as fast as you can. I do not keep nymphs imprisoned here, so the dogs will let you pass freely."

Cerberus is not his only guard dog. Just his personal one.

Minthe tries to move, and his ankle stays in place. He tugs at the invisible shackles, but does not look confused. Only disappointed at first. And then hateful.

"What is it about him that you like so much? His golden skin? His pretty lips and tongue? Or is it his youth? A virgin is only untrained for so long."

This is Minthe's version of pleading. Always, it is an attempt to draw Hades into a wicked, controlled fantasy.

When he grew suspicious long ago, he hoped it wasn't true. He didn't see Minthe's evilness right away. Like a thief, Minthe is good at distraction.

"You are banished to the upperworld, Minthe. And the punishment for ignoring banishment from now on is death. My sun-kissed colt had mercy on you, so do not waste it. Whether I kill you or Cerberus kills you—or if you jump into the pit yourself—I do not care. I have to look after Seph now."

This is spoken only so Minthe can hopefully understand that his words are true. There is no romance left between them, and Seph is his only concern.

I have wasted enough time on the murderer.

My husband is nearly dead.

So Hades leaves the nymph, setting his scepter to hover vertically close to him as he bends to collect his mate. Seph does not look so angry at him anymore. Only bewildered, weak, and frightened. He clutches to Hades like a scared babe as the god lifts him up. He can do some things to make this easier, like making Seph's weight lighter. But he cannot return strength to the young god's body. And most importantly, he cannot return his mind or restore his essence with the power that makes all things seem possible to a mortal's mind.

When he turns, Minthe is standing behind him, though a distance away. His hands are curled into fists, and he looks a mess, his chiton blood-soaked and torn in the front, a small corner of fabric folded over where the spear tip came out in front.

"I won't leave," he says, and Hades takes Seph to his horse. Cerberus is confused, and Hades snaps his fingers when the dog growls purposefully toward Minthe.

"Not yet," he orders, and tries to make sure Seph is steady on the horse.

He is not.

"I won't leave!" Minthe is louder. "Do you hear me, Hades? I'm not leaving! I am a nymph of the underworld! I was born here! I belong here more than you do!"

Hades glares at him.

He would not hesitate now to put Minthe down. He can't even remember feeling sorry for him.

Perhaps it is his apparent rejection of Hades' rare mercy that erodes all sympathy in him, picking it clean off the bone, like acid once did to Hades' flesh.

"Your terms are banishment or death, nymph," he says darkly. *So perhaps it is best to stay!*

But he controls his emotions before saying the last part. If Minthe knew he would see Hades again, he would certainly be here when Hades got back. While that would give Hades the opportunity to be cruel and remind Minthe and himself that he is, in fact, the God King of the Underworld and the Most Feared God Among Men—that manipulation would not be fair to Seph, who wants the nymph alive in the upperworld. He wants him to be spared for some goddamn reason.

And more importantly, Minthe is just not worth all that effort. If Hades leaves Seph again, after taking him to the palace, it will be as if Minthe's murder is more important than his husband barely clinging to renewed life.

Hades is not that kind of monster.

He levitates so that he can both hold on to Seph and mount the horse at the same time. He takes up the reins around Seph's torso, which leans heavily to one side. Hades calls invisible ropes out of thin air to bind the young god to him. While flying, he has to have absolute control over the horse, who tosses her head and dances sideways at first. She knows it's time to sprint and fly very soon.

"If you do not make it out of the gate, you will be killed by my dog." And he says this as factually as possible. He is a feared god, but not a wrathful one.

This whole day has been strange.

But Hades is certain that he's mitigated some of the damage witnessing Tartarus has caused. Seph has seen an act of mercy. It would not be good to tell Seph he is merciful or to present himself as such, but he does want Seph to realize that he is not Zeus. He acts with mercy, just a different kind. A mercy of logic and unhesitant action, whereas usually mercy is to *stop* action.

A leader has to take a difficult path...

He hopes he can make him understand.

"You can't leave me here! I'm worth more to you! I'm your mate!

Hey! Hades!"

Minthe waves his arms, beginning what looks like a tantrum. He's in a panic.

Perhaps Hades' attention was more important than his love all along. Perhaps that is why he abducted Seph—to be the focus of Hades' life once more.

That would explain why he wanted me to punish him at first.

So the best thing to do is to not look at him. Hades kicks the horse's sides and gives some slack in the reins, signaling that it's time. The horse bolts for the trees in the far off distance. His giants even farther off look over but do not pause in their task. Gentle, obedient souls. They knew nothing but toil in life and learned to enjoy it. Hades gives the horse her initial lift. Like the new human souls, the horse is unaware of what she can actually do. But once her feet are in the air, she knows no different, and Hades only has to use his magic occasionally to guide her up or down. The rest of his travel is effortless.

Looking back, Minthe's blue hair stands out in the distance. He shouts something unintelligible at the sky—"pig fucking" is a part of it—and he raises one fist, giving him the finger.

Hades whispers one last spell, aimed at Minthe's feet.

"Be swift."

Just in case the nymph waits until it's too late, or waits until he sees Cerberus return for him to start running. That would be just like Minthe, who had many endearing flaws at first. Nothing but flaws, in fact. His temper, his fighting, his playfulness, and later on... yes, even his cruelty.

That is why Hades felt like he could be himself around Minthe. He did not feel so unlikable around the little devil.

Maybe this is for the best after all.

Hades will avoid changing his mind and going after Minthe, even though a little voice whispers, *It's not like Seph would know.*

He has hunted someone into the upperworld many times.

But no. I can't. The deal I made with Seph has to be just. I will follow through and hope the damage to Seph can be undone.

The period with Minthe in my life is over.

Thirty-Seven

The horse runs at an all-out pace, her neck stretched out. Her hooves beat on invisible air but make the clatter of an angry guard charging down a cobblestone street, the kind of noise that calls mothers to leave their homes and bring their children inside.

Hades holds tight. He knows this is not the gentlest way to transport an ailing body, but it is the fastest. Once Seph is in a bed, he may never leave there.

What has Tartarus done to him? How everlasting can the damage be?

Seph is a god in every sense of the word, despite not being able to find his magic. Will that matter in his recovery? There are many like him, but none who have been to Tartarus. Nor are there any lesser gods who underwent the same kind of physical torture as Hades and his siblings. Who's to say Seph can't be physically killed like a mortal in extreme ways?

Gaia's heart consumes essence. It consumes and pumps new life through all.

How much of him do I have left?

He carries the horse low and does not slow down, a dangerous approach to all, and the horse's hooves act as a warning. His souls certainly can't be trampled to death, but they can be hurt.

There is only a musician or two at the palace's public entrance, where they most like to play, and those that are inside must pack and leave right away.

Hades guides the horse to the base of the steps. He would get closer, but horses are dumb, finicky animals. She does not see depth the same, and he cannot risk her rearing up in protest. Once they're on the ground, however, she takes the stairs at an amazing speed. She is not aware enough to understand that she has power in her spirit form and to use it to, say, completely ignore the paddock gate. But every intention of hers is met, and his horses have gained confidence in his care. They bound from one plateau to the next, jumping over sets of twenty stairs, not losing footing.

Inside the palace, he guides her to slow down, though reluctantly. They cannot careen through the dining halls and pillars at more than a controlled canter. Her hooves echo widely through the cavernous space, and Verah with her girls is already on the staircase leading to his private rooms. They run upward to reach the top of the stairs in time, though he slows the horse even further. He cannot rush through such tight corridors. Especially if they happen upon another soul caught in the hallway for some reason.

The girls flatten themselves to the walls. Thankfully, there are not many. Souls are staying away for a little while because of the hunt.

He takes his horse all the way to the solarium. At this point it seems to cost too much time to slow down, though he soothes and walks the steed when they get there. She looks curiously at the fountain and fresh flowers, unaware of the emergency that's brought her to this strange place. And Hades dismounts, using levitation and physical strength both to get Seph safely into his arms again.

His head hangs all the way back. He's fading fast.

As a god, he will recover, Hades reminds himself, but how long will he sleep? Some gods can sleep a thousand years before they come back, from illness or choice both.

What if Seph's fading means that he never comes back?

Verah appears in the solarium with four others poking around her back, as Hades magics the door open to his quarters.

"You need us, my king?" she calls timidly. His horse noses through the lush leaves of his plants, and she gives the animal a wide-eyed stare. Then she notices Seph. "Is he dying?"

"Send for Styx!" Hades yells back, because he's already crossing through the den with Seph. He sets the god on their bed as soon as he can, the covers flying back at his will. Then he grabs the blankets with his hands and pulls them back atop his husband, making sure the cloak is in place first. No need to waste those protections.

"Blankets will help," he mumbles to himself, going through a litany of care instructions in his mind. "Feel secure. Extra layers. Don't leave, Seph. Don't slip away."

First he was in danger of vanishing completely. But now that his body is so damaged and the spirit is missing so many connections? There are other places to sink. Deep, dreamless sleep.

Verah's head pokes through the doorway.

"The horse difficult to move—"

"Did you not hear me?!" Hades yells with rage. "Bring me the Goddess Styx immediately!"

Verah drops to the floor at once, performing the contrite bow of someone in her culture. She also grabs her skirt at the knees, performing a Greek courtesy. She has always strived to learn his preferred language and culture.

"Apologies, King. We are finding Styx."

"Good. That is all I need."

His voice is rough. He doesn't want to yell at Verah, but he'll yell at anyone right now. Every second passing by is like another year.

I should just go finish Minthe myself.

But then he would have to leave Seph.

Everything hurts, mostly his heart and his head.

He places hands on Seph like he's checking for a fever, but he doesn't know why. He doesn't know what good that's going to do.

"I am serving well, my king?"

She always asks this when he has a temper.

"Yes, Verah, that will be all."

She straightens with grace, trying not to make a sound. Then lingers in the doorway, looking back before leaving.

"I get the horse," she says, and who knows what that means. Probably that she is worried about his plants.

Hades waits until she's gone and leans over his beloved's face. Yes, even in this state, he's Hades' beloved, because Hades can't think of him any other way. He *was* so lively. So special.

His trauma in Tartarus did not pale his face, and Hades takes his features in his hands, wondering if this is a memory he will have to commit to keep forever. Did they have their last moments arguing over Minthe?

I should have left that little wretch with the spear sticking out of his chest. I could have sent Cerberus to finish my work after we got home.

And still, I could.

"Cerberus!" he calls, realizing the dog is not in the room. He meant to give Minthe a head start. An opportunity to safely travel to the gate. But now that Seph is unconscious, that time has expired.

Cerberus does not appear, and Hades is impatient. He stands from the bed, acknowledging that he can't do anything anyway. He's helpless until Styx arrives, and he might even be helpless then.

"Come back to me and wake up," Hades growls in the same tone he uses to command his dog. Then he leaves to find the disobedient hound, cursing him mentally.

He finds Cerberus with his ears back and three girls pulling on his collar. They appear young, only a few years apart, with similar traits. They look like sisters. But these ones are quite old and have mastered their abilities to not get bitten.

Cerberus does not actively attack them. He is only vicious when the hunt command is given. But his warning snaps are ignored, and he is not smart enough to realize that he can't be physically restrained. Even after growing three heads, he is still mostly just a regular dog.

Looking at them gives Hades an idea. A better way to protect Seph. But such a thing will have to wait and see if he recovers first.

"Girls, let him go," he says and kneels to greet the dog. His fur is wet with real blood, something Hades hasn't seen in a long time. Not since a satyr, compelled by a reward from Zeus, tried to sneak through the gate for the secrets to his wine. Now he has a much more gruesome mission. And if Hades was going to be fair, he would wait. Tartarus is so far away from the gate, Minthe can't even *hope* to be halfway there yet.

But that's why he whispered the spell as he left Minthe. He knew he would cheat.

"*Hunt*," he tells the dog, holding the middle head briefly, projecting an image of Minthe. He's careful to include the torn, bloody clothes. Dogs have a better sense of smell than sight, and with a command like this, Cerberus could make a mistake. A sock of Minthe's would be better.

But Cerberus is a smart dog, and Hades has trained him well. His heads tilt, thinking, looking curious, and Hades opens his eyes, ending the mental projection.

Cerberus tries to figure it out.

"Hunt," Hades repeats and stands, pointing to the door.

After only a second more, the dog is off, careening through the solarium and out the door with a lot less care than Hades had with his horse. An end table wobbles and gets knocked askew, the dog sailing over the nearby bench instead of going around.

And Hades takes a deep breath, reminding himself that it's over.

It doesn't *feel* over because Minthe's death is not by his hand, but now there is only Seph's care to see to.

I hope he makes it.

Thirty-Eight

Seph wakes up disoriented, his entire body aching in a way it never has before. Ever. He has not felt the strain of reaping wheat like the slaves have told him about. Fimus said that working when the fields are ripe and require long hours in the sun makes his arms weak and his muscles stiff every day. He said that any kind of movement hurt, even lifting them up over his head carrying nothing.

Concerned, Seph told his mother to not make the field slaves work so long to harvest. And she explained that halving their labor now would starve almost all of them in the winter, when they are fortunate to be given full rations still from her stores. Also, she gives them double rations during the harvest because hard work requires good food to keep illness away.

She talked a bit like the requirement of food and labor was the workings of a good machine from which everyone benefits. When Seph asked for lesser hours for the young slaves, or maybe just for his favorite slave only, she scoffed. She did not even respond, putting her back to him.

Seph remembers all of this in a strange way. Like a dream about a dream. A story that he heard from another man.

He cannot remember why he cared about Fimus. Only that his body ached, and Seph tried to fix it.

But I did not work in the fields for too long today, did I?

He tries to remember what he was doing yesterday. And his mind aches as well, muscles pulsing where he didn't know he had any.

He remembers all the pieces. He's just not sure if these are things that happened to him, or things that he witnessed happening to someone else. It's all very confusing, and for a moment he wonders if he was actually the blue-haired person, the one who was nearly killed.

He touches his hair, which is too short. The texture of it doesn't seem to match, and when he pulls a strand in front of his nose, he sees that it is a dark color. Ruddy, like clay dirt.

So I am Seph. Someone who cares about slave boys.

But why don't I remember what I look like?

He sits up, taking in the room, and nothing feels familiar to him. That includes the rather haggard face in the mirror against the wall.

I've been here before. I think.

I think...

I think the stories are real. Some of them.

A door opens, and Seph expects to see a woman with curly brown hair piled on her head, adorned by a laurel wreath. He expects her to be big, thick-limbed and tall, but to move with light steps and gracefulness. He expects a prominent nose and strong jawline—features that Seph very much likes on his own face.

Or, he used to. Seph has no opinion of it now. The face doesn't seem to belong to him, or to anyone important. It is just a face.

And the woman who walks through the door is just a woman. Seph tries very hard to remember which woman it is, but she is not in any of his memories.

"Oh, you awake now," she says, and leaves right away on quick feet.

Seph remembers another woman running once. She was smaller, with light skin, and she gathered up her dress around her knees to run in a bouncy way, with little steps. She had others around her, who grabbed his arms and pulled, trying to drag him away from... something dark.

He touches his head.

Am I real?

What is all this?

That, he decides, is the most important question at the moment. For he should be able to identify all the things about this room. Maybe that will help put his mind together.

So he begins.

Chair. Bed. Blanket on the bed. Window.

The next one doesn't come.

Blanket for the floor?

The thing for stepping on, what is it...

The word doesn't come.

He frowns with frustration and moves on.

Vase—no. Cup? No.

He frowns at the container at the other side of the bed. There is a cup in front of it, but Seph suspects it is not *only* a cup. The cup has a second name, and the larger container behind it has a completely different name than what he can think of.

But it is like a vase...

Three people appear in the doorway, striding toward him, and Seph forgets his problem. There are so many things to notice about them. He pulls the blanket up, covering himself, wondering if he should put it over his head. They quickly surround him, and Seph can't place any of their faces in his memories.

Well, except for *him*.

"It's you," Seph says, narrowing his eyes.

The pale-faced one does not look angry or cruel (only concerned, possibly frightened, and tired) but he is capable of great cruelty and does not have any love. Seph immediately begins to remember more, about a prison in the middle of a giant pit, and bodies—no, living people!—thrown to their deaths over the side.

That's why I hate him.

Rather, Seph—the identity in his head—hates him.

Seph himself only feels fear and uncertainty. But the *real* Seph, the person he's remembering, hates this man, and Seph purposefully changes his expression to match this emotion, pretending to be the individual he remembers.

He doesn't want to admit how vulnerable he is. He has no idea what he's doing here, or why this man attacked him.

"How are you feeling?"

Seph becomes confused as the hated man puts his hands on Seph's legs. He doesn't seem to be bothered at all by the events that took place before. Was it a long time ago?

No, it was yesterday.

"I am... disoriented," Seph admits, and then looks at the two women. One waits with her head down and her hands clasped in front of her. Her clothes are simple.

The other has straight black hair and green eyes. She's pale, but her skin has a more pinkish tone than the other, and there's a certain... healthiness to it that Seph can't explain. Her eyes are solid, the irises detailed, while the other woman's seem vague. Her breath smells faintly of smoke. Her hands fall on his shoulders, and then one cups his face. Bony and thin, but warm.

The woman he remembers speaking to about the slaves was heavier and very warm.

The voices also do not match as she says, "Young sir, do you remember your name?"

"Seph," he answers, narrowing his eyes to look brave. He does not think she's friendly. The woman he remembers is his family, and this one is not.

"And do you remember who that is?"

"Seph," he answers simply, and pulls his head back. The man he hates strokes his hair, and this is entirely too much touching from people he doesn't know. He moves away toward the center of the bed, pulling his knees in front of him. But he is not timid or afraid. He tries not to show it if he is. With aching limbs, he will fight if it's necessary.

"He'll make a full recovery then," says the dark-haired woman, looking at the hated man.

"What about his memories?"

"He might recover most of them." She snaps a finger and points at the door. The girl who was waiting leaves with soundless steps and returns quickly with a leather bag. "Or half of them, or very few of them, or none at all."

"That's not helpful," the man says.

"I remember everything," Seph says defensively. "You are a murderer who should be put to death. And you..." He shouldn't have carried the bluff this far. He cannot remember this woman anywhere. "You are his... slave. Or... or mine? I have a slave. Where is he?"

He is quite confident of this answer once he thinks of it, but the woman only gives Hades an uncertain look and shrugs her shoulders.

"You are Hades," Seph says, glad that the name came back to him. It is a good name, sadly, for such an evil individual. Seph likes how it sounds to say it, and his face is quite pleasant as well. His features are so perfect they're almost boring. But his eyes...

His eyes are haunting. Seph feels drawn to him.

But vivid images are coming back—boats going over the cliffs, hanging from chains, while people drop into the water.

It makes him so angry he starts to tremble.

"I must kill you," he whispers aloud, and his thoughts urge him to do it now, but he does not move.

"Well, he remembers you for sure," the woman says, and from her bag she takes several small objects and puts them by the bed. "An immediate recovery is not possible, I'm afraid. You can think of him as a very light wooden cup, and pouring too much too fast will cause him to tip over. He needs time to grow between every dose. We will give him these for today—spread them out. And I will look at him again tomorrow."

The man nods. "Can you stay? I need someone to look after him. I don't think he wants to see me anymore."

"No. You are the best one for him." The man starts to protest, and she says, "Seph, what do you remember about this god?"

She doesn't know!

"He kills people. Hundreds of them—probably thousands! It's happening right now. If we don't stop it..." He shirks, realizing he is about to be struck. Possibly speared or beaten with the staff. And he's too weak to successfully defend himself right now. But enough people have to hear this until someone believes him. "You can look for yourself if you go to the place called Tartarus. Thousands of them—every day—die going over a cliff."

"Such emotion!" she answers. "That is good. It means he's connecting with his mind. Hades, you're the best thing for him, whether he likes you or not."

Her response makes Seph wish he had enough strength to attack her. Doesn't she care about what he just said? His legs flex thinking about running, but his toes don't move very much when he asks them to. Everything aches.

"Seph, what other things can you remember about yourself? What can you tell me about your childhood? Or about your mother?"

"Mother?" Seph asks, confused by the word. "Oh, the woman." He looks around. "Where is she?"

He's not sure that she's a good person. He can't remember liking her. But she is important, somehow.

"You see?" the woman says. "His most recent memories will be the most real to him. The things going way back, the things that make up his core—those are the most precious memories we lost. The essence takes people from the foundation up. You may find that he's a bit different now than he was, even if he does come to remember everything."

Hades looks down at the blankets, his expression solemn.

"I see. Thank you, Styx."

"He'll be all right otherwise. He's mostly there." She seems more cheerful than the dark god. More factual, anyhow. "In a way, it's like he's been born again. Regenerating essence is like when the rains fill up a river. Some of the soil is lost, the shape slightly changed, but the direction and purpose should be similar."

She picks up a vial and stares at it.

"I'll miss my beauties. This one is common, though they're all quite special to me."

"I am grateful."

The man doesn't seem to say much. Can he really be as evil as Seph remembers?

Yes, I am certain.

But he doesn't seem hateful toward Seph. Maybe because Seph is a god and not just a human.

So I can't be murdered...

Yes, that's right. The gods don't treat humans well. That aligns with what he remembers.

"No need," the woman says with a sad smile. "His life is worth all of my beauties, of course. And I had better get to bottling the next one. It takes far more life to recover a person this way, but it has to be done."

She kisses Hades on the cheek. Seph can't believe it. After what he told her! And also... should she be doing that?

Why do I feel—

Like she's touching what is mine—

"We're married!" he says, realizing.

The woman looks back and leaves with a laugh. "Come, Adonis!" she calls in the other room, and a small hand takes hers. Seph can't see the child from the doorway before they're gone, to find out if he remembers who it is, but his mind is already reeling.

"Why would I marry *you*?"

Thirty-Nine

"Where are you going?" Seph asks, and Hades shoots him a lost and hurried look. He is not very expressive, but Seph thinks he's almost about to cry. Maybe. But Hades never cries.

How do I know that?

He looks for the memory, but he can't find it. There is very little he can recall about his husband. He certainly doesn't remember them exchanging I love you's... But... There is a moment with him in bed that Seph remembers very well. And he remembers being happy and pleased to have his hands on his husband.

How much time has passed since then? How can I remember him so differently from what he really is?

"You lied to me."

"Verah, please make sure Cerberus has enough toys and bones to keep him from scratching at my door and howling."

"Yes, king. Perhaps a meal for the young king? He has not had meal for days."

"Food this early will only make him puke. Perhaps a small bowl of broth though. Heat it up as much as you can."

"Yes, king." She bows again and leaves. Of the four women Seph can recall, she is his favorite. She has a strength about her, even though she is quite small in height.

Seph looks for memories, expecting happy stories. He would like it if he and her were friends. But he can't find anything, and that's disappointing. He also can't find anything about this room... Except that he may have had a conversation with a blue-haired person here once.

And this is the same bed he remembers with Hades in it.

Mostly he recalls Hades' face and the same pair of earrings the dark god is wearing now. Otherwise, he is dressed differently from what Seph remembers. They were riding in a chariot, Seph huddled on the floor. Afraid, maybe. Hades wore an all-black ensemble darker than any dye he's ever seen. It was like his form disappeared when he stepped into a shadow.

Now he wears a light blue shirt and simple gray pants. He wears his cloak even inside though, and that is odd. Seph does not feel so cold anymore.

Hades sits on the bed, and for a while he doesn't look at Seph or talk to him, staring only at his own knees. Seph almost feels sad. It is difficult to keep reminding himself that this man is a murderer.

"You tried to kill me. Why?"

"What?" Hades gives him an alarmed look. "What makes you say that?"

"You put me in that pit. And it... it ripped my mind apart. Why did you do that?"

And where is the woman I remember? My mother?

Most of the stories in his head are about her. But only her voice, and the moments are incomplete.

"I didn't put you in there, Seph. I pulled you out of that place. Minthe—the evil bastard—pushed you in. Don't you remember that?"

"Minthe... Minthe..." Seph looks very hard in his thoughts, his mind feeling empty. He can't find anything. He is about to say so, but he makes a guess with intuition. "You are working with him."

"Working with...?" Hades shakes his head. "I went to drop off your rabbit, remember? And I was only in the upperworld for a little while. Less than half the day. And when I came back you were gone. I nearly didn't rescue you in time. Minthe took you from me."

None of that feels familiar.

"No. You lied to me. I remember. Almost..." Seph doubts himself. Are the stories real? Is Seph real? Why can't he remember more than just Hades' face and how he feels?

It is one thing to remember some events of his life, but he can't remember why he did anything. Why did he care about someone named Fimus? Who is the other boy who chased him around the baths? Why does he have the feeling that Hades likes soaps?

Remembering facts does not make him feel like he knows who he is.

But he says, "I may not know who I am or... anything else. But I remember that you and him were together. And you—or he—pushed me? Or something." He lowers his head, looking around the room for help, but he isn't certain about anything.

"What am I doing here?" he whispers.

"Minthe is a jealous ex-lover of mine, and before you ask, we have not been together for more than fifty years. He is quite an old nymph despite all appearances, and you wouldn't have robbed him of very much time if you just let me toss him in the pit. I can't tell you how many times I've thought about tracking him down while you were sleeping. Someday you're going to appreciate the effort it takes for me to keep my promise. Especially since you can't remember me making it."

"You're a murderer. Explain that." And Seph picks up his head again. Hades does not look like a murderer, no matter what he knows to be true.

He looks pale. And delicate. And the exact opposite of everything that Seph is.

Have I ever seen him laugh?

Seph feels like he has, but he can't remember it and that bothers him. He wants to remember that even more than he wants to remember the things about this person called Minthe.

"What you saw is a... processing place. Seph, I cannot be the murderer of anything because the people you saw on the boats were already dead."

Seph pauses, his mouth slightly open with befuddlement and no response forthcoming. This is true. He could tell by looking at Verah that she was unlike the other woman who was here. She had features like she should be dark-skinned, but she was just tinged almond, and almost glowing. Her eyes barely blinked and always seemed to be unfocused. Sometimes it was like pieces of her would move without being attached to other pieces. For a human to walk forward, they have to push off the back foot. The girl's heels seemed to mimic walking while the rest of her body would float.

"But... this is the land of the dead. Right? So here they are people. They are not *dead* dead. I heard them scream." He swallows around a new lump in his throat. This part he remembers most vividly—the boats tipping over, and then a woman in the water transformed into a vanishing corpse.

"I saw a woman's body! So they are not all spirits. I saw her eyes rot away. And her skeleton exposed."

"Just an image, I'm afraid. The new souls retain a lot of their internal anatomy. Sometimes, you can even see them breathing. It is not something they consciously thought of when they lived in the physical world, but whenever they realize they aren't doing it down here in the underworld, they'll make themselves mimic the actions again. With organs they technically don't have. It's kind of cute, in a way."

Seph wrinkles his nose with disgust. He is talking about a woman Seph saw melt, and Hades' explanation of it includes the words 'kind of cute'.

"There's something wrong with you. If you don't feel remorse—or horror or guilt—over anything you've done, then you're a lunatic."

Hades starts, but he doesn't look particularly ashamed. He presses his lips together, letting out a frustrated breath through his nose, but always with the subtlest expression on his mostly passive face.

"I'm sorry. I haven't finished explaining. Let me finish explaining, and then you can..." He raises a hand and drops it. "Think whatever of me."

"I'm listening."

"The essence that makes up the souls, the Earth, and all living physical life will continue to grow. But in order to grow, it always has to maintain a base sum. There always has to be a certain amount of essence left in order for it to divide. If it divides too thinly, it is gone. All the Earth and everything in it could be gone, just like that, because I decided that Tartarus was too cruel for the little souls coming in.

"So, because I feed the ones who want rebirth back into Tartarus—for rebirth, by the way, I haven't lied about that—because I do that, the Earth continues to live. The number of souls that I have continues to grow. And life on Earth continues to divide and make new life. The Earth is growing ever more complex, and with it, I am building the eternal world as well.

"Eventually, I will have all of them. Trillions! And they will be of all personalities, but overall they will be intelligent and selfless and sweet. For they will grow more and more wise, the more lives they've lived in their essence, even if they don't have the specific memories."

"Your world is cruel," Seph says. He wonders if Hades could be lying. He doesn't know the man in front of him—not really, not anymore. And he doesn't know enough about anything to determine what is the truth or not.

He feels this hate and anger building up in him, but he doesn't know what exactly it's based on. Who is angry? Him? Or a memory of him?

Who is Seph?

I am Seph does not seem to be a real answer.

Hades smooths his hands over his thighs, then stands slowly.

"You will stay here while you are recovering. I am finding protection for you, but I haven't made the necessary adjustments yet. I haven't left this room for four days while you've been sleeping. But now that you're awake, I'll leave Cerberus in front of your door. Uh, he's tied up and I'll muzzle him, but don't try to pet him. For now, just leave him there, and he will incidentally protect you if anyone, like say, Minthe, comes back into the room."

"Where are you going?"

"To get your protection, like I said. I have someone in mind."

"Don't leave me, please." Seph reaches across the bed. He must get his knees under him to cross the bed the long ways to where Hades is standing, and every muscle is wooden. He keeps thinking, *This body does not belong to me. This body is not mine. Who is this?*

"If you go, I don't know what will happen to me. I feel thin. I feel... I feel like Seph sometimes, but I am not him. I am confused. And this body—" He takes Hades' wrist, then examines his fingers circled around the smooth flesh. He drops the hand to stare at his own palm. "Does that feel like me?" He looks up at Hades' face. "Do I look like me?"

There seems to be sorrow in his eyes, though overall his expression has not changed.

Seph speaks. "I don't know who I am. But I know who you are. So even if I'm mad at you, or something, please don't go. If you go, I'm not sure if... I'm not sure that I..." Seph finds it hard to talk, his eyes suddenly burning, his voice suddenly rough. "I feel so lost!" he gasps out.

Hades returns to him, arms around him, petting his hair. He pulls Seph close and tucks his chin over his head. Then, at first, there is only, "Shh, shh."

Rocking them gently, he explains, "Essence is supposed to grow with a body. When it is put back in, it takes a while to find all the pathways. But nothing is wrong, Seph, I promise you."

He leans back a little. His eyes are wet too.

And Hades says, "Just stay with me, Seph. Then it'll be okay."

Seph sniffs, then rubs his nose. It's a little bit easier to breathe now. He's aware of the oddest things, like the feeling of every blink and the wetness of his tongue. Things that he thinks are supposed to be normal, but nothing feels that way.

Except for Hades. Whether this is his body or not, he and Hades are married.

Hades is his.

And everything about Hades, from the sound of his voice to the feeling of his clothes—it's all exactly the way it's supposed to be.

"I just asked you to stay," Seph points out. "Now you're asking me."

"My meaning is entirely spiritual. Although, I don't think you can travel as a spirit anymore. It will help me a lot if you don't try. I won't be gone for long, Seph. You can probably sleep while I'm away. I'll stay with you until then, all right? You have to be tired. You're so weak."

There is a little flare of irritation, but it is like one of those fleeting thoughts before sinking into sleep.

He thinks again of the woman he knows—the mother who is missing.

He will ask more about her later.

"I would like that. Will you help me lie down? My legs are not moving."

"Yes. It will be a long time before you can walk again. But not too terribly long, Seph. You are a god like me, and in a matter of months, you will regain your strength and your memories. I know it. I haven't lost you yet."

Hades straightens out his legs for him and eases him down into the pillows. He kisses Seph, and more of that bedroom memory comes back. His hands all over Hades. The way they moved together.

"You are mine. And I am... Persephone."

Hades' thumb brushes his cheek. "You like to be called Seph."

Forty

Hades travels to the stable with his head low, his crown left behind and forgotten somewhere in the room with Seph. He assumes Verah knows where it is and has been keeping it safe. Just now, he can't remember where he usually keeps it. She's the one who always fetches it from some cabinet every morning.

Without his children, who knows what state he would be in. They keep things running without him. The new arrivals are looked after—and he has heard that already the boats are packed a little more than normal.

His palace has filled up with children again, many souls taking it upon themselves to simply be present, either to protect Seph or to express their condolences. From a distance, of course. They know not to bother him.

And if the palace had been filled like this on the day that he was taken, they probably never would've had this catastrophe in the first place.

Was Minthe behind the hunt that took place just before Seph was taken? Did he purposely empty the palace? The souls who ran were very new. Perhaps a bit too new to already be braving the run...

But there have been early runners before...

Lately, his thoughts often turn to Minthe. If not wondering where the nymph might be now, as though he plans to find out, he is always wondering where he went wrong. And how to make sure that such a thing never happens again.

That is the purpose for him leaving today.

It is an entirely cumbersome process, and while he answers, somehow, to the few who speak to him—*Is Seph all right? Will he be at dinner today? I hope he recovers soon*—that is Alfric, and Hades mumbles something along the lines of Seph still being in recovery—

Though all of this is true, his mind is always somewhere else.

And taking his horse high into the air, traveling almost vertically as though climbing a steep hill, he feels none of the freedom and gut-clenching adrenaline that he usually enjoys. Only impatience.

When he gets to the gate, an island that hovers in the air, the horse rears up, unhappy with the surrounding barking dogs. They are all hounds, of a very generic kind, since dogs seem to be unaware of their individual characteristics. And thanks to his own magic, they are black instead of gray or white. This magic sticks since the dogs are not aware of themselves enough to change it.

These ones do not change form at all. It was very rare for Cerberus to do so on his own and become one body. They are darkly colored by his hand to offer camouflage and protection. And being the guardians of the gate, Hades figured they ought to look intimidating.

They are ferocious, howling and yapping up a storm, making his horse dance as if she wants to bolt. But she's too well trained for that. He gives her a pat on the neck, speaking softly, before stepping down. And she scrapes at the dirt with her front hoof.

"It'll be alright," he tells his good steed, and repeats the words for himself and in his head as well.

Now it will be.

He wades through happy gazes and slobbering licks, every good dog sniffing his knees and waiting with their tails wagging. He pats them on the head as he passes, as many as he can. But he is not joyful to see them, as he usually would be.

He locates Hecate, the Guardian of the Gate and the mistress of the dogs. She rests atop the enormous, magnificent entryway, her hammock strung across the boughs of two ancient trees he has growing on either side of the arch frame.

He scolded her when he first saw this. The gate is supposed to be intimidating. But she scoffed and informed him that the job was quite boring. The souls come in a different way, wandering on their own through any forest around the world until real blends with spiritual and they find the River Styx. Through curiosity and mysterious beckoning, they follow the winding riverbank and gather themselves at the dock to await Charon.

Hecate will only have something to do when someone besides a soul wants to travel through. Gods will fly to the island with the dogs, and nymphs can summon her to ask for passage.

It is a long unfulfilling appointment. But no one has snuck past the gate since he put her in charge.

"I thought I would see you again." When she raises herself out of the hammock, walking atop the gate's arch without care for the uneven bricks under her feet and the slim ledge, a duplicate form of hers is left resting in the hammock. And that form turns its head to look at him—another face still resting with its nose pointed straight up.

Hecate thought Cerberus' new form was such a neat trick, somehow she practiced it and learned the skill herself. Only, she separates into what she calls her sisters, and they'll behave and speak as if they are one person.

Hecate's understanding of her own power and experimentation has always intrigued him. But he never thought he would have a use for her ability to split into three selves. Until now.

This one is the original Hecate, with her key resting on a necklace, atop her breasts. Her clothing is scarce and tribal, reflecting the dress of those cultures with a strong belief in magic. Hecate loves to do them little favors, keeping their superstitions alive.

"You had a brain parasite, I think. When I heard what the little blue-haired nymph had done and the fact that you spared him, I sent you a spell to eliminate it. Since you are here, I assume it worked?"

She smirks.

"It is not that," he replies, irritated, though he feels mostly angry at himself.

How easy would it be to send his hound, or any one of these, after the blue-haired twit? How easy would it be to at least tell Zeus what the nymph had done? Or Artemis? Or any one of the cousins who sparred over Seph?

While they wouldn't exact revenge with the passion or fury that Minthe deserves, they at least have enough family loyalty to do what needs to be done.

I'm keeping my promise to a boy who probably can't remember me making it. Because his presence changes me.

"I have a new job for you. So you may need to split yourself again. Or make one of these duplicates change whatever you've assigned them to."

This gets the attention of the other two. One rises and nudges the other awake, and both silently come alongside the original Hecate. They stand with their backs inward, facing out in all directions, the other two watching in an indirect way. They are submissive, letting the original Hecate do all the speaking for them.

Hades has always wondered how much autonomy each Hecate has. One carries a lantern, which she uses to appear at crossroads sometimes for a mortal summoner. One carries a dagger and a whip. She is the enforcer.

"About your... duplicates..." He's not sure if the other two will mind. "Do they carry all the same powers as you? Are they truly separate or do they have to stay within a certain proximity to be useful?"

Now the other two heads look directly at him, and the one with the whip crosses her arms.

"We are not slaves!" she says, and the key-holder looks amused. "I am Hecate. You may address *me* if you like. I am as powerful and strong-willed as either one of my sisters."

Hades nods once, keeping a frown from his features. Hecate is an odd one. She has never shared how she came to duplicate herself as more than just a mirage—anyone can make a mirage or a half-minded slave. But if it's true that she duplicated herself... that she made another god with her own powers...

Well, that shall be the first.

He has never tried to test her possible lie before.

"I have need of a guardian. One who is capable of great magic as well as having advanced skill with physical weapons."

"Well, we can all do that," says the one with the key. She and the lantern bearer lean on each other. There is barely enough thickness on the gate's ledge for them to stand.

"The job is constant. There is no rest and very little sleep. I admit, you will be a servant. Though, not a mistreated one."

The warrior version of Hecate looks intrigued, though the one with the lantern goads, "Then I suppose there will be great compensation for such a difficult job! Why, there must be. For otherwise, we would be slaves serving an ungrateful master."

Hecate with the key *tsks*.

That has been an odd little thing Hades has never figured out. They are all Hecate, and if they were to switch the items they carry, they could probably fool him into speaking to any one of them. He has no way to tell.

Yet, they are slightly different. It is like Hecate truly did make herself sisters—triplets—but she has insisted that they are all herself. She did not, say, birth twins and warp their form so terribly.

The crossroads Hecate often makes a sneer and snarl about payment. Hecate lives on this island, with the dogs and the trees and her hammock. She could have greater luxuries if she wished, but she has not asked for any such compensation. The crossroads Hecate still seems to think that it should be offered.

Hades says, "As always, if you have a request of me, I will evaluate it."

She cuts in, ignoring her sister's hand raised to stop her. "You do that for any one of your citizens, even the little wisps, so I do not see how—"

"Hush, sister!" says Hecate with the weapons. She falls from the gate with merely a step and drops straight down, landing curled over her knees, on bare feet. She stands with elegant posture and walks with small, balanced steps, as though invisibly wearing a fancy gown.

"What sort of protection job is this? Is there great danger? Is there an unbeatable foe?" Her eyes widen with delight for the last statement, her smile eager.

"I still need you here for the protection of the gate." He is not sure which of them to address now. Hecate must love the confusion. "If it is true what you say, I can borrow one of you for this job and the other two of you should be able to maintain the defense here. Is that correct?"

"As if I have a choice," says the crossroads Hecate. She swings her lantern back and forth, annoyed, and then eyes him through slits, as if she is considering hurling the flame. But her lips quirk mischievously and no action is taken.

Hecate with the key only looks serious and thoughtful.

The warrior speaks loudly and steps in front of him, commanding his attention away from the other two.

"I can protect the gate and take the job. You are not speaking to three of us, Hades. I have merely extended myself into three different bodies."

"They are the most realistic mirages I've ever seen." Did he have it wrong this whole time? Has the warrior, usually silent and impassive, been the real Hecate this whole time?

"No part of me is a mirage. No part of me is lesser. And I accept your offer. Though, understand that any god allowed to live under your rule is already an indentured servant. If I do not agree to your terms, you will simply cast me into the sunlit place and wait for me to beg to come back."

While he and Hecate are about the same age, she grew up in a world without a singular ruler who held any laws. Just an awful bull that trampled by once in a while, and the others would stay out from under his feet.

Unlike Styx, who is demure and quiet, Hecate will always talk about his authority as if it is a thing he claimed yesterday.

"I would try to convince you that this is something you want to do first," he answers honestly.

"Pah!" The lantern bearer rolls her eyes. "Such a *nice* tyrant!"

She is shushed by the one wearing the key, who steps off the ledge.

"Although this makes me seem as faithful and mindless as one of your guard dogs..." She gestures to the animals that have surrounded her, seeming to think she came down just for them. "...you are not an *utterly* despicable master. And I accept your request—if we can call it that."

She bows. Hecate has always had perfect balance. She challenges his rule with her tongue, but shows easy subservience in equal measures.

"Show me to my post, my king."

Forty-One

While Hades is gone, there is plenty of time for Seph to utilize the remaining strength in his body and perhaps try to escape. That would be if he *truly* felt unsafe, and if he *truly* felt like Hades was trying to harm him. Despite what he remembers, all the stories in his head, he no longer feels like Hades is a danger to him or anyone.

The story and the man he's met don't match.

Seph doesn't like Hades' explanation. He doesn't know why the world has to be so cruel. He wonders if maybe the people on the boats knew what was about to happen to them—if maybe they would choose to make the sacrifice anyway. They are dead, after all.

Whether Hades is bad or good confuses him. But he does seem to care about Seph, and Seph spends the time when Hades is away lying in bed with his eyes closed. He had pretended to be asleep just so the god could leave him and go wherever he said he needed to be (for Seph can't remember).

And when he comes back, after being gone forever it seems, Seph continues to lie with his eyes closed.

This feels familiar.

And as Seph hears the wine pitcher lifting, then liquid pouring into the cup, the sensation of this happening before only grows stronger...

Am I not real after all? Is this a story I'm living?

Seph opens his eyes and turns, reaching for Hades. He bumps the cup, making the liquid in the cup slosh a little. Hades' swallow is interrupted as Seph hugs the dark god around his waist and holds tight.

"I feel like there's something in my brain. A creature like a leech. And I want to reach in, right inside my skull, and pull it out."

Seph grabs the top of his head where the feeling is the strongest, right at his hairline.

"Here," Hades takes that hand and puts it on the cup stem

instead.

The name comes back to him. *Goblet.*

Seph swirls the drink and tips his head back for it.

"Oh, this helps," he says, wiping his mouth. Throughout his gut and stomach, the sweetness of the drink, all of these physical sensations overtake the mental tail-chasing in his thoughts.

It also brings back a memory. Yet another story. He doesn't want another one of those. But this one is not so bad. It feels right, like it's happening exactly where it's supposed to be. In the past. And it feels like it happened to *him* rather than some guy named Seph who apparently talked and had thoughts without the current Seph's input at all.

This one was him. And he didn't say much. He mostly just watched Hades eat and drink, dining from a large feast, leaning toward him on a couch.

That was a good night. Even if I was a little nervous.

"More."

His request is fulfilled.

"I've never seen you drink so quickly before."

"Am I doing it wrong?"

"No. You can guzzle it from the pitcher if you like. Watch."

His forming smile disappears behind the clay pottery, and he gradually tilts the drink into his mouth.

It's a lot easier for Seph to do without spilling, having his smaller cup. For a while, this is all they do, Hades refilling his drink whenever it's empty and then drinking straight from the pitcher itself. There is little talking and no savoring at all of the hearty, delicious drink. They down it like men in a hurry, and gradually, as the pitcher's bottom becomes visible under the dark liquid, Seph finds himself with the desire to speak.

It is little things at first. Questions he has that pester him as he's sipping his drink that then find their way onto his tongue somehow.

"Doesn't Seph usually curl his hair?"

"You *are* Seph. And let's say... when I met you, you had done up your hair like any young Greek noble. But no, I believe you personally did not curl it. You, Seph, do not have the patience to hold still for sixteen breaths and let the soap set. I highly doubt you had the patience for applying and setting rollers."

"Sixteen breaths? Soap set?" Seph lifts a hand, waving, lightheaded, and drops it. "What does any of that mean?"

"That you were looked after by your mother, and you'd have the stringy hair of a commoner if one of us more patient beings did not look after your grooming."

Seph dwells on the image of the woman, his mother, as he sips more of the drink. He can imagine her standing across from him, bangles on her wrists clattering and dangling as she props her hands on her hips.

She always does that, with a stern frown regarding him. She has a rather big pointed nose, his mother. But he can't remember her actual face. She's like a blur with hair and wrists.

He wants to ask about her. But she does not seem friendly.

There are some times when he imagines her that she's enormous, her hands twice the size of his head.

Children do not pick their own names!

You are my son and I will call you whatever I want, Per-sephone!

There is... something there. Some connection. But it's so wrapped up and muddled. He thinks that perhaps he'd rather be with Hades.

"Am I permanently damaged? Will I always feel like I don't know who I am?"

"No, a lot of it will come back." Hades leans on him then, rubbing his back, bumping his chin into Seph first and then kissing his head. His movements have more blundering to them, and his cheeks are rosy as he rests against Seph's shoulder.

"A lot of it will feel distant though. Once you've had enough of the essence Styx is bleeding from her old beasts, you will feel like you've discovered the world brand new. Like waking up from a very long nap and the time of day has changed. And you can't quite remember how you fell asleep or how you got there. But you will always be Seph. Only little things will change."

"Do you think I'll still love you?"

Hades was going to take a new drink, and now he stops. He lets the pitcher rest on the bed, and he lets a thumb trail up the long, looped handle.

"That is your choice."

He is quiet, looking fallen, and that answers a question for Seph. He wondered how loyal this marriage really is.

To make up for the hurt he may have caused by his curious query, Seph tries something *he's* never done before (but something he *remembers* doing). An action that may decide whether he is Seph who he remembers or not. And also, he wants to recover more memories like these. They are fragmented and incomplete.

He keeps the goblet standing up on the soft bed with a little help from his foot, as he takes Hades' face in his hands, kissing him.

This is weird. This is not very good.

Those were the old thoughts he had very long ago, recovered now.

I am finding pieces of myself in him. But only when he's around, like that woman said.

He breaks away.

"I want to do more with you. Is it okay if I do more?"

I want to remember more of that night after the feast.

Hades leans away. "Seph, you probably can't even walk right now."

Seph tries a smile, to show he's okay. Though, Hades is very right. His entire body feels achy and weak. With gusto he says, "Well, I'm not trying to *walk*."

Did you just—smack my ass?

His grin falters, then increases. He loves this new memory he found.

"Can I just... have your body, please? Maybe to do more of *this*, maybe just to explore... I don't know." He touches Hades' arm. There is another old whispering thought here, as his hand follows up to his shoulder.

Where did those scars come from?

In the present, he wonders, *What did he say when I asked?*

But no answer returns.

"I feel like I stored myself in here." He loosens Hades' shirt ties around his collar and slips his hand inside, over his heart. "I feel like if we are kissing and touching, I might find this Seph person again. And I might find out that he's me."

Hades says nothing at first. And then their lips touch.

"Please," Seph says when he can.

"You already have permission, my king."

And then the parts that he discovers are not words but emotion. Desire, want. But more importantly—the part that feels like *him* and not just a physical reaction to the beautiful body under his hands— he feels entitled. Hades' words are not just playful endearment. Seph feels like a king with a subject, a claim.

And he loves it.

He kisses the dark god's neck. He feels the wine goblet topple over his foot since he forgot about it, but when he lifts his head to assess the damage, the cup is floating in midair, unspilled, and Hades has a hand raised toward it. It floats to the table by the bed, and Seph appreciates that he doesn't have to fuss with such a menial thing.

He can focus on kissing the god instead. Hades threads their fingers together and squeezes his palm. The very magic that lifted the wine glass is Seph's to touch. He kisses the taste of wine off the god's lips. And more importantly, he smells the god's hair and runs his nose over his neck. He loves that icy, sweet scent. Minthe.

"What happened to the boy we were with? The one you were torturing."

"You don't remember? I sent him to the upperworld until the end of his days. I banished him."

"Hmm." Seph grabs Hades' head to tilt him aside, finding the area behind his ear. The king squirms.

"You told me to," Hades says. He shirks and shivers. "I made a promise. Remember?"

It is not important.

But Seph doesn't say so. He remembers the pretty-faced thing beaten and dying. He vaguely remembers that Minthe was responsible for his near death, but the details of it all evade him. Why was he out there?

It doesn't feel important anymore. That was all old Seph. The newest Seph is here with a husband who honors promises and smells amazing.

Oh.

There is one good skill he remembers. Barely. Looking down at his groin, wondering if he should do something or nothing, Seph unlocks a little bit of knowledge. A connection. Something old Seph knew that new Seph would like to experience also.

"I want us to touch. Like this."

He takes himself in hand, but he can't get close enough to Hades. He stretches out his legs instead and brings Hades on top of him. His husband goes along with it, looking a little perplexed. He lets the pitcher float off the bed and land perfectly on the table without a wobble. And Seph, holding Hades' hips, has him perch on his thighs, the accessibility perfect.

Hades is confused at first. But not for long. With a little guidance from Seph, taking those pale wrists, molding Hades' hands onto his stiff cock, Hades soon kneads and wraps and fondles, making Seph raise his hips a little. He can't afford much more movement than that.

Then he says, "I want to feel you with me."

He reaches far down and takes Hades in hand, his trousers already opened, perhaps with magic.

This doesn't feel familiar, though he knows the technique. This is all him—the real Seph. Not a memory of someone.

What he says is an echo though.

"I want you to cum for me, baby."

Hades' lips were parted and his eyes lidded in pleasure. Now his brows make a cute crease in the middle.

"*Baby?*"

"Mmm. Love doll. Plump cheeks. Squishy butt. What do I usually call you?"

His nicknames are terrible and without class. He knows this. But he also can't access anything. It's all new.

It's like I have to build myself all over again.

"I don't..." Hades rolls his lips together quickly, his eyes closing. He moves back and forth across Seph's broad cock. "We never really got that far. Just *my king*, I think, is something we call each other. And sometimes husband or mate."

"Hm. That doesn't seem right. Are you sure I didn't call you beautiful? I seem to remember..."

He stops speaking. Hades doesn't look displeased, his expression impartial, but he doesn't pipe up in accordance either. Seph is remembering someone or something else. Or maybe he just really wants to give Hades a nickname. It seems so natural a desire that he doesn't know why it wouldn't have happened already.

"I want to see you cum on my cock, beautiful."

Hades has no reaction. If anything, his features smooth themselves out.

That's okay. I'll dig.

"On second thought, I think I'll call you *Flower*. What do you think?"

Perhaps that was too playful. The dark god's eyes snap open, sharp and annoyed. Seph's hands stop on their own.

"You will not."

Seph makes himself chuckle. Though his body would rather not move at all, he forces his arms to use enough strength to lift himself up, and he kisses his husband, who moans and squeezes his hands around them both.

"I wish I could have you. Fully," Seph says, looking into his eyes. Then he shrugs. "But this is fun too. I want to see your face when you cum."

His hands help, taking over. Up and down, over and around their slick heads. He watches the pleasure spike and climb in his lover. Hades shuts his eyes tighter as he's feeling it, lost in his own thought-space. Maybe seeking out privacy, feeling self-conscious. But he's actually more exposed than ever, each moment causing a new frown, an inhale, or a small moan.

Seph sees the end coming when Hades curls his hands atop his knees. Seph leans forward again to lick over his ear and nuzzle through his hair.

"Cum for me, beautiful. And I'll be good for you."

What that means exactly, he can't say. But he knows what he wants, and he reaches around to feel Hades' backside. He slips low and pushes a finger into his ass.

His husband squeaks, quick like a mouse, his eyes flying open in surprise. And Seph pushes in hard and deep, because he knows Hades will lose control. He knows he has him. He moves his finger fast, the place tight but pliable, and all too soon it closes up on him.

Hades takes them in hand again, stroking their cocks and moving his hips into it, up and down on Seph's thighs. Through his cock, Seph feels his husband pulse and twitch. Hades' slick palm holds them tight against each other. His husband cums over them both, shooting up and spilling all over Seph's cock and stomach. Hades' own hands are coated and messy with himself.

Seph grins.

He isn't bad. He's just... the king of this place, is all. The underworld is morbid. There's too much grief. Here, existence pays its cost. And my husband—my king, my beautiful—runs all of it.

But not alone.

Not anymore.

That's something he remembers from old Seph's life... nothing much. No responsibility, no chores, no work. Lounging and laughing, rich clothes and fancy couches.

I want to help.

And I want to be partners with him.

"Have you ever taken a man into your mouth?"

Hades looks offended. "Please, only a million times."

He scoots back and lowers himself, opening over Seph's cock. Despite his wandering thoughts, Seph discovers he's more connected physically to his body than he realized. His head goes back. He drops against the headboard. And one of his legs bends, spreading himself wide.

There is no hesitation or lack of skill as the god's platinum head bobs over him, sucking hotly. And when Hades glances up at him, the look is sly and satisfied.

I'll get him.

He's not getting away with this.

"I know what I used to call you," Seph says, squirming because he's very close. Did the old him ever feel like this?

He needs more of Hades' mouth slurping and sucking, hollowing his cheeks and looking up at him deliciously—or he's going to die.

So he bites his tongue. Until at last the dark god is drinking him, directly, as Seph finishes in his tight throat. He swallows it all.

So greedy.

"Bunny," he says with a satisfied sigh.

The god's head lifts with a popping wet noise, saliva dripping from his tongue.

"Don't you dare. That's a misappropriated memory anyway, my stallion."

Ah. Stallion. That's what it was. Seph had the memory all mixed up.

"You must have a cute nickname you're not telling me."

"*Husband* and *my king* are suitable nicknames."

"I kind of like *bunny*."

Hades settles in beside him, pulling Seph close. Though their words have been playful, he can tell there is worry going on behind his eyes.

"Am I too different?" There is always the possibility that Seph won't make a home here and returns to the mother he barely remembers.

"No. You're just the same. I promise. I think I should have done better. A better king would never have faced this situation. It would have been prevented."

Seph scoots down and rests his head on the same pillow as Hades. He's falling asleep fast, and his eyes are closing as he says, "Maybe you shouldn't have to do everything alone."

Forty-Two

For two days Seph spends his time entirely in bed, sometimes talking to Hades with a tired smile and sometimes just resting in silence with his eyes half-closed, replaying fragmented bits of memory in his mind, but he doesn't like to do this. When he hears the whispers and imagines vague images and sensations, he always has a deep feeling that something is wrong. Something is missing. Something is wrong with *him*.

And there's always the feeling that he's not quite as he should be.

But he discovers with Hades that just talking to him can fix this unease. For instance, he learns that Hades was in a great war, the scar on his shoulder came from a Titan (a very old god), and Hades describes the battle to him, miming small actions with his fists stacked atop each other like he's holding a sword.

This feels new. There is no ghost associated with his story. And the more new, unechoed memories he creates, the more comfortable he becomes.

And as he learns about Hades, his husband who he finds out he never knew very well due to their nonexistent courtship and young marriage, he admires the mantle Hades takes upon himself as the dark king. He is the ruler of all that will ever be in the end, a time very far away.

Seph wasn't entirely sure what his old self was up to. According to Verah, he spent a lot of time just wandering around the palace or asking questions about things. When he asks Hades about himself, he mostly gets flattering descriptions of his body or personality.

Seph can't remember him. Who he was. Who he wanted to be.

But he remembers the last thought he had on the day when he woke up broken like this, and he decides that he wants to be Hades' husband. Not just his consort and companion, but also a king. He wants to have the burden that Hades has taken upon himself, and once this is decided, on the fifth day, the sixth and seventh days are not so sleepy, aching, and listless.

Seph wakes up on the eighth day alone, which is not the usual circumstance. If Hades leaves, he is always within shouting distance, and today he has a metallic taste on his tongue, like a coin. It is the listening spell he has placed on Seph once before.

"I am awake but not needing anything at this particular moment," he says aloud to an empty room. And then the taste fades. Hades is not all-powerful, nor omniscient, and the complicated spell only lasts for one phrase.

Then he flips the blankets off of him, revealing legs that have felt bony and weak the last several days. But Seph remembers them being strong, and he has suspected, though Hades insists on taking his arm and even levitating him a little bit for every trip to the latrine, that he is strong enough to start looking after himself for the most basic things.

Being a king is exciting! And the first thing he has to do is start learning about his subjects and exploring the palace.

Maybe that is why I was asking so many questions. Maybe this is who I have been all along, and I'm no different now, even though my mind feels split apart.

Styx said I would find myself again.

"Oof." His first attempt to leave the bed has him technically standing for a few moments, and then he collapses onto the end table, clutching dearly for support, and then wobbling for balance only to fall onto the bed.

It is not the great independent step he was hoping for.

Then he hears a scratch on the door and a whine behind it.

Usually the door is open and the chained dog is allowed to peer in. Hades shut it when he left, and he has warned Seph that Cerberus is not initially a friendly dog. He explained that Cerberus was there to guard the door only, and that an introduction might come later.

Well, that introduction never happened to the old Seph. Cerberus is new. The old Seph never even saw him face-to-face according to Hades. And as a measure of his own healing and achieving mobility, Seph decides to open the door. A dog on a short chain is easy to run from if necessary.

He winces as he gets his feet under him again. Now he moves like a toddler just learning to walk, clinging to the bed all the way around, grabbing the bedposts with both hands and then reaching far across the room for the door.

The extra steps required to reach his goal are a painful obstacle, but Seph gets a floaty feeling in his limbs, almost like Hades is levitating him again.

Hades explained that there's nothing wrong with Seph's magic. He isn't technically a weak god. There is merely something switched off inside, a connection that lets him control what he does, so that usually his magic is just sitting there doing nothing. Only sometimes, in a way that is unfelt, will Seph be able to do anything godlike. Hades explained it as being deaf for a human but sometimes able to hear a faint melody.

With his arms wide in case the melody stops playing, Seph toddles to the door and falls against it, catching himself with his hands.

"Whew."

It must be stupid to take pride in such a meager little effort, but Seph can't actually remember walking, which is a weird concept to him. Oh, he has a lot of memories about standing places, or moving around, or talking to people. But he doesn't actually remember the physical act of walking—of picking each foot up and placing it one step at a time.

He also can't remember, specifically, opening any doors. So this feels new to him. He takes the handle and pulls.

Sudden, furious barking has him slam the door shut, rethinking the logic of this endeavor, and he waits to hear the sliding claws of an angry beast on the other side. There's the metallic slide and clink of a chain on the floor, trailing then snapping tight. And then the growl of the dog itself, which rumbles lowly and then shouts some horrible, ego-stripping insults in dog language (probably).

Seph chuckles softly to himself, thinking that he's had enough damage done to the ego area. And healing from it hasn't been pleasant at all. Half the time he isn't sure if the world is real unless Hades is around. The other half he *knows* Seph doesn't exist. It's someone else's life he remembers.

Then he hears a woman's voice on the other side of the door. She speaks sharply to the dog, but she has a deep, smooth voice — one that matches his mother's!

Seph opens the door again, a few inches at first, and he peeks out. The woman stands out of view, speaking praise to the dog. Cerberus' big black tail thumps happily on the floor, and Seph sees a giant bangle held in the woman's hand. That is, until Seph opens the door wider, sneaking a foot out cautiously while holding on to the doorframe, and the beast whips his head around, erupting with fury again.

"Down, dog!" shouts the woman, and the voice is all wrong. Immediately Seph knows he was mistaken—his mother is not here. He's disappointed, and he doesn't know why.

The woman raises a coiled rope in her hand, and the dog falls silent at once. She didn't have to use it. He whines and his tail curls limply on the floor, his butt going down. He scoots closer to the woman with his ears back, hunched in submission. Seph blinks to see the three heads of the beast acting in unison, exactly as he remembered, exactly as Hades described. And he does not feel so much like an 'other' in this world.

It's as if he's floating sometimes, and Hades or a memory of this place will weigh him down.

For the women, however, there is no such familiarity. Seph examines her closely, but he can't find her in any of the stories.

She pets the dog with both hands, attention equally given, and says to Seph, "Hello, master. I am Hecate, your loyal servant." Then she regards the dog. "And this monstrosity is Cerberus, your husband's hellhound. He has no love for strangers, I'm afraid, but he's a slobbery, adorable goof for his masters. Come. Approach slowly with your hand low, and I will introduce you."

Her clothing is unusual. Her gown is shimmery, flowing and loose—but also, somehow, skintight. It clings to her so well he can see the indent of her navel, and though the pattern of the gown is a vivid red and gold, his initial impression is that she's bare naked. He can see every detail of her nipples through the thin material, though it is not technically see-through.

Around her waist is a golden snake belt that looks very expensive. And snakes seem to be her favorite animal. She has them on her wrists and dangling from her ears as well.

"You can trust me, master. I am your appointed bodyguard. Hades found me after your injury. And besides being unable to refuse the Underworld King—as long as I wish to remain in his lands I have to accept his rule—I have my own motivation to serve as your handmaiden. Protecting you is a great honor... *and* should find me many battles. It has become so boring helping my sisters train dogs to guard Hades' gate."

"Oh." Seph thinks hard. He doesn't have all the pieces of his most recent memories, but he's certain that trusting someone without Hades here is what caused the damage in the first place.

"Where's my husband?" he asks, wishing he had never stepped out of the door. He is too weak to fight off a goddess, especially one with a whip, and he knows enough of himself to remember that he never would've been a match for her.

I need Hades here. Or I'm not safe.

"On a hunt, my king. He is looking for that wicked nymph who tried to send you into Tartarus, making sure the rat is truly gone. I would've liked to go, but Hades was insistent on doing it alone. I guess he finds it to be a personal matter. But he left his two best enforcers—me and Cerberus—to look after you." She takes one of the dog's faces like she's pinching the cheeks of a favorite child. "Isn't that right, big smelly boy? Who smells like the barn, huh? Who's a big jealous boy?"

She might be entertaining two of the heads, but one of them looks back and lets out a bellowing bark.

"Hey. Down." She straightens up, and with the hand holding the whip, she points to the floor. The dog whines and immediately lies down, all the way to his stomach. His ears press flatly against his head, and he has a wrongfully chided look.

"I'm sorry, my king. He uses his nose to determine who fits or not. Troublemakers and trespassers are bound to have the smell of arousal—fear probably, or simply excitement. Your emotions are telling his instincts to execute you. It's what he's trained for. But he is a good dog. Come."

She reaches for Seph like grabbing for a friend. Seph can't help but notice that every part of her is delicate and beautiful, including the polished nails on her hand. Beauty and a friendly tone mean nothing though, and Seph moves back.

"No, I'm going to wait for Hades—"

And as he speaks, the door to the solarium opens. The very name he spoke walks through the door as if Seph summoned him.

He's dressed like the night, and for a moment Seph has the sensation that he's huddled on his knees in some kind of a carriage, Hades looking down on him with an impassive frown. His eyes were cold.

But that passes as the real god before him takes off his crown, his expression concerned.

"How are you out of bed? Has something happened? Hecate, you didn't let Cerberus wake him up, did you?"

"Mother hen," she says in a snide manner. Then, "Your timing is rather perfect. You haven't put a watchful spell on him, have you?"

"Of course I have. And he knows it."

Hades crosses to him at once, cool fingers inspecting Seph's cheeks, and his eyes are full of worry and love.

Everything about the old Seph just feels so different.

"Why are you out of bed? Did something frighten you?"

"*Cluck, cluck*," says Hecate behind them. Then she holds the coiled whip over Cerberus' three heads. "Stay." She moves toward them, her dress hugging every line and glinting as if her body is naked and wet.

She points the whip at Hades as if she is commanding another dog.

"Do you consent to this man's curse, master? Or do you wish for me to punish him?"

She smiles twistedly, like she's trying to hold back a huge grin.

Hades stares at her a moment, his frown deepening, then he turns Seph toward the room.

"Ignore her. It's too soon for you to be out of bed. Come on. I'll get you some soup."

"I don't want to be in bed anymore."

"Ha! You have heard my master's wish, and if you do not yield to his command, I shall have to guard him with my life! What will it be, Hades, my king? Will you let him out of bed, mother hen? Or will I draw my blade?"

She poses in a low fighter stance, one hand near her belt, and now Seph notices the large curved dagger sheathed there.

Hades does not sound the least bit intimidated.

"Hecate, the purpose of your position is not to annoy me."

"My position was made abundantly clear. You unclipped my leash and tethered it to another. You are not my master anymore, Hades. I serve the new king now."

Forty-Three

Seph does not want to return to bed. While Hades has the best intentions, Seph feels like it's time to start *something*—something about finding his life and who he really is. The old Seph is gone, and all that remains is an empty, confused shell. He feels like if he can start this journey, the separation in his mind and personality will heal.

And so he shakes his head and says, "I want to stay out of the bedroom. I'm tired of it in there... Maybe I can eat in the dining hall?"

"Why do you ask him?" Hecate says in a threatening manner, but when Hades looks at her she eases out of her fighting stance and lowers the whip. She tucks it into her belt by the dagger and clasps her hands peacefully in front of her. By her unassuming but generally satisfied expression, Seph guesses that Hecate is a bit of a prankster, and her threat to duel with Hades is only a joke.

He also wonders what kind of expression she saw in Hades' eyes, because Seph only sees a bit of tiredness and frustration, but overall, overwhelming love.

"Alright, my king," he says, and Seph is surprised that it's that easy. He half expected Hades to scold him and take his arm and steer him back to the bed. But that seems to be a misattributed story in his mind, one that belongs to someone else.

But something that happened to him supposedly in another lifetime. Seph feels that it was quite common.

But not here though.

"What about a bit of soup in the solarium? I'll have the tables and chairs brought in. Sometimes I eat there for a special occasion, and the subjects love it. We can have a small lunch, and the ceiling is glass, so you will not feel so boxed in"

"That sounds perfect."

Then Seph spends some time sitting on a bench in the solarium, side by side with Hades, watching the servants make preparations.

They are silent and extra careful to avoid unnecessary clatter and furniture scrapes as they bring the equipment in. Some planters and benches are moved out, giving them a wide area beside Cerberus' likeness, the statue dog in the fountain.

Only one person here will occasionally speak too loudly and too sharply—and he will be spoken to softly and quickly, reminded to be quiet again by his doting mother. Styx is joining them for lunch (Seph finds out she's staying in the palace for now), and she looks after a little one named Adonis.

"His mother was turned into a tree," Hades whispers, his knees touching Seph's, and they lean into each other like courting lovers. Seph likes the normal, quiet romance of this.

"She was said to be more beautiful than Aphrodite—and I saw her once; it wasn't true. But Eros, Aphrodite's foolish son, took it upon himself to defend his mother's honor. Myrrha's reputation spread too far and was too boisterous. He cursed her to fall in love with her father, and when the spell wore off, the father set out to murder his daughter for what they'd done."

Seph listens, frowning, as he watches Hecate take the hand of the boy. She produces spinning tops for them both, and then the boy sits manneredly beside her, both of them spinning the toys as perfectly as possible on the ledge of the fountain. The young boy blows at the base, trying to guide the spin and save the toy from the water.

"Myrrha accepted her father's sentence, but wished life for her son. Aphrodite brought him in a box to me, for the magic in place at his conception made the child unusually beautiful. She feared another Narcissus if he was left to be raised by mortals."

"How can Eros get away with that? Why isn't he in Tartarus?"

Hades' lips quirk on one side. "And why isn't Minthe there as well? Who can say."

Seph ponders an answer, but he has no logic to argue with, only the feelings he felt. He was certain Hades was a murderer, and he felt such terror for the pit that he didn't wish it on *anyone*.

Hades' expression fades, and he gives him a real answer without requiring Seph to speak.

"We make mistakes in life. Eros is still young. His mother caught him and tried to teach him better, but she could not undo all the damage he had done. To fix a mistake like that requires a massive amount of effort. She would have had to change the memories of everyone who had heard of the father and daughter's terrible act.

And magic done imperfectly can have terrible, permanent consequences. It is easier to let the mistake live, learn from the consequences, and move on.

"Eros was distraught after what he'd done. He was not raised with the humans as you were. He thought Myrrha would be horribly embarrassed, perhaps even disgusted with what she'd done. He didn't realize all of humanity would hold her accountable for a crime punished by death.

"He is a better person now. Though he is known for his youthfulness and not his discerning wisdom." Hades smiles at him. "He is spoiled, and he is not you, my king."

The brief hate Seph feels for Eros mildly disappears, equally weighted by understanding. Though, he is conflicted about this mercy, seeing the consequences of a god's curse before him. A boy without his real mother. And the gods do not regard her death in the same manner they would one of their own.

Persephone, why don't you get to know one of your nice cousins? Mortals die like that, you know. She snapped her fingers. She wore green bracelets and golden rings that day. *They are the only companions your age who will stay your age. So why don't you try getting along?*

"Tell me about Hecate," Seph says, looking at her. She has gold jewelry, though not golden rings on this particular day. Something about the adornments and how she secures her hair with glittering pins reminds him of the mother he's never met.

"She is your handmaiden. And your guard. And anything else you want her to be—besides your lover, of course." Hades' hand closes briefly. "I won't allow that. But otherwise, I have appointed her to be your enforcer."

"What does that mean?"

The meal arrives, and Hades stands instead, helping Seph up. Thanks to a little help from Hades or himself (he can't tell which), his body is light enough that he doesn't have to hobble like an old man, though his balance is unsure on his own. The couches are perpendicular with the heads put on the same end for private conversation. Everyone else eats a ways away from them, and there are several souls here, quietly dining as a gesture of support from the public.

Adonis cannot keep still, and Styx's patient tone does not seem to be the antidote. Hecate, fortunately, puts the small boy on her lap, and his boisterous voice is not heard over everyone else again.

There is chatter and pleasant laughs, but the meal is far quieter than the wedding reception Seph remembers.

Hades pours him a drink. They have both taken to it heavily in the past week, and Seph enjoys when his mind can relax as well as the aches in his muscles.

"You are my mate. My lover. And my everything." Hades taps their goblets together as a toast before drinking deeply.

It is not romantically spoken with longing eyes under a moon, but more like a heavy burden. Seph smiles into his cup anyway and plans to tell Hades that he feels the same, except the dark god speaks before him.

"But I cannot be your caretaker. Not faithfully. I have turned it over in my mind several times, and though it stresses me greatly—it seems that surely the task of your protection should be mine alone—I have appointed Hecate to take that position instead."

"Thank you. I like her. I think." He does not know enough of her to say for certain.

"Hecate is not just your guard, Seph," Hades says, and then they are interrupted by a platter of sweet grapes brought by Verah. She carries it to the other diners once they've taken their fill.

"She does not report to me. She is to be the source of your power and to use her magic however you like. She'll be with you constantly, and I have made her swear an oath to be the extension of your will. Through her, you wield the power of a true god now, Seph."

He plucks food from another tray carried by little Alfric, which they both have to reach down for. Alfric wears a proud, beaming grin, and whispers to Seph before moving on, "I'm glad you're okay!"

Then when he is gone, Hades says, "She is truly yours. That is why she's being annoying. I'm not her master anymore. Unless you order her to stop, she's going to use every opportunity to irritate me. She wishes for the old days of Kronos and anarchy. But don't worry. She's bound to you unbreakably, and her oaths are better than loyalty."

Forty-Four

As the days pass, the feeling of having woken up from a dream and being unable to discern what is real and what is merely a preexisting fantasy gently fades from Seph's consciousness. As does his desire to sleep, which is unfortunate for his ailing body at first. He becomes bored and frustrated, and while Hades is generous with providing physical pleasure, release, and much desired company, the needs of the kingdom pull him away more and more.

It is a bad winter in the upperworld, he says. And it has started early, after a cool summer and a lousy crop. The weakest are always the first to go, and there's already an influx of children who have to be looked after. Hades says his newest neighborhood, which is not yet complete, might be filled by the end of winter. The swell of deaths could be *that* bad, when usually he would keep all the newest Elysium citizens near the palace.

"What is happening in the upperworld will be as bad as a plague," he says, kissing Seph's forehead goodbye one day.

And so Seph is left alone for a long time, and while Hecate offers some amusing company and Cerberus will occasionally nuzzle his hand nowadays, Seph cannot abide being so useless. And his mind, left alone, only tries to sort the things that are fragmented and not in order—all those little broken pieces of a past life.

He orders the servants to bring scrolls, and soon it is common to see his bed covered in reading material. Fiction and memoirs at first. They are great for learning about the world's many cultures. And then he starts seeking more practical documents. The memoirs of kings. The writings of government, laws, and science.

He decides that to be a king alongside Hades, he has to educate himself. And while he recovers many memories of his life, an education does not return to him. Mostly, it seems that he was outside in the sun, surrounded by animals and friendly men, and helping in some task required of a farm. Or hunting.

"You will live forever. There is no need to learn it all now," Hades tells him one night, when he has a hand trailing up Seph's thigh, and Seph only has a few more turns of the scroll to finish his current text.

"Oh? Did you learn to be a king without reading?"

Hades frowns (pouts more like) because he knows he has to wait. "Well, I didn't read it all in one night."

Seph reaches under the covers and removes Hades' hand from his cock before he can wake it up too much, and goes back to reading with a smirk. A second attempt, however, and a nibble of his ear are deterred with a harsh tone.

"You will be patient, bunny, or you will get nothing."

The nickname always causes an enraged squint, and from his nose, the slightest wrinkle and twitch as his nostrils flare and he exhales a short breath. Watching his husband for minute changes in expression has become an art form. And Hades does rather look like a bunny after he's been called one. Or a bull, which would be more flattering, but *bunny* suits his purposes fine.

"That is a misappropriated memory. You do not call me that. And you should never call me that. I have told you—"

"That I used to have a rabbit, yes," Seph says, unwinding the scroll to reveal another block of text. He prefers the codices for reading, finding it easier to access each page of information, but there are not very many of them. "But who's to say you aren't lying? Who's to say you aren't the delicate bunny I cherished, and you're playing a trick?"

Hades huffs and his hands mind their own business atop the covers. Then he says, "You really don't remember Hibus? Still? Are you sure?"

"I know the name because you told it to me," Seph answers, and this is true. He has tried to picture a rabbit pet several times, white and fluffy like Hades says, but he has not had any success. "I do remember arguing with my mother about a rabbit though, I think."

He pauses, looking up.

"No. No, it was a cat. Something about a cat, and I was screaming, angry. I wonder what his name was..."

And so Seph's days pass in comfort and mental focus. His daily time with Hades continues to decrease, until Hades wakes him up with a kiss every night—and quickly sees to his needs—only to be gone in the morning before the lamp fires are lit.

"The neighborhood is full," Hades says one night, curled against him in the dark. "I never imagined I could fill one so quickly. This is worse than any plague I've ever seen."

"What makes it so bad?" Seph asks, whispering against his ear. "Why is this year so different?"

"It is winter all over the world. Usually there is an alternating balance. Winter in one place and summer in another. And then rotating again, so that the cold places are not cold too long. The plants have time to grow and the animals have time to raise their young. But now there are villages disappearing from the north places on the Earth. It is cold all over. Many creatures are starving, not just humans. And for the side of the Earth opposite Greece, spring never came."

"So you will speak to Zeus then? He will find—the god—" For a moment he wanted to say *my mother*, but his tongue tripped. "He will find her and make sure she follows the rules. That's what a king does."

"Yes. He's supposed to. I don't know why he hasn't."

"Sleep then, my king," Seph answers. "It is Zeus's worry to stop all this death. We will do as we're supposed to on our end."

And so it is for another two months.

Seph begins to walk without a god's help making him lighter, and while he finds that far travel, even in Hades' chariot, will quickly exhaust him, he's relieved and happy to spend his days in other parts of the palace. Mainly the stables, where he relearns to ride a horse and discovers that he can do so with ease. And then the library, which he pursues for both fiction and education, inviting the souls who wrote the books to be his tutors and storytellers.

Sefkh is not one of the scholars, but he is one of the oldest souls most readily available on a daily basis, and Seph invites him to translate scrolls written in Egyptian.

"There are two spiritual elements," he says, sitting with Seph at a table in the library, several Egyptian scrolls sprawled around them. "The *ka* and the *ba*. I am the *ba*—the soul. The *ka* does not really exist, but if it did, it would be like a physical body left in the living world that I depend upon in this place. We believe that we need to nourish the *ka* even long after our death, so we give gold and bread to tombs, to take care of our dead. Sometimes we speak to them as well, at the tomb. We might ask questions or seek a blessing."

Quietly, his thumb running over the papyrus, he adds, "It is all wrong, of course."

"Most cultures get some of it right. I think the Greeks guessed best simply because that is the spot on Earth Zeus chose to make his home. They had to get some things right."

Egyptian writing is complicated, but the many animal symbols seem to speak to Sefkh as clearly as the Greek does to him.

"But I am curious... So many human cultures present gifts to the deceased. Why do you think this is? Yours is particularly strict about it."

"We recognize that there is a journey, I think. So we offer provisions. Also..."

He considers a moment, touching his lip. Sefkh is handsome and young, appearing as an older teen, but his words often remind Seph he is speaking to someone much older than himself.

"Also, I think there is a pointlessness to life that we all feel while we're living it. We wonder about it sometimes, but not too closely. Because it's dangerous. And that is how the achievements we make as humans simply end. They are picked up by others of course, but for us, the progress is over. And humans desire progress more than anything. It's why most can't make it into this place."

He spreads his hands on the table, looking between his thumbs like he's gazing at a small picture projected by his mind.

"I lived a long time when I was alive. Over ninety! Almost no human, not even the pharaohs, can say that. But I was not rich. I was just lucky. I saw many of my sons die of old age before I did. And I think living so long helped me. It made me realize the pointlessness of money and achievements. That is how I'm here. But for someone who dies so young, they do not get to see it. And so it is important to them that they take their accomplishments with them. Especially their gold. When they get here, they want to keep working."

Then he shrugs. "Poor souls."

"Hm." Seph makes no comment because he has come to terms with Tartarus and what it means. He is also not afraid of it anymore. After all, he was mostly destroyed and reborn again. Nowadays he feels like a new person, but the *right* person. He's who he's supposed to be. And so he knows that souls who go into Tartarus come out okay again. And they are just as lively and loving as they were, glad to continue and to tackle new agendas.

The same way that Seph now is determined to be a rightful and wise king, whereas the old Seph was rather aimless.

"I think humans will grow old collectively," he says, after pondering his response for a moment. Sefkh is his subject and his *son*, a mindset he borrows from Hades. It is his job to guide him, though he is currently the novice learning from his son right now. "You are, in fact, one god split into many separate beings. There is no end to you, and you will all live and grow wise as one. Humans always do best when they borrow from each other."

And then he hears, from the level below, Hecate's bossy voice say, "My master has not requested your presence, and you're interrupting his studies. Be gone. Or fight me, rule breaker."

Seph grins as he hears Hades say, "Every time, Hecate? You are not tired of this game yet?"

"I think it is you who are tired! And cowardly."

"Go on," Seph tells Sefkh, giving him a nudge. "I guess we are done here. Thank you for spending time with me today."

"Of course, pharaoh." He wears the slightest smile as he bows. Besides Alfric, none of the souls Hades keeps close to serve him tend to be the personable type. So this new title must be a sign of friendship, and Seph briefly mimics the bow back (a playful attempt, for he is a king), and Sefkh leaves via one of the servants' passages here. There is a small door tucked in the corner between shelves.

"Goodbye," Seph says to him, and he nods before he disappears. And then Seph goes to the balcony to call below, "Hecate, let him pass. As long as he promises not to annoy me, he is fine."

Hades shoots him an unhappy look from below, and knocks Hecate's dagger away from his throat with an unaided hand. Seph leans against the railing, waiting for his husband to climb the many stairs up to him. And though he pretends to be nonchalant about it, he is always eager for Hades when there is a moment they can be alone. They do not come often anymore.

"How are you?" he asks first, before Hades has reached him, because it helps him determine his expectations. Hades might have the endless stamina of a god, and he never refuses Seph physically, but Seph would like his heart to be in it as well.

"Not well," he answers, and Seph wishes they would grab each other and move toward the bookcases instead. But this will not be that day.

"What is it this time?"

He draws Hades to lean into him instead. There is a tired dullness to Hades' eyes that Seph doesn't like, and secretly he makes plans to get out of the palace. As more and more of the upperworld's humans die, the need for Seph to help grows greater. Seph is trying but his recovery is too slow.

After a small silence and sigh, Hades confesses, "Perhaps I

should not tell you. It will only make you hate me."

"No. That is precisely why you should tell me. And I will not hate you. I am your mate, Hades, my husband."

Perhaps they should be over these endearments by now. Their marriage is not so new anymore. But Seph wishes to remind him that he's not alone forever, even if he has to do all the work for right now.

Hades seems shorter than he usually is. Smaller. He curls against Seph's chest and closes his eyes before he speaks.

"I am thinking of letting the good ones go to Tartarus. I cannot make room for them all. There is plenty of space, of course, but I have never had so many new children. How can I trust my souls to keep them safe when it usually requires several to one? They are adults—most of them—so they think for themselves and decide to run away. Or they don't acclimate right and they try to pursue past wars and old enemies. There was a hunt today. And there will be another tomorrow. And another, and another. They do not stay because they are not looked after."

The hunts. Seph knows what must be done. He has to share the burden and carry his weight. Perhaps even while he relies on a crutch sometimes, and he crawls into bed with his knees hurting. But this is Hades' plea, and he has to answer.

"I will do the hunts."

For a moment Seph is extra aware of his body, every limb placement, and his posture and the careful slack in his features.

Sure enough, Hades lifts his head and there's a critical gleam in his eye.

"You? You can't..." He doesn't finish his sentence. He has a reluctant frown as his eyes travel slowly downward, and Seph knows that while Hades may be thinking about his knees, which sometimes give out on him, and he's definitely eyeing the cane Seph left propped against the table where he was studying...

He needs the help.

Hades sighs. He's definitely considering it.

So Seph presses.

"I'll be riding. There won't be much for me to do, honestly, except oversee everything. Cerberus will do the tracking and the punishing. Hecate will command the dog and help me secure the prisoners to my horse. Then it's just a matter of bringing them in."

Hades is quiet, looking away from Seph, at the window far away.

"I can ride a horse fine. Hades, let me help."

His lips press together briefly. "I've never had help."

"I know. But I've just got here. You had to assume I'd be fit for something useful eventually."

"No. I just expected you to..." He shrugs.

"Be your stallion? Be your pretty bed thing?" Seph grabs Hades' waist and brings them together again. He kisses Hades. His husband's mouth barely moves as his thoughts seem far way and complicated.

"I can be," Seph says, thinking it over. "I'm not *un*happy being your bed thing. But I think..."

What he wants to say may come across as an insult. Seph cups the back of Hades' head. He needs his husband's attention for this, and his eyes seem so far away.

"I think you don't like to let people help. But just think of me as another one of your processes. You have the judges, the ferryman, and the giants, don't you? You don't expect yourself to crank the gears of Tartarus all day long."

Hades catches his hand and holds it. As if he'd like to remove his caress. But his thumb brushes against the back of Seph's hand instead.

"You've never hunted. Not like this."

And a memory comes back to Seph. Murky and dim, and the voice feels very faint.

Seph, a boar would be lovely at the feast, don't you think? And you haven't hunted for the table in months. Are you still depressed over that boy—what's his name? He hears her fingers snap several times. *Fen-something...*

The memory might as well be a phantom speaking to him now out of thin air. Seph has no attachment to what was said, and he can't remember his reply.

"I'm not the same as I was when you brought me here, Hades. I promise—I can hunt. Besides, nothing truly dies here that hasn't already passed on. I think it will be easy. It'll let me get away from these books. And I can finally start to care for *our* people, the way a king should."

Hades sighs again. He eyes Seph unhappily. But at last, tiredly, he says, "Alright."

Forty-Five

Hades stands outside in a barren land, the nearby wilderness presently being cleared of trees, and he has several scrolls spread out across a wide table. He draws with blue ink over red lines, now and then following the guidance of a leather strap marked with measurements. He brushes the paper quickly sometimes, or blows away the dust. The dye they use is like chalk and requires moisture. He dabs the end of a split reed against a soaked rag and then grinds the stalk into a little ink pot often. Then he resumes drawing.

He mutters about the ugliness of the initial plans while his gaze roams for ways to improve it. For the foreseeable future, his concern is only to build the most magnificent neighborhoods as efficiently as possible, and receiving first drafts such as these is an unacceptable setback.

The rough drafts his architects are giving him cover a wide area and certainly provide enough homes, but they are lacking uniqueness and a personal touch. His architects have been scolded, and they wait nearby with large rolled-up papers in their hands, their eyes downcast with shame. No one is eager to hand over what they've drawn and have him go over it in blue ink.

They will have to copy his revisions on new papers in the red pencil again, and he will have to review them for final additions in blue again. Their lack of effort has extended the process, and Hades lets his displeasure be known with a permanent scowl as he concentrates, adding measurements carefully in his head. His leather strap nearly draws the lines itself for how dirty it is.

Periphetes, who watches him go over his work, ignoring the red lines and drawing a completely new schematic, crosses his arms over his belly and looks put out, like he was wrongfully scolded.

He speaks quietly at first, but with growing assurance. He does not want to disrespect Hades, but he feels strongly that he is right.

"Little gardens and fountains do not make the new ones feel less homeless. We can deconstruct and add later. What they really need are personal rooms. They are plain boxes, as you said, but they can add their own furniture. And then when the famine and plague have slowed down, we can revise the neighborhoods up to your standards. We're all dead down here. We have nothing but time."

The other architects eye him with appreciation and wait for Hades' response.

Hades finishes his calculation first. To make this neighborhood more interesting, he's constructing several open prisms. Apartments make up the outer shell, and connecting them are decorated walkways over a massive garden. He wants a multileveled courtyard, trees growing all the way to the top and out of the homes. The community can mingle daily amongst seating areas, and the fountains for water supply are never too far from any home.

It's an entirely unique neighborhood he had an idea for a long time ago. It has been sitting in the back of his thoughts, and he did not know he would need it so soon. This is one of his more complicated projects, and now is not the time for a rushed miscalculation. The architects who should have helped him draw his visions came back with their own functional but bare designs.

"Do you think people look forward to sitting around in boxes when they reach the afterlife?" he asks when he can. "And do you think I am a king of dissatisfied subjects? That I am happy with achieving the most meager housing I can provide?"

"No, but it is only temporary."

This architect is old, though he looks young, and he's earned Hades' respect. So Hades patiently explains to him, "In life there is always the question of what will be. What will I become? What will I see and do? Who will I marry? But in the afterlife, all has been achieved. And all that *everything* will be... already is. They cannot sit in blank boxes, not for very long, before they start to wonder, 'Why am I even here?'"

"Yes, but it will not be for very long."

A breeze makes the waiting architects turn their heads. Hades glances to the sky and immediately knows who it is. He finishes his conversation.

"The plague will not let up. Not soon. Demeter is not a fighter, but she is a goddamn mountain. It will take Zeus some time to figure out how to move her." Without pausing, he addresses the god who has just arrived. His nephew. Hermes. "And what is the outlook in that regard?"

Hermes usually blinds him with his smile, which always makes him look a bit like a pleased fox. His teeth aren't showing today, though he manages a smirk and tosses Hades an apple. It is hefty, Hades notices as he catches it. Food from the upperworld always feels heavy compared to what grows down here.

"She smashed him right flat into a crater!" Hermes says, propping himself on the table opposite the side of Hades, careful not to disturb the documents while also leaning across it, pretending to have a disregard for Hades' important work. His elbow lands dangerously close to the wine goblet. Though he seems brash and clumsy, without a care, Hermes is known for elegance in physical feats and social tact as well. Nothing he does with his body or with the words he speaks is ever unintentional.

"Oh, you should have seen it! Lots of gods were lurking nearby, ready to see Zeus put the angry goddess in her place. But you called it right, uncle—she sits like a mountain, just weeping. A little bit of thunderstorms and zaps around her head aren't even noticed. She's gone far away from the mortals, where it's icy and cold and she can't hurt anything—well, *everywhere* is icy and cold now, but you know what I mean."

He's older than Seph by a few lifetimes at least, but from an ancient god's perspective, they might as well be twins. He is Seph's half brother, and Hermes inherited the same wavy hair, the same smile and physique. Though, none of the sensitivity and vulnerability that drew him to Seph.

"Stole that off of my mother's table, I did," he points to Hades' apple. "Might be one of the last ones ever in the upperworld. The apple trees are dormant for now, but in a couple more years, they might not exist."

Nothing is said for a moment. Hades turns the apple in his fingers and wonders why his nephew would bring him this. They have a working relationship, but they are not necessarily friends. Hades doesn't have any of those.

"Eat it," Hermes prompts him, and then turns the scroll on the table more towards himself, righting the image for a better look. "This is indecipherable."

"There are many levels designed on one sheet."

"And underneath it?" He follows some of the red lines with his fingers. "These are the streets, I see." He glances at said streets being laid with cobblestone nearby. "This is all a mess, isn't it? You have a map of the city underneath the drawing of your house plans?

And what is all this?"

"Bad ideas."

Periphetes shifts his posture and clasps both hands tightly in front of him.

Hades slides the paper back from his nephew so he can roll it up from the end and tie it with a ribbon. "The red lines aren't to be considered, and the blue drawings are to be improved." He hands the scroll to the waiting architect, who accepts it with a displeased expression but does not complain.

Hades waves his hand once, and all the architects turn around and leave. They will wait in the vicinity, understanding that they are not welcome company while he speaks with his nephew. And Hades sinks into the plush chair parked for him at the table, a sigh escaping him, his whole body stretching and slouching. He shuts his eyes a moment, wishing he could drift away.

Then he opens them and reaches for his wine goblet.

But it's already been snatched up by his lounging nephew, and his head goes back as he tilts the cup all the way up.

Hades glares. He doesn't have another pitcher nearby, because more than one these days makes him too tired.

Hermes smiles when he's done, wiping his mouth with an *Ah* and smacking his lips. Then he looks at the apple still on the table.

Hades picks it up and bites into it, the chewing giving his teeth and tongue something to do while his mind launches into an angry, imaginary explosion, summoning his scepter to frighten the stupid brat out of his kingdom.

But Hermes is one of the few relatives he keeps in contact with nowadays. And he is not usually so annoying.

"You have spoken to your father, I take it? And maybe helped put some ideas in his head? There must be some plan to bring Demeter in line. All the gods are watching, you know."

"Yes, well, for now he's playing up the delay as sympathy for my aunt. 'Poor Demeter,' and 'How could Hades do this.' You know, he's almost turned the whole marriage thing around. Of course, too many gods know the truth for him to outright lie. But when he talks about the marriage, it's like you snatched my young cousin up on his fourteenth birthday. Barely an acceptable age."

Hades snorts. Seph is young, but he isn't *that* young. His mother has raised him to be naïve, but twenty-six is considered middle-aged by human standards.

The apple is sweet and lustrous, and his stomach growls as it goes down. He was hungrier than he thought, so consumed with fixing the architects' mistakes that he didn't notice the needs of his physical body... which has been a bit weak and skinnier lately. He can sustain himself on the underworld foods just fine, but he would do better with more of the real stuff.

Hermes says, "About that extra task you set me upon..."

"Yes, what about it?"

Hermes sits up straight, crossing his ankles. He's good to look at, always. The sight of his short chiton pooled around the side of his buttocks and his muscled thighs sat heavily upon the table (like a good, fat roast) is always appreciated. But there's no hunger for the young man anymore, which Hades always ignored. Now there is only the awareness of physical beauty. Like all of Zeus's sons, Hermes is gorgeous.

He is also a thief and a charming charlatan when he wants to be.

He tilts his head. "Well... it's not that important, is it? I mean, the whole world is going up in flames—or ice, as it were. So who the heck cares about one little—"

"I care. And I've already explained why. Have you found it?"

"No. And forgive my rudeness—no, never mind, don't. Just hear me out—" he raises his hands like a man proclaiming he's innocent. "Are you smitten?"

"What?"

Hermes has never respected boundaries or formalities, but he has never been rude.

"Well, you have to see this from my perspective! Here I am on a dying Earth, completely frozen, and I'm running around as fast as I can—you have to understand, the job isn't easy. I go around the Earth in a few seconds, sure, but it's not like the lost souls are raising flags for me to find. All these new ones don't even weep when they go. They just kind of wander around moaning, all ghostlike—appropriate, I know. And then you come along—"

Hermes is also a bit of a rambler, yet another difference between him and Seph, and Hades has never second-guessed his decision to not ask for Hermes' hand in marriage. He was a consideration when Seph was nearly born.

What a disaster that would've been...

Hades interrupts him with, "It is one little pebble in a sea of pebbles. I get it. But the pet was a family member, and Seph's home here is forever. He should be able to bring one thing that makes him happy."

"But it is just a rabbit."

"It became more than a rabbit when it was adopted and named by a son of Zeus, the King of Mount Olympus. Unless you can think of some other rabbit who has managed that?"

"It is not really the rabbit that should get complimented for—"

"Do you have it or not? Did you fail the task? Or was the rabbit simply not there to find?"

Hades takes a larger bite from the apple. It crunches deliciously and he has to wipe juice from the corner of his mouth.

Hermes watches him for a moment and seems to almost look sad.

"Delicious, isn't it?" he asks, and his tone is subdued.

He's distracting him.

"Yes, it's fine. Now what about the rabbit's soul?"

"Zeus is making it out like you've gone mad," Hermes says instead and quickly rushes on, "Oh, I didn't tell him about the whole rabbit thing, but it would have started rumors and backlash, that's for sure. He's making you out to be an evil uncle, and the lecherous type too. For now, people still remember who you are, and Zeus *did* announce the marriage to the court after all—he's trying to say you persuaded him. Soon he'll say you blackmailed him! He's just not clever enough right now to find the words."

"That's precisely why I sent you to listen to gossip, Hermes. So I don't have to deal with it."

Hermes hops off the table at last, scratching his head. His nephew is someone always moving, always laughing, and it is desirable for most to just listen to him speak. As he rambles, he takes you on a series of stories, leading you down many paths. And in a short while, though you've told him nothing, you will feel like two friends who've shared many adventures.

Hades does not have the patience for it.

"If you haven't found the rabbit, then keep looking. Or get me one that's just like it. You can find *something* amongst all the humans."

"Oh, don't blow a tit, I've got your rabbit right here." Hermes also has fun inventing his own phrases. He takes off his shoulder bag, reaches inside, and pulls out a white rabbit by its ears. It kicks twice and just hangs there, its eyes huge with fear.

Hades stands immediately, reaching across the table. It looks just like Hibus—the right size and everything! Could it be?

But Hermes does not pass it over right away.

"How was your apple?" he asks instead.

"I see." Hades collapses back into his chair. "You wish to barter."

"Not so much barter as *lecture*, dear uncle... and barter," he adds quickly, for while Hermes is clever and thieving, he has never been dishonest with Hades yet. He puts the rabbit back in the bag, knots the top, and sets it up on the table. Hades is wishing Sefkh or anyone would appear with more drink.

"Apples will cease to exist in the upperworld if they aren't allowed to come back. Humans will be gone sooner than that. I know you're busy down here, uncle, but I want you to come up top with me, so you can see how bad it really is."

"I will not. I know it is bad."

"Do you know that snow is starting to swallow entire towns? Do you know there isn't a babe to be found in the cities? The children have perished, and the adults are eating from their bones. There's not a rat in Athens either. Nor a cat or a family dog or a chicken. Humans don't have *years* left on the Earth, uncle. Months are all I give it."

"That's a bit dramatic. Some places have been spared. And humans multiply quickly. When Zeus gets Demeter under control, the calamity will pass. I admit, it's nearly the apocalypse for the Earth. But Demeter has a kind heart underneath it all, and she will come to her senses on her own if Zeus cannot throw a lightning bolt big enough."

He reaches for the rabbit to see if Hermes will stop him. His nephew pulls it closer.

"Well, I don't think Demeter is the only one being stubborn here. Do you?"

"Seph is not going back."

Can he tell how much the gift means to me?

This might only be a rabbit, but he represents everything that Seph lost.

And maybe, if he can remember this pet, he will stop calling me 'bunny'.

Hades forces his expression to remain passive, and he maintains lounging indifference as well.

"Well, maybe let me talk to him? Maybe just that? If I can bring Demeter word from her son, that he is happy and safe or whatever, then maybe that will alleviate the mother's grief enough for her to grow smaller and warm the Earth with her love."

"Tell her so. And let me know if it works."

And then give me the fucking bunny.

Not yet. Hermes is clever, but he doesn't have a lot of patience. He will reveal all the cards in his hand to flaunt a weakness if his opponent refuses to play their turn.

"Well, I haven't spent significant time with Seph, you see. So I couldn't invent any words that are his. They ought to come straight from the boy. Something so that when I speak she knows only her son could have said it. That would go straight to a mother's heart and warm it, maybe."

He says nothing more. Even though Hades picks up the reed and taps the uninked end slowly on the table, something that makes the waiting seconds seem longer than they are.

So that's it. His hand.

And Hades decides how to play his turn.

Forty-Six

Seph's horse, Demeas, leaps over a log, and he holds on tightly with his knees, his hands making fists with the reins. It is difficult to get used to how a spirit horse flies over obstacles, overshooting the distance by several feet, or how they can change speeds in an instant, even coming to a complete stop with little more than a few steps and no slowing stride.

Spirit horses have no weight, but they use the same 'muscle memories', as Taushev calls it, to maneuver their bodies.

Demeas sails far into an open meadow, and Seph uses the voice commands, "Slow. Whoah! Easy there," to let the stallion know of his intentions as he pulls back gently on the reins.

Otherwise, the horse may take his signal to stop too suddenly, and his own momentum will throw him over the saddle horn or possibly unseat him. He manages to slow down with very little turbulence for both the horse and the rider, and he pulls Demeas into a circle with the extra momentum, his eyes scanning the trees for the dog.

Cerberus had howled and barked before, the signal that he's found somebody. But now he's gone silent.

"Do you think it was a stag?" he asks as Hecate arrives, her horse trotting and coming to a smoother stop. The animal and master know each other well, having ridden together for many years, and Taushev says that's more important than any training when it comes to taming a spirit beast.

"If that dumb dog has led us to a stag again, I'll..." She never finishes exactly what she'll do, and it would probably be an empty threat anyway. Hecate is a fierce trainer who is not above using her whip, but Seph has never seen her beat an animal.

"It may have been nothing," Seph says, turning this way and that, trying to get an eye into the trees and looking for crushed grass where the dog may have passed. He does not exactly sneak through the woods. "I told you, we need a better system. We shouldn't be out here chasing down ravens and stags and moving shadows. We look like fools. And we're putting too much responsibility on a dog with no brain."

Hecate picks the direction and they proceed. Perhaps she saw something in the grass that he did not.

"Alright, but what is the plan, master? Even if you do come up with a system for a—what is it called again? A *census*... What a stupid human thing. Even if we did do that, it wouldn't change the fact that we're out here every day patrolling these woods. Who cares if we know the exact number of the population missing. Someone will tattle and tell us they're missing."

"But they're not missing every day, are they? And we don't even know when the dog actually finds something or when he's just... chasing his tail, I don't know what."

Hecate is an excellent servant, always there when he needs her, but she is not an adviser. Any kind of law or policy is viewed as an unnecessary restriction of freedom or an overreach of power by others.

She's a much better hunter than she is a diplomat. But lately, though they initially took on much work and freed up many of Hades' hours, there haven't been many souls who come to Elysium and try to escape.

"Wait a second." She holds out her hand and they bring the horses to a stop. They huff, and Seph's horse shakes his head. There is a rumble in the trees to the right. They both turn in that direction, nudging the animals forward, and they find the dog digging at the base of an old tree. He furiously moves piles of dirt, and then the three heads push against each other to get their noses into the hole, sniffing and snapping.

I was right. Another rabbit, Seph thinks. But then he hears the voice of a young woman.

"Sirs, please come back! Sirs, please save me! Please, before he comes! He can't find me! I didn't do anything!"

And it is a good thing they slow the horses as they approach from within the shadows of the trees, because a man's voice answers from somewhere else far off.

"He's supposed to find you! That's the whole point of the thing!"

There's a laugh, and another man's voice says, more gently, "Don't mock her, Pirithous, the trap is working. We're the abductors after all—"

"Theseus! I think I see something."

"Search around the trees," Seph says quietly behind him, and Hecate nods, maneuvering her horse. She can move more silently than he can, and she's a full goddess with fighting experience besides.

He takes it upon himself to ride into the trap, whatever it is, and he calls Cerberus off with a whistle.

Cerberus is not used to taking orders from anyone but Hades, and Seph would swear he can read the disdain in the dog's eyes every time he issues a command. Sometimes he does not listen. And his growl grows louder even though he hesitates, a sign that this might be when he's stubborn.

Seph guides the horse quickly to the tree, using Demeas' body to block Cerberus from his target.

"Go on! You're done. Go on!"

The dog is reluctant, his hackles raised. Seph brings the chains off the back of the saddle, holding the iron the way Hecate does her whip, and giving them a shake.

The noise startles his horse and he does a skittering dance, but Seph soothes him with a quick, soft utterance and the reins held firmly in his other hand.

"Go on, dog. Don't make me tell you again. I'll call Hecate on you."

Cerberus puts his ears back and sulks. He moves a short ways away and sits lowly, though his demeanor communicates reluctance rather than shame. As Seph decides how he wants to dismount—his legs are not always steady, so he needs his hands free—Cerberus picks up his three heads again, his ears pointed forward, and his snouts turn to the side like nocked arrows finding a new enemy.

Sending the dog might be useful, but Hecate might still be sneaking in the shadows.

"No. Sit. Cerberus—sit!" His haunches were starting to lift up, his feet tempted to run. But this time, Seph's tenuous control of the dog maintains. "That's a good boy. Now stay."

Neither the praise nor the *stay* command happen to be very effective with him. Seph merely pretends that the words will be obeyed for now. For the sake of the girl and perhaps springing the 'trap' for Hecate, he has to move more quickly.

His knee is having a bad day, however, and he limps like an old man, heavily leaning on his cane, before he kneels by the tree and looks at the pit.

He was right, there is a young girl trapped under here. She is fairly new too, her eyes being the biggest thing about her face. Many bone indentations are visible on her entire form, and she managed to curl up in the dirt like a baby fawn. If she were a normal size, and still new enough to not have changed form, she wouldn't fit.

She has manacles on her wrists, and a chain leads to one of the thick heavy roots here, wrapped several times around and locked through the links.

"Who has done this?"

She shrinks back as Seph reaches for her. She tries to speak, but she's stuttering, and Seph's words don't seem to reach her ears.

"I-I-I didn't do i-i-it, sir! I-I di-didn't run. Why would I-I run? Oh, please believe me, I di-didn't run. Please don't let the dog eat me, sir. I am good, sir! I want to stay, please!"

Seph is firm about catching her and pulling her close. She's crying as he states sternly, "Stop that and get out of there."

Hades has repeatedly explained the dangers of being too soft. They have many to look after, and there is no tolerance for disobedience.

But once he has her, he holds the girl close and strokes her hair. The dog growls louder behind him, and Seph shields her from view, not even looking at Cerberus, entirely focused on her. And he pulls at her chains, wondering how he's going to undo this.

I need to use Hecate's power again.

As a substitute for the godly powers he doesn't have, Hecate has never failed to be useful. And Seph does not know why he went without help before now, for being a king in this place without being a fully abled god is impossible. Minthe was right about that.

"Who is in the woods? Who trapped you out here?"

"I don't know. They said they were kings looking for wives! But one of them wanted you instead. They were laughing about it! They said they would take *me*, but I am nothing. Not even enough meat for a twig, they said."

She tries to hug him, but the short length of her chains won't allow it. Seph examines the lock they put through the links, uselessly turning it in his hands.

"I'm sorry I did this! I tried to stay quiet so the dog—" In her sobbing, she hiccups. "So the dog wouldn't find me. But they threw rocks at me. And then I screamed. One of them hit me here—see?" She rubs her collarbone, and at first there is nothing to see.

While a spirit's form breaks and bleeds when the spirit perceives such an injury to occur, they do not visibly bruise unless they are looking at themselves in a mirror and they expect the imperfections.

Her flesh under her fingertips begins to purple.

"Here. I have magic. You won't hurt anymore." Seph lays one of his hands over the affected area. "Give it a moment. The medicine should feel warm. There you go. Can you feel it?"

She nods, her eyes blinking rapidly, and she wipes away the last of her tears. The discoloring disappears.

"Oh, thank you, my king! I was so scared you wouldn't believe me!" She bows over her knees, her long hair falling forward.

"Of course I believe you. I find it harder to believe that you ran away on your own and then locked yourself to this tree—"

"Oh, there he is!" she taps his shoulder and points.

Seph looks behind himself and sees an approaching man. A Greek man by the looks of it, and he has the bright vivid tone of skin that means he is *not* dead and he does not belong here. He's extremely tall. A god or a descendant of one, no doubt. And he wears a golden crown on his head, though a rather plain one. He's an older man but he smiles with the mischief of someone much younger.

"My beautiful prince! Forgive the summoning. I have come—"

Cerberus growls. The *stay* command held him for a time with his belly in the grass, but as the man quickly approaches, he tolerates his obedience no more. The black hound dashes from his position and stops midway between Seph and the stranger, his hackles fully raised, his three heads aimed low and his teeth bared.

"Ah!" The man throws open an arm to guard himself, a bit like a woman surprised by a rat. "That beast is, well—" He seems to become aware of how ridiculous he looks, and he rights himself. He takes a bold stance, one foot stepping forward, and his hands grasp the hilt of his sword in its scabbard. "Fear not, Prince Persephone. For I, Hero of the Lapiths, a noble protector of the defenseless innocent—"

"Who are you?" Seph asks, lifting one brow. For the defenseless innocent is in his arms right now, and the man seems to think he's in some kind of play performance.

The stranger takes this as a real question.

"I am Pirithous!" He makes a bow, though the dog growls louder and Pirithous stands quickly. He draws his sword. Pointing it, though taking a step back from Cerberus, he declares, "I am the famous hunter of the Lapiths! And I heard about your need of rescue! The story moved me to tears the first time I heard it!" He looks to the sky, a fist curling in front of his chest. "That is no way to be trapped for eternity, my prince. To be imprisoned in this cold, dark place! Raped by an old man..."

Seph's eyes grow twice their size.

Old man...?

This Pirithous guy has graying hair! Not to mention an enormous beard, which is well groomed and fashionable for a Greek man, but Seph much prefers the style of a clean shave, which is only worn by much younger men. He also has a bit of roundness hanging over his belt, though he is fit overall. He has a body of aging athleticism. And when he smiles, a gold band across his rotten teeth gleams at him in the dim light.

"I cannot stand to see one so young and fair trapped in this depressing world. Come with me, prince, and your every wish will be cared for. You will be married to the greatest king in history! And most importantly, I will bring an end to the long winter that has cursed the land."

Seph can't even begin to form a word. He's not quite sure what is really happening.

This man certainly has some kind of deity in his blood, but his aged features and imperfections show that he is not a god. And how could he be the greatest king in history? When he has never heard of the tribal Lapiths naming a king in the first place?!

He is wondering just how this conundrum came about. And the words he's thinking about forming are an order for Hecate to strike the damn fool where he stands.

But then he would lose the unraveling of whatever strange mystery this is.

Who sent this man?

Another person's voice calls from nearby in the trees. It is the nobler one, who did not want Pirithous mocking the girl. But apparently he is not noble enough to have stopped the rocks chucked at her.

"Pirithous! I'm calling it off! There's weird stuff happening!"

"What, eh?" says Pirithous, who half turns to look behind him. "What is it, man?" he calls back.

"I can't fucking move! I can't—fuck, I can't fucking see it, and I can't fucking move! What is happening! *Oh shit!*"

While the previous words were alarmed but not yet afraid, the last exclamation is a louder shout of terror, and Seph should have paid better attention to Pirithous. He moves faster than Seph could have imagined, his deity blood making him quicker than a regular man, and Cerberus roars as his blade meets his teeth. One of the dog's mouths drips with inky black blood as Cerberus turns around, Pirithous by Seph's side now.

Seph struggles to stand the moment he sees Pirithous move, pushing the girl away to keep her safe, but his knee gives out on him, and he has no weapons anyway.

It is time for Hecate.

But he finds that blade pressed tightly under his chin, making him put his head back to avoid being cut, and Pirithous' strong arms lift him up, capturing him close.

"Where is he, huh?" says Pirithous in his ear. He smells like liquor, and Seph forgot there was any other kind except the pomegranate wine that Hades makes. The scent is not pleasant at all. Hades' wine always reminds him of kisses and intimacy. This is something that reminds him of sweat and vomit, though he's lost those specific memories for why.

"Where is who?" Seph asks with a cough, for he finds it hard to breathe with this smelly man panting on his face.

"Your husband. The old bastard." Pirithous shuffles to look around, almost scraping Seph's throat as he looks with paranoia at the skies. And then into the trees everywhere. He even leans far over and tries to peer behind the one they are at.

The girl is left forgotten, and she pulls on her chains with a little cry of might.

Poor child.

She can be free of any chains or borders in this world, but the realization does not come for a long time.

"Are you afraid of my husband?"

You shouldn't be.

You should be afraid of me.

"How did he know we were coming, huh? The girl said he doesn't do the hunts no more. The girl said you would be all alone."

The girl and Seph make eye contact for a moment. She lied. But she's also fearful for her treason.

"They were hurting me, Your Majesty. Please believe me! I tried to tell them nothing at first!"

"I believe you." Seph cannot move his head very well to nod, but he shows her his palm to indicate that she should stop speaking.

She has done nothing wrong.

"I thought you were my rescuer, yeah? You're about to nick my artery."

"Your what?"

Seph learned about human anatomy in the palace library. Though it was only the very basics, it is more than even the nobles and royalty get among typical humans.

"My neck. You are about to cut my neck, dear rescuer." He almost chokes on the last two words, either from the sarcasm or the smell.

"Oh. Well, uh, I have to make it real, okay? In case he comes. Or we're all dead."

No, you're already dead. Seph almost rolls his eyes at the shady disgustingness of this man.

"Uh, where is he?" Pirithous asks, his head twisting to look in all directions at once, including up. Then he bellows, "Theseus! What's happening, man?"

And there is no answer at first. Seph rolls his lips inward, being bad at suppressing a laugh. Hecate found him and ended him, no doubt.

But then the weak and croaking words of Theseus are heard faintly through the trees.

"It's... coming... for you. My man. Look at... the ground."

The sword leaves Seph's neck and points at the grass, the end sweeping left, then right. Cerberus growls close by, his muscles taut to spring, but Seph whispers and gestures with a flat hand, "Stay. Down."

An attack from the dog might get him or the girl injured. He's certain Hecate has already incapacitated one of them, and this idiot won't be standing much longer. But while he is looking at the ground, Seph continues to look up.

There is something there.

Is Hades really coming for him? Did he have some protection spell Seph was unaware of?

He narrows his eyes to focus better.

It is as big as a horse, but it has wings, flapping.

Meanwhile, Pirithous shouts, hurting Seph's ears, "What is it, man? What is it?!"

"The ground..." Theseus says something, but it's lost to a rustle somewhere. Seph looks around. It wasn't the dog. There's something hissing.

"Theseus, louder, man! What the fuck is it?!"

Theseus does not sound like himself anymore. It seems that he is speaking with his last breath, but the word comes through, as the grass directly before them shifts and sways with a breeze that isn't there.

"Sss-snake!"

And a viper opens its mouth and lunges from the gray leaves. Pirithous throws his sword at it. He lets go of Seph, covering his face with his arms and cowering. But he does not protect the snake's target—his ankles.

Forty-Seven

Pirithous falls, and Seph for the moment forgets that the girl he's protecting is not physically real. He throws himself over her, and they both duck low to the ground as if the snake might grow legs, pick up the sword, and threaten to cut off their heads.

Belatedly, looking up from the grass to find the terrible monster, Seph thinks that climbing a tree would have been the correct action to take. And running away by himself while leaving the girl (for she can't be harmed by venom) would have been the best action of all.

But that wouldn't have made him feel very good about himself, would it?

There's a bit of irony and stupidity in caring about the moral implications of his actions more than the effectiveness of them.

But the snake is gone. He also can't hear the hissing anywhere. He looks carefully around Pirithous' body, but nothing moves, and the grass all around them is dead still again. The fallen man tries to speak ("Help me," is Seph's best guess) but he only makes a groaning sound. He's on his back with his mouth open, his eyes wide and staring up. A little piece of drool hangs from his bottom lip, and he's utterly still. Well, except for the fingers on his hand, twitching.

"What was that?" Seph asked breathlessly, still looking around. The snake was golden and shaped like a cobra, but the only kind he's seen are black.

The chains rattle, and the girl makes a tough, strained cry as she pulls on them. Seph pats her shoulder and rubs her back.

"I'll find the key. Do remember which one of them has it?"

"That man, I think," she says, sniffling, nodding her head toward Pirithous.

The groaning sound becomes louder as Seph digs into the man's pockets. His arms begin to shake and his feet kick a little as well, though his knees never bend much.

"Are you trying to speak to me? Are you trying to get back up?"

Seph asks, and he is not particularly concerned about the fear Pirithous might be experiencing. Rescuer or not, he held one of Seph's subjects hostage, harming her unjustly. She was nearly maimed by the dog too, who seems as alarmed about the snake as Seph is.

Cerberus snarls at Pirithous, but since the man is not moving and Seph clearly has the matter under control, the hound with his three noses sniffs around the body, searching madly for the reptile beast.

Cerberus and Seph have a working relationship. Gradually, in moments like this when Seph appreciates him, it seems to be growing into a bond.

"Good boy," he tells the dog and tosses him a biscuit he finds wrapped in the man's small travel bag. He also finds a hefty purse of coins, some kind of strong-smelling teabag, he supposes, and one old-looking key.

He returns to the girl, and it fits in the lock and the manacles both.

That thing from the sky approaches, and Seph keeps a wary eye on it as he tries to get the stubborn key to turn on her last wrist. She's nearly free. And what comes from the sky must be another attack. It's a monster.

He doesn't panic yet, since that doesn't help anything. And as Hecate arrives, walking her horse, he assumes she'll take care of it. She'll slay the massive thing, since she is a full god and an extension of his will. Seph will focus on where he is useful, staying out of the way and seeing to the poor girl.

The last manacle breaks open with a clink.

"All right then. Have you ridden a horse before?"

She shakes her head. This is not unusual for a woman or anyone of low birth.

"Well, there's no need to worry. You just sit there and hold on tight to me, okay?"

He gathers her up in his arms. Even the tallest, broadest spirits don't weigh anything. But it does pose an issue as he tries to stand from a kneeling position, needing to push from that weak knee without a hand free to pull himself up, and the pain just won't let it happen.

Styx told him he could have been the first paralyzed god in all of eternity if he hadn't reformed the connections with his legs. The left one in particular goes dead sometimes.

Seph, don't be useless, he growls at himself.

"I can walk, Your Majesty," sniffs the young woman. She's small, but older than Seph first realized.

"No need to." He suppresses a pained sound of effort as he manages to stand. "I'll protect you and carry you safely home." He smiles, glad that he didn't have to admit to one of his subjects he was unable to stand on his own.

Then he pauses, seeing the massive winged *thing* swoop down on them from the sky. He can hear when its wings beat against the wind, twice before gliding down, making a wide spiral overhead. For a moment he sees a different world suddenly. Extremely bright, blinding actually, and the ground is a vivid green. The sun is a blazing yellow, so bright that he starts to cringe and guard the girl before he realizes the vision is over and it wasn't real.

He saw a woman with brown skin wearing a white dress, shaking out bedclothes and pinning them on a rope to dry. It sounded just like the wings. *Flap. Flap.*

He hears it again as the monster comes down, its wings twice as long as his horse, who dances and widens his eyes for the incoming creature.

Spirit horses are better trained than any mortal steed. They've had centuries more experience, for one, and eventually they long forget that they can feel pain. But the old instincts of fear are still there, and they can make mistakes.

"Demeas!" Seph calls and makes a short whistle. The horse stamps a small circle, makes a nervous whinny, but trots to him and slows.

Why hasn't Hecate attacked the thing yet?

Her horse is better trained, standing calmly, though tossing its head once or twice as the creature lands on enormous talons. But Hecate does not draw her weapons, nor even let go of her horse. She stands facing the creature calmly, and Seph is fine with that so long as the enormous thing doesn't look over here.

He lifts the girl onto his horse in the meantime. And he asks his leg silently to just cooperate enough to get him settled. If they need to run, he doesn't want his injury to slow them down.

But he sees Hecate reach for the creature with an open palm, like she's greeting a large pet, and his curiosity makes him pause. Hecate's horse does not seem to mind so much anymore, now that the creature has folded its wings into its body, its back looking like a very large bird, but its head has hair instead of feathers. And its legs are like a human's too, at least the thigh and knee portion, which bend forward. The feet are the enormous talons of a raptor. And the thing has no arms that Seph can see.

It turns around and looks at him though, and Seph opens his mouth in horror. It is a woman's head! Twice as big as his own, but a beautiful-looking woman nonetheless. And Seph recognizes her. It is a likeness of Hecate's own face that looks at him with beastly, unintelligent eyes. It blinks, tilts its head, and then turns back to Hecate, who seems to be speaking affectionately.

The bird woman bows, and Hecate pets her in the same gentle manner one might treat a kitten.

"There is nothing to fear, master," she calls after a moment. The creature looks left and right quickly, its head twisting with unnatural speed and then stillness. Then the she-thing opens her mouth, and instead of a bird sound or a human sound, she lets out the most awful, the loudest, shrieking, unnatural, long noise that must carry through the entire forest. All of the underworld must hear it, and both Seph and the young woman cover their ears.

Thankfully, the noise ends. Seph's horse might have bolted otherwise, and he does not look happy at all that Seph secured the bridle to a limb on the tree, suspecting Demeas might walk away as he tried to mount. The horse dances too much to attempt it now. He throws his head, unaware of his free state of being.

"Shhh, shhh," Seph says, trying to regain control. Hecate waves, gesturing Seph forward.

"Approach slowly. I know she's big, but she is a shy creature. She's very scared of you, you know."

"What is she?" Seph asks, approaching with his cane. He pauses as the she-creature stares him down suddenly again. Seph lowers his eyes and stills for a moment. Hecate taught him to approach animals this way if they show signs of nervousness. *Let them come to you*, she said, as he was learning to work with horses and get along with Cerberus.

Cerberus does not approach the thing, nor does he growl at it, and that alone tells Seph there's nothing to worry about here. Not from the obvious monster anyway. From the man, on the other hand...

"Who are they, Hecate? And why did one of them say I needed rescuing? I assume it was bullshit, and he was going to ransom me."

He looks in the direction of the woods from where Hecate came. He can only see two boots sticking out from some shrubs a ways away.

"No doubt that is what they were trying to do. And for the attempt I assume they have balls the size of Mount Olympus. And a head as empty as the clear sky. They were kings, both of them. Wearing their crowns and everything. They must've thought they'd achieve infamy for this stupid act!" She spits in the direction of the boots, though he is too far to hit. "They weren't even a challenge. They didn't even fight."

The winged thing shuffles a few steps away from Seph and closer to Hecate, coming between them like it's trying to shield her. The creature has a woman's torso and stomach, fully bared, but then has feathers that grow out of her skin and the parts blend into a bird. The thing seems to mostly have the mind of an animal though, and she squats a bit like a chicken, down low to the ground, and rustles her wings. The feathers angle upward, which Seph assumes means that she is still scared.

"This is one of my daughters," Hecate says, stepping around her and trailing a hand down her feathered body.

"She's, uh, lovely."

Hecate gives him a dirty, offended look. But Seph does not offer an apology. He didn't say it meanly or sarcastically. Just with warranted hesitation.

"I thought myself above Gaia at one time. I saw the little humans come into the underworld beaten and battered. Broken to pieces, some of them. And at first, I didn't care for humans. I took the form of a snake back then, and I didn't have my sisters. I didn't work for Hades yet, and I wandered the Earth alone. But gradually I saw the cleverness of humans. I spoke to them sometimes. I heard that Prometheus gave them fire, and I scoffed at that gift. I thought I could do better."

She takes the large woman's head by the chin and touches her little nose to the enormous (though perfect) one. This seems to be an affectionate gesture, and the creature closes her enormous eyes. Her feathers smooth out.

"So I tried to make them perfect. Huge, so they would not be preyed upon. I gave them wings so they could fly and spread across the Earth more easily. I made them fierce with talons, so they could pick up and eat any food imaginable. And I made them soft in the heart, thinking that my humans would be loving creatures who lived in harmony with each other.

"Of course, something was missing. Something is always missing in every god's creation except Gaia's. I love my daughters dearly, but I was not willing to die for them." Hecate shakes her head. "Even then, I don't think it would've worked. Gaia was a genius, one of a kind. And the humans are perfect as they are."

"What is her name? Does she have one?"

"Podarge. But she doesn't recognize it." Hecate reaches for him. "You can approach now." And she soothes her daughter with cooing whispers as Seph approaches.

He doesn't really want to. While he's not afraid exactly, and he trusts Hecate completely, he finds the creature disturbing and simply too large to want to step into its shadow. But he does come close with small steps and lowered eyes. Because he also wants to ask Hecate a question.

"How did the man get in if you and your sisters are guarding the gate?"

"Oh, the gate is just a formality. Lots of kingdoms have gates. And lots of kingdoms have back doors and secret ways in, places that only the residents of many generations know. As for the underworld, we really have no border. The River Styx can be found by all. If you go into the woods with the right thoughts and the right heart, and if you wander long enough, you will always find yourself on the shore of the Styx. And then it is just a matter of crossing, and you are in our world.

"That is what Charon is for. To help people get across. But gods and exceptional mortals can figure out how to cross a river without a bridge. It's not exactly hard."

"So we don't have a guarded border?" Seph asks incredulously. "Why put guards at the gate at all then? I thought Hades said this place was safe!"

She shrugs. Her daughter seems to want to stare at Seph, so Seph respectfully takes a large step back, but she grabs her daughter by the hair and doesn't let her move her head so much.

"The underworld is not a place where gods or anyone really wants to be. It is difficult to achieve the right mind and the right heart to even find the river. And if you do find it and come here and make yourself enough of a nuisance that Hades should become aware of your presence—well, you'll end up like these idiots." She gestures lazily at the boots and props a hand on her hip. She lets her daughter go with her other hand, but taps her on the nose and says firmly, "No biting."

Hecate and the bird creature are caught in a stare. Her

daughter's expression remains blank.

When the creature looks away, Hecate says, "If you want to visit the underworld without pissing off Hades, you rightfully enter and exit through the gate." She points up. "And Hades does not like visitors. So when you get turned away, or chased off by my dogs, you had better damn well stay away. Anyone not respecting the gate is obviously a thug and an idiot. These men will go to Tartarus and wait in the prison for interrogation. That is why I called my daughter."

She walks away as she is speaking, her voice growing distant. The creature watches him, but Seph senses fear from her now, not malevolence. He waits without moving or making eye contact for her benefit. And Hecate begins to drag a man toward him, carrying him by his ankles.

He looks a lot like Pirithous, though he has a less wrinkled face and lighter hair. His eyes are half shut and his expression is still like a corpse. He does not twitch or make any movements.

"He looks dead."

"Only the snake's venom," she answers. She drops him near her daughter and walks past Seph to collect Pirithous. "It causes full body paralysis, and since it comes from me, it'll work until I give them an antidote. Which I will do when they are safely contained in a prison cell."

Cerberus trots alongside Hecate now, with a mild protective growl and a puffed-up chest, as though telling off the unconscious man.

Though it feels a little caution-worthy and new to him, Seph pats the dog on two heads when he stands close enough. It must be a sign of their growing bond that Cerberus sits kind of close to him.

"My daughter will drop them in the prison. She knows where. They're trained well." Hecate brushes her palms together, appraising a job well done. "Shall we continue hunting or take the tiny bird home?" She gestures toward Seph's horse. Then she pets her daughter on the head one last time and says, "Off with you."

The bird woman bends down to sniff at the bodies, her face still blank, and she even nibbles on the clothes of Pirithous with her huge human teeth.

Though Pirithous is completely paralyzed, Seph sees his eyes widen even further in terror.

"We have not found a runaway soul lately," Seph says, watching the massive bird dig claws into the grass as she takes both men in her talons' grasp. Dirt and weeds cling to the hooks, and he covers his face as the creature lifts up, flapping its wings wildly, creating wind and dust. Then she is gone, and quite suddenly at that. She's huge, but she flits off easily once she's in the air.

Arms dangle and flop like hanging puppets from the bird woman's feet.

"Let's go home. I want to spend some time at the docks."

Forty-Eight

Hermes thinks he's won. He's unnaturally silent now, not boastful, probably because he thinks Hades' ego towers high with an unstable, completely collapsible foundation—just like his father's. He also probably acknowledges that Hades is more powerful than his father, and he has made the dreaded God of the Underworld do something he does not want to do.

Hades admits it is not an easy feat. But Hermes has no idea how much the rabbit is actually worth.

The bunny spirit might be the true Hibus. It's impossible to tell, but it seems the right size, and Hermes swears the rabbit comes from the exact house. Hades hopes it is, and he hopes that meeting Hibus will help Seph recover more of his forgotten memories as well.

Hades leaves the gift with Verah and instructs her to procure a cage. She will find the right talented souls and see that it's done. Then Hades and Hermes travel to the docks, where he's told Seph has been for a few hours. Hades hasn't put any more protection spells on him since he's currently using all of his magic to stay awake and work around the clock, but he hasn't needed to. The citizens of Elysium track the young king with their eyes and ears and gossip, and Hades can usually ask anyone in the palace and get an accurate answer.

He does find Seph at the docks. But first Hades' eyes are lost, just scanning and scanning, seeing so many quiet, fearful faces. He has oath takers for every language here, and souls used to be guided into the temples, a few rings of ornate buildings constructed around the dock in enormous half circles. He thought the oath and religion should go hand in hand, since humans follow their religions quite faithfully, especially in death.

But Hades has agreed to focus solely on building while Seph sees to the day-to-day and other matters. He shadowed Seph for a while, and then checked up on his work weekly, and then realized he simply didn't have the time or energy to audit him any further. Seph excelled in everything Hades saw. In fact, Seph hardly seems to be the same young god that arrived here many seasons ago when he was governing over Elysium.

Seph has been in charge of the hunts and many other things for a while. And Hades had no idea how cramped the docks are now. Seph must have changed some things. For while the temples are open and new souls are being guided inside, the oath takers are more like merchants bartering wares.

There are many for each language. They each carry a copy of the oath on a tattered scroll. And they call on the newly arriving souls to come—"Come swear the oath and be a citizen of Elysium! Or get back on the boat and choose to be reborn instead!"

Hades stops one of the oath criers.

"We don't give them the chance to turn back."

The wise old soul bows. "It is orders, Great Emperor. King Persephone said that none who change their mind should be convinced. Only those with conviction will stay." Without looking up he asks, "Should I not do as he says?"

"No. Do as you've been told."

A change in orders needs to come from Seph himself, after Hades and Seph have talked about it in private. They have already discussed how these disagreements in rule will happen, but in this case, though Hades hates the thought of losing a soul over cold feet, he supposes Seph must be right.

There are so many!

And not only that, but the crowd is made even worse by the presence of many animals. Ponies mostly, who receive a lot of attention, and sometimes babes are put on their backs. Also dogs and even pigs. There are more animals here than Hades keeps in his barn!

"Uncle, are you having a festival?" Hermes asks beside him as Hades takes this all in.

He is right to ask. There's music too, though it is soft and not lively. There are no games and not too much moving about. But with the crowd, the animals, and the music, it certainly seems that Seph has changed the docks from a place of seriousness and religious faith... into the town market.

"I must find my husband," Hades says under his breath and pushes onward to do so. He's never had to walk in such a crowded area in his own city before! He doesn't have anyone to announce him or part the crowd, so many of the souls milling about are terrified to bump into him. Soon awareness of his presence travels, and a wake is created before and behind him.

Hermes is swallowed by it. Or perhaps just distracted. Hades doesn't care. He gets closer to the dock and the ship, where impossibly *more* souls are being brought into this crowd, and he hears someone singing above all the rest.

About a woman.

Hair so gold, lips so red, and a face to bring peace to wars.

And it goes on to say that she is dead and her husband weeps for her.

The bard has cleared a small area in the crowd and sits upon some crates, strumming a lyre.

I see her dancing with loving eyes
Come away with me, my love, my bride
I move the mountains for you, I say
But her eyes are empty
Her flesh decayed
And silently she whispers
Come away, come away

There are sniffs from the citizens nearby, all of them skeletal, clothes hanging off of them like rags. They cling to each other in small groups, looking up when he gets close like scared deer.

They try to make room, but on the dock there simply isn't any. Hades forces his way through a group of new citizens, who beg him for forgiveness or simply cover their heads as if he would strike them.

Over their voices as they scatter, Hades demands, "Who are you?"

The man is not dead. Therefore, he's an intruder.

Where is my dog?

Oh right, hunting with Seph. Perhaps he did not come home yet.

His fingers are tempted to go to his mouth, his lungs poised to emit the loud whistle that Cerberus can hear anywhere. But then he hears his husband's voice.

"Hades!" A hand raises in the crowd. Seph is further on, right at the new ship. There is another one approaching in the distance already, and this one is not unloading efficiently with the damn bard making the crowd stop.

"I am Orpheus!" Hades hears behind him. He chooses to ignore it and proceed to his husband. "I beseech you, Great Hallowed God of Death! Listen to my song!"

Hades hears an unpleasant pluck of strings as he continues to leave. The next note is musical, however, and another song begins. This one is about a woman dying—a young bride. And her husband arrives just in time to see that it's too late. Somehow she's fallen into a pit of vipers. He is on the part where the wedding guests prevent the husband from jumping in after her when Hades finally reaches Seph, and he's not sure where to start.

Hades doesn't want to tell Seph that he's done anything wrong, but the state of his docks is far worse than he expected.

Seph's expression also warns him that this might not be the right time. His young husband looks stern, even angry, as he's watching the bard with his arms crossed, leaning on a barrel.

"Can you believe this asshole?" Seph says, quietly so only the two of them can hear.

"You didn't send for him?" Hades asks, and he assumes he at least read part of the situation wrong.

Seph snorts. "No! Why would I? We have thousands of bards right among us and new ones are practicing every day. We compose some of the best music the universe has ever heard. Why would I ask a mortal man, of all things, to come down here and play?"

"He is an intruder then. Where's my dog? Why haven't you gotten rid of him already?"

Hades raises his hand to summon his hound, but Seph catches his arm.

For a moment Hades forgets everything. He hasn't been back to the palace in nearly a week, trying very hard to get this new neighborhood designed in time. And the deadline for the next one is like a constant migraine, always pounding inside his head. Even when he has come home, he hasn't touched Seph in a while, and he suddenly realizes how much he misses that.

Seph is saying something.

"—you'll terrify the crowd, and they'll cram their way back onto the boats. Do you want to start a mass exodus or something?"

Hades kisses him.

It is not publicly appropriate, nor is Seph prepared for it. Nor does he look particularly inviting, to anyone but Hades anyway. More and more Seph has seemed to adopt Hades' habits for scowling, and Seph's is more pronounced, possibly more effective as well.

Hades doesn't care at the moment. He grabs the front of Seph's shirt, tastes his husband's lips, and he just wants to curl up with him. Right there on the docks if they have to, if that's all the time they can get. He wants another conversation over wine, and to have Seph's taut round ass up close and displayed for him. Free for Hades to pet and admire and bury his face into—

They have to go home for that.

"Come on." He takes Seph's wrist, but as he turns to fly them home, his eyes fall on Hermes' face. He's smiling. And then everyone's face. They're *all* smiling.

"The king is moved by the song!" says someone in an awed tone, and a young woman claps.

"He will do it! Orpheus the Bard has swayed the king!" someone else says, and the clapping spreads and continues.

"Play more for him, bard! Your songs are magic!"

Said bard sings louder than ever, so loud he drowns out his own lyre, and this song is about the happy days of the two lovers, sneaking off together and him putting flowers in her hair.

The crowd watches the two of them with smiles, and only Hermes seems to be as confused as Hades, though he wears a small smirk as well.

"Cousin!" he exclaims, approaching, holding out his arms. And Seph is passed from one embrace to the other, though Hades is reluctant to let him go. Hermes uses his shoulder to wedge Hades out of the way, which Hades only allows because he finds the crowd's attention very strange.

Why are they staring at him so adoringly?

This is not normal.

"Uhh... Who are you?" asks Seph, unreceptive to the hug.

Hermes does not let him go but backs away, looking at him eye-to-eye. "You're kidding, right?" He looks back at Hades incredulously. "I'm your cousin!" Hermes shakes his shoulder in a friendly fashion, as if that will jostle the memory into him. "Oh my gods—really? You don't remember me?"

He looks back at Hades again, and Hades realizes that at some point he's going to have to give an explanation. But if there's one thing that will turn Demeter's heart cold enough to watch the entire Earth die, it will be hearing that her son almost fell to his death in Tartarus down here.

This is why Hades almost didn't make the trade for the rabbit.

"Wow, I forget how quickly the little ones grow, huh?" Hermes scratches his head in a sheepish manner. He upsets the helmet on his head, a bowl with two silly wings sticking up on either side like an owl's feather horns.

Then he rights it, saying, "I'm sorry I didn't come by more often. I'm the one who told you to put a rotten fig in your mother's slippers—remember? And then I taught you how to carefully draw a giant beard on her while she was sleeping. Which, of course, I'm sure you got in a lot of trouble for, but I had to leave, you understand. Business to do and all that. I run around the world helping lost souls for Hades! It's not easy."

Seph only blinks at the man who clasps his shoulder again as though they are friends. There is no dawning recognition in his eyes, though surely being left to take the blame for a prank should have been a significant childhood memory.

"Hermes is my messenger," Hades says, wishing he had told Seph more about him. More about all of his family, actually. He intended to, but somehow that task just got lost and forgotten. "He finds the souls that resist the call to the underworld and guides them here for me. He saves many millions of people every year."

And he's the one who protected you for me.

I will tell him soon.

"Oh," Seph says, and there is no recognition. "Yes, of course. It is nice to meet you... um, Cousin Hermes."

Seph offers his hand between them, which Hermes looks at strangely, and then takes it anyway.

Hermes then proceeds to put an arm around Seph, asking, "How has the marriage been, cousin?" And he begins to lead Seph away from Hades. Purposely, no doubt. They did not agree to that.

But Hades finds himself more perturbed by the attention of the crowd, an old man asking, "Will you do as he asks? If so, I have a wife I'd like to return to. She is still alive in Ephesus, and caring for her dear mother all alone. If I return to her, she will know there is nothing to fear. Not for her mother or for herself, and she may choose to come back with me, in fact."

The man puts his hands together like he's praying. "I will tell her there is food and no pain here. I know she is pure enough to come to Elysium! Why, she's better than me in all ways. Please, King Hades of the Underworld! Let me bring my wife back."

And he goes to his knees, bowing all the way to the planks.

The crowd cheers encouragingly, looking upon Hades with smiles. They wipe their eyes and more of them urge the bard to play. Hades only wonders where all this nonsense came from.

What the hell are all these people talking about?

Forty-Nine

It takes some time, but Hades orders a tent, a small table, and two chairs to be brought onto the ship that is now empty of souls. A new ship waits behind them, the poor frightened passengers unable to step off. And if his discussion with Seph takes too long, it may be awhile before the unloading happens as planned.

My docks are completely chaotic anyway, he reminds himself when they've erected the tent. Servants bow and step aside, and then Hades and Seph go in, two married kings. A ruling like this has never happened before, but little do the hopeful citizens know, they're actually gawking at a simple married couple's dispute.

Perhaps the first between him and Seph, if Seph's initial hatred of him after Minthe's attack is excluded.

Hermes and Hecate are left outside the tent, standing as guards at the ship's railing. (Though, Hermes slouches and sits on the railing like a lazy passenger.) They will be able to hear the gods speak if they raise their voices, but for now, the small tent gives the couple some privacy.

Hades goes first.

"Why is the mortal man allowed to play in the first place? Why was he not driven out immediately when it was clear he does not belong?"

Seph puts his hands on the table, leaning angrily over it. They do not raise their voices—yet.

"How did he get in in the first place? That's what I want to know."

Hades waves a hand airily. He does not like Seph looking at him like that, so displeased, so he sits as he says, "Anyone seeking the underworld can enter it. That's the way it works. But mortals aren't supposed to know how, and gods will find it very hard to achieve without using my gate. Unless they actually *want* to be here, which would be unique."

He hopes that sitting, remaining below Seph's eye level, will help keep the discussion reasonable. Hades can stay in control, but Seph would not be the first or the last young god to lose his temper publicly.

And I know perfectly well that he has the fires of a stallion...

Hades has long left his yearning adolescence behind, but he also wants the discussion to stay peaceful so Seph will not be averse to taking him tonight.

"Well, when I arrived he was already out there tearing up the crowd and singing about vipers. Vipers!" Seph throws up his hands. "How many damn people die from snakes and vipers?! Is it all the time or just today for some reason?"

Hades is confused. "Do we have a sudden influx of viper-related deaths?" That sounds like a god's plague, not a famine.

"No." Seph paces the short distance at his end of the table and then stops. The anger leaves his voice, and he sounds mostly concerned instead, perhaps worried. "Why is that man asking me about our marriage? Why is he asking if I find the bed *comfortable*? And if you provide for me well? Or if I have any 'untended desires'?"

Hades' eyebrows go up, though he is not entirely surprised. Hermes' concern for his cousin is genuine, but he would also use the opportunity to skim a little gossip. The spy, barterer, and messenger among the gods loves to trade whispers for favors.

Hades plans a vague answer. He wants the rabbit to be a surprise. He also does not want Hermes to overhear how much Seph doesn't remember, in case Demeter should find out how badly Seph was injured. That might cause a civil war among the gods, and already there is a dying Earth. By pure luck, Seph had the cane leaning against the barrels at the docks, and Hermes walked him away without the opportunity to pick it up again. Hades' magic has been helping him since.

"Your mother is the cause of all this. Like I told you. The seasons of Earth are long and harsh without her assistance, and she's still pitching a fit over the marriage. Seph, I don't want you to hate your mother, but you should know that you would find any private relationship difficult to maintain and be fruitful with her in your life. You are her son, and her only child. She keeps you as..." Hades winces. "... a substitute of sorts. I think she thinks that with a son she should never have to be lonely again."

And how are they talking about this and not the state of his kingdom? His ship dock looks like a farmyard. But he hopes he will get to that soon. Gently, in a way that doesn't put him in a cold bed tonight.

"I have thought about you every night and day we've been apart, Seph. I hoped that when we did meet, it would be with softer words, in our bedroom." Outside the tent, barely audible, he hears Hecate's "*Awww.*"

He chooses not to react to that and speaks a little quieter. "If you like, I can handle matters here, and we can talk more about the family—" *And the process of oath taking,* he adds mentally, but he does not wish to start a fight. "—in the morning when we are both rested. Does that sound good?"

Seph picks up his chin. "I already had this idiot figured out. Don't you trust me?"

Uh-oh. Not good.

Hades suddenly feels very, very tired.

It is not Seph's fault. Any man or god with a little power then wants to use and test that power. But meanwhile, Hades' kingdom seems to be crumbling, and the ferry behind them is still waiting to dock. The last thing he wants in this crisis is a queue of ships that never ends.

He will be very tempted to send more to Tartarus if that happens. He is doing as much as he can. He does not have time to let Seph figure himself out.

They say nothing, only look at each other, and Hades has the feeling he's going to make a great mistake if he speaks. So he must be careful.

"What do you have in mind, my king?" he asks inoffensively.

"Do I need permission? Or are we not equal kings?" Seph sits in his chair at last, interlacing his fingers and setting them atop the table like a man about to make a business deal.

Hades feels like he is staring at a little Zeus, one with full powers and a lightning bolt about to strike him on the head.

"You did ask me for *permission* to oversee some city matters," he says, still neutral in his expression and tone. Just stating a fact.

Seph reaches across the small table and turns his palm up. "Do you not trust me? Do you not see us as equals?"

Hades' hand goes to his, and now they are more like lovers than opponents. Hades can never forget how close he came to losing these hands, this voice. This beautiful soul.

He will not lose that over a crowded ship dock and some stupid mortal bard.

"I trust you. Do as you like."

Hades shuts his eyes briefly.

I've lost.

If they were even arguing to begin with. It is not clear. But Seph has been more independent since Hades gave him Hecate, and he suspects that stripping Seph of his responsibilities would be a mistake that ruins the rest of his life.

Seph has been trying. But somehow, I have to make sure he succeeds. For the benefit of my citizens.

Hades opens his eyes.

"But as your husband and also your king, I don't like to purposely be left in ignorance for dramatics and showing off. I am your mate. And I don't think my request for information is undermining your authority in the task."

"You're right. I was testing you. I'm sorry, I shouldn't do that."

Hades nod silently, and Seph continues, "I was about to act when I saw you arrive, so I waited for you instead. It will create a commotion, and I know you will not like my decision initially—until I explain it."

"Do so then." Hades lets go of his hand and leans back in his chair.

Seph does not sound nervous as he speaks, nor does he hesitate or stutter. Too soon, those cute shy habits of his are gone.

"Of course, I initially thought to solve it the way you would—by striking him dead with Hecate, or ordering Cerberus to chase him out. He got in somehow, so he can find his way back. But he already had the crowd entranced when I came, and I have been trying for weeks to increase happiness at the docks.

"I think it's working. I'm in the woods every day, but we haven't had a true hunt in over a month."

"That is impressive," Hades says with genuine awe. And a touch of confusion. The rate of souls coming in has only increased. So his trust in Seph must not have been wrongly placed after all. He's glad he didn't react too soon to this mess.

"Yes, but the idiot out there will cause ten, twelve, or thirty hunts tomorrow! That's if I run him off. Unless we wish to employ a militia—which I don't recommend, it would only work on the youngest souls anyway—we have to be sensitive to the wants and needs of our newest children."

"And I agree," Hades puts up his feet on the table, sinking in his chair. He longs to take his boots off. He is tired. And it sounds like

Seph may have a better grasp of the situation than he imagined. He has never done this with a partner before. Could it be that making Seph an equal king makes his life *easy*?

However, Seph warns him, "You won't like this part... but I'm going to give the bard what he asks for. I'm going to send him with his wife back to the upperworld. So they can be reunited and live out their days in love."

My husband should be an oracle, not a king, Hades thinks darkly, removing his feet and sitting up. For Seph is right—he does not like it. Not at all.

"Unacceptable. For obvious reasons. I do not give up my children to anyone who asks. I don't care how deep their love is or what poetry they spew. And Seph—I thought you knew this—a soul going to the upperworld is permanent death."

Seph holds up his hands. "I know, I know. Hear me out. If we run him off with violence, we will be the evil ones. He's won the crowd's heart, whether we like it or not. Running him off will save all the souls, true. But it may increase the number of hunts to more than I can handle. Especially in just the next few days. And Hades... I think you know we are overwhelmed by this population."

He is right. Hades looks at the rings on his fingers as he considers. He has never sent good souls into Tartarus before, but just this week he had thought again: *What if I have to?*

What if the good ones have to disappear as well because the underworld and its two kings cannot keep up?

And then he thought, *I'll listen to the architects first. I'll make their temporary boxes, as plain and thoughtless as slave quarters.*

But he always wanted to be a better king. Not a typical one.

"So you have a solution?"

"We give him what he wants. He takes the girl. We lose a few souls who follow. We don't try at all to punish or cage them here."

Hades narrows his eyes. "So then they all start asking to leave! And they all perish for nothing, which is even worse than sending them into Tartarus. Why don't we just put them all on a boat 'sailing to the upperworld' and call this what it is. A sacrifice to cover up our failure."

Seph shakes his head. "I don't think we'll have to do that. Most will choose not to go. We will only lose a few, and only for a little bit. You're forgetting one thing, my husband. For most of these souls, their loved ones are already dead. They're either here or they're not. And the state of the Earth is so bad most do not want to return anyway. We will lose very little, and the sacrifice will save a great many from the hunt. The ones staying after today will know that they chose to do so and they are not being forced."

"And what about the bard's wife? What about her? When she dies, he will be back. And I won't have another wife to give him."

Seph does not smile exactly, but there is a hint of smugness in his features. A pride over the decision he's reached. He looks like a true underworld king, even if he has tan skin and he chooses to leave his obsidian laurel wreath at home most days.

"That is why we lie. We tell him and the wife not to speak to each other. We tell this to all the souls who want to follow them out. Silence is absolutely necessary. And we tell the bard not to look backward as he travels on his journey. He's not to know she's there. We will help them cross the River Styx, but it is a long walk out of the underworld. If he fails in his task, even once, we make it clear that the journey might not work."

"And then he assumes the deaths are his fault..." Hades finishes, thinking over the plan. It is a good plan. In that it will work. It is not *good* at all actually, which makes him think Seph might have lost more than he realized to the waters of Tartarus. But is that because of lost essence and memories? Or simply the adjustment that must be made when one realizes the true dark nature of things, that death and life are a cycle, and individuals are made up of everyone else?

"What's the matter? You think the idea is too cruel?" Seph looks worried again. Perhaps he is fine with leaving an innocent bard to believe he is responsible for his wife's second murder, but disappointment from his husband king seems to matter.

"No," Hades says, standing and walking around the table. He takes Seph's hands and draws him up. They are the same height. Two equal kings in power and purpose. Exactly what the underworld needs to make it through this difficult time.

"I think it's perfect," Hades says and bows to him.

Fifty

Hades, Hermes, and Hecate stand at the bottom of the ramp leading up to the empty boat. A *third* boat is soon approaching the harbor, just a growing speck for now but it nags Hades' pride that his dock should be so sloppily run. And there's still the issue of the animals to address. Leaving the tent, eager to deliver the news to the bard and enact the decision he's reached, Seph briefly explained that the animals were to make people feel comfortable. He did not stay around to hear what Hades thought about that, or if he had any objections.

But... well...

It is not how I would have done it, but there is a certain peace.

A crowded peace for sure, the newly arrived souls having nowhere to sit or drink or for false sleep as they wait to take their oath. Which is their choice and theirs alone. There is also the matter of losing meek little souls who might change their mind once coming here, but Hades is satisfied for now to learn that this boat will not be sending any good ones back to choose rebirth instead.

That seems to be a rare choice, he is guessing, by the sheer numbers of the crowd.

And he can't argue with the results. No new hunts in over a month. If Hades was in charge, there might be six a day.

That does not mean Hades is a worse king. It only means Seph is willing to make sacrifices he is not, and for now, they seem to benefit everyone.

Of course, Hecate wears a displeased expression as Seph finishes his decree, and the crowd breaks out in lovely cheers. Hades manages a small smile for them, and even touches hands with a few who brave near. Tearful grandmothers and old fathers thank him for his mercy, but Seph gets all the credit.

"What a gentle young king," says one woman, her hands folded against her heart. "He's swayed the heart of Hades."

And others call, "Oh, Persephone, thank you for your mercy!"
"Great King!"
"Honorable Chief!"
"Majestic Emperor!"
The praises come in every language and every honorific.

Even the people far away at the temples seem to bustle more happily. For now, all eyes are on the bard, who breaks into a joyous jig (Seph hasn't told him the stipulations yet), and Hades can already feel the difference in the crowd. They will lose some. But more will be taking the oath all day, and the plaza at the dock will begin to empty.

"Tell everyone," Hades says, taking the hands of another brave man. Others are watching him and estimating the cost to express their gratitude. New souls are especially cautious. "Their happiness should be shared."

"Two kings are better than one," says the man with a deep bow and trembling hands. "Your wisdom is merciful. Thank you."

"It is quite unlike our old king, isn't it?" Hecate says, her expression and tone unfriendly.

"Hecate," Hades says in a warning tone.

And Hermes speaks.

"I don't like it either." A spell from him shuts out the sounds of the crowd at once. Seph dances with the bard's jig, grabbing for the hands of others to lead them into it.

They are a frail, knobby sort of party. It is heartbreaking to watch, knowing how their stomachs churned on emptiness and they died with the yearning for food in their thoughts. But there are big smiles everywhere. They beam and laugh like the children they are.

Seph finds a small one in the crowd. A little girl, much like the one Hades found in the upperworld before, and he twirls with her on his hip, looking like such a handsome father that Hades wonders if he should inquire about child siring methods for two male gods.

But while he's thinking all of this, Hermes watches the same scene and says, "I didn't know the child of Demeter was a cruel one. He was such a sweet boy when I met him. Oh, you should have seen him! He shared with slaves and rescued small kittens. An angel, I thought he was. I thought that's why you wanted him, dear uncle? Because he was so kind?"

Hades assumes that since the crowd is silent, they can't be heard either. No new ones approach to touch his hands or express compliments. They must sense that this is a private discussion happening in front of them. And while Hades *could* have done the same spell on the tent, with a bit of experimentation and effort, it did not occur to him. Different gods have different habits they find their powers useful for. To do this so easily, the trader of whispers must use this spell often.

"You think this is cruel? He's given the bard what he asked for. He's had mercy. It is the bard's own foolishness that causes the disaster to come. What does he expect to happen? His wife is dead. He should have accepted that. He's taking home a wife with no *body*, for hell's sake. If he thinks that's an acceptable way to do things..."

"Their love is for more than flesh," Hecate responds. "You've done the most wicked thing and spun it as kindness."

"We've taken a small sacrifice to avoid upsetting a great population. It is a politician's way."

"It is not *your* way," Hermes says. "Not usually. Your fashion of ruling this place is hard to stomach sometimes, but then again, Zeus is worse in my opinion. But Hades—one thing I have always admired about you is that you do not lie to your people."

"And I have not," Hades says, a rash impulse urging him to call the scepter. Of course, he won't. Not for this small thing. But he's deeply annoyed to be criticized openly. "Orpheus asked for his wife, and we're giving him his wife. We're telling him that she will disappear. Technically."

"If he *looks* at her, she will disappear," Hecate corrects. "And you know he'll—"

"He'll look. Yes. Of course. It is his own foolishness to think that he won't. He overestimates himself. This is a tragedy of his own ego." Hades gestures at the bard, who is listening to Seph's stipulations now. Hades can see the words form on Seph's lips.

You can't look behind you on your way. You can't speak to her until you cross the threshold of your home. You must always trust that she's there. And when you're inside and you turn around—she will be.

The crowd is happy, but the bard looks noticeably less ecstatic than before. Still, after less than a second of serious thought, he nods his head.

"He has asked for more than he can have. This story, when it's done, will be a great lesson for mortals. Some things must be accepted. Some challenges they cannot overcome. And the dead do not come back. It is a fair ruling."

"Well... it is different from anything I've ever seen," Hermes says, crossing his arms.

"And what will you tell Demeter about her son?"

Hermes considers and shakes his head. "Nothing she will believe." He rubs his chin. "Her son fits here. He's not the little scamp I used to know, that's for sure."

He shrugs and a bit of a smile breaks through. "I thought I'd find him depressed, gazing out a window in your gloomy palace."

Hades looks at the palace in the distance. It's not *gloomy*... sophisticated and elegant, yes.

"I never thought I'd tell you this, but I was half ready to engage in an abduction plan. Zeus put it in my head, you see, and Demeter called on me too, all grieving and begging."

"You would betray me, nephew? And you admit it so easily?"

"I'm not going to *now*," Hermes says without fear. "There was only a slim chance I would have in the first place! I mean, suppose I came and found my cousin horribly abused or something. I know you would never do that on purpose. But Hades, sometimes your rulings are unintendedly cruel. Sort of like this one. You solve problems in a direct but heartless way. I never imagined my cousin would be a match for you."

He gestures at the scene, the bard playing, the people dancing. A line exits the plaza like an army platoon on a mission. They must be the ones going to retrieve his wife, wherever she is, and many are offering clothing or jewelry or coins to the young couple.

"But I can see that he is happy here. Zeus is going to have to best my aunt whether he likes it or not. Do you think he's up to the task?"

"Pff. No. He can launch storms at her head and throw lightning bolts all day. Zeus is not going to move her. Eventually, Demeter will have to accept that her son is grown and married."

"And taken away from her..." Hermes starts, but Hecate interrupts.

"Do none of you care about the fate of the girl this bard married? And what about the others following them?"

"Seph and I will speak to each one privately before they go. We will tell them they are wanted and needed. If we cannot convince them after that... They have chosen to leave. And the wife will be the only one allowed to break her oath, any others I am not abiding. Only the newly arrived can change their mind and go. I am not giving them up easily, Hecate."

"This is why rulers should be struck down and prevented from ever rising up again. No matter how noble they seem in the beginning, no matter how good their intentions are, they resort to lies and murders eventually. Seph hasn't even lasted that long, and he is committing this murder 'for the rest of them.' My master is good, but no one should make decisions for everyone else. A king is always and only corrupt."

"Ah, Hecate. Your way is selfish. The few strong must look after the many meek. But this is an old argument and a waste of time."

After speaking, however, and noticing one of Hecate's rings, something Seph said comes back to him.

"My husband told me something about vipers today. He said there've been a lot of 'viper-related deaths' lately. And vipers are your favorite pet. What did he mean by that?"

Fifty-One

Though using his magic makes Hades feel a bit like he's trapped under a boulder, his magic straining, pushing to roll the giant rock off of him and keep from getting crushed, he likes Seph's suggestion that he fly them home in his arms. A horse won't guide itself out of the air and back onto the ground easily, and he is eager to get to the bedroom and skip the stables. So the best method to get home quickly and avoid a chatty, overly enthusiastic crowd between here and there is to levitate directly to their balcony, which overlooks the bathhouse courtyard.

Hades carries Seph in his arms like a bride, and his husband leans his head against his chest trustingly. They do not exchange words, though Hades lowers his lips to his hair once they're mostly out of the crowd's sight. The world up here is quiet, especially without the usual sound of horses' hooves, and the absence of wind. There's not even the slightest breeze. It is quiet with all the busyness and necessary stress seeming to have been left below them, on that surface layer of the kingdom. Above, it is only them, and Hecate disappears quickly with the horses, guiding them to the stables.

Hermes will stay in the palace another day or two, he says. To make certain that Seph is alright and not in need of unlawful abducting. His nephew promises he won't make an effort, and after his admission, he would not find an abduction attempt to be made without the utmost violence.

Hades may have let the moment go, but he already plans to have a future conversation with his nephew that will have some threatening overtones. He plans to have the other side of that conversation now, with Seph, but his young husband is out of his arms as soon as his boots land on the balcony tile.

"Can you believe it?" Seph says excitedly, making a turn with his arms spread. He couldn't look any happier with that big grin stretching his face. "We convinced all of them to stay! All of them!"

He laughs as he opens the door to their bedroom and disappears inside.

"Except the wife, of course," Hades says, and follows more stoically. He can't even begin to imagine being so expressive and moving around so much with his actions, no matter how pleased or surprised or devastated he might be. The emotion does not matter.

In this case, however, stoic fits his mood perfectly.

"Seph, I have to talk to you about something," he says, removing his cloak and tossing it over the back of an armchair. He hears Cerberus whine and scratch at the door to his living quarters. Briefly, since Seph doesn't seem to have heard him anyway, he leaves the bedroom to let in the dog.

The ridiculous, stupid dog.

Cerberus can fly as well, but having no consciousness of that fact, he followed at a running pace below them. At one point the dog must have ventured a guess as to where he was going (this isn't the first time he's come home this way), for he exceeded their pace and likely barreled through the palace to get to the door in time.

"Come in, mutt," he says, though he reaches down and kindly scruffs the heads, taking time to scratch behind six ears, and grudgingly murmuring soft affections.

"No. Get away from that," he says sternly when Cerberus sniffs the new addition to the furniture in his den. An enormous cage shaped like a house stands at waist-to-shoulder height, on a table. Even for royalty, he assumes Hibus must be the most spoiled bunny. The ghostly rabbit hops out of the hidden part of his home, a nest box, and sits on his haunches, sniffing.

He looks exactly like the old Hibus did, except that his eyes are completely white. And in the dimness of the underworld, a soul's eyes always emit a subtle, eerie light.

The rabbit is supposed to be a surprise, but he doesn't want to distract Seph any further. They have some things to talk about.

"Sit on your bed for now." He points to the new cushion where Cerberus stays. Which is plush and large and extravagant enough that Hades would feel comfortable sitting a mortal emperor there without causing offense. But Cerberus makes a dissatisfied grumble as he turns and lowers himself onto the cushion.

"I'll play with you in a bit," Hades says, retrieving a bone from within a cupboard. Another gift Hermes brought with him, but this one required no bartering.

The desk calls to him while Cerberus slathers on the bone.

Ugh. Work.

The work is necessary, but it is costing him. He and Seph have not been together as much as he'd like. And Seph is right. They are close to becoming overwhelmed.

Demeter had better come to her senses soon. She can't kill the whole planet just for her son.

Yet at the same time, knowing how much *he* cares for Seph, he also has the thought: *She might.*

"Seph, we need to talk."

He shuts the door to the bedroom since Cerberus might start barking, giving his opinion of the matters discussed if he senses tension in their words. Cerberus is tolerating Seph in his master's bed for now, but they have a ways to go before they bond.

"What about?" Seph asks, picking up the platter of fruit Verah keeps on Seph's end of the table. Now that he's recovering, Seph has an appetite. "Are you not happy with the decision I made?"

He nibbles on a pomegranate seed and pulls it away from his lips. "She was one soul, Hades. I didn't want to lose her either. I got on my knees and *begged* her to stay—I begged for her life! But I am still happy, overall, with the outcome. We cannot let our citizens wander away freely, of course, but I don't think we should have to hunt them down either. People should *want* to live here."

Hades waves a hand to dismiss his concerns, sitting on the bed next to him. Seph offers him a couple pomegranate seeds from his fingers, and Hades takes his lover's wrist, moving his mouth and tongue over Seph's hand, sucking the sweet juice into his throat, and eyeing Seph's body for more.

Gods dammit. Work can wait.

But can it? When Seph's life was nearly lost today?

Seph watches him with a dazed expression, his mouth slightly open. And Hades starts quickly on the buttons of his own shirt, recognizing that two bodily needs are warring within him at the moment. Seph looks very, very nice. And so do the blankets and the pillows.

So he says hurriedly, compromising by fitting in two tasks at once, "Hecate says you were attacked today. By two men."

Seph was leaning in for a kiss. But the words make him distracted. Hades takes his lips anyway, enjoying the surprised *oof* and clumsy start of the kiss. Only to have his lover give in and move his mouth and tongue against him fully.

"This is a really weird time to mention it," Seph says with heavy breath when they part. "But yeah. Yeah, I was. I wouldn't really call it *attacked* so much as *molested* though. I didn't see Theseus until he was already on the ground and disabled. I'm guessing Hecate turned into a snake and bit him? Or perhaps she summoned a snake. I didn't see her transform. Can she shapeshift?"

"Hecate mostly keeps her powers unknown." And Hades thought he would never say her name as he was undoing the crotch on his pants. He stumbles and toes out of his boots as well, saying, "What I want to know is why you didn't tell me first. You should've come to me immediately. Dear husband. And I am ashamed that you thought I was too busy to hear about this attack and make sure you are safe."

Seph hasn't been undressing at all. Lazy boy. Whether dressing or undressing, he lets Hades or the servants do it for him. He always used to seem put off by Verah or Sefkh wrapping a chiton around him, but since Minthe's attack he has become more comfortable letting others do things for him.

Hades doesn't mind at all. He doesn't even get his trousers undone all the way, just loosening them to make room for his erection, and then he goes to his knees in front of Seph, his hands reaching up and under his clothes.

"I will always make time for you, Seph. It doesn't matter how busy I am. You should always come to me." *And cum for me* would have been added as a joke for his own amusement, if his mouth was not already open for something else.

He is disappointed. Seph, always so modest before and after, is wearing underclothes. A design he's borrowed from one of the human cultures.

"Why do you wear these?" he asks, irritated.

Seph chuckles, taking the crown off of Hades' head. He holds it with two hands, glancing from the crown to Hades' face, and then up and down Hades' body.

He says, "I didn't avoid telling you. I would've told you now—or before." He shrugs. "I've just been very busy. One thing right after the other seems to take our attention. And those guys barely touched me." He sets the crown aside. With his thumbs, he removes the stupid, pointless underclothing. "I can tell you all about it now if you like. One of the guys, Pirithous, put a blade to my neck. But he could never seriously hurt me."

Seph curls over Hades, holding his chin and stopping him from wrapping his lips around Seph's cock (for now). They kiss at an awkward angle, and Seph puts his chiton up around his waist with his other hand.

Hades hates multitasking. Seph has a beautiful cock, and it's thick enough to fill his entire mouth, long enough to almost make him gag. But from down here, he has to say, looking up at Seph sternly, "I will always make time for protecting you. I am never too busy—"

With the little souls, Seph has endless patience. With Hades, he has none. And by his smug expression, he quite likes having Hades on his knees in front of him. He tugs Hades' head close, and Hades does not deny his husband. The pillows still call, and his eyes are so tired they're starting to blur, but first he wants this. All of this.

He is sweet. Verah's fruit platter has been the extra sugar in his dessert. The cock is soft at first, and easy to wrap his lips around. But soon it pokes the back of his throat. Hades sighs through his nose, letting his eyes drift shut. He pushes Seph's knees wider and lets his hands drift wherever they want.

Belatedly, he realizes he did not spend as much time exploring as he should. He and Seph are still early lovers and should be having long, amazing sex. But the last several times have been rushed.

I owe him more than that. I need to be a better lover.

Yet he does not slow down or tease. The decision to make weighs on him. Finish Seph now and taste him in his mouth? Oh, Hades wants to do that so much. But he also needs Seph hard and demanding inside him. It won't be satisfying unless he gets it. So somehow...

If Seph had god magic, he could stay hard...

A spell. I need a spell. No, an herb. Magic on someone else's body is too risky.

I could come up with something...

Someday, if the work ever ends...

Seph pushes him back. The smugness is gone. He is so focused and wanting, he looks a bit like the determined god Hades faced back inside the tent. And Hades is so small on his knees right now. Seph pets around his face. A wetness of something dribbles from the corner of Hades' mouth and he licks it off. But Seph hasn't finished yet.

"I love you," his husband says, and Hades hurriedly agrees.

"Yes, I love you too. Take me now. And never delay information like that to me again."

He hates to ruin a perfectly good moment, but he's afraid this will be another thing that gets buried underneath all the work. This is a serious discussion that has to happen. He won't have Seph putting off news of an attack again.

A second time will make him extremely angry. So Seph has to agree to this.

His husband only frowns a little, not speaking at first.

"Tell me, Seph. Tell me it won't happen again. And then take me. Please."

Seph looks like he's considering something. Then he picks up Hades' crown and puts it back on his head. Balancing the weight would make it rather difficult to start sucking again, and Hades is considering it. He doesn't want to fight. Or to give a scolding. He just wants his glorious husband to have pleasure with him and to never make that mistake again.

"I didn't do anything wrong. And I had every intention of telling you. When there was time."

Seph scoots sideways, and Hades wonders how he's going to fix this.

"Seph, please don't be difficult. I'm not mad about anything."

"Get up," Seph says, and offers his hand. Strangely, he smiles. Are they going to be mean to each other? Will Seph try to impress on him again that they are equal kings?

Eventually, Hades will have to set the boundary. Yes, they are equal kings, but Seph may not be able to do hunts anymore if he thinks this responsibility means he can keep things from him. He will have to accept that.

But I can't say any of that now without hurting him.

Seph orders, "Against the vanity. I've wanted to do this for a long time, but you're always busy when you're headed off in the mornings."

"Evenings are good too," Hades says, planting himself on his hands in front of the mirror. "Just tell me where you want me, anytime."

Seph positions himself behind him. There will be no preparation, but Hades won't need it. He's eager to feel stretched, and Seph will quickly find the place inside that makes him push his butt out eagerly. His stallion has an eager mate, and Seph's cock seems to be shaped for Hades specifically, the head and length nudging back and forth on that area, making Hades whine and pant for it sometimes...

They haven't even begun. Seph *does* slow down, and he does use a finger first, testing Hades' tightness. The king sighs impatiently and wonders if he should say something. Many times, he has told

Seph *I am fine*, only to have the younger man take his time anyway. Maybe he prefers it this way.

But meanwhile that finger simply won't be enough, no matter how open and displayed Hades is. He needs it deep.

Then Seph speaks. "You know, I was never in any danger. You gave me Hecate to keep me safe, and to have some of my own power. That's exactly what happened. Her magic manifested through me, and I protected myself, in a way. It depends how you look at it. But I don't want you to see me as a weak king who needs protecting."

Can we not speak about this right now? Can we finish the discussion later?

But he knows that wouldn't be fair. He's the one who brought up the attack in the first place. They might as well finish it. Even if Seph is finally satisfied with his inspection (it wasn't thorough this time, thank god), and he positions to give Hades the real thing.

His lower back sinks. He arches up otherwise and lifts his rear end with his toes.

Seph is *big*. He always has to force his way into Hades' tight little hole.

"I just—have to know if—have to know—" *Fuck.* Hades' eyelids flutter.

Seph might be cautious to start before they've begun, but once he's inside it's like he can't help himself. He pushes deep and hard, forcing Hades open. The dark king winces. But he wouldn't have Seph stop for the world. He'll be loose and slick soon enough. His muscles clamp down on Seph, and (right or not) somewhere a primal part of him is saying, *Seph is mine. Nobody takes him from me. If someone tries, they'll rot in my dungeons for eternity. And I want to know about it because I want to punish the bastards.*

But of course, that side of him might be insane, like his father. It is the side Hermes spoke about when he said the god was oftentimes *unintentionally* cruel. Oh, there is plenty of intention behind it. He simply loses his mind when someone tries to harm someone who is his to look after. Or if that subject harms themselves under his care.

The protective part of him is a beast to be tamed and controlled. So for Seph, he says, "I have to know so I can get information. Uhh." He finds his top half sinking as Seph begins to thrust into him completely. His pace is slow. Hades needs to relax and offer himself up. His stallion will get what he wants soon.

His crown makes a little *tink* against the mirror as he lowers his head. He pushes it to keep it on for Seph's amusement, but when he looks into the mirror, Seph's gaze is downward. Watching Hades stretch to fit him in.

"Zeus, he—might be—" Hades can't even remember how he would have finished that sentence. Something about protection. Unlawful abduction. Something, something a bounty and bribes.

Seph nudges against that spot inside him, and keeps brushing past it with excellent aim. Hades has been trying to last longer, for it seems that Seph can last forever but Hades is often over too quick.

It's been a long time. Over a month.

Heh, like one of Seph's hunts.

Ohh, it feels like an eternity.

The moaning part of that thought comes out of him, and at last the animal part of Seph's mind takes over. He whispers something, kissing Hades' shoulder, and then large heavy hands pin him down to the vanity. There's a ring or something trapped underneath Hades. His face knocks aside one of the tonics for cleaning his skin. His nose pushes against the bottom of the mirror, and strands of hair fall into his eyes.

But Seph's enormous cock fits into him, and his stallion ruts against the back of him, finally using Hades' body for his own selfish desires. His balls are so huge and heavy they slap against the back of his own, and Hades' insides spasm around the enormous cock, his climax coming on too soon.

"No. Not yet."

He is speaking to himself mostly. It isn't a command. But the first *no* makes Seph pause, and Hades does everything he can to hold back. To let the waves pass unspilled. He knocks something over as he reaches underneath quickly and pinches himself.

"Are you okay?" Seph asks, and there is no amusement in his tone, only concern. His stallion is an animal when he lets himself be. But the man inside is considerate and careful. Exactly the sort of person Hermes remembered him to be.

"Yes, I'm fine. Don't stop, Seph. I can hold myself back when you're inside me."

Seph breaks into an easy smile. He leans over Hades, wrapping him in a hug. He starts moving again, but his shaft stays deep, avoiding rubbing that sensitive area too much for now.

The tease somehow makes it *worse*.

"I don't want you to finish early either. I've heard there is a way of tying the balls—well, we can talk about it later. There's a lot written about sex practices in the library, you know. And a lot of erotic fiction as well."

"I love that you have taken to studying." Hades knows everything there is about coupling, of course, and perhaps a little too much. He will enjoy playing innocent to let Seph teach him though.

"I want to turn you over, okay? I want to see your face. And not just in a mirror."

"Uh-huh—mm." That sound is supposed to be a yes, and Seph interprets it correctly. Losing the connection to him is a disappointment though. It takes so long to leave. Hades just wants to thrust himself back down on him and keep going. But he grasps a necklace lying atop the vanity and lets Seph turn him around.

Leaning backward over the desk, he catches his breath, every limb relaxed to let Seph position him however he wants. But Seph doesn't move him yet. His gaze travels down Hades' chest to his fully erect, flushed cock, and Seph touches himself, pinching himself as well.

So Hades is not the only one with the problem.

But Seph's cock is so wet and glistening, it almost seems he could be finished already. He drips when his fingers pinch.

I want all of that inside me.

Hades pushes himself up onto the desk, sitting on it, and Seph closes in on him at the same time. Their mouths meet. They breathe into each other. And Hades is tasting pomegranate, his tongue pushed selfishly into his lover's mouth, as that cock returns and there's nothing shy or considerate about it.

Hades whines when it hits, lifting a leg to wrap around Seph's hips. Seph fits easily, and at this new angle, he is always deep, driving hard, greedy, and never close to leaving Hades. He's just too damn big.

He could probably fuck me with half his length, and it'd feel just the same...

Seph finishes. He's first, for once. Then one of Seph's hands wraps around him, and Hades' hole begins to spasm and clench, all around Seph's cumming cock. The waves build up and Hades doesn't fight it. He spills over.

Several breaths later, Seph pulls out of him.

"I don't want you to worry about me. That's what I was going to say. At some point. Protecting myself from murderers and abductors is my responsibility first and foremost, you know."

Hades cannot even begin to continue the discussion right now. He feels Seph's cum dripping out of him. And he is slightly concerned for the surface of the vanity, which may need to be cleaned immediately. He can't have Verah do it, and when his head hits a pillow, he will forget.

A little splatter of cum reached the pendant he wears today. He is both impressed with himself and bemused that he has never seen cum-covered beryl before. Not in all these millennia.

"I am worried about you. You're doing as much as you can," Seph says as he leans close, his fingers touching near Hades' lips. "And I think you will work yourself as thin as a wraith before you consider the possibility of maybe resting a little."

Hades blinks a few times, a loopy sensation coming over him as he feels the physical exhaustion of his body temporarily. It is not common for a god, and it's a sign that Seph is right. He'll put himself into a century's long sleep if he keeps this up.

A regular sleep is overdue.

"Help me to bed. I think... if you are watching over the boats and looking after the citizens... I think I can rest for a day. Or two."

Fifty-Two

Seph carries Hades back to bed, kissing him on the forehead as if he were a small child. It is strange to hold the mysterious and powerful god, who is limp and weak as a kitten in his arms, and then to move the sheets aside and set his pale, delicate body on top. He has shadows under his eyes from lack of sleep. He gazed at Seph with a loving, dazed expression when they were finished. But now his eyes are solidly closed. He turns his head against the pillow a little, but otherwise doesn't move at all.

He seems asleep. Or even dead.

Seph pulls the covers over him and tucks him in. Then he goes to the latrine to clean up.

Is he tired?

No, no more than usual. Lately Seph has actually felt like he's gaining strength, as his knee gets stronger, and he no longer feels like he's grasping for memories all the time. The reading has helped. It used to be that Seph might forget the words for common things, like the laces on his sandals, or even body parts like fingernails. But slogging through the books with the help of Hecate and some of the scholarly souls has built his vocabulary up again and even made him feel normal.

He can picture the farmer fields described in some of the texts. He doesn't remember his mother well, but he's relearned family labels and he's heard quite a lot about her. He has no drive to reconnect with her, though he's not heard anything to think she's cruel. His memories, however, are of her always towering over him, looking after him, telling him *don't do this* or *you must do that*. She protected him the way Hades does now, but she did not give him as much freedom.

Seph is happy where he is. And his learning is always pointed at how he can do better in his role as the second king of this place.

He emerges from the latrine refreshed, his chiton righted, and he slips on a new pair of underclothes. He thinks Hades might like underclothes if Seph took to wearing *just* them. His dressed-for-cold-weather husband likes to look upon Seph's naked form, always. And while Hades is a jealous mate, he likes others to envy what he has.

Seph smirks with amusement as he thinks on this. But... there is also a sense of satisfaction in covering up, even just a little bit extra. It is like...

I don't want Hades to own me completely.

I want him to trust me to take care of myself.

He wonders what this means for them, because he knows they didn't come to any agreement in their recent discussion while they were having sex. Seph shouldn't have to run to his husband, falling, every time he has to defend himself. Especially if the need is as frivolous and simple as what happened with the two strange men who came to abduct him.

Seph doesn't want to keep secrets but...

There has to be trust.

How do I get him to listen to me and understand?

Cerberus whines at the door, and Seph lets him in. The dog looks all around suspiciously, slinking and with his heads down, and once he's passed Seph he sneaks to the bed and hops in on the side where Seph isn't. Perhaps he tries to look nonchalant, settling his chins near Seph's pillow and not making a sound. But his eyes roll back to check on Seph. Just staring at him. Watching wherever he goes and not moving a muscle, just looking up when Seph comes near, feigning to be relaxed. But really, Seph knows the stubborn hound is acting like a child.

I'm not moving. What are you going to do? Seph hears from those 'innocent' eyes.

And sure enough, as Seph sits on the bed and finishes his snack from the fruit platter, the dog doesn't budge. Even though Seph nearly sits on him.

Seph scratches the dog's rump. He'd move if Seph wanted him to. A king cannot be run over by a dog. But there's no reason to force Cerberus into obedience without purpose.

Hades is just going to have to get used to me not being helpless anymore. It'll be a gradual thing. Nothing to fight about now.

He sets the platter aside and hears a strange sound in the next room. A shuffle. Or a footstep. Perhaps just Verah cleaning? Or Hecate doing something. But they are not permitted into the rooms whenever they'd like, and this is not their time to be useful. Hecate's room does have an adjoining door to the den, so maybe she came in for some reason?

In any case, Seph gets his cane to walk. It's just better to have it if he's by himself. And he's well aware that he can't magic the simple thing to him, not even the few feet from the window to the bed. That's the kind of god he is when he's by himself.

But as long as I have Hecate, I'm not helpless.

An older memory speaks to him, just a whisper, *I'm a man, Mother!*

He can't remember what she said back, but he knows it wasn't an agreement. Both Hades and Demeter don't see him as fully capable... and that's a problem.

There's no one in the den.

But there is a large covered something in the corner, table legs sticking out from under the sheet. There was no table there before, and Seph hears the little shuffling sound again from under the cloth as he hobbles near, leaning on his cane a lot. He ignored his knee when he was with Hades, and now his spent energy combines with the injury to affect his gait.

He lifts the corner of the cloth. Something inside scuttles about. And as he peels the cloth halfway back over the top, he sees that this is a cage. A well-done, ornamental cage with two levels for a creature inside, a nesting box with carved ornamentation, and a straw floor that pulls out for cleaning.

"Hello. What are you?"

He peers at the dark entrance of the nesting box. Something moves inside. And Seph eyes the vegetables in the food dish.

"I'm guessing you are not a rat. Do you want to come out and meet me?" He picks up a piece of lettuce from the bowl and holds it in front of the door. He wiggles it with his fingers, and also wonders what Hades would want with another pet. Especially since he's mostly into dogs and birds, and the predatory kinds of those. He likes hawks, not so much doves.

"I'm not going to hurt you, little guy. Come on out."

A little twitching nose appears in the darkened box. And then tiny teeth grab onto the lettuce and tug to bring it inside, trying to steal the bribe without stepping out as payment first. Seph moves it just out of his reach.

Soon a rabbit's face peeks out of the hole. Seph smiles to see it, holding in an excited noise. His worries about Hades' possessive and overly protective nature are forgotten.

He got me a present! A white rabbit!

He suppresses his laugh, for the bunny looks rather nervous.

If Hades thinks I'm going to stop calling him Bunny for this gift...

The rabbit steps out of the box.

And suddenly, Seph has a new life. The room is sunny and warm. His mother is behind him. Not just a voice, not just a ghost of something that *might* have happened. She is behind him, solid, wearing a blue dress and some red stone that comes from the sea. Her hair is messy but beautiful atop her head, and she has broad cheekbones and a largish nose. She is a gorgeous and strong-featured woman. Almost the perfect female version of Seph.

And for the first time, Seph feels like he knows her. They have a vivid, visceral connection.

I am your son.

He wishes she was really here. He would run and hug her.

But in the memory she only says, *Make sure he doesn't get out of the box. The cats might eat him.*

That is all, and then in a few seconds the sense of being in this other world disappears.

The rabbit has lost all shyness, fully out of the nesting box now and standing as close as he can get to Seph, his little paws up on the bars. His neck is stretched out high, his nose seeking another treat. He finds the opening to the cage very interesting. And he does not startle or run away as Seph gently scoops his hand underneath him.

"I remember you," Seph says. "Hibus."

Fifty-Three

Seph sits at Hades' desk, the rabbit cradled in his arms, and Hibus (this must be him) seems to cuddle against his chest. Seph would swear the rabbit recognizes him, even if Hibus is supposed to be a simple animal. There are very few mice and rats in the underworld, and only a couple bunnies. The simple animals just don't make it.

So is this the real Hibus? If not the real one, he is very tame and friendly. His appetite sated, feeling perfectly safe, Hibus makes a great yawn as Seph smooths down one of his ears.

"Are you my bunny, little pal? How did Hades find you, hm?"

It must be. But where did Hades find the time? Seph tried gently to wake him up, to thank him for this amazing gift, but the dark god hasn't moved except to breathe since Seph put him down. Cerberus, fully stretched out against Hades, remains unwilling to leave his master's side, even while seeing the small creature in Seph's arms. He's devoted.

And so Seph sits at the desk instead, and while his entire life doesn't come back to him, Seph feels like a piece of himself has clicked into place. Demeter's son. A boy who grew up spoiled and happy but also uncertain of his future and unfulfilled. Not having a place to belong.

"You are my only friend," Seph says, with the feeling he has said it before, or at least thought it.

More memories come.

"You are an old bunny, aren't you? I raised you from a little tiny rabbit. Little children used to swarm me for a peek at you, and I would cradle you securely in my hands, passing you around to pet. But carefully."

Hibus does not feel warm anymore, not that Seph's hands mind. He can still see that small helpless creature burying its face where Seph's palms pressed together. His fur is not the same texture either. There are no actual strands to brush back, only the essence of what was. With horses, dogs, and any kind of animal, they always feel sleeker and smoother than they did when they were alive.

"And I had to scoop your poop and urine out of a box every day. I remember my mother..." It is still hard to picture her completely. He gets glimpses, but nothing he can closely examine. "She scolded me at first, but I think... I think... that was just her way."

She always seems to be saying negative things, speaking to Seph sternly. But with Hibus, the feelings are quite different. They are warm toward her, even if phrases like *filthy animal, barely better than a rat* don't sound very generous or kind-spirited to him now.

He's not sure about her. Hades has always said she is kind, but clingy with Seph, and greatly missing him. Seph has silently held the opinion that no mother should let the innocents of the world wither and die for her selfish grief. He imagines her as being too possessive and controlling, the same symptoms as Hades but scaled up to a mountain.

And he remembers very clearly, two days after his marriage, the level of freedom and gratitude he felt.

But this bunny, the real Hibus or not, creates warmth over the colder memories.

"I'm going to say you are you, little Hibus," Seph says, touching his tiny nose with his finger. "You are a smart bunny to come back to me. And I bet Hades knew just where to find you."

There is a small knock at the door. It is not Verah, who taps too lightly, and it's not from Hecate's room. It is someone in the solarium, so Seph shifts the rabbit to a one-armed hold and goes to greet the visitor.

Hopefully it is not a little soul asking to leave. Hades worries that he set a precedent.

It is Hermes.

"Oh, hi. Hello," says the young-faced god. He is taller than Seph, and their chitons are about the same size, exposing miles and miles of shapely legs. Seph is sure more of him would be exposed by a very slight breeze or a certain pose. And the god who is his cousin would not mind.

"I would like to set an appointment with you." His eyes dart side to side, and he seems to be trying to look in, maybe to find out if Hades is with him. "Usually there is a house slave to speak to, or I put in a written request with the mistress of the house. But, uh, none of that applies to you, soo..."

"What do you want to talk about?" Seph asks, letting the door fall open a little wider. He'd rather get this over with.

"I see you found Hades' precious gift! He was not easy to catch. I spent an embarrassing amount of time stooping to reach under bushes, and I even crawled under a house! How do you get him to hold so still?" Before Seph can answer, the god is already speaking again.

"Well, the appointment is rather useless once I explain why I'm here. I want to know if there is anything we can do to ease Demeter's grief enough that she'll consider helping the Earth into the warm season. Humans are not well suited for the icy cold. It took them thousands of years to populate and learn and build their cities. Right now the cities are already in dire trouble. And if I don't convince her soon, I'm afraid some of the greatest places of achievement and learning for mankind are about to be empty rock. You see, the humans themselves may come down here and live and prosper... but up above, the constructs of their imagination and wisdom, the very achievements that make humans so amazing—are about to be lost."

Seph does not find him so annoying now as he did when they first met. He wears the most ridiculous helmet Seph has ever seen, and his wavy hair and good looks make Seph think his bright smile is because he's full of himself. But perhaps that is a touch of jealousy. While Seph's hair is brunette with a sheen of red now and then (nothing to brag about, especially on a man), Hermes is a golden blond. And it looks much better. His face is flawless as well.

And he's known Hades a lot longer than me...

But these fears are unfounded.

"Come in, Cousin Hermes. We don't make appointments or hold hearings in Hades' palace. We are not like mortal kings."

"Ah. Thank you. I love, uhh, this place." He looks up at the mural on the ceiling of a stag fleeing through the forest, hunted by wolves. "I always have. Are you, uh, doing any decorating? To make this place your own? You know, usually the one married is the mistress— or the master, I guess—of the house. I don't see too many of your own things in here. Are you sure you're happy?"

Well, there he goes being irritating again.

"I am perfectly happy. And if I'm not, I will change whatever is needed so that I will be." Seph sits and puts his feet on the desk. He lets Hibus wander on his stomach and fences him in with his hands.

"Wow. You look just like him. The two of you must be taken with each other, I see." Hermes takes a nearby seat, but instead of sitting he only leans over the chair toward Seph. "I have to put a stop to your mother. I need your help."

"I'm not returning home, so I don't see how I could help. Before you do anything dangerous, you should know that Hecate is already aware of your presence, and while she's not spying on us or anything, you should act as if she's already in the room." Hermes looks surprised and even mildly affronted, but his unasked-for concern is not altruistic. He would've come to the wedding or visited Seph right after if they were close as cousins.

"And besides, I don't see what the goddess's grief has to do with me. I am married now. I am happy." Seph shrugs. "I have no wish to leave."

Hermes' eyes widen. "You're kidding, right? You don't see what Demeter's grief has to do with *you*? Persephone—are you even aware that the entire world was covered in ice before Demeter carried you? The entire world filled with humans and cities and great green fields, all of those things exist because of you! Before you were even born, Demeter set out to create a paradise for her son to prosper and live in. Before that, humans were huddled up in caves, fighting off enormous predators and hunting with pointed sticks.

"They did alright. They even made music and poetry, some of them. But it wasn't very good and their language wasn't sophisticated. Humans didn't start to put themselves together into a civilization until their basic needs were met. That meant seasonal warmth and food. Prometheus gave them fire to cook with, but farming and sunny seasons were the real catalyst to forming the humans we have now. Demeter is responsible for that. She made the winter short and taught humans to plant the first seeds. And that was all for you."

"I didn't know that," Seph says, letting Hibus hop onto the desk as he gets restless. "It must have been a long pregnancy. I am only twenty-six years old."

"Yes, well, gods come into being in all kinds of ways. Demeter never once looked heavy with you, and it wasn't something that she talked about. But she knew you were there, and she may have held you inside her until she determined that the world was ready. Who knows."

"That does not sound like a mother I want to go back to," Seph says, drumming his fingers on his stomach, wondering how uncomfortable it must be for a baby to be trapped in the womb. Could he ever remember such a thing? He hopes not.

"Hades says that if I go back, she won't let me return. He says Demeter will hide me and keep me in a prison or something. He says my father Zeus is dangerous as well."

Hermes avoids looking at him and doesn't deny it.

Seph says, "I think the safest place for me is here, at my husband's side. I am happy, and I won't leave him."

"And that's fine, Persephone. But isn't there *something* we can do?" Hermes offers a hand to the rabbit to sniff, and Hibus hops away from him. So he isn't friendly with everybody. And that settles it. He's the one. The real Hibus.

I got someone from my family back.

Seph gathers Hibus again, and the bunny is as tame as a house cat.

"I have everything I need here. I'm not happy that people are dying, but that is neither my fault nor my responsibility. That lies with Demeter and Zeus. My father especially. I understand that he is supposed to be the king up there, is he not? Why isn't your appointment with him?"

Hermes' fingers tap the chair, fidgeting. "I did do that. And that's why I came down here to assess... uh, the situation. From what I can see, you are doing well and Hades is doing well. But the upperworld is still freezing and dying off slowly. Humans can still make it in their caves, but Seph... have you forgotten the beauty of human cities? Don't you remember your home with fondness? Perhaps if I could show you what it's like there now—we could leave very quickly, you know, and just come straight back and then you would—"

"Do you think I'm a fucking idiot?"

Hecate.

Seph merely has to say her name. He would have already if Hermes moved toward him. But surely an abduction would not come with such an obvious request first?

Maybe. He thinks Hermes must be considering it, even now.

"Hades is in the next room. He's asleep, but that can change." *I'm certain the dog would protect me too. If I called for him.*

Seph is maybe a little hurt that the hound isn't interested in him and their company one bit.

"What about a letter or something?" Hermes asks. "Or you could give your mother some kind of gift? What if you asked her, even begged her, to stop these freezing winds and let the crops come back before they're gone forever? Could you do that for me? You're very selfish, you know, saying that this is Zeus's problem only. That this is all your mother's fault.

"You and Hades are not just the kings of the underworld. You are the kings of everything! That's why I serve Hades first and foremost in our family. Someday, if Zeus doesn't overthrow you, you two will be the only kings there are. And I think—I *know*—we are going to need humans to survive if we are to live together as one kingdom. They're going to teach us how to govern, the way they've already taught us some of the most magnificent songs and stories in history. Humans should not be left to freeze like this. All the gods in existence—you, myself, even our crazy old uncle Dionysus—all of us need to be concerned that we're about to lose the greatest creation we've ever had."

Fifty-Four

Seph pets Hibus for a long while, just staring at nothing. Sometimes he looks at the wolf mural above him, for it's the only picture of the upperworld available to him. At one point, he cocks his head and wonders, *Why does Hades have this here? He doesn't even like the upperworld.* But he can't deny that it suits the room, with its elegance, beauty, and grim presence.

Seph loves how Hades comes undone in his hands. It is like the god becomes younger and untroubled. More like himself, and he loses the presence of a dark underworld king. But only for a little bit, when they're all over each other, which is Seph's favorite time.

He smiles thinking of the new memories he's made, and then the innocent, unsuspecting rabbit hops onto his chest and bumps his head against Seph. Hibus becomes insistent on brushing up against him, and even gives Seph's chin a lick.

Leaning back in Hades' chair, his feet up on the desk (exactly the way his lover likes to recline also), Seph cuddles the rabbit and muses on what he *almost* remembers. Almost.

There was another lover before. Fimus? The slave?

No. Maybe...

"Come on, little guy. Back you go. I love you too, but another calls me."

He carries Hibus to the cage, thinking, *I am happy here. That is not an illusion. I don't want to go back, do I?*

He closes the door to Hibus' cage, a frown creeping onto his features.

But the letter I write will certainly not dissuade an upset goddess from a tirade of murder.

He was going to rejoin Hades in the bed, but now he redirects himself to the desk again. He sits properly and grabs a scroll and ink for writing. Slowly, he draws sentences onto the paper, each word mechanical and unfelt.

Dear Mother. I am well.

It lingers there a long time, then picks up speed with the following lines:

You have created a lot of work for us, starving mankind until they eat their dogs and cats. We have even taken in a few who have consumed the already dead corpses of their children. Though it caused them great sorrow. Hades thinks they can heal from this trauma, especially those who have reunited with their children here, but I am not so sure.

All the new souls brought to Elysium have deep sadness for the things they suffered before coming here.

And then there is so much he wants to say but he doesn't. *How could you do this? What sort of monster are you? Are you punishing me by killing the whole world?*

There is a whisper of wrongness in his thoughts. He disagreed a lot with the mother he remembers, but when he held Hibus, there was a new warmth to his previous life he can't describe. He doesn't think this is solely due to the love he imagines from a pet bunny.

So he ends the letter instead with:

I am learning to be a king, and I find my life fulfilling here. Please help the crops come back this summer, or I'm afraid the great cities we've come to admire from mankind will just be stone and wood again. Think of what we will lose, Mother. The teachings of philosophers have been profound even to our oldest gods. These accomplishments, which may be with or without material form, are the consciousness of the humans, and the end of their advancement is a great loss.

He thinks, and decides to let it be. So he signs it, *Persephone, King of the Underworld, Ruler of the Dead, God of the Harvest's End.* And lastly, though he pauses a long moment, *Your Loving Son.*

He rolls it up, secures it with wax and twine, and there it sits on the desk as he wonders if he should redraft it. The words are not compelling enough. He sort of remembers her warmth and the connection they shared, but he can't create that same emotion with unspoken words on a page.

It's that warmth that she misses. That love she had.

This letter might actually make the winters on Earth even worse. She will know I've lost whatever was there.

And so Seph returns to Hades thinking a great many things, all of it so large and interconnected he isn't sure where to begin solving the issues that nag him.

"Move, dog. Cerberus, please. Off you go."

Cerberus does not move at all, acting like an enormous sack of potatoes on the bed. Nor do any of his heads snap or growl, which is an improvement. Seph tries to forcefully wedge himself between the dog and Hades, but doing so begins to disturb his husband's sleep too much. So, kneeling on the bed, shoving a rump that won't budge, Seph says sternly, "Don't make me get Hecate to hold a whip over your head."

Then he gets an idea. He makes a fist, no whip visible, though he calls on his magic (pretending he has it, because he's never felt his own magic before) and hopes a whip will appear. "Get down. Now."

The dog takes a moment to decide, his ears flat, his shoulders sulking. Then he scuttles off the bed, looking ashamed.

Seph takes his place, relieved. Perhaps if Hades did not work so much he wouldn't care, but in this instance, he won't let an opportunity to sleep beside his husband be usurped by a dog.

Cerberus does a short circle and looks over the bed at him. He utters a pathetic whine.

"Alright, come back in." Seph pats the open space beside him. He is going to snuggle up on Hades' side anyway, leaving a large space empty.

Cerberus makes the mattress dip with his massive weight, enough for three dogs even if he's only using the body of one. He licks Seph once, and then he turns a fast circle, disrupting the blankets, digging at them and winding up the covers to leave Hades exposed now.

Seph tries to pull them back. Cerberus gives him a beseeching stare.

"Oh, alright. You big mutt. With a big butt." He shoves Cerberus fondly and scratches his rump. They're learning to get along with each other. And Hades loves his dog, so automatically Seph wants to love him too.

Hades makes a small disgruntled sound. He explained to Seph that all gods have innate powers, things happening without thinking about it. Most acts require intent, will, or even a spell. And many more feats require such massive effort, they may be impossible to do, even if it is as easy as breathing for another god. Their magic finds unique pathways to wield miracles, and powerful gods simply have more innate abilities than others. The gods must lean into their powers, as he put it, and not fight against whatever advantages and limitations they may have.

Seph cannot control his powers, but his innate magic creates warmth. For himself.

"Do not worry, love. I will keep you warm."

He covers Hades with his arms and a leg, pulling him in close.

"Your stupid dog took all the blankets," he mutters and falls asleep.

Fifty-Five

He wakes up feeling particularly good, dreaming of Hades' tongue inside him, his hands parting his ass, his wet tongue, impossibly long, reaching inside him and stroking—

And his eyes open realizing that it's actually happening. He's sprawled, mostly on his stomach, his husband's form absent underneath his limbs, and Cerberus has disappeared from the other side of the bed next to him. Instead, there are familiar hands holding his ass open, a familiar, dreamy, but real tongue poking inside him, and his erection is trapped against his stomach, hot against the sheets.

Seph blinks the sleep out of his eyes, yawning, looking around himself bewildered.

"Are you not impatient?"

He's not quite sure what he's asking, or accusing, exactly. He hasn't remembered how to speak yet, and Hades' tongue feels just as good as it did in his dream. He can only see the top of Hades' head back there. He slept in his jewelry, which Seph hadn't noticed before. He feels a cold and rigid jewel brush against his ass, and he lets out a moan, burying his face in the pillow.

He takes a few breaths to just process that this is happening. He's awake. And Hades is doing the most wonderful thing to him. His nerves are lit up, his muscles jump as Hades licks a very personal place, and he flexes his hole, wishing he could draw his husband inside him…

While his cock wishes to be buried in his husband's ass, letting that velvet squeeze the milk out of him…

"Hades…" he moans, turning his face against the soft pillow at last, needing to breathe.

Hades replaces his tongue with two fingers. It does not feel as good as Seph imagined. He is not used to it yet. Though he has asked Hades to switch roles with him before, the god says he is content to play instead and Seph may take a long time before he is ready for it. Hades is in no hurry. He says he prefers their current arrangement anyway.

But Seph imagines that he would very much love to have Hades inside him, and he urges himself to relax around the god's fingers.

"Yes, my love," Hades says in a lazy, disinterested way. "You said my name? You're requiring something, I presume?"

"You're supposed to be sleeping. It hasn't been enough time, has it?"

He intended to keep the bedroom extra quiet and let Hades sleep an entire day. The god should need it. Though Hades looks vibrant and healthy, and his smirk is like a satisfied cat. His hair never tangles in sleep, inexplicably, but it looks unadorned and bare without his crown. When Hades wears his crown, you don't even notice his hair. You are talking to the King of the Underworld, after all.

Without it, his hair is simple. Straight, long, platinum.

Seph watches him, half his face buried in the pillow, looking back coyly.

"Get back to sleep with me. You are going to wear yourself out even further if you continue."

Of course, he only says that because he knows his strong, stubborn husband will not be stopped. His cock is greedy and twitches already. He knows that body will wrap around him in all ways, his ass and limbs both, and Hades will squeeze him and rock against him until he's finished. He wants it now.

But for the moment, because it suits him, Seph will play the protesting virgin.

"You need your sleep. Stupid king."

"I have had ten hours. It's more than enough for the week."

Hades' eyes lower and his mouth returns. His tongue sticks out first, making Seph draw himself up tight with anticipation. And then it's moving on him, in him, and lapping incessantly. Seph gulps and lets go of a heavy breath, squeezing the pillow under him. Hades should *stop* and Seph shouldn't like this so much. The god is *licking his anus* like he's enjoying the flavor. Like he's hungry for it. Like there's nothing disgusting or dirty about it, and Seph is a delicacy.

Seph makes fists on either side of his pillow. His cock is heavy and needy, but he ignores it for now. It's easy to let it wait. His hole is flexing and mouthing back, all the nerve endings there alive with pleasure. He doesn't desire to cum so much as he desires *more of this.*

And he wonders...

What is Hades getting out of it?

Is this Seph's pleasure alone?

But his husband's eyes are lidded with pleasure, and he has Seph parted in his hands like this is his specialty. Like he plans to do this for a while.

And Seph begins to wonder...

How much more of this can I stand?

"Hades?" he moans, the name a question, but he isn't sure what he wants to say. "How long are you going to do this to me?"

The tongue leaves. It's mind-boggling that something so normal should get to do these dirty things to him. That tongue speaks decrees and powerful spells. And it also laps inside Seph's ass eagerly, devouring him like a sweet.

Hades tilts his head, getting the perfect angle, and his tongue reaches impossibly deep. It's not so much the *pleasure* that makes Seph wild (makes him moan and almost cry out, blushing), it's the fact that Hades licks so intimately against him without hesitation. With only desire and want, and his fingers follow after the tongue, poking deep, going in to open him up.

And Seph knows then. It's time.

He lifts his head out of the pillow, panting, and looks back.

"I want you."

There is a telltale smug smirk. Perhaps this was the dark god's intent all along. But in any case, he continues licking. There's no hurry for now. Seph lets him for a little bit, feeling nervous, but also adventurous.

He's not worried about pain. He just worries about being good at it, for it seems like a lot to take in, and what if he has to ask Hades to stop? Won't that be disappointing for his husband? Won't Hades want to wait for a long, long time after that, like he said?

So Seph does not ask again, even though everything happening to him feels very good. He urges his body to unwind instead, like he's getting a massage. He forgets about the dirtiness and just lets himself go into pleasure.

His needy cock is perhaps disappointed to be ignored, but Seph knows Hades isn't done with him. Hades just hasn't had his fill of this yet, which is amazing.

He must be getting something out of it. I'm going to try this on him.

And then it becomes a lazy game to memorize his moves. Hades takes to prodding and licking, both. At one point, a single finger opens him up, hooking slightly to make it feel bigger than it really is, and Hades moves his mouth on the open hole, making Seph lift his head and gasp, despite how sleepy and calm he's become.

And then Hades magics the slick oil to his waiting hand, the drawer opening by itself and the vial flying through the air. Seph waits, focused on everything he hears happening behind himself, prepared to like it but nervous still.

Hades' slick fingers in his hole feel like they belong. And Seph bunches the pillow up under him, hoping it all feels good but prepared for some discomfort.

He's surprised to feel his insides warming up unnaturally. There's fire in the gel from the vial, but not the stinging kind.

"Is that you doing that to me?"

"Just a little. Don't worry, my magic is safe."

"I wasn't worried."

You would never hurt me.

Quietly, though it is a problem for later, he also has the quick, impetuous thought: *You won't let me go, either.*

"Are you ready to be taken by me, stallion?"

Hades bites his ass cheek gently, just nibbling the flesh between his teeth. It makes Seph's body seize up with ticklish impulses, but Hades only waits, and Seph manages to hold still until the feeling subsides. He looks back, and Hades' teeth are visible behind his rosy wet lips. It is a sharp-toothed cat's smile.

"Yes. I'm ready. Please."

And he's still so nervous, but he's glad Hades doesn't slow down to prepare him more.

Maybe this is why he's always in a hurry, telling me not to bother with opening him up—

Seph groans. Hades' cock is a lot bigger than his fingers and tongue. And he eases in without stopping. Until he's about halfway, all of Seph's muscles tightening like mad, and the deeper he goes, the tighter he gets. It feels like Hades stops right before it's about to hurt.

And then he moves in and out. Slowly.

It's hard at first. Then easier and easier.

Gradually, Seph realizes he doesn't have to worry at all. He can let go and just trust Hades to do this to him.

Fifty-Six

His stallion is gorgeous underneath him, tanned thighs thick with muscle spread out and knees bent, propping up a round ass that's gaping wide to take him in. A push forward makes those muscles clamp down on him, and Seph makes delicious heavy breathing sounds.

Soon his stallion eases onto him, and Hades is a doting master, brushing his hair off his shoulders, kissing the nape of his neck, propping himself up and leaning over his lover's back. Then he drives gently, his hips moving in and out. He leans to one side to rest on an elbow, gathering up Seph's hair with his other hand, gently tugging and imitating dominant games while his lips continue to seek and dip and kiss. Then he reaches underneath Seph and hugs him like that.

He moves faster. Seph is getting fucked for his very first time. Hades will not disappoint. But he is kind and romantic too, as much as he can be, while selfish desires well up in his mind.

He wants Seph to be soft and accommodating, mewling, and he wants Seph to take all that he has to give him, *however* he wants to give it to him. As his mind drifts, he imagines Seph on his back, blushing shyly, biting his fist. He sees him bent over his desk with his back sunk low and his shapely ass pointed up.

Or maybe just standing at the balcony. Hades would lift up the hem of his chiton and push inside.

I will make you weak for me.

But such fantasies will have to wait. As a virgin, it will be easiest for them both this way.

"I look forward to having you in all sorts of predicaments," Hades says, kissing him and moving his lips over the perfect skin. Seph's tastes like salt and smells like one of his soaps. And he radiates heat, his body always warm like embers after a fire.

Strangely, Seph says, "You will never let me go."

Hades supposes this is a romantic thought, so he says, "Never, my love. You're always safe with me."

"I don't want to go," he says.

"You never will. I will always be here for you." And he wonders if this has to do with how much he's been working.

I have to make time for him somehow.

But he also knows that time may not come for a hundred years. And he knows what kind of state the humans, or this place, will be in when it comes to that.

"I will find time for you, love. I promise."

He decides he can't wait any longer. One fantasy will have to happen now. He turns Seph over, laying him on his back, and enters him again with Seph's thighs wrapped around his hips.

Seph looks at him with lidded, lustful eyes. His cock is the masterpiece of this vision though. Heavy, huge, and pressed between their bodies against his stomach as Hades lowers himself over Seph, kissing his cheek. He reaches between them and down to play with the head by feel alone, letting the ridge of Seph's cock slip up and down on the sensitive inner arch of his thumb. Then he pulls the shaft in rhythm as he drives into him.

Seph cries out and grabs him hard around his shoulders, fingernails digging in, his expression almost of pain. The utmost pleasure.

And Hades' pace slows for this technique, but it's worth it. He feels the muscles spasm around his cock, wringing him for cum. Seph pulls the corner of his pillow to his mouth and bites it. Hades laughs, taking it out of the way, and forces Seph to kiss him instead. He can feel the frustration of such a romantic gesture to counteract a massive need.

Then Seph throws himself on Hades. Bucking into him with his own hips. Encouraging Hades to go faster.

But Hades only stills.

Let the stallion do the riding for his own pleasure.

Hades rather likes taking the more 'submissive' role in bed. He knows that oftentimes the penetrating partner is the one looking after the other's needs.

His stallion will learn a new way to dominate.

It does not look like he will cum this way on his own though. After a bit, Hades has mercy on him. Letting him go and pulling out, Hades takes Seph's hands to quell any complaints from him, pins them up by his head, and raises his body over Seph. Hades' hole is still prepared and comfortable from their activities before.

Initially, there is a bit of catch and slip, Seph's cock being too wet with precum to fit in his tight entrance. But he moves his knees wider and he makes it happen, sinking and pushing backward. He drags his hands down Seph's muscled chest as he sits up, his fingers kneading his taut stomach and splaying around his navel when they get there.

Then it is only a matter of when Hades wants to let him cum. They have changed roles, but he is still the master.

Seph touches his knees, petting. He's a bit lazy when they do it like this, but he's good in that he stays hard and lets Hades take his time.

Not today, love.

Even in this moment, flexing around Seph to find the right angle, using his body to milk him and find pleasure for himself also, there are thoughts of the work to be done. He said he could rest, but now the cost weighs on him heavily.

He sighs in real life and in his thoughts. But then banishes the notion of work and lets himself focus fully on the sensation of his lover instead.

Seph lifts himself up and kisses him. Again, they change positions, Seph holding him as he pushes Hades all the way back, and then begins thrusting into him, grabbing his legs to hold him open wide, kissing him continuously so that he struggles for breath.

The work does not invade. Hades gives up all fantasy of being the master and becomes the submissive instead, arching his back against the bed, moaning and clenching down on his master's cock as Seph drives it into him.

He's breathless as he cums. And Seph never stops moving inside him, his pace picking up as his climax comes over him as well.

Trying something different was fun. But Hades has never had as much pleasure as he gets from Seph's massive fit form pushing into him, holding him, keeping him secure and warm. He shudders as Seph finishes inside him with a final surge.

Seph chuckles and pushes his fingers into Hades' hair when they're all done.

"Well, that was interesting."

"Hm," Hades responds, unable to make words.

"I think we did it every which way in one go."

"Mmm, we can do it lots of ways."

Then they are apart, but not for long. Hades rolls lazily to the side, and Seph comes up behind him, holding him to his chest.

I can fall asleep again just like this.

And distantly some demon in his head taunts, *Work*.

The seconds feel like missed opportunities. He won't get to rest for a couple days like he initially said. There's too much to do.

And then Seph says, "I have to talk to you about something."

"Talk? Now?" Hades asks, not opening his eyes.

"Yes. Because I know you're either about to go to sleep or you're about to leave me. I never get to hold on to you after for very long, you know."

Again, the guilt assaults him. That demon. But what is Hades to do when his kingdom needs him so? The new human souls are scared, alone, and needing his help. Hades took on the task of being their father. He can't rut all day like Zeus.

"All right." He forces his eyes open. He turns a little and looks at Seph as much as he can. "What do you want to talk about?"

"I think I have to go back. To the upperworld."

Fifty-Seven

Seph's arms around Hades are tense, like he is waiting for something in the room to explode. Or maybe he's expecting Hades to grow, like his mother. He now remembers talking to her waist, or her knee, her giant hands big enough to swat him like one of the errant flies in the room. And to make matters worse, he remembers that Demeter grew more animated the more furious she would become, stomping the ground or waving her fists. She certainly flattened a barn or two in their home city when the offerings were meager that year.

She would never hurt me though...

He thinks. He still can't remember her well enough to say he knows her.

And he does know Hades, and he knows of Hades' love for him, but that is not comforting at this time. What he knows about his husband, most of all, is that Hades does not like things in the underworld leaving the underworld. Ever.

His domain is here. This is where he looks after what he cares about most. And once things leave, they are out of his control.

Seph runs the back of one finger down his lover's face. An affectionate gesture, and a test to see if it's bitten off. It would not be out of character for Hades' head to twist all the way around and for his lips to lift in a snarl. Cerberus does that sometimes.

"Did you hear me?" He checks that the god's eyes are open, and they are. That feeling again pressures him as if the walls are closing in on the room. As if the ground is shaking, and something is about to burst out from underneath the bed.

But Hades' voice is cool, almost tranquil enough to be called untroubled, as he finally asks, "Why do you say that?"

"I wrote a letter to my mother to appeal to her pity, but it's not going to be enough. I don't know how I know, but I just know. I think I remember trying to get away from my mother all the time..." He says this to pacify Hades, for his instincts tell him it's necessary. In truth, he is not sure what he felt around her. Apprehension. Irritation. Sometimes a kind of trapped seething, but always in mild quantities. What he knows for sure is that he wants to see her again. He's curious, if nothing else.

"But at the same time I want to see her. I couldn't put the right words on paper because I don't remember enough about her. If I see her, my memories will come back, and I think I'll be able to speak to her in such a way that she stops this evil that seems to be killing everything in the upperworld."

"No." Hades closes his eyes as if they are done.

"What do you mean *no*?" Seph picks himself up to hover over his husband's face, wanting to see his expression.

Hades mimics sleep with closed eyes and a slack expression, but his words are spoken clearly and he does not sound tired.

"Supervising you on such a journey will put us more behind in our work. And besides, Demeter is not your responsibility. Or mine, like you said. The Elysium citizens are ours to look after, no matter what Hermes claims."

So Hades figured out where Seph got the idea. But that doesn't change what Seph knows. He needs to go back.

"It's not just for Hermes or Demeter or even entirely for the poor humans—who are dying by the scores, you know. They are disappearing off most of the continents. You know that. But it's also about me."

His husband's eyes open. He's listening.

"I'm missing most of myself, Hades. You know this. I can barely remember anything that happened before I woke up."

"Well, you weren't here very long. We talked about that."

He sits up, his back to Seph, his elbows put on his knees. And when Seph looks around, he holds his face in his hands as if he's weeping. But when Hades lifts his face, he only appears worn. And slightly mad.

Seph chooses not to use a soft or comforting tone. He speaks as the king now.

"It's true, I told you not to worry about Demeter. But I've changed my mind. A matter of death is a matter of ours, wouldn't you say? And I think we should want our citizens to lead prosperous, fulfilling lives before they come here. They should learn and develop as much as they can, unless you want them with a half-starved nature, wild and unthoughtful. You know that the temperament of humans is equal parts consequence and spirit. I've read from many scholars in the library, and a lack of resources teaches them to fight and steal when they're young. Abundance is necessary for sensitivity."

"This is all Hermes," Hades says, standing up. Even while they're arguing, Seph notices the signs of distress in his physical form. Hades may very well be able to stay awake a week with ten hours of sleep, but he has a physical body while the souls don't. Without illusions cast to hide his imperfections, shadows and lines of stress stand out starkly against his skin. More so than before.

What used to be a round and perfect but dainty little ass now has a lean look to it. The dimples behind each hip bone have become knobby instead of muscular and alluring.

They especially protrude, along with the line of his spine, as he bends down and pulls on his northerner pants.

"Hermes was an adviser. I am the king and the decider."

The scoff Seph hears, for Hades doesn't look at him, makes his jaw close tightly. He rises out of bed too, though it is just to sit up for now. He feigns a relaxed pose.

There is something simmering here. Something old. Talking about Seph's mother and Hades' disregard for his opinion has brought it back.

"Our kingdom is here," Hades says right before he pulls a shirt over his head. His hair is tousled, and he does not look kind as he scans the floor for his socks.

"Stop dressing and speak to me. Our kingdom is everywhere."

To his credit, Hades does pause as requested, in the act of leaning over even. There is a faint old memory playing over this one. His mother, again in a blue dress, moving around the room, waving her hands as he tries to tell her something important. The frustration he's experiencing is both present and past.

"You do not have any pull over Demeter," Hades says. "You never have."

And that is true. Seph feels it in his very soul, as if these words are a beacon to all those memories he's missing.

"Nobody does, really," Hades continues. "Not even me. I might have to kill her to sway her. And Seph, how do you kill a mountain? What do you do with it after?"

"I'm certainly not saying kill her. I'm saying I have to go back."

"And tell her what?" He resumes dressing, but it is not so hurried. He sits on the bed by Seph to put on his socks.

"That is what I'm going to improvise. When I see her and remember her, I will know how to address her with all the right reasoning. I will persuade her. We were..." He tries to put a label on it. "Not enemies. We were close. Fighting... but close."

"You were family. And trust me, in this family, that is no benefit."

"She will listen to me."

Hades' fist thumps the bed, though not with furious force. "No. She won't. Do you know why I came to get you in secret? Usually collecting the 'bride' from the parents' house is a public ceremony. But I stole you down here like a thief in an alley. You know why? Because you don't move a mountain, that's why. You go around it."

"I can move her. I'm her son. Hermes told me something... He says that the Earth was cold before I was conceived. He says my mother made the upperworld warm and taught the humans how to farm specifically for me. She made the world for me to live in it."

"Her affection for you is a danger more than it is a benefit." Hades goes to his vanity. He picks up bottles like he's searching for something, occasionally untopping one to sniff. Seph knows he is looking for the serum he applies before brushing his hair. Something to keep every strand straight.

"Hades, do you think that because I am not kept in this bed by chains what you're doing to me now is any different than what she would do to me up there?"

Hades pauses, the correct bottle in hand, and stares at him for two seconds.

"Well. It is different."

A second later. "We are married."

"I do not want to be your bride, Hades. Not in the Greek sense. You told me on my first night here that you despised men who rape their wives."

"And you disagreed with me."

"Yes, because I didn't understand it then. I'm not sure why. I must've thought all gods preferred only Greek culture, and that human culture would never change. I was naïve. Stupid even. I was not very educated, I think. I can't remember." Seph picks at the blanket a moment, wishing he had a better memory of that night. Who was he?

But he also recognizes a distraction from the main topic at hand.

"I understand it better now. And you are right. Men can rape their wives. And husbands can hold their spouses hostage. Even though they have the best intentions. You know that's what you're doing to me, don't you?"

Hades drops the bottle of serum rather suddenly. He did not finish corking it, and so it rolls and spills oil across the vanity wherever it goes.

It smells lovely. Like him. Seph imagines standing where his husband is now, pulling his hair back, inhaling deeply, and kissing his neck.

He is relieved to see that Hades has some strong reaction to what he says. The god's expression is still mostly impassive, though he spreads what's on his hands hurriedly through his hair, taking none of the time and care that he usually does. Hades does not even seem to notice the mess or the bottle, which finally, loudly, drops to the floor and clinks against the wall.

The mess will be cleaned and the bottle replaced by Verah by next morning.

"Is that what you think? I am sorry then, Seph. Deeply sorry. Especially after what I've done." He faces Seph finally, his impassive mask breaking to show sadness. His eyes are downcast and his frown subtle, but the emotion in his voice is true. "I suppose you are right. I am one of the bad ones. I... never expected us to be close. I didn't hold out hope that we would consummate the marriage even. But I never had any intention of letting you leave."

Quieter, he admits, "I still don't."

Seph takes a long, slow breath before he responds. That old and new frustration is brewing, but he's only confused by how he has let it persist for so long. He can't remember why he did. With Hades' admission, the actions needed of a king—an equal king, Persephone, King of the Underworld, Ruler of the Dead, God of the Harvest's End—are clear.

He only has one question to ask first.

"Why?"

Hades looks miserable. And tired. And half-starved. And while he may have applied the serum, he's already forgotten to pick up the brush, so his hair is in disarray with its natural waves. He sits on the vanity stool, unsuspecting of what's next for him.

This will be my best chance.

"Seph, you're born to a family of extremely powerful gods. And yet, you are..." He makes a vague gesture in the air. "There's too much risk," he says with his palm up and a shrug. "I could overthrow anyone who tried to harm you. I will in a second. I will even eliminate Demeter—and that would be a terrible thing. Talk about dooming the Earth! That would not only upset the balance she's created, it would cause a civil war amongst the gods. And while Zeus and I are not friendly, we are united in a single goal. A better world for everybody."

"You are worried because I'm weak." Seph feels like he's doing an impression of Hades, though it all comes naturally. A closed-off expression, a calm voice. He's learned well.

His heart beats faster under this shell because he knows what's coming. He knows he might lose. And he knows that no matter how it happens, the relationship between him and Hades will be shaped forever.

"I still love you, husband. Even if you lock me up in Tartarus or chain me to the bed. I want you to understand that I'm not betraying you. I'm not trying to leave you permanently. I am simply standing on the ground you've given me. And I have to do this. Hades—I remember what the nymph said. And he was right. The King of the Underworld cannot have a meek mate."

"What are you saying?" Hades asks, looking confused.

He'll figure out a challenge is coming in moments. So Seph has to take advantage of the first strike. While he can't feel his own magic, he pretends that he does as he uses a command spelled to his tongue.

"Hecate. Subdue him. So that I can leave."

Fifty-Eight

Hecate appears before the first syllable of her name has left his lips, the spell somehow detecting his intention to call her before he actually speaks. And though she may have been doing something personal before he had need of her, the spell must have some sort of detection for the nature of the task he's called her for.

She arrives kneeling, her hair bound at her nape in a warrior's knot, one hand clutching a dagger and the other her whip. Her skirt is short, like a male warrior's chiton, and her breasts are bound by a simple red wrap. She wears Greek sandals laced high on her calves so that they won't slip.

"My enemy...?" she asks, rising and turning at the same time.

And there is Hades, dressed but messily, his hair in disarray and the laces on his trousers still undone. He sits on the vanity stool looking rather stunned, uncomprehending. But the stupidity clears quickly from his eyes. He refocuses on Seph, intention honing his features, and he opens his mouth to speak.

But Hecate comments first, smirking, "Ah. I see. I knew a domestic squabble would benefit me soon."

She lowers herself into a fighting stance and raises both the whip and the dagger toward Hades.

Hades doesn't look ready to stand up from the vanity, much less fight a war that determines whether Seph is a god of the underworld—or merely a warm body to entertain its true king.

Seph has given Hecate the best chance she has. Hades is run down, exhausted, and they've just finished making love for the second time in one day. If there is a good time to challenge Hades' authority, it is now.

"Seph, Hecate cannot raise a blade against me."

"Oh?" she says, her battle stance unaffected. "Did you not make it clear that I am the extension of Seph's will? That I am to be the source of his magic? And that he is to wield control over me as easily as he would call flames to his fingers."

"You are putting words in my mouth." Hades ties the front of his pants and tends the laces on his shirt. "I said you were to be the source of his abilities, and that is it. Since he has none."

"And you said his protection was my utmost duty."

"Yes, I—"

"I knew that someday protection would mean guarding him against you."

"Yes, but that..." Hades stands, looking perplexed. His boots slide out from their places by the bed and prop themselves up in front of his feet. He steps in. "That is not what I meant."

"I remembered the words of our agreement very carefully. I can repeat them back to you if you wish, exactly as they were spoken. I am the extension of Persephone's will. I am his guardian, his servant, and his tool. I am whatever he needs me to be, for I have given up personhood to be the force of Persephone, the underworld's second king."

She ends, in a less grand voice and with a quick half shrug, "It is slavery. But I figured I shall get to fight something, at least. And if there's one thing every married couple does, quite often..." She smiles. "...it's *bicker*."

Hades looks past her. And when he takes a step toward Seph, her whip unfurls.

He does not take a second step.

"Seph, I am afraid Hecate cannot stand between me and you. I am far, far more powerful than her. Don't you think if Hecate could kill me she would have done so a long time ago?"

Seph lets his alarm show. He is doing his best Hades impression otherwise, trying to be a strong, assertive king, while he worries and his gut twists itself in loops. Hades will see this as a betrayal, whether Seph means it that way or not. Hades does not want anything under his domain leaving that domain. Ever.

But Seph must act as he has decided, or he is not truly a king.

"I don't want to kill you!" he explains. "In fact, Hecate, you are not to cause any permanent damage to my husband. No matter what happens. Not even to defend yourself. You must run or otherwise wound him in a manner that can be healed completely. Those are my orders."

She frowns deeply, but does not protest. As she said, her position is like that of a slave, and she has willingly given up all free will of her own. But as she told Seph once, when they were patrolling the woods behind the palace...

I am bored of a long existence down here. I have no ambitions, nor any true enemies of my own. I am not burdened by being exercised by your whim. Actually, all your tasks are quite easy. And I think as you grow into a king, you will make a great many enemies. I will fight a great many battles.

Finally, I will raise my whip against something other than a dog.

"I can make it work," she says with her unhappy expression. Seph has made her job far more difficult.

Hades sighs and looks around the room.

"We can make amends by speaking, my love. Let me explain again how Zeus, his wife Hera, and several of your cousins are a danger to you. Your own mother is a danger to you. This is the only realm where you are safe to go and act as you please. Have I not given you every freedom among this world?"

It is time to get dressed. Seph throws the blankets off himself, exposing his nakedness, and crosses the room to the wall with the wardrobe. Somewhere they have a full storage place of nothing but their clothes, and Verah rotates a few outfits for each of them to choose from inside the wardrobe.

"You did more than that, my husband. The love of my life." He throws Hades a smile as he chooses a chiton. But at the last second, he changes his mind and picks up a shirt meant for Hades instead. It will be tight on him.

"You made me a king. A king! And not a prisoner." He pulls the garment over his head. On Hades, this would drift well past his waist, giving him extra material to tuck in. Seph decides it will be best letting the hem stay out of his pants.

He chooses one of Hades' traveling pants as well. It's made of a dark hide, but thinner than usual leather, and soft.

Hades' legs are much too slender for these to fit him though. He holds them up for Hecate.

"Make these bigger so they can fit me."

Hecate makes a quick sigh. "I am not a tailor. My magic is imprecise for such things."

Hades' hand lifts slightly away from his side, and the pants' waist sags as it grows larger. Seph shakes out the newly resized garment, holding it up to his legs.

This will be his first time wearing clothes such as these. He always wears the short chitons because he knows those are Hades' favorite. But he is traveling as the King of the Underworld, and he needs to look like it.

"Ooo, you can badly stretch fabric and ruin good leather." Hecate rolls her eyes. "That does not mean you'll best me, Hades, King of Nothing."

Somehow, Hecate's personality allows her to hold opposing views. She hates kings and does not believe government should rule over anything. She does not let that conflict with her service. She has said that Kronos had too many powerful sons. And she implied that it would be better if he had succeeded in absorbing them.

Seph does not let her views bother him much. Her oath is binding. And Hecate is a strange one.

"I will not best you," Hades says, "because we are not fighting. Hecate, if you think an attempt to take my husband away from me and let him leave this realm does not violate your oath, you are wrong."

"I am the extension of his will, not the judge and jury of his will. Who am I to decide when my master's actions are a danger to himself? You made it very clear that I was not to be his nanny. I was not to be his 'second mother,' as you put it. I was to enable Seph to be the powerful god that he would be if nature had not somehow stunted him."

"You are his guardian, it is in your oath!" For the first time, Hades lets his anger through. He straightens his hair with his fingers quickly, and his crown flies to him next.

He is just a frustrated, tired husband. Until the crown goes on.

His face is the same, but the spires of dark stone make him taller. His impassive expression usually looks soft to Seph when they are alone in the bedroom. When the crown goes on, it becomes chilling. He calls his cloak to him, and it is like a shadow beast rushes across the room to envelop him.

Cerberus has no idea what is going on, but he does not have the notion to attack Hecate, the master Seph assumes trained him and all the hounds. With Hades dressed, the hound stands at alert, watching from the den, understanding by their tense tones that they might be doing something important. Maybe going on a hunt.

One of the heads yawns. He lifts one leg and scratches behind his ear while the other two look ready to receive orders.

"You forget that I am a crossroads god as well," Hecate says. "I crafted the little nuances of striking a deal, great Hades. The very spell we used to bind me was one of mine."

"There was no deception," Hades says quickly, his eyes

narrowed. He looks down and his lips move with unspoken words. He is going over the spell to himself, making sure there was no mistake.

"No deception," Hecate agrees. "But the nature of the oath is that the first spoken law is the most binding, with every promise being less binding after that. That way, if a circumstance should break one phrase but honor another, the earliest phrases are truest, and the very first is always the great truth. The very first is the absolute binding oath. Otherwise, in circumstances where a debtor's actions seem to contradict half his oath and uphold the other, the binding spell would fall apart. The debtor would break free."

Hades lifts his head. "That is how you created the greatest binding spell the gods have ever known."

Hecate looks smug, her anger and unhappiness changing to a look of confidence, especially as she raises her nose in the air.

"That is why you should expect to lose this battle, old king. I knew to prepare for a moment like this. And your little brother Zeus should have taught you already that wits can always outsmart brute strength."

Something hits Seph and makes the world go dark. It is like the wardrobe collapses on top of him, but there is no clatter of wood on stone. There is no weight pressing down on him either. Instead, there is the sound of rushing wind in his ears. The sensation that he is falling very fast, very far, and into the dark. And something suffocates him.

Then arms around him.

He knows it is Hades even though he can't see his face. He leans into him, clutching a pair of boots that he was about to put on, and he shuts his eyes. Even while very afraid and knowing that Hades will do anything to stop him from going anywhere, he has the ultimate trust in his husband.

They land. The force of it sinks him to his knees, and Seph's hands seek the ground. The solid, sturdy ground. And shakily, he pushes himself up.

The darkness still present is Hades' cloak. Perhaps they were falling and the wind was rushing in his ears, but now the sound is louder and different, and it is from the rushing water of Tartarus and the sails creating gusts and waves.

The cloak falls free as he stands. Comparatively, the sky here is bright. The landscape expansive. A tower casts a long diagonal shadow in front of him. He hears the creak of wood, and there is the sound of screaming all around. It is so distant and dim amongst the ruckus that it sounds like cheering at the athletic games.

He sees a ship a lot larger than he remembers from his accident. Back then he was standing on the outer rim, looking across at this place. Now he is on the flat roof of Tartarus, made of a smooth stone like clay of some kind.

The screaming is loud and constant. It does not die off as he remembers.

There is a continuous stream of swimmers falling down as the boat is pulled underneath the water to go back upstream and collect more doomed souls. There are never less of them. And the helm of the next boat appears at the ledge above, even as the empty boat is just vanishing under the water.

Seph finds his expression transforming to cry.

He has thought about Tartarus almost daily as he went about learning to be a king. For this is what it is to rule the world of death. The god of death kills many. It is endless.

This is the blood to Gaia's beating heart.

And through it runs the life of all the Earth.

But seeing it is another matter.

He whirls on his husband, who only stands nearby and watches his expression.

"Why did you bring me here?!"

Hecate! he nearly calls in a panic, worried his commanding spell will be broken. But there's a commotion off to one side, and Hecate is climbing up from a crawling position, coughing, thumping her chest, and brushing off her knees.

Seph begins to feel small and afraid. If Hades can bring him here so suddenly...

He can do anything!

He doesn't even need me!

But then he sees his husband again, and the details make it through his panic.

His husband is bent forward, clutching his own stomach like he's deeply wounded. He's panting, and there's moisture beading on his forehead. His neck glistens, and his chest as well where it's visible through his shirt laces.

He is not infallible. He is not all-powerful. Nor is he as impassive as he likes to pretend.

Seph approaches, reaching out to embrace him. He touches gently, for Hades clutches his gut as if he's been stabbed.

"Why did you bring me here? Why like that?"

"So he can kill me," Hecate answers for him. She gets to her feet, and she is in a better state than Hades, though there is a red scrape up one side of her, from how she landed.

"No, Hades." Seph makes sure his husband is looking at him. "I like Hecate. I need her. I don't feel like I can be a god and your true mate if I don't have her power acting as mine. She is the greatest gift you've given me, and I feel like I'm only of use to you if I have her help."

He is still so unshowing. So untouched.

How many years must he have stood here in Tartarus and watched these boats go down until he was able to seal up his heart?

Hades looks at him. Amazingly, he makes a small smile. Barely there. He touches Seph's cheek, and his hand is clammy.

"That is why we will do it this way. If I don't let you go, you will never love me the same. And I will lose everything. And if she doesn't best me on this rooftop, then I cannot trust her to keep you safe under the eyes of Zeus or in the clutches of Hera. This is the only way I'll let you go, Seph. And I have put her life at stake so that she doesn't hold back."

Their foreheads touch, and his hand travels to stroke the side of his neck.

"Thank you. I will still love you," Seph says, because he knows Hades is terrified to do this. There is nothing in the world that scares his husband more than letting someone he loves out of his kingdom.

He risks losing Seph forever.

"I will not disappear. The upperworld will not take me."

"But she must defeat me. Or she is no match for Zeus and Hera."

Fifty-Nine

You are not as good as he deserves.

Hades uses his magic to move Seph to the edge of the rooftop in an invisible bubble, holding him there safe so he won't be struck by the gods' magic. Hecate cannot harm him. By the binding spell she swore, an action that harms Seph (even at the cost of her own life) will not be permitted.

Hades did not require the same spell for himself. And he knows she chose her oath well.

"You are clever, Hecate. I want you to know that no matter how the battle resolves, I admire this move by you. You are perhaps the only loyal servant who has devised a way to overthrow her master by obeying the orders of the same king."

She is scared but hiding it.

No god has ever done what he's done.

To a simple human, a god seems all powerful, yes. But there are rules of any physical realm that they must obey. Otherwise, things like flying wouldn't make sense. A creature who vanishes and appears somewhere else suddenly has no need to be floating around the sky, sharing the space with insects and wind.

The concept of gates and borders and guards would also be unnecessary. Physical movement is something all beings must master for themselves, for space and time are the canvas upon which existence is the paint.

Hades is not an all-powerful god. There is no such thing.

And without doubt, moving them through the realm just underneath the underworld—the absolute void in which space does not exist and life is impossible—well, that has been an impressive secret that Hades has never had to use until now.

They went under and up like a needle through fabric. Or a fish skimming the surface of the lake.

She is right to be afraid.

And perhaps Hades has earned *some* forgiveness. Hecate never had any hope of standing up to him before. He could've killed her the moment she appeared before Seph, before he even finished speaking his phrase.

Getting them here cost him. It feels like the internal organs of his physical body are burning and pulsing, pushing to keep him from disintegrating—a side effect of that void.

But she still has no hope of defeating him. The fight to take place is a show to placate his lover and keep Seph from hating him forever.

Quietly, his conscience whispers, *So what will you do? Continue slaying Seph's protectors? For you must find him someone else after this murder. How will that help him?*

Shut up, he tells that part of himself, narrowing his eyes and focusing on Hecate. *I can't give him back. He's everything to me.*

"Do you understand the significant risk of this battle?" he asks. And he still has not called his scepter to him. He will wait and rip it through the void at the last second, giving Hecate no warning for the weapon he might choose.

"I understand," she says, and her voice is shaken. She resumes her fighting stance anyway, and she forces her features into the same fierce expression as before. But the confidence is gone.

"Let's do this then. Hera would not have mercy on you, and neither will I."

He pulls the scepter to him. To Hecate, it will appear to have materialized instantly. To him, it is sitting in its special protected case, in a vault where he keeps magically imbued items. His family might be the powerful rulers of the universe, but they're also greedy thieves.

He pulls the scepter down to him, down into the void as a fish might snap a baited hook and pull it to the bottom of the lake. And then the nature of physical things is to 'float', using the same analogy. There cannot be existence in the void, after all. Left longer than a few seconds, both matter and energy disintegrate in the void.

So he moves it, a paradoxical and extremely quick task in a realm with no space. And he lets it go.

It shoots to the surface. And he catches it out of the air.

"I am not going to die today!" Hecate shouts, and charges him.

Her physical dagger is only a channel for her true weapon. She closes in on him, slashing, and a magical thin cutting blade slices through him like a wire.

But it causes no damage. Her strike is successful. Her strength is not.

Hades calls on his scepter to become a long and deadly sword. Its blade is made out of his favorite stone—diamond. Its hilt is leather-wrapped obsidian. And the magic around it is like burning ice. It wouldn't just cut Hecate in half. Even a touch or a passing blow would absorb the power from Hecate like a trapper lost in a blizzard, every minute feeling his body grow colder and colder.

It is not her body or her life he will destroy first. He will tear gushing wounds in her magic.

Another strike. Another and another. The ground at his feet has become swarming with a mirage of vipers, their physical forms a shell but their teeth deadly and venomous. To a mortal. Their attacks are insignificant. Only their bodies are a nuisance, preventing his own charging counterattack.

Hades lifts himself up, the fake snakes snapping at his heels.

You must fight better! he wants to snarl at her.

But he does not bother to speak as he levels his sword and runs at her. Down and forward, he sees her eyes widen, and she rolls aside.

But Hades intended her to. The sword catches on her ankle. The physical blade does not cut her skin, but he has made a gash in her powers. She will not run as quickly now.

"You should have made protecting Seph your first oath" he says, repositioning with no hurry. "Then you would not be about to lose your life."

Why do you speak? It is not necessary to chide her. Finish the action and be done with it.

Somewhere, a part of him must hate himself. For it whispers sarcastically, *'Great' King*.

I am not losing Seph today, he reaffirms, and prepares to charge again.

His feet running against the stone, even passing over a biting snake on the way, he expects his sword to plunge right into Hecate's chest—destroying her magic, her body, and her soul all at once.

But while her torso and waist should be straight, an easy target, it seems that they twist and bend out of the way. She moves like a dancer twirling. And then there is a great crack in the air, and something claws across his face.

Her whip has struck him. And it caused no magical damage, but creates a deep and annoying physical agony. It is poisoned too, he discovers as he tries to use his magic to close the wound. It won't close, not immediately. It will take several minutes, maybe an hour, the magical poison burning like acid.

It is not a residue he can wipe off or banish. And he can feel his flesh disintegrating and rebuilding at the same time. The same feeling he suffered every day inside his father's stomach.

"You underestimate me," she says, a lot closer than he thought she would be. And he realizes that he has been touching the wound in shock for perhaps too long a time.

"I am accustomed to physical agony," he says, and he rushes at her with the sword again.

There is no more pausing, no more evaluation. They attack.

He likes Hecate. Sort of. There is no true desire to end her, but then, Hades doesn't know if he's ever felt the true desire to end anyone. There is only cause for action, and while sometimes that cause is vengeance, the emotion of vengeance alone is not reason enough to act. His one personally satisfying motivation for this death?

Preventative measure. His mercy for Minthe turned out to be disastrous. He cannot allow one so prone to traitorism to cause a catastrophe that puts Seph's very life in danger.

What if she found a way to circumvent the second oath, doing much like Minthe did and causing Hades to attack her?

No, what if she framed Seph for something, and waged a war that way.

You are reaching.

He pauses, panting, wiping the hurt side of his face and spreading blood everywhere.

He senses something is off. He might be wrong.

"Have I miscalculated?"

He turns in time to deflect her attack, the whip's end flying overhead. He raises a hand and sends out a force that throws her. Tossing her over the side of the island and into Tartarus' pit should be easy, now that he has her grasped. He rises into the air, intending to take her with him, and perhaps to question himself before the act is really done. To make sure he hasn't missed anything.

But Hecate still has her strength, even if she's caught in the net. And her whip is more than leather. The end of it becomes a viper's head, and the snake bites into the stone, anchoring her to the building.

"Come now, Hecate. You knew when you started this fight that you would not be a match."

He tugs to get her free. But of course it won't be that easy. So he approaches the whip with his blade.

"Why did you not attack me through all these centuries, if you wanted a chance like this the entire time?"

"I have been training," she says, grabbing at her neck where his power is like an invisible collar. The whip is wrapped several times around her other hand, and even Hades' magic would have a hard time separating her. Magic clings to its owner. Magical items are strongest when they're held by the person who created them.

I could just cut her open now.

He considers it. This is an easy 'win'.

(As if they were even having a contest.)

But while he considers it, he also looks down at a distant form and faraway face.

I don't want him to see that side of me again.

"You should have kept training. What made you think this was a wise course of action?"

She kicks her legs in the air, uselessly. She throws herself side to side. But this is a crippling hold, and she will not get out unless Hades says so.

He wants to hear her answers, so he waits with his sword instead of cutting off the snake's head.

"My sisters stopped me from challenging you earlier. They've kept me under your boot for years. But I am not afraid of you." She shows him her teeth, much like a snake exposing its fangs. "And I will win this fight. You have not bested me."

"I have you helpless. And soon you will be gone. It did not even take all morning."

"No, idiot. You have been bested. And you're right, it did not take a long time. Seph is so moon-eyed over you, I thought I would wait a thousand years for the honeymoon to wear off. Fortunately, he is smarter than the rest of your kind. When you are gone, he will be the only underworld king there is. At least he will be better than you."

A game of wits, she said before.

Hades plays with the weight of his sword, shifting it subtly in his hand, feeling the possibility of severing the whip right now and ending this game she hopes to win. He knows very well how a conversation can end a battle that should've gone the other way. He would not be here if his little brother Zeus did not have a smart tongue.

But he is curious...

"Very well. How have you bested me?"

"Not me." She coughs. "Him. He's bested you, you fucking idiot. Don't you get that?"

"You cannot drive a wall between us," Hades says simply, and he decides he is through with all this. She was foolish to take her oath the way she did. He told her to obey Seph and to only report to him. He did not want Seph to think she was his keeper or his spy.

But her purpose was to guard Seph. Not to wage challenges against Hades.

The snake is cut. He's surprised that it bleeds, the head lopped off with evidence of a spine, and its jaws continuing to snap. Hecate must have cast some morphing spell on a real animal.

Her ways are strange.

"I've killed you then," she says and smiles. Her laugh is nervous. She doesn't struggle anymore, and both hands futilely grasp the invisible collar on her neck. "It will be a long, slow death. You're welcome."

I've missed something.

Her confidence is not a bluff.

"What is it then?" He brushes his cheek against his shoulder, the pain irritating. Was there something he missed in the poison? "Enlighten me, Hecate, how will you kill me?"

With her eyes and a nod of her head, she gestures downward.

Seph has left the place where Hades put him, and he's picking up the end of the whip, wrapping it around his hands and holding tight.

She is right. I might be gone.

Hecate's whip is long, and they are suspended in the air together. Seph shouts up at them, "Hecate, fight back! Do not let him do this!"

"Yes, master," Hecate says with limited ability to breathe, and she kicks her legs feebly. Then she smiles at Hades. "I just wanted the chance to fight you. That is what I get out of this deal. And my sisters will benefit from my death. Do you expect your little husband to continue to love you when I'm gone?"

"I see. You think the depression from him not loving me will be what kills me."

"I know it will. You were fading already. It was a waiting game. That is why my sisters and I never attacked you. And I was training.

In case the wait was too long for us."

"And you bound yourself to my husband, looking for an opportunity to wedge us apart."

"That too. But I am better with my weapons, and I knew you would mess up eventually."

"I only want to protect him."

Seph pulls without effect on the whip. Hades can actually feel some of his magic come into play. Seph would be a considerable force. He might even best Hades, if he was able to feel it. Hades can ward off an immature, inexperienced blunt attack such as his.

"Demeter wants to protect him too, you idiot."

He has made an error. He feels it in his gut.

His mind still can only think that Seph cannot leave. He won't let him go.

So he says, "I told you, you have to best me, to prove that you are a match for Zeus and Hera."

She smiles cruelly. "My blade is in your belly, Hades. You haven't won."

Sixty

Seph watches as Hades finally releases Hecate, her body falling several feet to the ground, where she painfully sits up on her side. She gets to her knees. And as Seph passes her, she says, "I have completed my task, master," kneeling to the ground with her head low.

But Seph runs directly past her, to where Hades has landed on his feet, his back to them both.

He cares about Hecate as well, and he worried dearly for her life as she was suspended in the air. He regretted his decision, and he was nearly about to beg Hades for her life, taking back his challenge. His independence was worth fighting for, but not at the loss of her life.

And he worried that Hades wouldn't be merciful. And that with this challenge he had killed the loving bond between them.

But now Hecate is safe! He spares a look backward for her, where she's huddled. There are no visible injuries besides scuffs and red marks from the stone ground.

And it is Hades he worries for now. His back is bent. His sword touches the ground, barely grasped in one hand. And as Seph approaches, he hears…

Sobbing?

He is timid for just a moment, his feet halting his momentum, but then he remembers that this is his husband—the man he should fear the least.

Only for a little while, during this battle, has that not been true.

He touches Hades' back.

"I am not leaving you. Not for long. I promise."

As Hades looks at him, his eyes are tear-filled and sad. It is shocking to see. He looks so young, displaying emotion like this. For the first time, Seph gets the sense that they are not so different in age, and Hades does not wield so much wisdom and power over him.

He embraces his husband fully, making sure that they are faced away from Hecate, for he knows Hades doesn't want the sharp-tongued goddess to see him like this.

"You're being quite dramatic over the whole thing," he whispers quietly against Hades' hair. But his touches are soft and comforting. He knows his husband is struggling with very real fear.

"You were born helpless into a family of rapists, thieves, and murderers."

"Has Hecate passed your test? Are you confident she can protect me?"

"She has passed, yes. Against me. I don't know how she would fare against Zeus or Hera. Or your mother."

"But you are the most powerful god in existence at the moment, yes?"

"Yes. For now, at least. In our realms."

Seph can only imagine what that means, but he stays focused on the problem at hand.

"Then she has passed the greatest test you can give her. If you're not confident she can protect me, then please, test another. But I have to go, Hades. I can put a stop to all this senseless death and make the upperworld balanced again. Well, if there's a chance I should try! And you should be able to trust me on my own somewhere. Otherwise, we are not truly equal kings." He makes sure Hades looks at him and their eyes meet. "And I want to be. Please, if you let me..."

Hades makes a vague and angry gesture toward Hecate.

"She may have cheated. She's known me many years. But I suppose that means she's known all the other gods just as long. She's older than Zeus. Older than Poseidon, and a little bit older than myself as well. She's almost a Titan. And if her weapons aren't good enough... I suppose she's honed a clever tongue. I suppose she's the best option we've got, though I don't like it."

"Hades, thank you!" Seph squeezes him tightly, jubilantly. He kisses Hades' cheek, and then his lips as well.

It is more than just them being equals. When he sees his mother, he may recover a piece of his old self as well. And he is hoping that with these memories he will devise a solution to the suffering of humans, dying on the Earth that does not warm enough for crops and livestock.

His joy is one-sided, however. Hades stops crying, but what's left are empty, dulled eyes.

"I can't live without you. Not for long. That was her blade."

Seph is only mildly confused. He heard enough of their conversation to know that it was about him, and he heard Hecate imply Seph would not forgive him.

Perhaps.

Perhaps the resentment of being kept would grow slowly over time.

But, at least initially, Seph would forgive Hades of anything.

"I will love you for eternity, Hades. And I will only be gone for as long as it's necessary. My home is here. And nothing will keep me from you."

Sixty-One

Seph steps out of Hades' chariot, accepting his husband's guiding hand. Mount Olympus is huge, monstrous. Beautiful too, in a way, but it is the loud sort of beauty. Bright and boastful. The palace itself sits at the mountaintop, towering over everybody, and they must climb a steep set of stairs. The gardens before the palace are admiringly lovely as well, lots of flowering trees and fruitful hedges.

But Seph forgot how utterly garish and gleaming the color green could be. Or any of the plants and scenery, for that matter. In the underworld, another presence is always what shows best. You can spot a person or living thing at a great distance for their vibrancy.

Here, the animals (some red deer and a few wild ponies) are the same as the scenery. And while they are attractive, Seph notices how imperfect they are as well. When they move, it is not effortless. When they graze, he can hear the stems of grass tear. He can hear the chewing.

It seems rather violent to him, for the grass is a living thing being destroyed and processed.

The way of physical things is new to him, and he spends some time petting the noses of tamed beasts, wild but without fear.

Hades is with him all the time, of course. And so is Hecate.

"Do not fiddle with your dagger too much, Hecate. And pretend that your whip is only for the horses. If we strike, the poison will leave Zeus in shock, but only for a short time. Hera, I believe—I hope—will be incapacitated. She is not a warrior. But she is a devil about certain things where Zeus is concerned. Let me handle my little brother. I don't want him killed. And you do whatever is necessary to subdue her."

"If it is within my master's orders, I will do as you say."

"It is," Seph says, leaving the stag that has come up to them. He is a gorgeous animal, but weak. Weighed down. In his essence form, he would be powerful, limitless. But he is trapped in this mold, this shape.

He finds the physical world beautiful all the same. But it is not the quiet, everlasting beauty he prefers.

"Where is Zeus? I thought he would be here to greet us?"

"No, that is not my little brother's way. And his nature is also why we have to land down here and we are not allowed to ride the chariot directly up to the front door. Everybody but himself must walk."

"You should be more respected by him," Seph says, unhappy about mounting the steps with his feet. "This power play seems petty and rude."

"Gods are not as obedient as Elysium subjects. And this is the upperworld, his domain. I cannot choose to fight every battle, or I will have no time in my own realm to rule over things."

"I suppose you're right," Seph concedes, and they climb the long, steep steps. He left his cane at home, unwilling to appear physically weak, so he relies on Hecate's magic and Hades' guiding arm.

He begins to notice hints of death that previously his wonderment missed. Flowering trees have lost all their blooms, their naked branches pointed at the sky, and a pink or white carpet lying all around them. Certain plants are bent over, wilting. And the sky above is a deep, stormy gray.

The wind that blows through is like ice. Seph would be fine either way, but he's presented in northerner's garb now, to match Hades, and he holds the cloak closed out of habit and for keeping the warmth. They're dressed in matching black outfits, and Seph wears his obsidian laurel wreath. He appears somber, having left the pastel colors at home, like Hades. They are a set. They are partnered gods and equal kings.

The palace atop Mount Olympus seems to grow bigger as they approach it. And while it is technically open, the front of it mimicking a Greek forum, there is nobody else here. There are no children on the steps or in the garden. He sees a human or two, but they are well-dressed slaves tending the plants and things. They are silent and do not acknowledge the gods when they pass. They don't even look at them.

And while Mount Olympus may give the appearance of being a bright oasis, underneath the roof it is all shadow. Standing at the foot of the columns, Seph looks onward with apprehension.

There are no lit torches here. No fireplaces, no couches, no tables. Not for guests, anyway. This looks like a court, not a home.

The only furniture of any kind is for the king god himself to sit on, and whoever he's dining with. The forum is expansive, the columns perfectly spread out so that he can't see the upperworld king plainly at first. Walking through the vast space of columns is like walking through a forest, and gradually, the dining king becomes visible.

Seph doesn't know who any of the others are. But Hera and Zeus are plainly visible.

Zeus sits on a blue couch, the largest, and immaculately carved, patterned, and stitched. Hera sits on a much smaller couch next to him, leaning over hers and onto his, but she is diminished. Everyone is.

She's smiling, and Zeus, who is not noticing her, meets Seph's eyes instead. He is surprised. The wine goblet he was tasting leaves his lips early. And as Hera turns to see who he's noticing, the joy fades from her expression. Outwardly, she does not show hate. But the very slight narrowing of her eyes and the dip of her brow reminds Seph of a cat hissing.

The other gods seem to hardly be worth attention. They sit lower than Zeus, their couches all small and brown. They are curious but bored, paying as much attention to the newcomers as they do to the feast. They spend a lot of time watching Zeus, as a matter of fact, like actors on a stage seeking their cue.

Around them, sharing a couch or resting on the floor, picking scraps and morsels off the table like pets, are many naked nymphs. All women and all lovely.

Zeus does not have eyes for any of them as he stands up and opens his arms. He says nothing, but he beams as he steps around others and around the table laden with their feast.

"Do not worry for me," Seph says, stepping away from Hades' side. Hades has closed himself off and looks as impassive as a stone statue, but Seph knows enough of his husband now to recognize that he's seething.

His fingers twitch on his right hand, which should be still.

Seph does not want to embrace the approaching god, his father. He swallows down his reluctance. But he lets the sky god get close—knowing he can call on Hecate anytime. And then he reaches around his waist and mimes the hug his father wants.

Zeus hugs for a long time. Seph hangs in place and wonders when it will ever end.

He's enfolded in bulky, impressive physical power. Zeus must be as heavy as a horse, all of it in his massive muscles. He has chest hair, which Seph doesn't like. And the smell of him brings back memories of mortal men. Men Seph can't remember the names of, so they might have been nice, but this is a physical smell. An animal smell.

It is not the calm scent of Hades.

In fact, Seph can only compare Zeus further to Hades and rank him worse in every way.

But then he sees a little bit of Hades in his eyes. They have the same eye color almost, his father's a bit more blue than gray, and they both (while physically young and smooth-featured) look very, very old.

"Brother," Zeus says, barely looking that way. And holding Seph's shoulders, beaming down on him like a proud parent, he says warmly, "Son."

Seph senses himself leaning into that warmth. The desire on his father's features might be plain to see if he didn't wear that thick beard. And a desire of his own surprises Seph. He never knew his father. He's not sure if he was close with either of his parents.

And now it seems they might have something special...

If not for Hera's gaze just visible over one of Zeus's shoulders. There is nothing inside *her* that is warm. He gets the sense that she may be threatening him with her eyes alone.

She bites harshly into a fig as Seph separates himself.

"I can hardly tell it's winter in the upperworld," Seph says, gesturing behind him.

He wishes his father would let them stay apart, but instead the god puts an arm around Seph's waist as he guides them forward, away from the dining table and toward the garden. Seph thinks he is awfully brave to stand between him and Hades. But seemingly, he does not care about Hades' presence at all.

"Well, I can do some things like chase the clouds away and keep the snow from falling. But the damn cold is persistent, no matter how long we bask in the sun's rays." Seph realizes where he might have gained a natural ability to keep warm. Zeus is right about it being cold, and Zeus only wears a barely fitting chiton wrapped around his muscled frame. "I believe your mother brightens the sun or something. Look at it!"

He points upward and they walk forward until the sun is visible beyond the forum's roof.

"It's as small as a star. And it barely offers any heat. It is good you're coming home. The deer have started to pick the gardens clean. And so I've had to butcher several of them for my table. There is not enough warm land to keep the herd fed."

"We are not staying for long," Hades says quietly, only looking down the hill. He yearns for the chariot, Seph knows, and he might be considering calling his scepter to him as well.

"No?" Zeus says, and Seph finally manages to step free of his touch. He takes Hades' hand instead, going to the side opposite Zeus.

Be patient, he thinks, squeezing.

"I have only come to assure you that I am well."

"Why would you do that?"

"Because I heard you were worried about me, Father. There are whispers that I'm in need of rescue and that Hades' abduction of me wasn't lawful and with your consent."

Seph chides himself. He meant to be far more blunt than that. But his father seems clueless and pleasant. Friendly. His tone and his expression are nothing but joy when he regards Seph, and Seph is finding himself falling for it—a little. He hasn't forgotten his purpose here.

"Uh. Well..." Zeus shrugs his shoulders and scratches the back of his head with one massive hand. "Was it?" he says, surprising them both. Hades actually turns his head and looks at him.

"I was pressured and perhaps acted too hastily. And Persephone, I did not truly give you away as your father, for I have never known you like a father. Now you are here, and the opportunity is given! I did try to get to know you, remember? Only a true father can marry a son, so..."

"No," Seph says firmly, stepping out to face Zeus directly, with Hades in the middle but not impeding his confrontation.

"Uh, what?" Zeus asks, blinking. His eyes dart to Hades quickly, and Seph can tell he is measuring a prediction of the dark god's next action.

"No, your consent for Hades to marry me was lawfully binding. And even if it wasn't, I am a god anyway, and we both know that gods are only bound by the laws that can be enforced."

Now Zeus's eyes are mostly for Hades though he speaks to Seph. And there is some calculation there—some little sign of Hera or Hades or even the controlling tactics of Demeter. He is not just the simple, overjoyed father he pretends to be.

"Persephone, perhaps I acted too rashly. And you are right, you should not be bound by my decision alone! We should take some time to think about this. Come." He reaches far across and touches Seph's shoulder. "Let me take you to your mother. And when she's done crying her tears, we will discuss this as a family—"

Seph can sense Hades is about to pull the scepter to him. It is a strange feeling, again like he is standing on the surface of a lake and it goes impossibly deep.

He speaks firmly before the scepter can appear.

"I am not bound by your decisions anymore, Father. That is what I came to say. And there is no need to send rescuers after me, or to spread rumors—"

Zeus waves a hand, and though the point of this conversation is for Seph to establish his independence while he's in the upperworld, he finds himself naturally falling silent. Zeus dresses like a simple man, and he has none of the jewels of a rich person. He is like a commoner who just happens to look amazing.

But he is a great and eternal being of immense power. Seph can sense it in him, even if he pats Seph's shoulder again like there was no offense taken.

"I have not sent any rescuers. Though I admit, I think I should have. Where is this coming from?"

"Two mortal kings, possibly with some magical aid, traveled to the underworld to abduct me. While I was riding in the woods."

He feigns shock. Seeing a king's face so animated is new for Seph, and he can tell immediately that these are mimicked for dramatic effect. The small shifts and little tells might make Hades seem unfeeling, but they are more genuine than this.

"I did not know this!" He puts a hand on his breast. "I didn't help them, if that's what you think. You haven't come to harm, I hope?" He looks Seph up and down, but rushes ahead, not waiting for any answer. "But Persephone, your mother—and I—have missed you. Your mother has been inconsolable, actually. So regardless of what you say about your marriage to Hades and all that, well..."

With one hand he waves to the air frivolously. But his grasp on Seph's shoulder is a little firmer. A little more purposeful and unmoving.

"Well, I'm afraid I simply can't allow it to happen. Anymore." He fixes his gaze on Hades as well. "You see, I am the god of the upperworld and all the creatures in it. And your mother's grief for you, well, it's causing a lot of *dying*. I'm sure you noticed, being down there and all." He looks backward, towards Hera. "Come, have lunch with us and discuss this more. I have to hear all about you, dear boy! I'll have couches brought up. Come on!"

He tries to bring Seph forward and hold him around the waist again. No doubt, he's masking an evaluation—his side versus their side. At the dinner table, Hades is likely to notice that he's outnumbered.

Seph pushes his hands away, deciding to be done with the polite games.

"I am not here to discuss anything. Especially not with you. You are not a true father, which you've even admitted."

Zeus is a good actor. When he shows hurt, too exaggerated to be real, Seph must ignore his instincts telling him he's overstepped. But he also knows that he's right.

"Your mother never let me—"

"Being a father is more than just looking at your son occasionally and making sure he's fed alright. If you are a parent, you should have had an equal partnership with my mother. But you do not. Not for me or any of your sons and daughters."

Zeus makes a light scoff at first. Then he thinks it over. Beseeching, like he regrets having to give the bad news, he says, "Well, I have *a lot* of sons..."

"No. You have offspring. You do not have any sons. And even if I was your son, I don't wish to give you the right to marry me. Or, in this case, to *un*-marry me either."

Their eyes meet, Zeus's delicate features contained behind thick bushy brows and a thick bushy beard. He looks more like Hades than he wants to let on, only the broadness of his muscles and the wideness of his neck being the starkest differences. He has fully embraced human Greek culture, even though there are many to choose from, and Seph notices now, for the first time, that this must be why so many gods follow the same fashion.

Only Hades is noticeably different, staying in his northerner's garb, even here.

"Before you challenge us, Father, I would like to remind you that you are the one who gave me away. You are the one who caused this to happen. And you are the one who is incapable of calling Demeter to obey your laws."

"I understand you're upset with me, boy..." His expression is mostly frozen and not furious or threatening—not yet. But his voice is mildly losing its friendliness.

"Now, if you can't command the simple Goddess of the Harvest—your own sister, your ex-lover, and the woman you claim isn't as powerful as you—if you can't command her to listen, what makes you think you can command me?"

"Do not speak carelessly with me, son. A war amongst the gods is bad for all of us."

"Then do not think you can remarry me, and you won't start one."

"But son, apparently your mother cannot live without you." Zeus is sounding like he could live without Seph very well. His hands have drifted back to themselves. Seph's first impression, whatever it was, has been rescinded.

"And that is the second thing I've come to tell you. I am going to convince my mother to warm the Earth again since you cannot. I will be here in the upperworld, going to see her, and any sort of assistance from you is not necessary. I do not want to see an abduction attempt made on my life. I do not require any visits from you at all."

Zeus chuckles mockingly. "Well, you're just a little Titan, aren't you? You know, I've had plenty of gods both young and old tell me to stay out of their business. And you know what I say?"

"No," Seph admits, though in reflection he wishes he had stayed quiet.

He leans forward in what he must imagine to be an intimidating way. But Seph is unaffected. He still has Hades by his side.

"I am the King of the Earth, boy. And it is not you who gives me an ultimatum."

Seph does not tower over him in kind. Nor does he call upon Hecate to strike him with her acid whip. It does not seem necessary yet.

"And I am Persephone, King of the Underworld and partner to my husband—King Hades of the Underworld. Tell me, King Zeus, why did you become desperate when my mother refused to listen to all pleas for mercy?"

He pauses, but does not hold out for a reply.

"It is because you are only a king until the Earth dies. You have taken a temporary position. And who controls the time span of that position? Why, it is us. If I choose, I will bring all the souls of everything home for their final rest. You will watch your kingdom be covered in snow and finally die."

"Is this your plan all along?" Zeus addresses Hades, who doesn't answer. His husband is being quiet, letting Seph control the conversation. He didn't expect this, but he hasn't felt like he needs help yet.

"Hades, you know the world can become so much more beautiful in time. You know the humans shouldn't be called home yet! And you are letting this one spout declarations of war!"

"No, not war. It is an empty threat. Before following through on such an ultimatum, my husband and I would replace you first. Or did you forget, King Zeus? Hades lets you have this place up here. We can claim it any time. Since it has not been managed effectively—"

"I am about getting tired of your bullshit."

"Since you have not managed it *effectively*," Seph continues, "we would seek to replace you before dooming the Earth entirely. Or we can start a war now. On behalf of your hurt pride."

"Brother," Hades says, speaking for the first time, "remember what you told me after we defeated our father? You want to be the protector of the weak. If that is still true, see past these aggressive words. Nothing needs to change. You know I am content to keep the eternal world. And a war between us now would damage an already ailing Earth. I think we would annihilate it."

"You have come into *my* home..." His tone is reserved, but Seph does not think many get to see him with a stern face. In the arguments with his mother as Seph was growing up, he was always mocking, never truly furious.

In the distance, Hera stands from her couch.

Seph says unapologetically, "Prevent your wife from interfering in our discussion. Or it will be said Zeus the Thunder God is spineless against women."

Zeus shouts over his shoulder, and Seph trembles invisibly.

There is power in him. Raging, uncontrolled power.

And Seph gave it a command.

"Hera, go back to your place and wait for me!"

Her obedience is far more reluctant. In fact, she is not fully obedient at all. She stays at a distance, just out of hearing, and crosses her arms, watching.

"If I've convinced you I don't want to be friends, Father, then perhaps this will be easy. Don't visit me. Certainly don't remarry me—that won't go well at all. We would have to prove to everyone who the strongest power is. And in the underworld, you are facing two kings instead of one."

"Get out of my house."

"Gladly. That is all we've wanted since we stepped in it. Just make sure you stay out of my business and away from me and my mother." He could leave it there, but the moment to assert himself is now or it will forever escape his tongue.

"Do a better job convincing us that you are the all-powerful king of the land in the upperworld. If more of your subjects contest your rule—successfully—well, then you're not a king at all, are you? We will have to appoint someone else."

He leaves. And the sky above the garden grows dark and cracks with thunder. The red deer and the ponies move away. The gardeners also cover their heads with shawls and run to the nearest shelter.

Seph walks calmly, his head exposed. Hades protects them from a little rain that begins to fall. A lightning bolt at his head might be very tempting for the thunder god, but Zeus is not entirely evil.

It is true what Hades said and what Zeus himself believes.

He wants to be everything he pretends to be. Cheerful, untroubled, the protector of the weak. He's trying to be perfect, and he doesn't want that war among the gods.

But he has no affection for Seph or anyone individually. That part is true as well.

Sixty-Two

Leaving Mount Olympus, it seems that the chariot flies level and the rest of the Earth gets farther away underneath them. The upperworld looks almost exactly like the underworld from this vantage point, though a lot less colorful. It is all white and bleak. And somewhere, among a memory of Seph's, while he's thinking that the air and the wind smell familiar somehow, Seph realizes that it isn't supposed to look like this. The Earth isn't supposed to be buried in snow and blank everywhere.

He looks for one of the human cities, but does not find one. They are too far up. And Hades takes him into the clouds where the ice particles are like little needles stinging his cheeks. Seph lifts his cloak to protect himself.

Hecate huddles miserably behind them in the chariot, but she's shielded by their bodies. Hades does not dodge the ice at all, and he begins to look like a true mythical king of the underworld as snow begins to collect on his features.

On his stony, somber features.

Seph angles his back toward the horses and the barrage of icy flecks. With his hands, which are always warm, he brushes at Hades' brows and his cheeks, wondering if he should command Hecate to guard his husband from the cold for them both. Hades is not unable to spend his magic, but he is lost in thought.

"That was dangerous," Hades says, never letting go of the reins or putting up the hood of his cloak.

"You know my reasoning. He would've been a nuisance. And you never would have been able to trust me and focus on your work while I am gone if I hadn't stood up to him."

"Yes, but I did not realize you would imply that I would *replace* Zeus. Replace him with whom? There are not any gods suited for the job. Except maybe Poseidon, but he is…" Hades shrugs. "He prefers the sea over people. He has disdain for the land. Zeus is not the best, but he is all there is."

"And if it came to it, I would let death take the Earth now, and Zeus—and Poseidon—would become our subjects. Now my father knows that I know that. That is all I wished to communicate." Imagining he enacted such a threat makes Seph sad. He understands why his husband might be disturbed by this. "I didn't wish to remove Zeus from power. I just wanted to remind him that we *could*. That is all."

"And you did." Hades grabs him around the waist with one hand, managing the horses with the other. He pulls him close, and while Seph acknowledges the sheer frigid temperature from the outer shell of Hades' clothes, his body contained warmly in wool within, Seph's less dressed physical form absorbs this and exudes heat.

Seph cuddles close, pushing his chin above Hades' shoulder, wishing he could share this innate magic with another. He tries to force it to happen through his physical touch.

And Hades says, "That is what surprises me so. You left Zeus at a loss. He was not expecting you. And I was not expecting you."

"You've made me stronger than what I was. I can feel it. There is the sense that... I was less. It's hard to explain. But I'm more now."

"You were not so willing to seek power. It is true. But you are still everything else."

"Then I am glad the nymph tricked me. Because you deserve a mate who doesn't depend entirely on you. I am your instrument as well as your partner."

Hades picks at Seph's hair. While his body is warm, ice has been collecting. It clings to the golden chariot and thickens the harnesses of the horses too.

"Just be sure you are not like that fool Icarus. Do not reach too far for power, my lovely-but-young king. Zeus did not expect you this time, and so you won. I think you are his only son to publicly stand up to him. The rest are smitten or cowed. But Zeus defeated our father, Kronos, and I did not. Don't forget that."

"I think I have enough of him in me that we would defeat Kronos together. But do not worry—I hear you, my king. My Hades." Seph cups his face. "I think Zeus will leave me alone. And if he does not, I will come to you before I face him again. I was not fearless in our meeting. Zeus was terrifying. He is a great god. But he is heartless in a lot of ways."

Seph continues, thinking on what he felt as he spoke to his father, "He does not want to be a bad person. And so, he is a dishonest one. He tries too hard to be perfect." He blinks twice, realizing the depth of an early lesson. One that justifies Tartarus and everything else about Hades. "To be good kings, we have to enact cruelty sometimes. To be kind to everyone is a selfishness."

"I am still selfish," Hades says, and kisses him. But it is not a good or even passionate kiss. It is far too cold for that. It is claiming and possessive and matter-of-fact.

"Then I must be cruel to you, Hades, in equal measure. When you drop me off, I want you to leave. You must go back to the underworld and wait for me. I will send Hermes with a message if there is something urgent to say. Otherwise, you must manage the underworld by yourself and let me solve the problem up here. If you come with me, it will only cause my mother and you to fight."

"I would kill her..." Hades mutters, but it is off to the side and without intent. He is hiding much behind his blank expression. He hasn't cried again since that day he lost Hecate's duel, but Seph knows his husband well enough now to notice all the little signs that he's hurting. Hades isn't a mystery to him anymore.

Seph takes his hand and they face forward together, the ice rushing at them and making it seem that they are going faster than they really are. To Seph, it is like he's gazing ahead into the long years of his reign with Hades.

They are only just beginning, but the time will fly at them just as fast, and side by side, Hades and Seph will stand steady. They won't erode to the discomforts of ice, darkness, and a little pain.

"When I come back, the balance will be restored, and I want to marry you all over again. That way I'll feel like I have the real marriage in my memories. And also, it will remind you where my heart really is... while I'm up here trying to solve this shit."

Sixty-Three

Their departure is short. Hades embraces him. Kisses his cheek. Then tells him he loves him and climbs back into the chariot alone. Their eyes never leave each other as he takes up the reins, snaps them, and then he is gone. Seph looks up after the dark horses for as long as he thinks there is a chance he might still glimpse them through the gloom and the snow.

But those are only seconds. He is well and truly gone.

"Which way?" he asks Hecate, and miserably, silently, she points forward.

Seph gathers his cloak around himself and begins the trudge. Uphill in the snow, his steps sinking halfway up to his ankles. They would sink even farther in all this endless snow if not for Hecate's magic to elevate them both and keep his knee functional. While this is not a great challenge, it is annoying, she says. Like carrying two distracted babes on either side of her hips. Since Seph wanders autonomously, she must always be tracking him, following him, and lifting him. As well as herself.

She is not dressed at all for the blizzard they walk in. She wears another thin lovely gown like the one he met her in, and while Seph's magic warms him without even thinking about it, her skin seems to glow and her miserable expression may also be from the concentration that she must maintain all the time.

"How much farther?" he asks when they have walked a long time. He continuously has the urge to offer her his hand, his polite inclinations forgetting that she is the truly powerful one of them both.

"Hades could not come too close," she says loudly over the wind, holding her hair to one side. Both of them, though warm, are collecting ice, and some of it is melting into their clothes. Seph's cloak is heavier than it ought to be, snow clinging to the bear fur.

"Onward then," he says, and the trudge continues.

All he can think about is Hades and the lovely days he used to spend with him. Even if Hades was not there, he knew his husband wanted to be, and that was enough. Seph loved spending time in his husband's vast home, every room and art piece a reflection of the man himself. Elysium is their world. And the Earth, while beautiful, is really just a mess. There's no design to it, unlike Elysium.

He can only think of how much he misses his home already.

But Hecate will help them get back when the time comes. And he is certain this is the right thing to do. This is best for all the realms.

He also worries that he won't have any better luck than Zeus. He hasn't been able to come up with a plan for being out here. He doesn't even know what to expect! He doesn't know what his mother will say, or if she will look exactly the way he remembers.

He's nervous about meeting her, but the physical discomfort of climbing a snowy mountain in a blizzard is enough to bury those concerns. Even missing Hades gets turned and layered upon and obliterated by the blanketing snow.

His breath becomes a little heavier than it naturally would be. His climb slows due to the wind and ice. Though Hecate's magic strengthens his knee considerably, he loses his balance, and Hecate catches him by the arm, straightening him.

"Not much farther now, master. She senses us, and she's curious, I think. A little closer, and you shall make yourself known."

"She can see us?" Seph asks, looking all around.

"No, she senses us, I said."

And they march forward again. Seph assumes this sense is a god thing, and he doesn't find it within himself. Minthe was right. He's practically a mortal.

But you were wrong about me being weak.

They reach a small flat area atop a steep incline. The mountain ahead is straight up and won't be possible without magic or ropes.

"We are here," Hecate says, taking his elbow. She pulls his hood down and combs her fingers through his hair, twice. "Call out to her and see if she answers."

Seph looks around. There is nothing here. Not even a human-shaped boulder like he expected to see.

"Mother!" he shouts vaguely at the sky, watching the scenery. "It is I, Persephone! Your son! I've come home to visit!"

There is nothing, but his questioning glance at Hecate confirms that she is here, somewhere. This is his chance.

"I've come to talk to you about this long winter. Mother, there's too much death to sustain the Earth. There are not enough boats in the underworld to take them, and we are losing too many wandering souls to the ether. You've created too much work for Hermes to do, so I've come to beg—"

The voice comes from everywhere. From underneath his feet perhaps.

"My son?"

And then he hears a great crack, almost like the thunder when his father was mad. But instead of lightning, the snow from the top of the mountain comes down in an avalanche, and Hecate jumps in front of him, throwing her hands up.

The air shimmers, a ripple spreading out from Hecate's palms. But it is unnecessary. The snow misses them.

And the mountain... moves? It is hard to see since the top is nearly obliterated by gray clouds and falling snow, but the shape of the mountaintop awaiting them is different.

"Persephone, is that you?" The sound booms from the very center of the Earth. The entire world must hear! His legs shake from the noise vibration. And he grabs around Hecate's waist briefly, feeling unsteady.

"It is me, mother," he calls out, though a little more quietly. He's afraid. But he has to confront her, the same as he did with Zeus. "I understand you are unhappy to have me gone! But you have killed too many! I have come to ask you—to bargain with you, to beg— please stop! This wind, the snow—please do not bury the Earth in ice!"

They move. The snow shifts underneath them like sand. A giant wave of it rises, and Seph is swept off the mountainside with it, clinging to Hecate now. Together, they barely maintain their balance. But the entire land falls away around them, and then they are lifted up.

It seems to Seph they are looking at a great cave surrounded by magnificent stone. It is all perfectly circular and too smooth to be naturally made. There is a strange light glistening from the portal.

And then Seph realizes—it is an eye!

He moves in front of Hecate and takes off his cloak. He lifts the black diadem from his head as well.

"I've come home, Mother. Please."

It seems that all around his feet is a great icy white plain. And further on there are rock walls that go up, too hazy to be seen clearly. But these must be her hands.

"My son!" The eye disappears behind another avalanche. It seems to Seph that the entire world is coming apart, snowdrifts diving and falling off the mountain into oblivion. "Oh, my son! You've come back!"

And then they are falling with the snow, though the ground underneath their feet stays steady. It is like they are on a plummeting, shrinking plate, the other mountains, just shadows in the distance, rushing up all around them.

And then, though his mother is monstrous—a giant!—Seph can see her face. He can make out the details of her hands. She glows warmly vibrant, and he feels that same warmth through the soles of his boots. Through his hand also, as he reaches down and touches her skin, going to his knees during the fall.

The snow becomes rain all around him and around her. Light from above goes dark as her other hand folds around the top and cups him.

"My son, I've missed you," she says, and her lips are like entities unto themselves, moving in such a strange way, teeth like trees becoming visible.

But she is still shrinking. And down, down they go.

Snow continues to fall off of her. She is wearing a blue dress, like from one of his memories. She has elegantly carved bangles on her wrists, jewels hanging from her ears, and gold necklaces around her neck. While resizing clothing does not come easily to Hades and Hecate, she seems to do it without thinking, expanding riches out of thin air.

Down, down they go. And he and Hecate hold on dearly as she moves them to a place beside her knee. First she is an impossible giant. A mountain still! And then she is half that size, but still a giant. And then her knee, covered by her dress, is as tall as Seph is. And then Seph gets the weird sensation that he is actually growing taller over her.

She gets smaller and smaller. Until Seph is standing over a huddled Greek woman, her hair messy, wet, and neglected, frayed and falling out of the decorative hairpins. She is thin too, much thinner than he remembers. She does not look any different from the new souls that Seph looks after, except that she is alive. And she emanates warmth.

It is just the same as what Seph can do, but it is melting the snow all around them, even on the ground far away.

And she weeps.

"Persephone! My baby boy!" She crawls and clings to his knees. Seph picks up his cloak and puts it over her. In her unaided form, she is skinny and weak. Her dress is soaked and filthy too.

"Mother... Mother..." He can't think of anything to say to her. So he squats beside her and holds her in his arms.

She must be scorching with heat, but Seph's magic seems to resist this as well as the cold. He sets his cheek atop her hair, feeling her soaked, bedraggled features. He holds her and soothes her, for she cries like a child. And then she kisses him all over his cheeks, his hands, his head, and everywhere. She checks over him, tugging on his clothes. And she smooths her thin frail hands across his face. She smiles, but it is like a grimace of pain too.

"Y-you aren't hurt, a-are you?" she stutters out, and Seph shakes his head, trying to give her a happy expression. But this is strange for him. He expected to see her as something other than 'the Greek woman'.

He waits. Surely the memories will come back.

But nothing more is there.

I have everything I'm going to get, he realizes.

And also, *I want to know her.*

While Zeus's interest in him was insincere, his expressions exaggerated and his heart hollow, his mother only looks at him with desperate, genuine love.

"Let's go home, Mother. I want to speak to you."

Sixty-Four

Hades returns to his quiet world, and it is without any of the dramatics that he was expecting. Every question he anticipates, of *where is our other king?*, he expects to be a mild stab reminding him that his lover left him. His husband, his mate.

But even though he's inclined to give into dramatics and helpless thinking, he notices even on the way back, before he has touched down in the stables, that it won't be allowed or necessary.

He flies over Charon's boat, which is now as big and long as a warship, steered by his magical pole and carried by the current into the marsh. The judges are as busy as ever, unable to hurry with their work, but the souls crowd onto the island so much that now they are up to their waists in water if they cannot quickly decide to take their turn. Here they linger, some of them up to their chests, not even having ground to stand on.

And he is reminded yet again, as always, there is work to be done.

He does not fly the horses home. He scours the woods instead and finds Styx tending young Adonis with one of her daughters, Bia, who is Hecate's favorite sparring partner. They have the same fiery desire for violence and competition, but Bia grew up under Hades' rule and is loyal to him.

"I need help from you," he says directly after landing, without even a hello. And soon, Bia offers to take up the hunts in Seph and Hecate's stead.

The little boy Adonis also eagerly wants to help, but he is turned down.

"When is Hecate coming back?" he asks his foster mother, though the question is clearly meant for Hades.

"When she can," Hades answers, for he is not in the mood for longer detailed explanations.

He contemplates the answer though, as he flies off to his

unfinished neighborhood. The architects still need him to make revisions in blue ink. He goes to the table, sits in the familiar chair, splits open a new reed with a small knife, and waits.

His people will come to him.

First there is Periphetes, who has made dramatic improvements since that time he looked over the plans last. And then Verah appears with a pitcher and goblet in hand. She takes a comb from her belt and briefly tends his hair, making it perfect again, while he drinks gratefully from the goblet.

"I send for God Hermes?" she asks in Greek, anticipating one of his needs, though his mind hadn't got there yet.

He is reminded again that he speaks Verah's native tongue, but she strives to learn Greek for him, because on some level they are family.

"Simply deliver a message for me that he is to return to the Earth immediately and continue his good work of collecting lost souls. Our King Persephone does not need protection from Zeus any longer."

She nods once and replaces the crown on his head. There is no surprise in her expression nor a questioning gaze. While Seph was quite naive when he first came to Hades, he has proven in a short time to the citizens that he is a capable king.

And he has proven himself to his husband as well.

I made him like that.

On the one hand, Hades would not have minded being Seph's protector (and jailer) forever. He was prepared for it when he asked for the young god in marriage. But that was when the world didn't have so many deaths. And admittedly, he now has seen that he could not have managed this place for billions of years anyway. Not without some innovation or help stepping in.

Humans had been prospering, and they will cover the Earth if they aren't accidentally destroyed by ice first. All the gods visit their cities and admire. Certainly, there are no such marvelous things as the Olympic games between gods, though Zeus has been tempted to try.

The gods are too few, and they disagree too much.

So it is good that Seph will sway Demeter's heart and make her realize that we do well together. Humans will grow and spread and achieve much. More than the gods alone ever would.

Hades draws a blue line and stops. He picks up a fresh scroll, unfurling it over the table. He wets the pencil tip with his own tongue quickly, dabs it in the powder ink, and inspiration moves his hand, a simple yet elegant dwelling design appearing in his mind's eye. A place of far-spaced homes in a rolling meadow, adorned by a magnificent enormous stallion statue in the distance. Towering.

He doesn't have to worry about Seph, nor look after him anymore. He will return when he is able to.

And in the meantime, I will make many more homes for our children.

Sixty-Five

With Hecate's magic, driving her to exhaustion, Seph and his mother fly to the nearest human city where Demeter is recognized by the priests. A nobleman takes them in his chariot along a winding road through the barren trees. Demeter says they are going to the manor, which is six days away, but eight given the poor state of their horse and the conditions of the roads.

It is crowded with four people on the back of the chariot, but Hecate is exhausted from flying and her duel with Hades, and Seph's mother does not look well. She's healthier now with fresh clothes and clean hair, but she's older than Seph was expecting. Physically, she seems older than Hades by a decade at least, and this must mean she's exhausted since Seph has only seen goddesses who look young.

They take shelter at night in the houses of humans, which are roughly worn, cold, and almost always empty of children. Yet, they welcome the god of their faith with tired but happy smiles. Some even grasp Seph and kiss him on both cheeks, like they are welcoming a friend.

And then some seem to know him.

"We have a wolf hunt for you," says one farmer, sitting beside his son. "The packs crowd close to the village now. One tried to take my boy!"

And Seph knows this has something to do with him, some memory he's lost.

His mother says, "My son has had a long journey and will spend some months at the manor. But your fields will be safe soon, I promise it."

And then there is the strange fact that many of the common human folk know to address him as Seph and do not use his longer name, even though it is all his mother speaks.

The closer they get to the manor, the more people address him correctly. And when they arrive at a small city, humans gather outside their homes, some stepping into the street, their arms raised and making offerings, or kissing their hands and showing them up again.

Seph remembers his first ride through the city of Elysium, one of his first memories with Hades. This is nothing like that. Though they cry tears of joy, they do not get close to the horses or the chariot wheels.

His mother does not acknowledge any of them, though some cry out, "Great Goddess Demeter!"

"These are your children?" Seph asks, and his mother gives him a suspecting look. Though they have spoken much about his time in the underworld and Demeter's grief for him, she has held back many worrying questions, it seems. She suspects that Seph is not the same as he was, and Seph has not explicitly explained it to her yet.

She says in a manner of stating the obvious, "You are my only child. And these are not my subjects. Their ruler is Synesius, who lives in the highest house there."

Seph did not even notice that the large building was supposed to be a small palace of some kind. It is nothing compared to the palace of Elysium. In fact, there it might be a regular house.

"But I am their goddess, and that means I look after their livelihoods, yes."

Seph keeps his remarks to himself. For the humans she is 'looking after' are fit for the underworld, and Seph can even recognize by the hollowness in their eyes and their protruding bones which ones will be on Charon's boat soon.

His tongue is very tempted, and he weighs the cost of challenging her in public, something no ruler likes.

But he cannot hold back.

He tries to be gentle, since she has shown nothing but overwhelming love for him.

"Why are they not looked after *better*?"

She pats his back, which may be a signal of some kind. It feels familiar.

"Wait until we get home. We're almost there."

And so the horse continues past sad, decrepit homes with smoke rising from fires. He has never seen orange fire until now, and Hecate has stopped him from touching it once or twice. His mother told him the story of how a god named Prometheus gave humans the ability to create fire of their own, different from the underworld nymphs, and she seemed perplexed the entire time she was telling it.

This was something he was supposed to already know.

So Seph supposes there is a difficult conversation coming up. Often his mother looks into his face, or even grabs him by the elbow and turns him, like she's looking for differences. She has found none, except for what's missing in his mind.

They come to a place with a large decorated gate and a winding cobblestone path that takes them past many storehouses and fields. It is all neglected. But gradually humans arrive, peering at them, looking down the road, and then several run toward the large house. Now this looks like an acceptable home. This is something Hades would make for Elysium, but inside, he already notices the ways it is different.

There are a lot less flowers growing in planters and pots for one thing.

A lot less windows, sitting areas, and shelves for scrolls too.

There are no dogs that greet them in this place, though they did go by a pen of cattle, a pen of goats, and more. For some reason, despite the fact that the humans are starving, they did not slaughter these animals of hers.

Withered slaves clothed in rags guide them into the dark home. The lamplighter is an old man, and he struggles with his chore. Seph offers to help, but his mother takes him to a couch instead.

"Slaughter one of the bulls," she tells the servants. "We will have a feast and then retire to our beds. Draw baths for us as well."

"Mother, I will draw the baths," Seph says, for he can't imagine the stick humans carrying much of anything.

"Oh, Persephone," she says, and puts her hand on her hip the way he remembers. "Sometimes I know it's you. And sometimes it's like I'm talking to another man. You didn't always call me 'mother,' you know. Unless you were mad at me or there were others around."

"I will see to the baths," Hecate says, though her voice is weary. Seph nods to her, acknowledging, and then addresses his mother.

"Well, I am mad. How can you just let your people starve and die like this? How can you not even care?"

"Shh," she tells Seph, patting him on the back again. Seph is reminded of how mothers hold and pat their babies when they get fussy. She looks at the servants, clearly concerned that they may have heard. "Let's go upstairs and talk there." This is more like an order of Zeus's when he's decided to stop being friendly.

Seph climbs the stairs. He does not know what Hecate's limits are. But he trusts her. Neither she nor Hades would have let him come to Demeter if he was in true danger. Zeus was always the most dangerous threat. The Goddess of the Harvest was secondary.

And so he goes alone, and his mother climbs up after, grabbing her dress up around her knees.

It is strange to see physical beings behave in physical ways. Most of the girl souls forget this habit, and their dresses drift instead of catching under their steps.

They arrive at a room Seph immediately knows is his. There's a cage in one corner. He becomes fascinated with the furniture for a time, putting his hands on everything, opening every drawer. There is a mural of a fruit tree on one wall and many grape vines trailing up another window.

"Did I paint?" he asks. And he knows she knows.

"No, Seph. Why would you ask me that?" She looks lost, shaking her head.

"Something happened to me since I last saw you..." Hecate's name is on the tip of his tongue. He turns away from the murals and looks at her, expecting to see an accusation. He thinks her eyes will be narrowed and her lips will form a scowl of hate. *You deceived me!* she might say.

But instead it is a sad look. A horrified look, almost. And she wipes her cheeks.

Her tears do not seem fake, though her reaction is strong.

"I knew it." As she approaches Seph, it is not to attack him but to embrace him. Seph puts his arms around her uncertainly. Having seen her enormous form sitting between two mountains, he wonders why she chooses to be smaller than him.

"You're not the same boy anymore, are you? Come, sit over here," she leads him to the bed, and she sits close.

Seph can't remember her in this room, though he looks at the simple bed and the fine (though dusty) bed coverings, and he thinks that he should. He grew up here. And he almost feels like he can see her kneeling there, at a time when the room was warm and she was looking healthier than she is now, telling him stories about his family and all kinds of strange things.

But he can't *actually* see it, so maybe it is just his imagination.

"Tell me what he did to you," she says, touching Seph's cheek and petting down one of his arms.

There are things about her he doesn't like. Her lack of concern about the humans almost makes him certain she can't be a loving mother. But she is warm and concerned otherwise, and it seems genuine.

"Your father will get him back," she says. "Whatever Hades has done—I'll make sure Zeus listens. There has to be retribution. How did you escape him, dear boy?"

Seph almost laughs at her suggestion. He gathers up her hands and holds them in his lap, trying to reassure her.

"It is not Hades who hurt me. And I am still happily married. Mother, I was attacked by a nymph."

Confused, she echoes his words. "Nymph? A nymph working for Hades? Who would do—" She shakes her head. "No, not a nymph. You are a *god*. Their species would not…"

"It was a nymph, Mother. An ex-lover of Hades." And he tells her all about Tartarus, how he was lured out there, how he saw the boats, and how Minthe tempted him near the edge with the threat of harm to himself.

"And where was Hades?" she asks angrily, squeezing Seph's hands tightly.

"In the upperworld because I sent him. He discovered a pet I had, that I brought with me. A small rabbit."

She looks at the cage.

"He had to send the little rabbit back because living things cannot subsist in the underworld, and I wanted Hibus to go to a good home. Minthe used the opportunity to lure me away, and I suspected Hades was hiding something from me in Tartarus. I wanted to learn the truth. And so I did."

"I've never liked that place," she says, shaking her head. "It keeps Gaia alive, for one thing. I don't know if she can still feel pain in her state, but to keep her blood running like that…" She looks around the room solemnly, and Seph knows she is measuring the essence of Gaia. The beauty of the physical world versus a goddess she may have met as a babe. Gaia slew herself shortly after Zeus was born.

"You do not want the world to continue?" Seph asks, and he knows her answer will form his opinion one way or the other. The hard part will be convincing her to cooperate with Zeus when the powerful god himself has already failed.

"It is not that. I love this world. But Gaia was…" She has no words. "Well, she was just as beautiful and magical as all her little creations now. These are her dying dreams, you know. Everything that's taking shape is her invention. She was a storyteller in the old world. In the darkness that was bleak and empty, I sat in her lap and heard stories of color and magnificent things. I don't like to think of her dying. That is all."

"Then you should want the world to continue," Seph says. "For she is not dead until the Earth is gone."

It is time, and Seph bites his lips nervously.

"Mother, I came back for one reason only. I need you to stop punishing the world and letting the humans starve and freeze to death. Even if you miss me, the suffering you cause is not justified. I..."

He realizes he is going to lose. How can he argue with such a fanatical mindset? He shrugs in his own thoughts and decides to ask.

"How can I convince you that all this human suffering is not worth it? That the world and everyone in it, even the mortals, are worth more than your attachment to me?"

"Is that what you think of me?" she asks, surprised. She does not let go of his hands yet, so he assumes he hasn't offended her deeply. "Persephone, you knew this about me before you left. How much of your childhood is gone now? What do you remember about me?"

"Not very much. So please explain."

She nods. "Persephone, you and I are the same. I don't know if the other gods realize it yet or not. It's something I never talked about. I was born into a powerful family with dueling brothers. Fortunately, the attention was not on me."

"What do you mean? I saw you turn into a mountain."

"Yes, but my magic manifests without my will. The same as you. When I am upset, I grow. When I am happy, my warmth spreads. The plants and animals thrive around me. That is how I am the Goddess of the Harvest, my son. And truthfully, I'm not even sure if it's I who am doing it. I never had the ability to warm the Earth until you came along! I thought it was you, working your magic through the womb within me. I thought you would be the God of the Harvest when you were born. I thought you would be powerful and magnificent."

She smiles at him. It is proud and not disappointed at all.

"And you were." She squeezes his hands, reassuring him. "But not powerful." She shakes her head. "That part remains a mystery. I only know that I became the goddess of the crops and the fields while I was waiting for you. And then I thought you might be creating it still, but your magic has not manifested in any noticeable ways. Besides your warmth. Seph, I don't know if you are doing it or I am doing it, but the entire world was ice before you."

Sixty-Six

As the weeks pass, Seph learns to plow again. He learns to sow the crops and the different methods of tending them. The sun is out every day, and though the area is still frigid for a while, snow and gray skies disappear.

Humans gather outside the manor boundaries, and they are the sickly, desperate sort. His mother worries about him going out there, exposing himself to filth and diseases, whether he is a god or not.

"You may spread it to our healthy staff here," she says as an excuse, but Seph ignores her, and she never presses too much.

Seph shares what he can with the people outside every day. And it is not enough. It is never enough.

But Seph looks into their yearning eyes, he sees their skeletal forms, and he does not despair. These will soon be free of all suffering. He only goes and shares so that the citizens will remember how Persephone is a good king, and they might like to stay with him for eternity in Elysium.

He meets a man one day in rich but frayed clothes, shadows around his eyes, but an optimistic expression.

"I heard what happened to you," he says. "The nymphs told stories of your abduction all over the countryside. Are you okay? Was it bad?"

"The underworld is a beautiful land of peace," Seph replies. A practiced response, for he does not want any of these frightened children to pass away crying. The food does not grow quickly enough to save them, though the Earth is growing very warm, very fast. Neither he nor Demeter have direct control over this magic, but it seems that urgency is applied.

"You will like it so long as you're dead first," he says with a little bit of joviality. "Hades is a stern king, but so long as you stay within the borders, you will pass eternity untroubled there. You will find many loved ones and be without suffering."

The man nods once and slowly reaches for his hands. Seph gives them, and the man says, "I understood when you had to leave. And I understand now why gods and humans should not mix. Here I was worried about getting gray alongside you—and now you're a king of the underworld! I can't keep up with that."

He smiles, and Seph wishes he could say the man's face is familiar. They must have had a connection. But there's nothing there, and so Seph says, "In the underworld, gods and spirits are nearly the same. You don't ever grow old. Only your physical form on Earth does."

And later in the day he asks his mother if he ever had a mortal lover or close friend while he was here.

"You fell in love with the boy who delivered apples. But Seph— you fell in love with a *lot* of boys."

She makes Seph laugh.

While she is grating in certain ways, there's a lack of decorum that Seph has never had with anyone else. Not even with Hades. His mother speaks bluntly and sometimes thoughtlessly, and Seph finds himself becoming comfortable around her.

He learns the reasons for her apparent cruelty.

"Persephone, they die so fast, it is nearly worthless to be attached to a single one."

"They are each unique and special, Mother. And if they don't return to Gaia to be reborn, if they choose Elysium instead, they might live longer than you and me."

He sees a mild look of surprise on her face when he tells her this.

"Huh," she replies.

And though it is a quiet victory, Seph gets the sense that he settled something longer between them. Some fight he cannot remember. Possibly about the man he may have had a love affair with.

Demeter is nicer to the humans around him after that. She is also still quite spoiled and every bit a noblewoman god who expects her baths to be drawn and her mantle to be dusted. But she was never outright cruel to begin with, just indifferent, and now she is simply more personable.

Several times when some task is performed, Seph sees her notice the human doing it and she says, "Thank you." She is even making an effort to learn their names.

They have disagreements sometimes, such as the sharing of food beyond the manor boundaries.

"We need *our* slaves to be strongest," she says, "For they will be working the grain mills and harvesting the crops. Honestly, there is nothing we can do for those outside right now. Some will survive until summer, and those will be the ones we feed after. They will repopulate."

But Seph finds himself able to deflect her arguments. The words come to him easily.

"Perhaps you see them as only human, spending brief lives in your existence. But they are my subjects, Mother. I will rule over them in Elysium. And I say they are fed whatever we can spare, as long as I think it will help. I will choose the ones. I can see who is almost alive and who is almost dead."

He can tell she is uncertain around him sometimes. But she never asks him to leave. And she never expressly criticizes all the ways that he is different. Instead, she tells him a lot of stories about the old Seph. And he gets to relive himself through her.

"Hey," he says one evening, "did I ever have a pet cat?"

She blinks several times and her lips roll inward as if she's thinking of words she'd rather keep silent. Until she says, "Yes. A cat. Leto or something. He lived a good life. Why do you ask?"

"Huh. Well, I just remember being mad at you about him. I don't know why, but I was quite worked up about it. Do you remember that?"

"No, I can't remember..." she says vaguely. But moments later she confesses a sad tale in which Zeus surprised her in the courtyard and his cat hid under a bush that got crushed.

"I am so, so sorry."

"Oh, that's all right," he tells her, and he refills her cup with wine. It is different in the upperworld. Worse. But it helps him get through the evenings when all he can think about is Hades. "It was a long time ago. And you didn't mean to."

"I liked that kitty..." she says quietly, sipping. And Seph is reminded that sometimes he sees a youthfulness in her, and in all the gods actually. Even Hades, and of course himself. For the mind does not truly age the same as the body does.

And then comes a long night. There are many long nights.

Hecate prods him sometimes, saying, "Are you still fawning over that jerk?"

And he can always force a laugh for the dismissive way she says it. But then one night, when it is very warm and no one in the house sleeps with a blanket anymore, Hecate sits up on her sleeping mat in his room and admits, "I miss spending days with the little one. Adonis. He was a little angel, wasn't he?"

Seph musters a sleepy snort. "A typhoon, more like. Assuming he isn't talking to you—at the top of his lungs by the way—I can always find you two in the library by following the trail of paper and forgotten scrolls."

"He is lively," Hecate says with a smile. "He will grow into a beautiful man. With passions."

And Seph is only mildly curious at how she would think of him like that. To a god, the lifetimes of humans go quickly, and so if she is interested in Adonis, ten years or so must not seem a terribly long time to wait.

"Hades is a beautiful man with passions," he says to get a rise out of her, and it works. He and Hecate have become great friends while they wait for the crops to grow. In the entire upperworld, he and Hecate are the only ones who miss the realm of shadow, coldness, and death.

Well, not the *only* ones, as he discovers one day when he wakes up to his mother rushing around the house, getting ready for travel.

"Persephone, please stay here and look after the fields without me. I'll be back in a week." She kisses his cheek hurriedly. "Promise me you'll keep safe here. And see that the cows get fed plenty, since I think they're all carrying double."

Seph doesn't wonder much about where she's going until Hermes visits the next day.

"Your mother's not here? I guess she got the news early then."

"What news?" Seph asks.

Hermes looks hesitant to tell him, but after a little silence he says, "Ohhh, it's nothing. Just a... a little rumor about a nymph acting as a guide to humans who want to travel to the underworld. She asked Artemis to find *him*... in the mountains."

And Seph nods, evaluating his options. Should he strive to protect his enemy again? Minthe is meant to be paying for his crime with his exile, and Seph could use Hecate's power and see that his word is followed. But in the end, he goes with the advice of a scroll written by a wise ruler.

Execution laws do not teach future criminals, but they do ease the suffering of families.

He decides to let them both be. And then he inquires about

Hades.

Hermes likes a bit of romance and dramatics, so his words are always especially entertaining

"He looks out his window with a long sigh every evening and thinks about your round tush and your strong shoulders." Seph punches him in the arm, and they jostle a bit, mock wrestling. But secretly, later, Hermes' playful words will be thought of by his lonely heart. "He whispers your name while he's picking flowers! And once I saw him break down crying on the balcony. 'Oh, Seph, my love!' he said, and he held his face in his hands, in tears!"

"Tell him I'm coming home soon," Seph says when he manages to pry himself out of a headlock. He still loses to Hermes, but he's getting better. "Three more weeks and we will finish harvesting. Then I will be gone."

Finally. At last.

Sixty-Seven

The night is warm and dark, and Hecate leads Seph further away from the house and even out past the fields. The bugs sing and the frogs are loud here. They're near the giant pond. And Seph scans the stars for any dark shapes that might be blotting them out overhead. The sky is perfectly clear, so they're probably not looking for his father. And Hermes wouldn't land out here so far away from the house. He just left two days ago. So it's not him.

But Hecate says a god has called her. She says she feels it the way a dog feels a tug on a leash.

"There are only a few people who could do that. Hades, my sisters, Styx and any of her children, maybe the god Poseidon—he's powerful enough—and you."

And so Seph is scanning earnestly, but he's trying not to get his hopes up.

Hades is far too busy in the under—

Seph takes off running as Hecate calls to him, "Master, do not rush!"

But that is only because he saw the figure first. Four black horses and a chariot are parked under the distant tree on a hill. His knee has not given him any trouble in weeks, and his own god magic must propel his feet. He feels like the wind! Almost like he could jump into the air and take off by himself the way Hermes does.

Hades stands next to his chariot, still and dressed regally with fur around his shoulders. His earrings are extravagant and his necklace is as hefty as a whole ore deposit. But Seph crashes into him without hesitation, throwing his arms around him, and then kissing his cheek. And then his lips, inserting his tongue, for he has forgotten that Hecate might be watching. Or that this might be a trap and a cruel mirage.

Fortunately, none of that is so. Despite having embarrassed Zeus publicly on Mount Olympus, his summer has been quiet. He hasn't even heard a whisper of Hera.

And oh, Hades is so *real* under his fingers. And soft and warm under his cloak. Seph is quick to slide his hands under the layers of fabric and feel his husband's waist (and his ass) with remembering hands. Hades also holds him tightly, and in the hot and humid weather of a Greek summer, Seph is not wearing the underclothes Hades despises. He does wear much longer chitons, however. Ones designed for a man and not a showing-off athlete.

"I expected your hair to be in curls," Hades says, lifting a lock with one finger.

"You should try it sometime if you want curls," Seph says, grinning ear to ear. "It is agony."

"She did not overpower you." It almost sounds like a question. Or a statement. Seph is unsure.

"No. She couldn't. I've been wanting to tell you something, but I didn't want to share the secret with Hermes. I wasn't sure if it was safe to share or not, and you know how he sells to others."

Hades tilts his head, intrigued. "I am glad I came early then. What secret do you have? And you know, you could have sent a coded message to tell me. I would've figured it out."

"It is not that urgent, but... my mother is the same as I am. She is not a powerful god."

Seph hears footsteps behind him. It is only Hecate approaching. She wears an unpleasant expression of dislike, but after their battle six months ago there is dislike *and* trust. They would have worked together to protect him from Zeus if it was necessary.

She is like my hound, Seph realizes, thinking of Cerberus.

He misses the grumpy, fierce dog back home. But it is not time, and even as he speaks to explain his mother's magic, his hands are traveling over Hades' clothes. Treasuring him.

"She confessed to me something I already knew—or I mean, something I was already supposed to know. She has the same defect I have. Neither of us can feel or command our magic. She didn't want to kill so many humans and animals and freeze the Earth with her grief. She wasn't doing it on purpose to pressure Zeus into capturing me. She was just sad. And when she is sad, the Earth is not warmed by the sun."

He adds, though he feels it is an unnecessary detail given the solution he's worked up:

"Or I am doing it. I am always warm, you know, so it is an option. Neither of us will ever figure it out since we are magic-mute. But either way, it changes nothing. She can't be happy unless I'm here. So, in order for the humans to prosper..." Seph shrugs, but that does not mean he is cavalier. Feelings of depression are rising again, even though he was joyous just moments before. There is nothing he loves more than the underworld, or more than Hades, the man who embodies it. Elysium is Hades, and Seph loves him.

He explains, more sadly, "The humans have to prosper in order to grow. In order to become wiser and more accomplished. They eventually will come down to the underworld, so it is like I am building up our kingdom as well. Just, from this side."

"Seph, don't do this to me." Hades looks like he's trying to control his features, but his frown is deepening. "I did not know this about Demeter, and I suspect she might be lying to you. She might be trying to take you from me. I don't want you to hate me, so please don't ask me to—"

"You didn't let me finish." Seph shushes him quickly and manages a smile. "I'm not leaving you. And also, I don't think she is lying. There are little things about her that are very human-like—and very *me*, come to think of it. Like how she takes the chariot everywhere. Can you think of any other god that rides a human chariot to go between cities? You don't count, obviously. Your horses fly. But her? Even long distances she must go by chariot or with Hecate's help.

"And then there are her temples. My mother makes collecting from the temples look like running a business, whereas Zeus and Dionysus and all the other gods treat them like curiosities, sometimes appearing for the offering and accepting the acquisition, but only when it amuses them. Do you see what I mean?"

Hades admits slowly, "No one is particularly close to Demeter except for you. No one has observed her personal life with any great interest. I suppose... when she is upset, her magic causes her to grow big? She has tried to stomp on Zeus a few times, you know. But come to think of it, I have never seen her hurl magic or enchant weapons before. I've always thought it's because she is gentle."

"She is," Seph says. "And I'm truthfully the only family she has. I'm the only one she cares about. Whether I am the one warming the Earth or it is her for her happiness to have me, my solution for the matter remains the same."

"I won't let her keep you," Hades says, tightening his hold on him.

"No, Hades. She won't keep me the entire time. Just until the

Earth warms enough for the crops to grow. Then I can come back and help you look after the underworld again. That is how we will prosper. Not just the humans, but the Earth and the underworld together. I will spend half the year here to make sure that the summers are warm. And when the crop is ready to harvest, I will return to you. The winters will be a little colder from now on, and Elysium will see a mild surge of citizens each year. Our harvesting time will be opposite the upperworld's. And I will look after the whole thing, making sure the yields on both ends remain stable."

Sixty-Eight

Hecate strolls off in the direction of the human houses, told to stand where she cannot hear him unless he yells, and ordered to use her magic to make sure no one interrupts them. She mutters, grumpily, "Yes, master." But there is also a subtle smirk on her features, as though she finds her orders both laborious and amusing.

Seph can't take Hades' clothes off fast enough. And he wears so much of them! Initially when coming here, Seph wanted both kings of the underworld to match, but he's spent so long in the tropical Greek weather that he can't remember why anyone anywhere would ever wear pants.

He gets them off though, and they kneel together in the grass. Hades pushes him to lie on his back, and then his limber lean lover straddles over him, taking both their cocks in his hands, rubbing against him.

There is never a better look for Hades than when he is dreamy-eyed and panting atop him, his long hair straying messily, or draping onto Seph's chest whenever he leans close.

Still, despite this being everything he's ever wanted all summer, Seph feels like he's rushing to put his physical needs before other concerns.

"Why did you leave early? And how did you get time to get away?"

He rubs Hades' thighs and thinks about kissing his nipples. He has missed every asset of Hades' while he's been away.

"I have not been so busy lately," Hades says and lifts himself up. He aims Seph's cock underneath and lets himself down slowly.

Seph wants to force him on faster. There is sometimes a selfish, evil part of him that likes being called stallion and wants to use Hades. But today it won't get to play. He curls an arm under his head and lies back, being the spoiled, expectant prince instead.

"And why are you early?" he asks with a bit of a haughty,

unappreciative tone. "I said three weeks, not three days."

"I couldn't wait," Hades answers, holding himself on his hands over Seph, and his body begins to move. Their eyes lock, and Seph finds himself trapped here, as much mounting Hades as Hades is mounting him. He loves the tight squeeze on his cock. How Hades quivers when Seph reaches the best place inside him. And he loves that Hades moves him in and out, finding so much pleasure for himself on Seph's cock. It makes him feel submissive, in a way.

And he also likes to be showered in ego-boosting compliments.

"Ah, my stallion. You're so big. And so full as well. You haven't had your king to look after you."

"I miss you every night," Seph answers with a smile, loopy with needy emotions. There is nothing better than Hades in the moonlight, even if his horses make a lot of noisy jostling and shuffling sounds nearby. Even in the shade, they find the starlight uncomfortable.

And Seph says, thinking of them, "But you must go back to wait for me." He groans and grabs on to Hades' hips. He is starting to move much too fast, and Seph never wants this to end. "It's not time yet."

"Then I will make it a mandate to sneak in time with you, whenever I can. Seph, if you think I am going to be fair and share you with your mother half the—"

"No, don't say *mother!*"

They both laugh breathlessly, and then it is nothing but physical movement, and Seph discovers one enormous disadvantage to the underworld... He has never tasted Hades' sweat before. As soon as he notices a gleam on his husband's neck, Seph picks himself up and laps his tongue across his husband's skin. He is not content with just that. He rolls them so that he is on top, a hand behind one of Hades' knees, holding him open, and he watches his cock buried and thrusting in his husband's little ass. And then sees Hades' long and lovely cock spurt with cum.

He arches his back and bites into his fist when he does it, somehow looking shy and cute despite having no concept of modesty.

Seph decides to plow him hard then. Purposefully, he holds back and lasts as long as he can because he knows when this is over, it is over. He will have to wait a long three weeks to see Hades again.

He falls over Hades so that they are face-to-face, nose-to-nose. He still keeps that one knee in the air, driving into his husband.

"Every month at least. You will see me. Your king demands it."

"My stallion, I won't forget."

But Seph decides he still has to make this time count. He pulls out and positions Hades again, this time on his knees with his butt pointed up at Seph. Seph spreads him open, looking at his wanting, pliable hole. And he remembers what his husband did to him, what he wanted to do if only he had stayed around long enough to have the chance.

He lowers himself and licks over that hole. One extensive, lapping sweep. And then he pushes his slick cock inside again, broadening the space, making sure Hades will feel him for nights to come. He stays on the edge so long that when he finishes, it is not so much a release as it is a final extension of pleasure, his peak already reached and sustained, but the climax letting him find satisfaction from it.

He can feel himself fill Hades as the hole sucks on him tightly at the same time.

As they both roll into the grass, Seph catches his breath, and he feels something minute crawling around his knee, but he is too exhausted to bother with a flick. His cock lies against his stomach, thick, heavy, and fully milked.

"I miss you," he says. "Did I say that? I miss you, I love you, and..." He doesn't just want to use his husband for sex and then dress and say goodbye. He wants Hades to know about the emotions as well. The love. The combined adventure and misery of this long separation.

A mangled mix of Hermes' mockery comes to mind.

"I look up at the stars at night and cry about you. I hold my face in my hands and sigh, 'Oh, Hades!'"

He rolls onto his side then so he can laugh and look at his husband. But also, he finds a thumb moving a strand of hair away from his Hades' lips. Then Seph kisses him.

When they part, Hades asks, "Have you been spying on Hermes with a listening spell? That would be impressive work against the God of Whispers."

Seph chuckles. "I knew he would tell some bullshit about me."

But both of them know by their loving gaze that Hermes spoke the truth to each of them.

Sixty-Nine

The day finally comes. Seph stays a little longer and works almost entire days and nights to fill the storehouses up faster. He sees that his mother's staff and slaves are well provided for so they can continue working long hours without him, and then he works a little more. Just to provide extra bread that will save a dozen humans from entering the land of the underworld this winter.

It still seems there's so much work to be done while he is leaving, but he knows Hades has already been generous with his patience. He won't accept another delay, and though Seph has come to be friends with many of his mother's servants, the same way he's become friends with Verah, Sefkh, and Alfric...

The upperworld is no substitute for his real home. His place in darkness.

Saying goodbye to Demeter would be easy except that she makes it difficult. In the days leading up to his departure, Demeter has nothing but evil things to say about Hades. Particularly, about how he's failed Seph and damaged 'her baby boy'.

She gets to utter that phrase one time in front of him, and then Seph towers over her and says once, firmly, "I am King Persephone of the Underworld. And you will not disgrace my name again."

She is silent then the following day, the very last day before he is to leave, and Seph spends much of it feeling guilty, but he does not let himself make amends for that guilt. He is willing to call on Hecate to curb his mother's tongue, even if calling him *baby boy* was a slip into an old habit.

She doesn't seem to treat him the same. She certainly hasn't tried to curl his hair or choose his clothing for him yet. So it was probably just a mistake.

Morning comes, and he and Hecate rise early and don clothes for travel. Seph will take nothing else with him, leaving all his possessions in his room to be picked up when he comes back. And they travel out to the edge of the farmlands, Seph admiring the yellow sunlight through the trees, joyously saying goodbye though finding it beautiful at the same time, when he and Hecate turn to the sound of distant yelling behind him.

"Wait! Wait, Seph! Don't leave yet!"

His mother runs toward him with bare feet, wearing a plain beige frock secured hastily around her waist with a belt, and her hair is a mess like she just got out of bed. She has yesterday's makeup smudged around her eyes, and it doesn't look bad at all in Seph's opinion. But he was certainly not expecting her here, so he and Hecate share perplexed glances.

"You can't go yet!" Demeter says as she reaches him. "We still have the roof to repair. And the cows to feed. And all the hungry people out there. Seph, you know—" She grabs his hand and goes to her knees on the ground. Seph's eyes widen, for he's never seen a goddess of any kind kneel in the dirt like that, ruining her dress. She begs him, "—you know that I can't stop the world from becoming ice again! It's not me, I think it's you! Zeus is going to come after me again, and he's going to beg me, and he's going to say—he—he's going to say you're responsible! He'll only punish me for letting you leave. Please, come back to the house with me."

Seph recognizes this game of manipulation and stalling, but he also sees that his mother is terrified he won't come back. The same as Hades.

Either I am extremely unlucky to be trapped between two insecure gods... or I may be the only son of Zeus to be this well loved by my family.

His family excludes Zeus himself, of course. His mother never manipulated him into believing lies about his father. She truly has his best interests at heart. And for that, Seph loves her and is grateful to her.

He helps her up out of the dust.

"There will always be those things to be done," he answers. "And Mother, the date has been set—"

"But half the slaves have died already! We have more work to do, and less than half the hands to do it! Seph, you are holding this farm together—"

Seph begins walking, though now he guides his mother alongside him. Hecate heaves a little unhappy sigh, letting him know her opinion about these last-minute dramatics.

He agrees. But he is more patient. In a way, his own mother is his subject too, no different than any of the humans he's looked after while he's here.

"Buy more slaves if you need more slaves, Mother. There aren't many on the market, it's true, but their prices are lower than they've ever been. The slave masters have to feed their families. And if you wander to the poor places of town, you will find mothers willing to give away one of their children for a loaf of bread."

"The hunger is not averted, Persephone! Humanity is still in great danger. Not everyone will get to eat, and the winter may bring the flu. You realize the winter will be hard, don't you? Without you here—"

"It has been a long summer, Mother. The winter will be mild and short, since I will come back after the first snowfall in Greece—for *this* winter. I think it will be a decade of long summers to bolster humanity and make sure the Earth is thriving again. But then there will be long winters too. There will be times when Hades has beautiful homes sitting empty, and those will be the times that the harvest is in the underworld's favor."

"Seph, you're killing *children*," his mother says, as they climb a cobblestone road up a hill. It is too early to see other farmers heading into the city market. They are glutting and stashing their own feast from the tax collectors before they share with everyone else. But no fruit, vegetable, or strip of meat will go to waste for many summers.

Ahead, at the top of the hill, the shadows from the trees grow long and dark. They are slanted slightly wrong, as if there is a prick in the fabric of the world that draws them that way.

Hades will be just over that hill.

"Seph, did you hear me?!" She grabs him by the arm and tries to stop him. She also eyes the hill.

Seph does not hurry, but he also will not be stalled anymore.

"Why should the deaths of children bother me? I love children. Hades does too."

"Oh, I see. You don't care about the babes now? You don't care about slaves suffering or mothers so hungry they're willing to trade their babies for grain? What happened to you? Is Hades so evil he's been able to penetrate your heart?"

She is sounding desperate and heartbroken. She stops walking beside him, and so Seph allows himself to turn back and address her. Only because he cares about her.

She is about twice the height he was expecting, and looking

levelly at him, though she stands at the bottom of the hill and Seph has started climbing.

"Mother, I love you. I'm not leaving to hurt you. Someday you're going to come to the underworld with me—with all of us—and you're going to see all the beautiful things Hades and I have made together. You're going to look back on this moment with regret for discouraging me."

"Why don't you care about the children? Where is your heart for the slaves? Convince me, Persephone, my son, that this man hasn't gutted you of your good qualities."

She doesn't say it, but Seph can read the unspoken threat in her eyes. *Or I will send Zeus after you.* His father may not like him, but if Demeter continues to blame the marriage for the summer season not returning, Zeus will care enough about the entire world to make some sort of nuisance. The agreement Seph has reached with him will not hold.

And though Demeter might be defective like him, no god magic has been able to harm her when she is in her giant form. So Hecate likely cannot subdue her either.

The only one who can get through to her is Seph himself. And he has tried.

"Mother, nearly half the children who die go straight to Elysium. They are the best kind of souls, actually. They have no ambitions, and so they usually do well in a world where achievement is at its end. There are many orphans in Elysium who await their mothers. And there's great happiness there, for the little souls love babes to look after. As for the slaves—there are none in Elysium. No one is truly a slave, not even here."

"He's brainwashed you!" she exclaims, and Hecate taps on the whip in her belt. She wants to try. But that would unravel more family dramatics that Seph is trying to avoid.

"Sefkh, one of my sons in the afterlife, explains a concept where the afterlife is sort of a mirror of Earth, but with a lot of dead people in it. I think it is the opposite. I think all humans are connected, and somehow, through their essence, the knowledge and ideas gained from the ones who stay in the underworld reach the ones who are reborn here. And I believe that together, all of Gaia's children will reach wisdom and happiness. It is not my job to care about the slaves. Humans will resolve the issue themselves."

She has become her normal size again, a tall-ish but disheveled noblewoman at the bottom of the hill. And Seph can see the familiar look of loss on her features. It is times like these he knows he speaks in a way that her old son never would.

So Seph holds out his hand to her. "Come see me off. Please." And he waits for her to catch up to him.

Then they go together toward Hades, who waits on the other side of the hill. Seph wanders off the road, following the ever-darkening shadows, and finds an overhang from a rock ledge nearby, where Hades has parked the horses.

Demeter hugs Seph and gazes coldly beyond him.

"He left me to burn. I was only a babe."

Hades says nothing and makes no gesture. But Seph knows it is only because he can't correct what is already done.

"If there was a way to take it back, he would."

"Then why hasn't he said so himself?"

"Would you like to hear him say it now?"

Her answer is to turn away. Gods do not forgive for a long, long time.

As Seph reaches his husband, embracing him also, they hear her yell from the trees, "Take care of my son this time! Or I will crush this entire Earth in my fist!"

Seventy

"Welcome home, my stallion," Hades says in his ear, and Seph feels a smile against his neck. He reaches up to grab his husband's shoulders and to feel his hair as well, that wonderful sweet winter scent taking over the smell of earth and sweat in his own clothes. And a little bit of horse manure. Seph thought he picked something clean from his room, but he must have been mistaken.

He won't wear these clothes for long anyway. He sighs and leans into his husband and they kiss.

Somewhere Hecate makes a single smooching sound, but otherwise her attitude is properly submissive.

"Master, may I meet you there?" she asks after a long time has passed, and Seph is not nearly done kissing Hades yet.

He makes a waving hand gesture behind his back. And since he doesn't hear another word or an impatient sound from her again, he assumes she's disappeared somewhere. If anybody knows how to travel in and out of the underworld as easily as Hades, it would have to be Hecate.

"I've prepared a wedding feast," Hades says, smiling more than Seph has ever seen as they stumble and fondle and kiss each other back to the chariot. "Have you worked on your vows for me?"

"I was only going to say how I miss your ass in leather. And that I'm weirdly attracted to your hair soap."

"Don't worry. Verah conspired with the poets to write you some short traditional vows. This is more of a party than a marriage, and everyone is brainstorming a name for the holiday. Right now they're calling it Persephone Comes Home Day, but don't worry, it may not stick."

"I like Persephone Cums Day," Seph says with a grin as his husband picks up the reins. The horses make a sharp turn to face a break in the trees, and then Hades snaps the reins on their backs and they charge. The chariot plunges directly into what should be solid earth, and the ground rolls with ripples out around them. There is a race of wind and colors and a cold sensation. Like jumping into a lake from a far height, something that Seph did this summer.

And then there is so much vastness underneath him. The air is clean of heat and smells. The light is no longer in his eyes.

Seph leans far over the chariot and scans the dark woods for wandering souls, finding their way to the docks where Charon will guide them. Or for the occasional animal who shows up.

There is nothing to be seen. No birds and no flowers even. Hades has to cultivate anything unique. There is no color or light out here in the endless unclaimed woods.

But Seph stares down into barren land and feels excitement. "The Earth is going to grow very old," Seph says, and already he's thinking he might like to add this to his speech later tonight. "We are going to grow fabulous things down here and up there both, happening at the same time. And this eternal world is going to be the most vibrant, beautiful, and complicated place."

Author's Note
November 2019

Thank you for reading! I hope you enjoyed this modern and classic blend of Hades and Persephone.

I became interested in the myth when I saw a reddit post criticizing a digital painting of Hades gazing at Persephone for romanticizing rape. And when one of the comments refuted it, explaining that abduction is part of the ancient Greek wedding ceremony, I became curious and started doing research.

This was while I was finishing up Pykh 1, over a year ago! I waited patiently to start this novel.

The number one thing that called me to write this story was Hades' character. A bad boy with a soft heart? Who doesn't love that? But also I became more interested in Seph as I realized his modern depiction doesn't suit him at all. (Or her. LOL)

Persephone is usually represented as the good side of Hades, the one who reins in his evil. But in truth, Persephone is the bad bitch you call for curses and morbid favors. She usually sees to the punishment of men.

Or, that's how it *was*. Nowadays she's a flower princess, always depicted as the damsel in distress.

From the very start, I wanted to show Hades and Persephone as equal kings, being a perfect union. I did not want Seph to become Hades' moral compass, since I felt like that would lead to him overruling and overpowering his husband. I wanted the older interpretation, in which they are partners, not opposites.

Though, I suppose Seph does tempt Hades to be a *little* better. And Seph does sort of overpower him in the last act. But overall, I hope I wrote two badass gods who complement each other. Their setting is morbid, but hey, it's the underworld.

This is likely to be my one and only dabble in the world of Greek myths. I hope I did a good job! I'll be starting Pykh 4 very soon, which is a humorous sci-fi story and nothing at all like Hades & Seph. But I have at least one more dark fantasy world I want to write someday… an underwater world full of monsters. Styx would approve!

You can follow my blog to see what I'm up to, and I've also started a Patreon page. I'll be posting chapters of Pykh 4 there in December.

- Eileen Glass
eileenglass.com
patreon.com/eileenglass

Also by Eileen Glass

Omega Society Auction

Chapter 1

BREEDERS WANTED.
EXCHANGE YOUR ORDINARY LIFE FOR LUXURY, FAMILY, AND SPACE...

The words are imposed atop the photo of a smiling human man hugging a pink-haired baby with the moon behind them. The first word on the sign changes every couple of years from 'Breeders' to 'Omegas' and back because the Earth and the Moon bicker constantly over what it should say.

"Not thinking about getting your ass pounded, are you?" Cory laughs. "Remember, as bad as it gets scrubbing toilets, nothing is worse than that."

He touches his stomach and shudders. All men have the same reaction, mental or physical, when they stare at it for too long. Most don't even look at it anymore, but the signs are posted everywhere. Every business of a certain size is required to display them in highly visible areas. They also have to keep them in good condition, clean of graffiti.

Thus, there's a man currently climbing a ladder with scrub gloves and a wash bucket. Someone drew a dick over the baby so that the man seems to be cradling, and smiling at, an enormous prick. They also added ASS CUNT over 'Breeders'.

"You seem quiet, man. Everything alright?" Cory asks.

"Yeah," Rourke says, distracted, as the woman at the pharmacy counter calls for next in line.

He gives her his identification card, which she scans to pull up his record. The pain medication is for his mother, but he's an authorized buyer on her account. She scans the list of the many medications he's allowed to pick up.

"You're here for..." She guesses the one that's low due to the bottle capacity and the time of his last pick up. They monitor these things exactly to stop dealers.

"Yup," he confirms. Usually, she'd be off to retrieve the prescription. He sees her about three times a month for different things. But just this once, she lingers on her computer, her eyes affixed near the top of the screen. She clicks once.

Rourke's heart picks up a beat. What could she be looking at? Could he be approved so soon? He checked his account status on his lunch break, and it was yellow—'In Review'.

Her glance from Rourke and back to the computer screen could be coincidental.

Cory leans backwards against the counter, oblivious. "Remember Rourke, as it bad as it gets mopping floors for the corporate slaves that keep laying us off to save *their* paycheck... at least you aren't spitting babies out of your ass. It's a good thing they put those signs everywhere to keep life in perspective, huh?"

Rourke drops his eyes, unable to look at either of them. Everything Cory says is true. He and Cory have joked and talked shit over so many lunch breaks and just hanging out. BS-ing their lot in life always comes with a footnote: *At least we aren't spitting babies out our ass for the alien overlords.*

In Rourke's city especially, when life gets hard there's pride in never taking the easy way out. *Suicide is preferable*, Rourke heard in school once, and the whole class 'hmmed' with agreement. The teacher didn't chime in, but he looked proud.

Earth, in general, protests against the alpha aliens' rule. But Rourke's city is where they brought the harem towers down. Where they killed several alphas and alpha children in a war. Where they suffered massacres as a result.

Death before slavery is still the motto.

The woman—Audrey, her name tag says—gives the back of Cory's head a very long and obvious stare. She knows. It must be on her screen, the little infinity symbol next to his citizenship ID.

His application got approved. Rourke's thumbs itch to bring out his phone and check, just to be doubly sure, but he can't with Cory watching.

"Who the hell even calls that number?" his friend muses aloud with a bored sigh.

Almost no one... and Rourke. Their city has the highest number of omega-compatible humans and the lowest number of applicants. What would Cory say next if he knew?

"I'll get this from the back," Audrey says and leaves the computer. Her tone is neither friendly nor unfriendly. Rourke is probably reading too much into it, but it did seem that she was a *little* more personable before.

Thankfully, the law prevents anyone, professional or otherwise, from outing an omega status on someone's personal record. Rourke remembers his mother throwing a fork at the TV when they announced the alphas' ruling ten years ago. Protests were held for months, but the Earth Coalition backed the ruling due to the violent 'bitch hunt' that had happened.

Audrey returns. "Here you go." She passes the bag across the counter and interlaces her fingers, making an attempt at a polite smile. "Do you have any questions about the medication or anything?"

"No," Rourke mumbles and produces his wage card.

She looks at it and opens her mouth. Rourke can see the words forming. *That's not necessary.*

He cuts in. "*Please.*"

Alpha government is absolutely efficient. The moment his application got approved, he doesn't pay for any medications, government services, or even housing. The allowance is temporary, until he gets auctioned. His winning alpha foots the bill when it all gets finalized.

It's illegal to charge an omega for these services. She looks at his card like she can't figure out what to do with it. Cory, who still has his back against the counter, looks over his shoulder to see what's up.

The card wobbles in his grasp as Rourke prepares for the worst.

"Oh! Of *course!*" Audrey play-slaps her forehead and breaks into forced chuckles. "Man, it's been such a *long* day..."

"We hear that," Cory remarks.

Rourke exhales with relief and gives her a grateful smile. She gives him a little one in return, tapping away on her keyboard. She slides his wage card, and a short receipt prints for the bill. Rourke takes a pen from the cup on her counter to sign his name. Then she trades the little receipt for his invoice.

"Have a great day! And thanks for being honest."

Rourke crams the invoice and the pills into his coat pocket. A whole half sheet of paper for the secure purchase of one tube of lip balm. Fortunately, Cory has no reason to be suspicious and doesn't demand to see the bill.

"Hey! Let's hit up the game store next," his friend says. "I want to try out *Quests and Mages* on the Perception console. I hear it's kick-ass."

That is one good thing about the alien alphas taking over Earth and enslaving the human race to have babies. With their advanced technology, video games have become *amazing.*

~

AMAZON.COM/AUTHOR/EILEENGLASS